A Deadly Deletion

Lorna Barrett

BERKLEY PRIME CRIME
New York

BERKLEY PRIME CRIME
Published by Berkley
An imprint of Penguin Random House LLC
penguinrandomhouse.com

Copyright © 2021 by Penguin Random House LLC
Excerpt from *Clause of Death* by Lorna Barrett copyright © 2022 by
Penguin Random House LLC

ISBN: 9780593333488

Berkley Prime Crime hardcover edition / July 2021
Berkley Prime Crime mass-market edition / May 2022

Printed in the United States of America
1   3   5   7   9   10   8   6   4   2

CAST OF CHARACTERS

Tricia Miles, owner of Haven't Got a Clue vintage mystery bookstore

Angelica Miles, Tricia's older sister, owner of the Cookery and the Booked for Lunch café, Booked for Beauty day spa, and half owner of the Sheer Comfort Inn. Her alter ego is Nigela Ricita, the mysterious developer who has been pumping money and jobs into the village of Stoneham.

Pixie Poe, Tricia's assistant manager at Haven't Got a Clue

Mr. Everett, Tricia's employee at Haven't Got a Clue

Antonio Barbero, the public face of Nigela Ricita Associates; Angelica's son

Ginny Wilson-Barbero, Tricia's former assistant; wife of Antonio Barbero

Grace Harris-Everett, Mr. Everett's wife

Grant Baker, chief of the Stoneham Police Department

Becca Dickson-Chandler, former tennis star, ex-wife of Marshall Cambridge

Mark Jameson, Stoneham's dentist and head of the committee to recruit a new Chamber of Commerce president

Louise Jameson, owner of Louise Jameson Photography Studio; wife of Mark Jameson

Terry McDonald, owner of All Heroes comic-book store

Hank Curtis, leader of a homeless encampment

David Kirby, federal deputy marshal of the Witness Protection Program

Dan Reed, owner of the Bookshelf Diner

Larry Harvick, owner of the Bee's Knees specialty shop

Ava Campbell, Marshall's assistant at the Armchair Tourist

Russ Smith, former owner of the *Stoneham Weekly News*; former president of the Stoneham Chamber of Commerce

Marshall Cambridge, owner of the Armchair Tourist and Tricia's friend with benefits

A Deadly
Deletion

ONE

"**Are you** out of your mind?" Tricia Miles said, raising her voice. She had good reason to do so, too.

Stoneham Police Chief Grant Baker stood before her in stunned silence. His marriage proposal had been the second Tricia had received within fifteen minutes—and she hadn't expected either of them.

Tricia's relationship with Marshall Cambridge had pretty much been "friends with benefits." She enjoyed his company, he encouraged her independence, but there had been a distinct lack of passion. She hadn't given him an answer, but she had an answer for Chief Baker.

"Absolutely not!"

"Why won't you marry me?" he asked, sounding like a petulant child.

Tricia kept her jaw from dropping in shock, but only just. "You couldn't commit to me when we were together, and now you've jilted your fiancée weeks before that wedding to ask me to marry you. What are the odds you'll have cold feet again?"

"Zero," he asserted.

"Yeah, and I've got a bridge for sale in Brooklyn," she said sarcastically. She pointed toward the door. "Go."

"Tricia, can't we talk this over?"

"There's nothing to talk about. Go!" she repeated. When

he didn't move, she stalked off in the direction of the door, threw it open, and gestured for him to leave.

Just as Baker reached the threshold, the roar of a powerful engine thundered somewhere on Main Street. At first, Tricia wasn't sure which direction it was coming from, but as it grew louder, she realized it was heading north. Baker pushed her aside and darted onto the sidewalk outside Tricia's store, Haven't Got a Clue, just as a big white pickup truck—with lights out—veered toward the sidewalk and Baker. Tricia grabbed him by the back of the shirt, pulling him into her store as the truck swerved into the street. Before either of them could react, they heard someone yell and the terrible sound of a thud before the truck disappeared down the darkened street.

Baker was the first to recover and dashed up the sidewalk with Tricia in hot pursuit.

Up ahead in the middle of the street lay a crumpled form. As Tricia approached, she recognized just who it was.

"Marshall!" she cried.

Baker fell to his knees in front of the supine figure, searching for a pulse, first at the man's wrist, and then reached for his throat.

"Do something!" Tricia cried as tears welled in her eyes.

Baker rose to his feet, his expression one of shock.

"I'm sorry, Tricia. He's dead."

The blue-and-red emergency lights still flashed out on Main Street more than an hour after the accident.

But was it an accident?

Of course it was. It had to be.

"Did you say something, Tricia, dear?" Tricia's sister, Angelica, asked, sounding worried.

The rotating colors from the flashing light bars on the police SUVs below came through the second-floor windows, looking gaudy against the living room's pastel green walls.

Tricia held a glass filled with whiskey, ice, and soda—her second. For some reason, she found the cold condensation beneath her clenched fingers to be of comfort. Well, not comfort, but it proved to her that she could feel something besides the terrible numbness that had encircled her soul.

Marshall. Dead.

"I can't believe it. I . . . I just can't believe it," she murmured.

"I'm here to listen," Angelica said softly from the adjacent chair. "That is, if you're up to talking."

Tricia looked up to take in her sister's worried gaze.

"He asked me to marry him." The echo of that proposal kept rattling around in her brain.

"And you were going to say no."

"I was," Tricia said. "But that didn't mean I didn't have feelings for the man. If nothing else, he was my friend." And lover.

Tricia absently petted the soft fur atop Angelica's dog's head. Every so often, the bichon frise raised his head, looked up at her with soulful brown eyes, and whimpered. He knew when one of his human friends was in pain.

"He had so many plans," Tricia lamented.

"What will happen with the sale of the *Stoneham Weekly News*?" Angelica asked. "Did Marshall sign the final paperwork?"

Tricia shrugged and took a sip of her by-now-watery whiskey. "I don't know. Why do you ask?"

Angelica suddenly stiffened in her chair. "Uh, no reason," she said, but for some reason, her voice had risen in pitch.

Tricia shook her head. What would happen to the women at the little weekly newspaper? They'd been nervous when its owner had put it up for sale—and was now destined for jail. Surely nobody else would be interested in buying the horrible little rag. Marshall had planned to resurrect the dying enterprise. Earlier that evening, over dinner, he'd outlined the plans he'd devised for the paper. Tricia now wished she'd paid more attention to that conversation.

Suddenly, she had a lot of regrets.

"Are you sure I can't get you something to eat?" Angelica asked. Offering food was her way of showing concern. She put such care into the dishes she prepared for others—and, of course, herself.

Tricia shook her head. "We had a lovely dinner at the country club outside of Nashua." She frowned. Marshall's last dinner. And then she'd gone and spoiled his evening by refusing to give him an answer to his proposal. But then, maybe he'd died with his heart full of hope.

Like her ex-husband, Christopher?

Yeah, she'd promised him moments before he died that she'd again wear the engagement ring he'd given her years before. And she had, but for only a few months and mostly on a chain around her neck. She wouldn't get the chance to do the same with the ring Marshall had offered.

"I suppose Chief Baker will want you to make a formal statement," Angelica said.

"It'll be brief, that's for sure. I didn't see much of anything. Just that white pickup careening down the block." She shuddered at the memory, slopping the last of her drink onto poor Sarge, who didn't seem to notice. Another wave of anguish assaulted her. Tricia hadn't taken the time to do more than drag a comb through her hair and freshen her makeup for her (last) date with Marshall.

Her mouth trembled.

"Why don't you stay here tonight?" Angelica suggested, and reached to place a hand on her sister's arm.

Tricia looked down at the boot her sister still wore on her right foot—part of her recovery from bunion surgery. Although Angelica was getting around better, she was in no position to host a guest. And if Tricia was going to have to change sheets, she'd rather do it on her own bed—and certainly not that night.

"It's good of you to offer, but I think I'll just go home."

"What if the chief wants to get hold of you?"

"I'll text him to let him know I'm going back to my apartment, but first I'll take Sarge out for a tinkle break."

"Oh, you're so good to both of us," Angelica clucked.

Tricia got up, taking her now-empty glass to the kitchen

and placing it in the dishwasher. Then she headed for the door, slipped on her jacket, and reached for the dog's leash. He knew that sound and came bounding across the room like a gazelle. "We'll be back in a few minutes," Tricia called.

"I'll be here."

Tricia reached down and picked up the dog, carrying him down the stairs. Not that he couldn't handle them, but he sometimes tended to try to trip whoever was at the end of his tether.

Tricia disabled the security system and exited the Cookery's back door, still carrying Sarge, finally setting him down when she reached a patch of grass on the other side of the alley.

Knowing this was his last foray outside for the night, Sarge took his time sniffing for the perfect spot to christen. "Speed it up, Sarge. It's chilly out," Tricia chided him, but Sarge was not to be hurried.

Tricia gazed up and down the alley. It was illegal to park vehicles after hours behind the businesses that lined Stoneham's Main Street. And yet . . .

Tricia squinted. Could it be a white pickup truck parked at the south end of the alley?

After what happened to Marshall, Tricia wasn't about to investigate.

She yanked on Sarge's leash. "Ready or not, it's time to go in," she told him.

Sarge dug in his heels.

"Sarge!"

The vehicle's headlights suddenly flashed to life—instantly switching to the powerful high beams—and the truck was immediately on the move, heading straight up the alley.

Tricia bent down, grabbed Sarge, tucking him under her arm like a football, and made it across the asphalt and up the concrete steps behind the Cookery just before the truck would have hit her.

It roared past, heading for Hickory Street. Surely Stoneham's best would catch the driver and arrest him—or her.

Breathing hard, and with shaking hands, Tricia reentered the Cookery. She set Sarge down and fumbled for her phone, quickly texting Chief Baker.

The same truck that hit Marshall just came after me in the alley behind the Cookery!

Seconds later, Baker answered. *Stay put.*

The sound of a siren broke the night as Tricia turned on every light in the Cookery and planted herself by the store's entrance, peering out the door's plate glass window to watch for Baker. He was there in seconds. Tricia fumbled to unlock the door.

"Did your men get him?"

"It's too soon to tell," Baker said as Sarge, who was no fan of Stoneham's top cop, began to growl. "Are you sure the truck was aiming for you?"

"There was nobody else in the alley."

Small though he was, Sarge had sharp teeth, which he bared, looking like he might pounce at any second.

"Can you put that damn dog away?" Baker barked.

"This is his home," Tricia remarked, "and he's protecting it. It's what dogs do."

Baker's lip curled, but he took a step back just the same.

Tricia picked up Sarge, who launched into full-throated barking. "I'll take him upstairs. Then, if you'd be so kind, would you walk me home?" It was only a few steps down the sidewalk, but Tricia felt rattled.

Baker's eyes lit up. "Of course," he readily agreed. "I'll check in with my team and be back in a minute."

"Thanks."

Tricia turned the lock on the door and, still holding on to Sarge, headed for the door that led to Angelica's apartment. She had a feeling her evening was about to get a whole lot longer.

TWO

 Tricia awoke late the next morning, surprised she'd been able to sleep at all—and dreamless at that. No nightmares about seeing Marshall's lifeless body. No terror of the white pickup aiming to run her over. Nothing. Maybe that was good. Perhaps her mind was trying to give her ragged emotions a brief respite. Or maybe she'd just been exhausted.

Although it was nearly time to open Haven't Got a Clue, Tricia didn't feel like meeting the public. She'd let her assistant manager, Pixie Poe, and her other employee, Mr. Everett, handle that. But what was she supposed to do all day? Hide in her basement office? She could run away to a hotel or a resort for a few days to try to heal, but she'd be carrying her feelings of remorse and sorrow with her. She didn't even feel like retreating to her bedroom nook to read the day away—especially not stories filled with death and misery.

Though it was much later than her usual morning walk, Tricia decided not to forgo that ritual. Yet she would have to at least face Pixie and go through her tale of woe once again. Unfortunately, she'd probably have to repeat the story over and over again to friends, family, and colleagues for the foreseeable future—something she wasn't looking forward to.

Pixie arrived just as Tricia was making the coffee. "Morning, Tricia. How are you today?" Pixie called brightly. Obviously, she hadn't heard about Marshall's death.

Tricia turned to face her assistant manager. "Uh, I—I didn't sleep well last night," she lied. Was the fact she slept well damning in itself?

"Oh, I'm so sorry. Reading 'til dawn again?"

"Not quite." Tricia braved a smile. "When I finally dropped off, I woke up late and I haven't had my walk. Do you mind if I go now?"

"Oh, sure. Get it over with before it rains. It's supposed to be a gloomy afternoon."

Tricia already felt gloomy. "Thanks. I'll get my jacket and be off. I shouldn't be more than half an hour or so."

"Take your time. We haven't exactly been inundated with customers this week."

That was true enough, although that would change any day now once the tourists returned in force to witness New England's spectacular fall colors.

Tricia was tempted to head out the shop's back door, but then remembered her near-lethal encounter with the white pickup truck. When he'd returned to the Cookery the previous evening, Baker had warned her to be careful. The someone who'd killed Marshall might be determined to take her life, too. That said, she felt pretty safe walking the village streets in broad—if dreary—daylight.

Pixie had taken off her coat and the women sidled past each other near the reader's nook. "Have fun!" Pixie called.

Fun? Feeling the way she did, Tricia wasn't sure she'd ever have fun again.

June, the Cookery's manager, had already arrived and gave Tricia a sad, tentative wave as she passed the store's big display window. Since Angelica's surgery, if Tricia didn't call or stop in early, June would take Sarge out to do his business. After what had happened the previous evening, Tricia was sure Angelica wouldn't expect her sister to show up for dog duty that morning. From June's expression, she must have heard what happened to Marshall—and probably from Angelica.

Instead of a brisk walk, Tricia's gait more resembled a

slow drag, and after covering only half her usual three miles, Tricia turned back for home.

She'd taken her usual route around the village, going up and down streets, but eventually, she'd have to pass by Marshall's shop, the Armchair Tourist. The store had done better after Tricia had loaned its former owner, Chauncey Porter, money to invest in the business, but it had positively flourished under Marshall's guidance.

Tricia's gut tightened as she turned the corner of Cedar Avenue and walked up the west side of Main Street, nearing Marshall's store. But as she came closer, she noticed someone on the sidewalk ahead of her: Ava Campbell, Marshall's assistant.

Ava's gait was jaunty, and she swung her purse as she walked. She caught sight of Tricia and waved.

Oh no oh no oh no! Tricia did not want to be the bearer of bad news, but there was no way she could avoid Ava—and not to tell her about her boss's passing would be the ultimate betrayal.

"Hey, Tricia!" Ava called.

Tricia braved a smile and waved, slowing her pace.

The two women met outside Booked for Lunch, which wouldn't open for another two hours, its usually cheerful, blinking OPEN sign dark and lifeless.

"You're awfully early for work, aren't you?" Tricia asked.

"Uh-huh. We got a new shipment of electrical items in yesterday, and Marshall asked me to come in early to do an inventory. I don't mind. Overtime is overtime," she said, and laughed. "You can't go to Europe without those adapter plugs, you know."

"Yes. We took some on our trip to Ireland last month."

"Marshall had lots of cool stories to share when he got home." Ava laughed. "He's a great storyteller. I almost felt like I'd been along on the trip, too."

"Yes, well . . . there's something I need to tell you."

"Sure. What?"

Tricia let out a breath. "There was an accident here on Main Street last night."

"Oh, yeah, I saw what was left of some crime tape in the street. I picked it up and tossed it in the trash."

"You're a good citizen," Tricia said quietly.

Ava shrugged. "Just doing what anyone would."

Not these days.

"What about this accident?" Ava asked.

"It was a hit-and-run. A big white pickup truck."

"That's terrible."

"The victim was killed instantly."

"That's even worse," Ava said, her breath catching. "Was it anyone we know?"

"I'm afraid so. It was Marshall."

Ava's expression turned from concern to disbelief. "You're messing with me, right?"

Tricia shook her head. "I'm afraid not."

Ava's mouth began to tremble and her eyes filled with tears. "He's dead?"

Tricia nodded.

"But that can't be," Ava cried. "I just spoke to him last night at closing."

Tricia reached out and pulled the twentysomething young woman into an embrace as Ava began to sob. She held on for long moments wondering why she wasn't crying in commiseration. She felt the same terrible loss, but for some reason, she still couldn't cry. Was it shock or guilt? She wasn't sure what exactly she felt besides the cold numbness that didn't seem to want to leave her.

"Why don't you come on over to Haven't Got a Clue and have a cup of coffee with me?" Tricia asked.

Ava pulled back and shook her head. "I've got to open those boxes of stock before we open for the day, and—"

Tricia shook her head sadly. "Ava, you won't be opening today."

"But . . ." Ava wiped her sleeve against her tearstained cheek. "No, I guess we won't. What am I supposed to do?"

"I'm sorry, I don't know."

Ava cleared her throat and stood straighter, shaking her

head. "No. I *am* going to open the store. I mean, I need to. I need to keep it going for . . . whoever now owns it. Wouldn't they expect that of a good employee?"

Tricia sure wouldn't, but it was a testament to Ava's work ethic and loyalty that she wanted to. She gave the woman a sad smile. "I'm sure Marshall would be pleased."

Ava nodded and swallowed hard. "It must be really hard for you. Especially after last night."

"Last night?" Tricia asked.

"Oh, then he didn't ask you to—" She stopped herself. Ava had known Marshall was going to ask her to marry him, whereas Tricia had been blindsided. She pretended she didn't know what Ava was intimating.

"Never mind," Ava said, and withdrew her keys from her jacket pocket. "I'd better get to work."

Tricia was about to say *Have a good day*, but stopped herself just in time. "It'll be a hard day for both of us. Let's try to think of all the times Marshall made us laugh."

Ava nodded bravely. "Okay."

"We'll talk again soon," Tricia promised, and patted Ava's arm.

Ava nodded and carried on to the Armchair Tourist. Tricia watched until she entered the store and closed the door behind her, then carried on down the street. She had intended to go directly back to Haven't Got a Clue but wasn't sure she was up to going through the whole story with Pixie and Mr. Everett. Not yet. Instead, she decided to walk a few more blocks to try and shore up her courage.

An SUV was parked in front of the Happy Domestic, its gate open, displaying pots full of cheerful chrysanthemums in gold, brown, yellow, and a few pink ones, too. Nigela Ricita Associates paid for the flowers for a second time that year, since the now-ex-president of the Chamber of Commerce had slashed them from the budget. Since she'd begun her walk, the urns in front of a number of shops were now decked out with fall color. It was a bright spot on a very gloomy morning.

As Tricia approached the *Stoneham Weekly News*, her

steps slackened still more. Marshall had practically gushed the evening before when describing his plans for the horrible little paper.

Tricia frowned. He would have turned the business around. With Russ Smith no longer at its helm, Tricia might have even tried to enjoy the little weekly rag. She wasn't sure she'd be willing to give it a chance . . . if it survived.

As Tricia approached the paper's modest display window, she noticed the lights were on inside. They suddenly winked off, and Russ's girl Friday, Patti Perkins, backed out, locking the door before turning with a start. "Tricia! You nearly gave me a heart attack."

"I'm sorry."

Patti's shock soon turned to dismay. "Oh, Tricia, I was so sorry to hear about poor Mr. Cambridge."

News sure traveled fast.

"Thank you," Tricia murmured. "You must be as devastated as me. Just when it looked like your jobs at the newspaper would have been saved . . ."

"Oh, but they have been saved. Thank goodness Nigela Ricita has bailed us out," Patti said with relief.

Tricia's jaw dropped. "What?"

Patti grinned. "They've bought the paper and if they can iron out the details with the attorneys, we'll be back to full speed by next Monday."

"But—who's taking charge?" Tricia demanded.

Patti gave an exaggerated shrug, her gaze suddenly dreamy. "That divinely handsome Antonio Barbero."

Tricia's eyes widened and the heat of a blush rose up her neck to color her cheeks. Why hadn't Angelica mentioned this to her? Had she swooped down like a vulture to pick at the carcass of the plans Marshall had left behind?

"How did you find out about this?" Tricia asked, her voice strained.

"From Mr. Barbero—Antonio," Patti corrected herself. "He popped into the office about an hour ago to tell me the good news."

Tricia's mouth twisted into an annoyed frown.

"Is something wrong?" Patti asked.

Tricia shook her head and struggled with her emotions. "Nothing. I'm . . . I'm so happy for you and Ginger."

"Can I call you on Monday about reserving some ad space?" Patti asked eagerly.

Tricia struggled not to cry. "Sure."

"Aw, you're the best! Talk to you soon." And with that, Patti scurried down the sidewalk with a decided spring in her step.

Anger fueled Tricia's pace as she briskly resumed her walk south on Main Street. She pulled out her phone, flipped through her contacts list, and stabbed Angelica's number.

"Hello, Tricia," Angelica sang upon answering. "I sure hope you're feeling better after what happened last night."

"We need to talk. Now!" Tricia said.

"Oh, dear. I don't think I like your tone," Angelica quipped. "Have I upset you in any way?"

"Oh, you know damn well you did."

"Whatever are you talking about?" Angelica said in all innocence.

"We'll discuss this in person. I'll be right up," Tricia said, stabbed the end-call icon, and entered the Cookery.

June looked about to speak, no doubt to offer her condolences, but took a step back upon seeing Tricia's furious expression.

Tricia stalked to the door marked PRIVATE, threw it open, and took the stairs two at a time.

Sarge was barking up a storm of pure joy, but then abruptly quit as soon as Tricia entered the apartment. He was good at sensing the moods of the humans around him and quickly vamoosed to the safety of his bed.

"Why is Antonio taking over the *Stoneham Weekly News*?" Tricia began without preamble.

Angelica sat on one of the kitchen island's stools, still clad in her pink chenille robe, with a pink fuzzy slipper on one foot and the ugly black boot on the other. She gave a nervous laugh. "Oh, that. Yes, I was going to let you know about that—this afternoon, at lunch."

"You know there are no secrets in this village. Why would you let someone else leak it to me?" Tricia demanded.

Angelica's expression darkened. "Who's the blabber-mouth?"

"Patti Perkins. I just spoke to her and—"

Angelica scowled. "It isn't quite a done deal—not until we turn over a Nigela Ricita check," she hedged.

"And when's that going to happen?"

"Um, this afternoon."

"So fast?"

"Yes. As it turns out, Russ hadn't cashed Marshall's check, so there won't be a delay."

Tricia pursed her lips, feeling as though she might explode. "How could you swoop in and buy the *Stoneham Weekly News* without even consulting me first?"

Angelica shrugged. "Because I knew it would upset you—although, for the life of me I can't see why."

"Marshall's not even cold in his grave and—"

"And what?" Angelica objected. "We saved a Stoneham institution and the livelihood of many people."

"Many?" Tricia challenged. "Patti and Ginger are not 'many.'"

"There are the people who actually print the newspaper, the paper and ink suppliers, the US Postal Service . . . The list goes on and on."

"Losing one account wouldn't have hurt any of them. Much," Tricia amended.

"We don't know that," Angelica said reasonably.

Tricia couldn't argue with that kind of logic. She changed tacks. "Why on earth would Antonio want to run a newspaper?"

"Well, he minored in journalism when at university," Angelica pointed out.

Tricia frowned. "I didn't know that."

"Now you do. And you know he's been itching to do something other than managing the Brookview Inn. And now that we've brought in Hank Curtis to run the place—"

"He's only had the job for five days!"

"He won't be there on his own. I've got a crack team, plus the fact that I *am* his supervisor. I can give him direct guidance."

"You mean Nigela Ricita is his supervisor."

Angelica waved a hand in dismissal. "Same thing."

Tricia felt herself deflating. It still seemed wrong that Marshall's dream of running the paper had been snatched away. The fact that he was dead and would never see that ambition fulfilled was beside the point. Kind of.

"You're upset," Angelica simpered. "Why don't I make you a nice soothing cup of tea? I've got some apple cinnamon scones in the freezer. I can pop one in the microwave and it'll taste just like it came out of the oven."

Tricia thought it over. Most people found comfort in eating. For years she never allowed herself to do so. Now was just as good a time as any to start. Besides, she hadn't had any breakfast. "Well, okay," she said, feeling defeated.

Angelica put the electric kettle on and brought out the pretty rose-patterned teapot. Next, she collected several tea bags from a glass jar on the counter. When the water boiled, she made the tea and set the dishes on the island. Tricia would have helped, but she was still angry at her sister. And, besides, she was grieving. It wasn't a good excuse, but it was all she had.

Angelica popped the scones into the microwave and less than a minute later set them on the plates before shuffling over to the island. "There you are."

Tricia had to admit, the scones smelled wonderful. She took a bite as Angelica poured Tricia's tea. Delicious.

Angelica sat on one of the stools and poured milk into her cup before pouring the tea. "Are you terribly angry with us?"

Tricia took another bite of her scone, enjoying the flavor, making her sister wait for her answer. "Yes. No. Definitely."

"Will you get over it anytime soon?"

"Send a couple of these scones home with me and I might."

Angelica grinned, but it was short-lived. "What are you going to do today?"

"I don't know. From what he told me, Marshall had no

family. I don't know who will make the funeral arrangements. Maybe his lawyer? As a businessman, he had to have
a will." It suddenly occurred to Tricia that although she and
Marshall had been sort of a couple, there was a lot about the
man she hadn't known. Maybe that was another reason she
hadn't wanted to be more than friends with benefits. They'd
been intimate—but failed to share the kind of intimacy she
and Christopher had at the beginning of their relationship.

She took another bite of the scone, wishing Angelica had
come up with some clotted cream, and contemplated her previous thought. Would she forever compare every man she
was with to Christopher?

Probably.

"You never did tell me why Chief Baker came to see you
last night before . . . before the accident."

Tricia picked up her cup and sipped her tea. "He asked me
to marry him."

Angelica nearly dropped her cup. "He what?"

Tricia shrugged. "I told him no."

"I should think so," Angelica said. "Why on earth would
he think you'd marry him?"

"Completely delusional," Tricia muttered, and polished
off the last of her scone. By now Baker had to know about
the engagement ring Marshall had slipped back into his trou-
ser pocket. It would have been listed as a personal effect by
the medical examiner. Would Baker interrogate her about
that when she came in to make her statement? She hoped
another officer would be assigned to that duty, but one never
knew. Baker would know she hadn't automatically accepted
Marshall's proposal. Would that give him false hope that he
could again try to pursue her? If so, she'd nip that notion in
the bud without delay. And she didn't yet have all the answers she needed from her sister, either.

"Why didn't you buy the paper the minute Russ put it up
for sale?"

"Antonio and I talked about it, but we certainly didn't think
Marshall would snap it up within a day or so of the announce-
ment."

It had seemed a hasty decision to Tricia, too.

"Patti said Antonio intended to start work on Monday. Isn't that rather soon?"

Angelica shrugged. "As Marshall proved last night: life is short. Why wait?"

Tricia felt herself deflate. Why wait indeed.

THREE

By the time Tricia returned to Haven't Got a Clue, word had reached Pixie concerning Marshall's death. She rushed to the store's entrance and threw her arms around Tricia. "I'm so sorry," she whispered over and over again. "I'm so . . . so sorry."

Suddenly, it was Tricia comforting Pixie. "It's okay," she said. "Well, no, it's not okay . . . but . . ." She ran out of words. Mr. Everett had arrived for work and lurked in the background, looking quite upset.

Pixie pulled back. "Can I get you a cup of coffee? Do you want something to eat? Would you like me to find a book you haven't read? We have that set of 1940s Nancy Drews. I always find them a comfort to read when I'm upset."

"That's very kind of you, but . . . I don't think I can even read right now."

Pixie nodded and dabbed at a tear welling in her left eye.

"Is there anything we can do, Ms. Miles?" Mr. Everett asked sincerely.

Tricia shook her head. "We just have to get through the day and then . . ."

"Happy hour?" Pixie suggested.

Tricia had nothing to be happy about. Alcohol was a depressant, and six o'clock was seven hours away, but she was already craving her usual martini.

"Maybe you should take the day off," Pixie advised.

"And do what?"

"Well, you could bake. When you do, it seems to make you almost as happy as Angelica when she's conjuring up a sweet treat."

Tricia considered the suggestion. She could make some cookies for her customers. And maybe she could make some canapés to share with Angelica before dinner. . . . Goodness only knew, she now had no one else to share them with.

"That's a good idea. I could make thumbprint cookies—"

"Please don't make them especially for me," Mr. Everett protested.

"I'll eat some, too," Pixie piped up.

"Okay. Thumbprints it is, although I'm not sure what kind of jam I have on hand."

"Then it will be a surprise," Mr. Everett said hopefully.

Tricia almost laughed. "Yes, it will."

The shop's door opened, and a heavyset man of about fifty with what looked like dyed brown hair entered. "I'm looking for Tricia Miles."

Something about the man made Tricia feel uneasy. "That's me."

"Ms. Miles? I'm Deputy Marshal David Kirby." The man brandished his ID.

Tricia felt every muscle in her body tense. "What can I do for you?"

"I'd like to have a word with you—in private," he said, his skeptical gaze taking in Pixie, who that day was wearing a khaki skirt and matching jacket, looking like one of the Andrews Sisters and at any moment about to burst into "Boogie Woogie Bugle Boy."

"What's this about?" Mr. Everett asked, moving to step between Tricia and the government agent. He was at least a foot shorter than Kirby, and probably fifty pounds lighter, but Tricia appreciated his protective gesture.

"Mr. Marshall Cambridge."

Tricia knew that federal marshals tracked down fugitives. They transported prisoners. They were responsible for protection at federal courts and enforcing the decisions made by those judges. And they were also responsible for the security of witnesses.

A cold fist of dread seemed to clench Tricia's heart.

Federal marshals were also in charge of the federal Witness Protection Program.

Tricia's mouth felt dry as she answered, "Of course. My office is on the lower level." It sounded so much nicer than saying *the basement*. "If you'll follow me, please."

Tricia started for the back of the store with Kirby following in her wake.

"Call me if you need me," Pixie hollered.

"And me," Mr. Everett echoed.

Tricia flipped the light switch and led the marshal down the stairs. She ushered him into her guest chair and turned her own from in front of the desk to face him.

"First of all, I'm very sorry for the loss of your"—he hesitated—"friend."

"Thank you."

"I've spoken with Chief Baker of the Stoneham Police Department and he gave me your name."

She figured as much.

"Why are you here, Mr. Kirby?"

Kirby hesitated. "I was the agent in charge of Mr. Cambridge's case."

"Was he enrolled in the Witness Protection Program?" Tricia asked. She didn't have the patience to waste time fencing.

"Er, yes. How did you know? Did he inform you?"

Tricia shook her head. "I read and sell all kinds of mysteries, Mr. Kirby. I'm well aware of what federal marshals do when carrying out their responsibilities. What crime did Marshall—or whatever his real name was—do?"

"Unlike most of the participants in our program, Mr. Cambridge was not a convicted criminal."

"Unconvicted?" she asked.

Kirby shook his head. "I'm not at liberty to say."

"May I assume everything Marshall told me was a lie?" she asked, trying to stay calm.

"I don't know what he told you, ma'am," Kirby said matter-of-factly.

"That he was a former college professor."

Kirby shook his head.

"That he was a widower."

Again Kirby shook his head.

"He was married?" Tricia asked, startled, although she knew the WPP had an all-or-nothing policy when it came to families.

"Divorced before he entered the program."

The terrible yoke of grief became that much lighter with every new revelation.

"Was his death an accident?" Tricia asked, dreading the answer.

"We don't think so," Kirby said, his voice level.

"You believe the man he helped convict was responsible?"

"More likely a relative or a business associate."

Tricia nodded, trying to make sense of everything she'd just learned. "What was his real name?"

"Eugene Marshall Chandler."

"So at least one thing about him was true." His middle name.

"We encourage those under our protection to assume a name they'll readily answer to."

Eugene. Marshall would never have struck Tricia as a Eugene. Gene maybe, but not Eugene.

None of that mattered anymore.

The fact that Kirby had dropped by meant he hadn't come simply as a courtesy call. "What is it I can do for you, Mr. Kirby?"

He pulled a small notebook and pen from his suit pocket. "Please tell me exactly what you saw last night at the time of the . . . incident."

Tricia gave a brief description, trying to keep her emotions in check.

Kirby jotted down a few sentences. "What did Chandler tell you about his upcoming plans?"

"That he intended to stay here in Stoneham and take over the local weekly newspaper."

"Yes, we've ascertained that. Anything else?"

Tricia hesitated before answering. "He asked me to marry him."

Kirby's gaze dipped. "Yes. A box with an engagement ring was found on the body. I assume you said no."

"Is it any of your business what I told him?"

His gaze hardened. "I'm investigating a probable murder, ma'am. Everything is relevant."

"And you suspect me?" she asked, aghast. "You must know I was in the company of the Stoneham chief of police when Marshall—er, Eugene—was struck by the pickup."

"I understand that. But apparently, you were the person closest to him. We'd like to know Chandler's state of mind at the time of his death."

Really?

Tricia sighed. "I didn't say no. In fact, I didn't give him an answer. His proposal was totally unexpected and caught me off guard."

Kirby nodded. If a thought balloon suddenly appeared over his head—like in the comics—it probably would have sarcastically said, *Sure*.

Tricia suddenly remembered Ava. "Will you be talking to Marshall's employee at the Armchair Tourist?"

"It's my next stop."

Poor Ava. Unlike Patti and Ginger, she would be out of a job sooner rather than later. That is, if Angelica didn't rush in to buy that business, too. She already owned half of the village under her own and Nigela Ricita's names.

"What will happen to Mar—Eugene's—remains?"

"His lawyers have been notified of his death. Whatever arrangements he made will be carried out."

"He led me to believe he was alone in the world. Will the lawyers carry out his final wishes?"

Kirby's face remained immobile. "I don't know, ma'am."

Tricia despised being called ma'am. It made her feel so *old*.

"Will you be in charge of the investigation into Marshall's death?"

"We'll do a preliminary investigation, but we'll likely turn it over to the local jurisdiction. Officially, Mr. Chandler left our protection the moment he died."

Wow. Talk about cold. But then Marshall had been just another cog in the program's machinery.

"Is there anything else I can tell you?" she asked.

"If I have more questions, I'll be in contact." Kirby rose from his chair and turned to leave.

"I'll show you out," Tricia said.

Kirby paused at the stairs. "I can find my way. Thank you for speaking with me today."

Tricia merely nodded. She watched him go before turning to collapse into her office chair.

Everything Marshall told me was a lie, she thought. But those lies had kept him alive—until the evening before, at least.

Tricia frowned, unsure what to feel. If she'd committed herself to Marshall and then found out everything about him was a sham, she'd have felt shaken to the core. She wasn't sure she wasn't already that shaken. But the terrible grief and guilt she felt had been muted by Kirby's revelations.

Now she simply felt numb.

Tricia must have sat staring at the floor for nearly half an hour, thinking about the past—the present—and what was to be her future.

Her talk with Deputy Kirby hadn't been all that informative. But Tricia knew someone who could probably tell her a lot more.

Grant Baker . . . that is, if he was still speaking to her.

Sure he was. He'd been quite concerned after the pickup had come after her the night before. He'd told her she could call him day or night. He could afford to be nice to her if he thought he had a chance to get back in her good graces.

It really wouldn't be fair to prey on that hope. But then . . . how was she supposed to find out what happened to Marshall? Deputy Kirby wasn't likely to keep her in the loop. She would just have to be honest with Stoneham's top cop.

That decided, Tricia rose from her chair and headed back to her store. As she rounded the top of the stairs, she grabbed her jacket, donned it, and headed for the front entrance.

"Going somewhere?" Pixie asked, looking anxious.

"I need to see someone."

"About Marshall?"

Tricia nodded. "I'll be back as soon as I can."

Pixie nodded.

"We'll be here," Mr. Everett assured her.

Tricia left the store and headed north, crossing the street at the village's only traffic light. It took less than two minutes to reach the Stoneham police station.

She entered the station and, as usual, the receptionist, Polly Burgess, looked up from her computer and scowled. She was no fan of Tricia's. With no real knowledge of her relationship with Baker, the older woman had assumed that Tricia had broken the chief's heart when they'd broken up several years before. If the cop pined for her, it had been his own fault, not Tricia's.

She didn't want to waste another second thinking about it.

"Is Chief Baker in?"

"No."

"Then why are his car and his service SUV sitting in the parking lot out back?" Tricia had learned to take note of such things, as Polly usually tried to blow her off.

"Oh, are they?" Polly asked, playing innocent.

"I'm here to make an official statement. The chief will want to know I've arrived."

Polly frowned but pressed the intercom key. "Sir, Ms. Miles is here to see you."

Instead of answering, seconds later the door to Baker's inner sanctum opened.

"Come on in, Tricia," Baker said gently.

Tricia strode past the receptionist, who she was sure

would stick out her tongue as soon as Tricia's back was turned.

Baker closed the door and gestured for Tricia to sit in one of the chairs before his steel-and-Formica desk. "What can I do for you?"

"What can you tell me about Marshall's death?"

"You've no doubt already been visited by Deputy Kirby."

"Yes, and he didn't seem to have many answers."

Baker shrugged. "I probably don't, either—not now, at least. Maybe in a couple of days I'll know more once the feds wash their hands of it."

"Does that mean you aren't expecting me to give an official statement?"

"Sure—for our records. Did Kirby ask for one?"

She shook her head. "He took notes, but didn't ask for anything more." She shrugged. "Maybe he figured I'd turn into a hysterical female."

"He'd be wrong about that." Baker looked down. "I, uh, didn't have an opportunity before now to express my condolences to you on your loss."

"Thank you," Tricia murmured. "Did you know about the . . ." She couldn't bring herself to say the words.

Baker raised an eyebrow. "The engagement ring?"

Tricia nodded.

"I assume you said no."

Tricia frowned. "You assume wrong."

"Oh, so that's why you blew me off so explosively."

"Explosively?" Tricia echoed. "Your proposal was just ridiculous."

Baker ignored her. "If you said yes, then why did Cambridge still have the ring?"

"I didn't say no or yes. I said I'd think about it."

"That's pretty wishy-washy."

Tricia's frown deepened. Baker always seemed to know which of her buttons to push. "Unlike some people, I take the idea of marriage very seriously."

"So do I."

Tricia felt tempted to laugh and say something snide but

decided not to go there. She rose from her chair. "Can I write out my statement and go? I have a business to run."

"Yeah, I have crimes to solve."

Ha!

"Polly will help you with the paperwork."

"Fine. I'll talk to you later, Grant."

Much later.

FOUR

Tricia spent the rest of the morning wandering from task to task without really accomplishing anything. She just couldn't seem to concentrate. In her mind's eye, she kept seeing Marshall's hopeful expression when he'd asked her to marry him. Thinking about it, she was glad she hadn't given him an answer, and she knew in her heart she would have eventually said no, but it would have been after careful thought and with words meant not to hurt.

Because of the many deaths that had plagued the village since her arrival, some of the villagers considered her a jinx, which was ridiculous. Those unkind souls could have applied the same moniker to any number of booksellers who'd opted to move to the village that had become known in the New England area as Booktown. It just happened that Tricia had an uncanny knack for finding the newly deceased. In this case, those trolls might well brand her a black widow, as well. Except . . . that Baker still lived. Would he, too, eventually be doomed?

Though they had parted several years before, and though there was still a kind of magnetic pull she sometimes felt for Baker, there was no way she would ever commit herself to him, and although he had a penchant for annoying her, she would never wish him ill.

Such thoughts clouded her mind, and though she helped several customers during the morning, she felt the need to think and contemplate. She canceled her usual lunch with Angelica and ate alone—save for the company of her cat— then made the dough for the cookies for her staff and possible customers, but decided to let it chill in the fridge overnight.

Tricia spent the rest of the afternoon giving her apartment a thorough cleaning. She finally returned to Haven't Got a Clue only minutes before closing. Mr. Everett had already left for the day and Pixie had just finished washing the cof- feepots and cups.

"Feeling better?" Pixie asked sympathetically.

Tricia shook her head. "Not really."

Pixie nodded. "We heard a whole lotta vacuuming go- ing on."

"Yes, well . . . it was mind-numbing work and just what I needed."

"You know, you could take a couple of days off," Pixie offered once again. "Maybe go somewhere fun."

Tricia shook her head. "I just need time. Besides, we're starting to get busy again. I don't want to leave you and Mr. Everett at such an important time of year."

Pixie nodded. "I placed the day's receipts in the safe. Ev- erything on the sales floor is set up for tomorrow."

"Thanks, Pixie. You're a gem."

The women grabbed their coats and headed for the door. Tricia turned off the lights and locked the door. They walked together until they reached the Cookery. "See you tomor- row," Tricia said.

"You bet," Pixie said, and gave a wave as she headed north.

The Cookery had already closed and Tricia let herself in, heading for the back of the store to the door marked PRIVATE that led to Angelica's apartment. As usual, Sarge heard her plodding up the stairs and began to bark in happy anticipa- tion.

"Oh, hush!" Angelica called, but doggy joy knows no bounds, and it was only after Tricia tossed him a biscuit that the dog quieted.

"I missed you at lunch," Angelica said by way of a greeting as she stirred the awaiting pitcher of martinis.

"I'm sorry, Ange. I just needed some time," Tricia said, and draped her jacket on the back of one of the kitchen island's stools. "Do you need help with that?"

Angelica shook her head. "Thank goodness for my little knee scooter. I should have been using it more. But the good news is, I can put a little weight on that foot. Hopefully, I'll be back in the pink in no time."

"And to think you'll have to go through all that suffering again when you have the other foot done."

"Oh, no," Angelica said fiercely. "I've given it some thought and—much as I hate to admit it—stilettos are just not that important to me anymore."

Tricia blinked. "What brought on that revelation?"

Angelica retrieved the chilled glasses from the fridge. "I've been stuck here at home for weeks on end. I could have been doing so many useful things—but instead, my foot is killing me. I've had time to think about just how frivolous—and painful—those heels are. It was difficult, but I boxed them all up and will give them to the thrift shop on the highway. They serve the homeless. If they can make a few bucks off the shoes to help feed or clothe somebody, all the better. And I ordered myself five pairs of flats online. They should arrive in a couple of days. I figure I should get used to wearing them as soon as possible."

Wow. She really was making a lifestyle change. "Good for you, Ange."

"I made some sausage rolls. They should be ready just about—" *Ping!* The stove timer went off. "Now."

"I'll get them and bring the drinks out to the living room. You go sit down—take a load off that foot."

"With pleasure."

Tricia set the sausage rolls on a plate and ferried them and the stemmed glasses to the big coffee table. After the sisters had settled in, Tricia grabbed her glass. "If anyone deserves a martini, especially after the day I've had—it's me," Tricia said.

Angelica raised her glass. "I imagine Antonio will pop open a bottle of wine," she said sadly. "It's too bad Ginny's pregnant. I'm sure she needs a glass or four about now. We should drink to Antonio's new job and to Marshall."

Tricia raised her glass. "To Antonio and Eugene Chandler."

"Who's that?"

"It was Marshall's real name."

Angelica blinked. "Run that by me again."

Tricia took a sip of her drink. No doubt about it, Angelica made one damn fine martini.

Tricia started with Kirby's visit and the news that Marshall had been part of the Witness Protection Program.

"Oh, well, then it's no wonder he was killed."

"Ange," Tricia admonished.

"I'm sorry, dear, but we all know there are loose lips and they do, indeed, sink ships—or at least can cost lives. If I was that Kirby fellow, I'd be looking within my own organization to chase down the leak."

"From what I understand, the program has been very successful—as long as those in it adhere to the rules."

"And you don't think Marshall did?"

"I don't know. Somehow, someone must have tracked him down."

Angelica looked pensive. "Maybe it was a good thing you didn't want to marry him."

"I never said that."

"Of course you did—from the moment you didn't accept his proposal. Anyway, someone might have come after you, too."

Tricia hadn't told Angelica about the truck in the alley. It would have just worried her.

And Tricia wasn't really worried about being targeted anyway. Marshall had never told her about his past life so she didn't have any information to pass on.

Then again, if someone had *tried* to run her down, maybe they thought she might know or have something of Marshall's that could still be incriminating.

Suddenly Tricia didn't feel quite so glib about her safety.

Angelica shook her head. "Well, with the day you've had, it's no wonder you needed to skip lunch for time to think. Did it do any good?"

Tricia shrugged and reached for another sausage roll. "At least I have a clean apartment. What happened in your world today?"

Angelica shrugged. "Just business as usual."

"I suppose now you're planning to buy the Armchair Tourist," Tricia said, and drained her glass.

Angelica shook her head. "Not interested. Although I wouldn't mind getting my hands on that building."

"To buy or lease?"

"I'm not interested in leasing it. But if I could buy it, I'd knock down the wall on the first floor and expand Booked for Lunch's square footage."

"You've already cut into the Bookshelf Diner's clientele. Is it fair to be so cutthroat?"

"Who's being cutthroat? It's the customers who'll make the ultimate judgment on where to eat. Besides, I only do lunch. The Bookshelf is open from six in the morning until nine at night. They're not suffering."

"Could you justify that kind of investment?"

Angelica seemed to muddle over the question. "Maybe. Maybe not. I'd have to give it some careful thought—and, of course, consult Antonio." She looked thoughtful. "Maybe we'd just launch a completely different restaurant. There is only one fine-dining venue in the village." Yes, and she owned that, too. But then she shook her head. "No, I think I'd stick with the lunch crowd. The bulk of Booked for Lunch's customers are outsiders. Local support isn't as great as I'd like."

"What can you do about it?"

"I'll have to give that some thought, too."

"Maybe take out advertising in the *Stoneham Weekly News* once again."

Angelica offered a half smile. "That would help. Maybe I'll offer a discount coupon. It could be a test for Antonio to measure the paper's local reach."

"Now you're talking."

Angelica pulled the last olive from her frill pick, chewed, and swallowed. "Time for a refill."

Tricia got up and did the honors. When she returned, Angelica once again raised her glass. "Now what do we drink to?"

"World peace," Tricia said, thinking of a scene from *Groundhog Day*.

"I'd settle for peace in Stoneham," Angelica muttered, and took her first sip. She looked thoughtful. "Do you think we drink too much?"

"Of course we do," Tricia said, taking a sip. "Isn't that what all unhappy people do?"

"No. And speak for yourself. I have plenty in life to be happy about. In fact, I imbibe to celebrate. You're just unhappy because of Marshall's death and the fact that you didn't love him."

Tricia winced. Angelica could be the epitome of tact . . . except when she was being tactless. Still, Tricia could forgive her because she was absolutely right.

Tricia *did* feel guilty. And she also felt torn. If she'd accepted Marshall's proposal she'd be living a life built on lies. No, she'd been right to trust her gut feelings. Something about the man had always been just a little off, and now, finally, she knew why.

Despite the sparkling-clean apartment and the crisp clean sheets on her bed, Tricia ended up reading until well past two that night and then slept only until six the next morning. She got up and, still in her pajamas and robe, baked the cookies from the dough she'd prepared the day before. She chose strawberry jam for the filling. Mr. Everett would be pleased.

After showering and dressing, Tricia applied her makeup, relying far too heavily on the tube of concealer for the dark circles under her eyes. She breakfasted on a couple of cookies with a cup of coffee while Miss Marple savored her tuna-and-egg surprise, before grabbing the container of cookies and heading down to the shop half an hour before opening.

And it was a good thing, too, because no sooner had she raised the blinds on the front display window when Mary Fairchild walked past and paused at Tricia's store entrance, wildly gesturing for attention. Tricia unlocked the door and Mary, looking efficient with a clipboard in hand, and ready for autumn in a granny-square, hand-crocheted poncho of blue and gold, charged into Haven't Got a Clue.

"Hey, Mare, what can I do for you?" Tricia asked.

"I'm here on official business," Mary said gravely. "But first, I heard about poor Marshall. I'm so sorry for your loss."

"Thank you," Tricia said solemnly.

"Is it true you two were going to tie the knot?"

"We hadn't firmed up any plans," Tricia hedged, not exactly lying, but not telling the truth, either. "What brings you to Haven't Got a Clue today?"

"I've volunteered for the recruitment committee for the Stoneham Chamber of Commerce."

Tricia sighed. She knew where this was going to go.

"I'm very flattered, but—"

"About what?" Mary asked, sounding puzzled.

"About being asked to step in to—"

Mary waved a hand in dismissal. "Oh, we weren't going to ask you to run for president—just to be a part of the recruitment process."

Tricia frowned. But just a week earlier Mary had told Tricia if she decided to run for Russ Smith's job as Chamber head, she would have Mary's backing. What had changed in the last seven or eight days?

"Oh." Tricia couldn't think of another response. "Uh, what's your criteria for finding a replacement?"

"Someone with an open mind, for one. Someone who won't mind cleaning up the mess Russ Smith left behind. Someone willing to spend the next three to five years rebuilding everything we lost."

That was a pretty tall order.

"Who else is on the committee?"

"Dan Reed from the Bookshelf Diner, for one."

"I didn't realize he'd rejoined the Chamber." The man

hadn't forgiven Angelica for opening Booked for Lunch, and when she'd become Chamber president, Reed had quit out of principle. He must have been the only new member during Russ's tenure as Chamber chief.

"He may not want to work with me," Tricia offered.

"Oh, he's fine with it. As long as *you* aren't the one being recruited."

Lovely.

"Anyone else?"

"I'll be talking to Terry McDonald next. But in addition to finding someone to take Russ's place, we need someone who will sweet-talk our old members to rejoin. *You* could be that person," Mary said, looking hopeful.

Tricia considered the offer. Now that Marshall wasn't going to be in her life, she'd have more free time on her hands. She supposed she could make a few phone calls and perhaps visits to former Chamber members. It might make her feel useful. She hated how all Angelica's—and her own—hard work for the Chamber had been undone in just under a year.

"Well, what do you think?" Mary asked.

"How much time do I have to think it over?" Tricia asked.

Mary glanced at her watch. "A minute."

She had to be joking. Tricia asked.

"No, I need an answer right away. I've only got twenty-five minutes before I have to open By Hook or By Book. We want to get the ball rolling ASAP."

Nothing like putting Tricia on the spot. "Well, I guess I could help out for—"

"That's great!" Mary said, and immediately headed for the door. "I'll be in contact." And with that, she practically flew out the door.

Tricia, feeling distinctly unloved, watched Mary scurry to the All Heroes comic-book store next door to talk to Terry, its owner.

Tricia wandered over to the reader's nook and sat down on one of the upholstered chairs, resting her elbow on her knee and her chin on her clenched fist. Miss Marple jumped up on the big square coffee table and said, "*Yow!*"

"Indeed," Tricia told her cat. "Did you hear what Mary said? They don't want me—who has experience working for the Chamber—to be its leader."

"Yow!"

"I know! It's ridiculous."

Of course, she'd been ready to reject an offer to run, but now Tricia felt insulted that the powers that be—whoever they might be—had rejected her out of hand. Was she a glutton for punishment to have agreed to work to find a replacement for Russ Smith—someone, anyone, who was *not* her?

Maybe. Just maybe.

FIVE

 Mr. Everett was the first to report to work that morning, arriving with fresh bagels from the Coffee Bean for himself, Tricia (poppy seed, her favorite), and Pixie.

"You're such a dear," Tricia said, "always thinking of ways to spoil me—and Pixie," she amended.

Mr. Everett blushed. "I wish I could take away your pain. But as I can't, I thought . . ."

"You thought you'd say how much you care with breakfast, and I thank you for it." And especially after the ego-dashing visit with Mary. "Why don't you hang up your coat and I'll get everything ready. Pixie should be here any minute."

And as if on cue, Pixie arrived just a little breathless—as though she'd run the last block—arriving one minute before the store's official opening. That was okay with Tricia. The first hour after opening was usually slow—even during leaf-peeping season. They could afford to spend the time chatting and sipping coffee. Tricia could never be called a cruel task-master.

"Hey, Pixie. Look what Mr. Everett brought us."

Pixie smiled, her gold canine tooth gleaming. "How does he always know when I run late and don't catch breakfast?"

"It's a gift," Tricia agreed with a laugh.

The trio was settled in the reader's nook, enjoying their bagels and chatting, when the shop door opened and the bell over it rang.

A tall, attractive woman with short-cropped blonde hair, who looked to be in her early forties, entered Haven't Got a Clue. Her athletic build was not disguised by the navy tracksuit she wore. Her shoes were the kind some paid hundreds of dollars for, and when she stepped forward, she had a noticeable limp.

"Welcome to Haven't Got a Clue," Pixie called cheerfully, leaping to her feet. "Can I help you find a book?"

"Uh, no, thanks. I'm looking for Tricia Miles."

Tricia stood and stepped forward. "I'm Tricia. How may I help you?"

The woman gave Tricia a thorough once-over before speaking. "I'm Becca Chandler."

For a moment, the name meant nothing to her, but then Tricia remembered her conversation with Kirby the day before.

"Chandler? Are you any relation to Eugene Chandler?"

"I'm his ex-wife."

Tricia blinked. Marshall had described his so-called deceased spouse as a jogger. In that outfit, this woman fit the bill.

"How . . . how may I help you?"

"I just wanted to meet the woman Gene chose to take my place."

Tricia took in Pixie's confused expression. She hadn't shared Marshall's secret with either of her employees.

"Uh, why don't we take this conversation to my office," Tricia suggested, feeling decidedly rattled.

Becca shrugged. "Fine with me."

"This shouldn't take long," Tricia told Pixie and Mr. Everett.

"Take your time," Pixie said with a wave of her hand but didn't immediately return to the reader's nook.

Tricia led the way down to her office, which seemed like it was becoming a habit when visitors arrived.

Once downstairs, Becca took in the space. "Wow. Great light for a room with none of the natural kind."

"Yes, well, I took that into account during the design phase. Won't you have a seat?" she said, waving a hand toward the visitor's chair, à la Vanna White.

Becca took the guest chair Kirby had occupied just the day before. "So, you told him no," Becca said matter-of-factly.

Tricia blinked, startled at her visitor's blunt question. "I didn't. I didn't give him an answer."

Again Becca shrugged.

"I'm surprised to see you here. I thought once someone went underground with the Witness Protection Program, they cut all ties with their old life."

"They're supposed to," Becca said nonchalantly. "Gene got lonely."

"But you were divorced," Tricia reminded the woman.

Becca drew back. "That didn't mean we were enemies. Gene thought long and hard about turning state's evidence against Martin Bailey—for a couple of years. There was no way I was going to give up my career—everything I'd worked for—to live in some corner of East Podunk and become an unassuming nobody."

Tricia frowned. "You mean like me?"

Becca shook her head. "From what I understand, you once ran a powerful nonprofit in Manhattan. What made you want to give that up to come *here*?" With the hint of a sneer she looked around the basement office/storeroom.

Tricia took a calming breath before answering. "I thought the pace would be a lot slower."

"And *is* your life quiet and peaceful?" Becca asked pointedly.

How much had Marshall—er, Gene—told her?

"Not exactly."

Again Becca nodded.

"You seem to know a lot about me, whereas I know nothing about you," Tricia ventured.

Becca blinked incredulously. "You *don't* recognize my name?"

"I'm sorry, but . . . no."

"Rebecca Dickson-Chandler," the woman said pointedly. When Tricia didn't react, she clarified her response. "The tennis player," she said as though to avoid calling Tricia a complete dunce.

Tricia's eyes widened in recognition. "Oh, yes. The two-time US Open women's singles champion."

"*Three*-time," Becca corrected, "among other just as prestigious titles."

"And what are you doing here in Stoneham?" Tricia almost added the word *slumming* to the question, but held her tongue.

"Once the marshals contacted Gene's attorney, he immediately contacted me. I'm the executrix of his estate. He never changed that when he went underground." Becca pulled out her phone and tapped the photo gallery icon. She turned it and flipped through a number of pictures Tricia readily recognized as the Armchair Tourist and the *Stoneham Weekly News*. Something about them seemed off, but she wasn't quite sure why. "Although," Becca continued, "from what I gather, we dodged a bullet—if you'll pardon the rather bad analogy—when it came to that little newspaper. It turns out the owner hadn't cashed the check, so we're off the hook."

"*We?*" Tricia inquired.

Becca gave a little laugh. "Me. Gene seems to have done all right for himself these past few years. I was glad when he dumped that horrid little porn shop for a more respectable business."

"You seem to know a lot about his time here in Stoneham," Tricia said, suddenly feeling ignorant of the finer points of her lover's time in the village.

"We weren't supposed to keep in touch, but like I say . . . Gene got lonely. He found a way for us to communicate."

And was that how whoever killed Marshall traced him to Stoneham? Did Becca realize she might have been of use to her ex-husband's killer? Her attitude so far seemed rather remote, as though attending to the aftermath of Marshall's death was just another item on her list of things to do.

"How long were you married?" Tricia asked.

"Eight years. Probably six of the best years of my life."

Were the first or last two years of that marriage unhappy? Tricia wasn't prepared to ask.

"I don't suppose you'll be staying long in our"—again, Tricia bit her tongue to keep from saying *crummy*—"little village."

Becca shrugged, her expression bland. "I don't know. Gene liked it here. Maybe I would, too."

"We're rather a quiet hamlet." Except for being the murder capital of New Hampshire, that was. "You'd probably be bored in an hour."

Becca nodded. "Maybe."

"Where will you be staying?"

"I booked a room in a place called the Sheer Comfort Inn, but I may just bunk in Gene's apartment for a few days. Is it nice?"

"Yes," Tricia answered guardedly.

"Did you help him decorate it?" Becca asked, her voice hardening.

Was Becca on a fishing expedition?

"Uh, no. The former tenant had a hand in it. Marshall, er, Gene, kept it as it was."

"I understand the former tenant was your ex-husband. He, too, was murdered . . . wasn't he?" Becca asked, her tone suspiciously innocent.

Tricia answered honestly. "Sadly, yes."

Becca cocked her head and squinted at Tricia. "Maybe you *are* the village jinx," she said, her voice growing hard once again.

Tricia stood. "It's been nice speaking with you, Becca," she said, and glanced at her watch, "but I have a business to run. Perhaps we can talk again another day."

Becca's mouth twitched into something that resembled a smile . . . or was it a smirk? She rose from her chair. "Oh, we'll talk again," she said rather snidely, and turned for the stairs. Tricia hesitated before following.

She didn't like Becca Dickson-Chandler.

* * *

It was late in the afternoon when the phone rang at Haven't Got a Clue. Pixie answered it. "Haven't Got a—" She stopped. "Oh, sure, she's right here. Tricia!"

Tricia had been helping Mr. Everett restock shelves, but approached the cash desk.

"It's Ginny," Pixie whispered, and handed Tricia the phone.

"Hey, Ginny, what's up?"

"I'm sorry, but I need to postpone our Thursday lunch. Can we do Friday instead?"

"Sure."

"Great. I've been trying to sweet-talk the owner of a new-to-us print shop to give us a price break for all the printing costs this holiday season and I finally nailed him down. He wants to do a lunch meeting over subs and soda. I want to talk shop on my lunch hour like I want a tooth pulled, but if it saves us ten percent, it will be well worth it."

"Friday's fine. Anything else new?"

"Just the usual. We'll catch up on Friday, okay?"

"Sure thing. Talk to you then." Tricia hung up the phone.

"Ginny's always so busy," Pixie commented.

"Yes, she is. I always feel like our lunches are stolen time from her job. I don't know what they'll do when she goes out on maternity leave in the spring."

Pixie shrugged. "Cope."

Tricia glanced at the clock on the wall. It was nearly time to close. While Pixie cleaned the beverage station and washed the pots and mugs for the next day, Tricia finished stocking shelves with Mr. Everett.

The shadows were growing long as they all donned their jackets and headed for the door.

"Are you sure I can't drive you home, Pixie?" Mr. Everett offered.

"Aw, thanks, Mr. E, but it'll only take me ten minutes to walk and the sun won't set for another fifteen minutes after that. Give me a couple more weeks, though, and I'll gladly take you up on your offer. I intend to keep walking to work as far into the fall as I can. It keeps me toned—and I don't have to feel guilty if I eat a handful of chips."

Tricia liked that kind of thinking. "You two have a wonderful evening. I'll see you tomorrow," she said, and watched as her employees waved and started up the street.

The door to the Cookery swung open as Tricia approached and its manager, June, stepped onto the sidewalk.

"Don't close the door," Tricia called.

June turned. "Oh, Tricia." Her smile quickly switched to a frown. "I haven't had a chance to offer my condolences on your loss. It was such a shock."

"Thanks, June. Marshall was a good man." Yeah, and he was also a man with a past. Had news of that past started making the rounds? Tricia wasn't about to ask.

"Sarge went out about an hour ago, so he should be good for a while," June said, sounding just a little nervous. Maybe she did know the scoop on Marshall.

"Thanks."

"Well, uh, have a good evening," June said, and practically fled down the street, heading toward the municipal parking lot.

Tricia entered the store and locked the door behind her, headed for the door marked PRIVATE, and up the steps to Angelica's apartment. A joyful, barking Sarge greeted her at the landing.

"Mommy's little boy loves his auntie Tricia," Angelica simpered. Usually, she just implored the dog to "Hush!" She must have been feeling pretty chipper.

Tricia hung up her coat, gave Sarge a couple of biscuits, and settled onto one of the barstools. "Something smells good."

Angelica's knee was once again perched on the little scooter. "I made us garlic cheese dip and didn't spare the garlic. After all, we're not kissing anyone tonight." Then she winced as though suddenly remembering Marshall's untimely death. "Oh, Trish—"

Tricia raised a hand in dismissal. "Don't worry about it. How about our martinis? Can I give you a hand?"

"Of course. You know where everything is," Angelica

said as she removed a ceramic bowl from the oven and moved the steaming dip onto a waiting platter that already contained a stack of crackers. "I'm sorry we don't have a baguette. We'll just have to make do."

"I'm sure it will be fine."

Tricia placed the glasses and the platter on a waiting tray already decked out with napkins, and they moved into the living room, taking their favorite spots.

"How was your day?" Angelica asked as she grabbed a cracker and dunked it into the goopy dip, its aroma intoxicating to any garlic lover.

Tricia passed a glass to her sister. "Just the usual. I took my walk, opened my store, met Marshall's ex-wife."

"What?" Angelica cried, nearly dropping her cracker.

"Yeah. And you won't believe who she is."

"Who—who?"

"Rebecca Dickson-Chandler. She introduced herself as Becca Chandler."

Angelica's mouth dropped open, her eyes wide with delight. "The world-famous tennis player? Rod," her ex-husband, "and I saw her win the US Open in Flushing Meadows." She shook her head, her gaze dreamy. "What a power player she was —probably still is, although she retired from the game a few years back after her terrible injury."

"I don't remember."

Angelica rolled her eyes. "Rock-climbing. She fell. Really messed up her leg."

"I didn't know you followed the sports celebrities so closely."

"Back in the day, I was a pretty good tennis player myself." She clasped her hands together as though holding a racket. "I had a wicked backhand." She sighed. "But then I got a wicked case of—"

"Tennis elbow?" Tricia suggested.

Angelica frowned. "Tendinitis. I'd stop playing for a few months until it healed, but it kept coming back. I had to give up the game." She sighed again, this time wistfully. But then she brightened. "What in the world was Marshall doing married to such a wunderkind?"

"We didn't get into that. But she didn't seem terribly upset to learn he was dead."

"Some people hold in their grief," Angelica remarked.

"She didn't seem to be grieving at all," Tricia said, and took a sip of her martini. "She booked a room at the Sheer Comfort Inn."

"Oh? That's funny. Marina didn't tell me we had such a distinguished guest."

"Maybe Ms. Dickson-Chandler isn't as well remembered as she'd like to think."

Angelica scowled. "Oh, Tricia. That's rather catty of you."

"I'm sorry. It seems like someone ought to grieve for poor Marshall."

"Even if it isn't you?" Angelica prodded.

"I'm grieving. In my own way," Tricia amended. If nothing else, she'd valued Marshall as a friend—and a good one. A man she could talk shop with. Who'd understood her. Or at least he'd given her that impression. She'd have to Google his former persona to learn what he'd concealed from her and the world at large.

"So, what's new with you?" she asked her sister.

"Nothing." Angelica gave a weary sigh. "Until I get rid of this boot, I'm more or less stuck here at home. You can't imagine how lonely and isolated it is to be in the same place day after day, week after week."

Tricia didn't want to contemplate it.

"But thanks to my phone, I'm in touch with the people I care about most and can talk to and text them throughout the day."

"Then, is there anything new in *their* lives?" Tricia asked.

Angelica's mouth quirked into a smile. "The architect has given Antonio and Ginny the preliminary plans for the renovation of their house."

"Wow, that was fast. It was only a week or so ago that they even started talking about it."

"Well, I may have helped in that regard," Angelica said with relish. "I knew they'd eventually want to renovate that little cottage into a big family home. I had seven—count them—seven Pinterest boards just devoted to the project."

"Have you shown them all to Ginny?" Tricia asked.

"Well, no. I didn't want to come off as pushy or anything."

"Of course not," Tricia agreed sarcastically.

"But after we spoke the other day, Ginny and I had a Zoom meeting with Trevor Hanlon, the architect."

"Admit it: you already had the plans half made up in advance," Tricia accused.

"Um, that may have happened, but you'll never get me to admit it in court. Besides, Ginny loved just about every idea I pitched to them last week."

"I suppose you've already picked out the furniture, too," Tricia stated.

"I *do* have good taste, don't I?" Angelica said, and looked around the room as though to illustrate how she'd decorated it.

Yes, Tricia had to admit that her sister did have good taste. In fact, Angelica did just about *everything* well. If she weren't her sister, Tricia might hate her just a little bit.

"With Ginny and Antonio working full-time, and me just killing time for the foreseeable future, I could be on-site and act as general contractor."

"Have you ever done that before?" Tricia asked.

"Twice, as a matter of fact." Angelica pointed to a folder on the coffee table. "I've already done the preliminary work of gathering up the contact info for the various trades. Once we have some finalized plans, we can get the building permits and get going. My new grandbaby will be here in six months—and we've got the weather and the holidays to deal with. I want that job finished weeks before Ginny goes into labor."

"Sounds like you've got it all planned."

"Rather exciting, isn't it?" Angelica gushed, grinning.

After living with a whole-home renovation the year before, Tricia wasn't eager to go through it again anytime soon. Angelica, however, seemed to thrive on that kind of thing.

"My lunch with Ginny tomorrow is off. She's working," Tricia said, and sipped her drink.

"I swear I'm not an unreasonable employer," Angelica said defensively.

"No one said you were. Apparently, she's going to sweet-talk a vendor into a lower price."

"I wish her luck. I'm sure she'll tell me about it after it's a done deal. I'll act duly surprised. But if she's busy, we can have lunch together."

"Here or at Booked for Lunch?"

"At the café. I'm sick and tired of looking at the same four walls." Angelica picked up another cracker, plunging it into the dip before taking a bite. "So, what's Becca Dickson-Chandler like? Can I meet her?"

Tricia shrugged. "I don't know. She gave me the impression she was only going to hang around the village until she can pick up Marshall's ashes from the funeral home."

"Did she mention what's going to happen to the Armchair Tourist?"

"I don't even know if the store will stay open. I guess Becca will make that decision."

Angelica shook her head sadly. "There are always so many loose ends when someone dies."

"Even more when it's unexpected. But I got the impression Becca will handle things just fine." Tricia waved a hand in the air. "Let's talk about something different. Tell me more about Ginny's renovation."

Angelica took the subject change and ran with it with glee, although Tricia only half listened. Marshall's death and everything she'd learned about his past had cast a pall. In contrast, everything about Tricia's everyday life seemed so trivial. What she'd taken for facts about her relationship with Marshall had proven to be false. It made her look at her life through a filter. Could she trust what she had come to consider truth?

At that moment, she just wasn't sure.

S I X

Tricia arrived back at Haven't Got a Clue just after eight, but instead of heading up to her apartment, she trundled down the stairs to her basement office. After switching on the computer, she wiggled out of her jacket and sat in front of the big monitor. Out of habit, she checked her e-mail first and found a note from Mary Fairchild announcing that the first meeting of the Chamber recruitment committee would be held the next morning at eight thirty in the makeshift office Russ Smith had established in a warehouse at the edge of the village. That gave the retail members some ninety minutes until they needed to be back at their shops for a ten o'clock opening.

Tricia sent Pixie a text telling her she might be late for opening Haven't Got a Clue and could she come in early?

She could.

Next, Tricia opened a browser window and did what she'd proposed hours before: typed in Marshall's real name and hit the search button. In no time at all a number of links flooded her screen. She clicked the first, which was a news story about Eugene Chandler testifying against business mogul Martin Bailey, a sleazy Baltimore real estate developer who had a habit of neglecting to pay the people who worked for him—contractors, plumbers, electricians, etc.—and made dubious financial transactions with scores of unsavory businesses in the US and abroad. Marshall had been asked to cook the books, and he'd done it for a couple of years until he apparently grew sickened by the depths of depravity Bailey was willing to delve into. The account said it was Marshall who'd gone to the feds with copies of the incriminating second set of books. Bailey had been convicted and sent to jail for twenty years.

Digging deeper, Tricia found links to Eugene's high school and college yearbooks, and, of course, his courtship and marriage to tennis star Rebecca Dickson. She'd been a globe-trotter, winning tournament after tournament, open after open, while Eugene had apparently been content to remain in her shadow. There were no pictures of him at the red-carpet events Becca had attended during their years of marriage, and she'd often been accompanied to those affairs by her coach, one Sandra Bailey—ex-wife of Martin Bailey. Was that how Eugene got the job working for the Baltimore Kingpin, as Bailey was known in Maryland?

A small article dated six years before noted the amicable dissolution of Eugene and Becca's marriage, and she'd been seen in the company of several well-known actors and movie moguls, but none of those relationships seemed to have lasted—if, in fact, they were relationships and not just photo ops. A year after that, Eugene had testified against Bailey. It had taken a jury less than five hours to convict Bailey on all counts, and he went to jail vowing revenge. By that time, of course, Eugene was apparently already in federal custody himself and then disappeared, whisked into the Witness Protection Program.

Tricia typed the name of her favorite online encyclopedia into her browser search box and hit the enter key. Next, she typed in Martin Bailey's name and read his bio, skipping over his early life and heading for the personal life section. It listed his several wives and the name of his only child, a son, who had changed his surname some years before so as not to be associated with his father. Sandra Bailey—Becca's coach—had divorced the man before the trial, perhaps to recoup some of the couple's assets before they could be swallowed up by lawyers, creditors, and the ever-powerful IRS.

The son who'd distanced himself from his father, and a wife who'd decided to grab what she could and let the man face jail alone, didn't seem like the type to perpetrate an act of revenge. Bailey Junior was the product of the old man's first marriage. His mother was replaced by a younger, prettier model and had not made out well when it came to a divorce settlement. She'd had to take her ex to court on numerous occasions to get the child support she was granted by the decree.

So, it didn't look like Marshall's death was a simple case of revenge. Then again, Tricia knew only a few sketchy facts about Marshall—Eugene—and the people he'd been associated with in the past.

Tricia sat back in her office chair. When would Chief Baker have the inside scoop on what the feds suspected?

Poor Grant.

Tricia shook herself. Now she was feeling sorry for Baker? They hadn't spoken since she'd given his department her statement. And after her unequivocal rejection of his proposal, perhaps in the future he might be reluctant to speak to her again. That was too bad. While she wasn't interested in pursuing a relationship with Baker, she realized she was going to miss male company.

Hers and Baker's relationship had always been rocky. He couldn't bring himself to trust her completely. He'd even suspected her of being capable of murder—and on more than one occasion.

She let her mind wander to the times when they'd been in sync. At one point, she even wondered if she loved him, but their relationship had gone sour one time too many before she'd called it quits. It hadn't taken him long to replace her with the beautiful, high-powered attorney Diana Porter.

Tricia shook herself. Why was she even thinking about Baker when there were so many other subjects she could pursue?

She reached across the desk to pick up the phone to call

Marshall to ask his take until she remembered she'd never hear his voice again.

Evenings were going to be the hardest. That's when they'd go for a drink at the Dog-Eared Page and then to his place for a final nightcap. Sometimes she stayed over, sometimes she didn't. Sometimes he came to her place. Sometimes they'd just chat on the phone for an hour or more, comparing notes on the day or just commiserating over the lack of sales in their businesses during downtimes. Yes, she was already missing Marshall Cambridge . . . Eugene Chandler, she reminded herself.

Then it occurred to her . . . she'd neglected to ask Becca what, if any, arrangements were being made for Marshall's burial, and if not that—his remains. Would she scatter his ashes here in Stoneham or take them somewhere else? Would she hold a ceremony of some kind? And if not here, where? Back in Baltimore? Would he be remembered in death by his birth name or the name he'd acquired when he'd dropped out of sight after the trial? They were all questions Tricia wished she'd thought to ask.

Becca had said they'd speak again.

Tricia decided she wouldn't wait for Becca to seek her out. The next morning, she determined, she'd seek out Becca.

SEVEN

The morning sky was steel gray and gloomy when Tricia donned her jacket and left Haven't Got a Clue, clutching her pink floral umbrella in one hand and settling her other on the purse she'd slung over her shoulder. If one had to use a bumbershoot, it might as well be pretty and colorful.

The walk up Main Street took less than ten minutes, but by the look of the cars in the gravel lot, the rest of the Chamber's nominating committee had chosen to drive.

Russ Smith had chosen a terrible location to house the Chamber offices. It was only a brass padlock that kept the warehouse secure—and this one looked brand-new. No doubt someone on the committee had changed it since they'd probably had to cut the old one off to gain access to the building.

It seemed Tricia was the last to arrive, although by her watch she was two minutes early.

Tricia didn't bother to hang up her jacket and joined the others at a folding table and chairs that had been set up in the drafty, wide-open space. She greeted the others, who all looked appropriately somber—especially Mark Jameson, a more recent member. He'd opened his dentistry practice in the new professional office park near the Brookview Inn and had apparently appointed himself head of the recruitment committee. The others were Mary Fairchild, of course, Terry McDonald, and Dan Reed, owner of the Bookshelf Diner.

"Now that we're all here," Mark said, "we can start. Mary, will you act as secretary and take notes?"

Weren't any of the men capable of that duty?

"Sure thing," Mary answered wearily.

"Now, I've spoken with the Chamber's attorney and he's looking into how we can get the organization up and running again as fast as possible." He leveled his gaze at Tricia. "Since you were in the running for the Chamber presidency during its last election, and got thirty-one percent of the vote, it's likely you could be named the interim president."

"What if I don't want the position?" Tricia asked.

He leveled his laser-like gaze upon her. "Then why are you here?"

Tricia bristled. "Because Mary asked me to be a part of this committee. She also made it clear that it wasn't *me* the Chamber wanted as president."

"Oh, I'm sure I didn't put it that bluntly," Mary said defensively. Oh, but she had.

"Once a judge gives us the okay, we can hire back the old secretary—oh, what was her name?"

"Mariana Sommers," Tricia supplied.

"Between the two of you, you could have the Chamber up and running so that the new president can step right in."

"It may not be that easy," Tricia cut in. "Mariana was extremely competent. When Russ fired her, my sister wrote her a glowing reference letter and she found a well-paying job in Nashua. I'm not sure we'd be able to lure her back."

"Well, then we'll find someone else," Mark practically growled. What put him in such a bad mood—or was that just his regular state? It made Tricia appreciate her dentist and the friendly people who staffed her office in Milford.

"What's the state of our finances?" Tricia asked.

"Not good," Terry piped up. "In addition to a murder rap, it looks like Russ Smith could be facing additional charges of embezzlement as well."

Russ was broke, or at least that was what everyone assumed. He'd said he was saving the Chamber money by giving up their comfortable digs for the warehouse and firing the secretary, who undoubtedly would have noticed the lack of funds by merely opening the envelopes the bank statements came in. The temps who came and went on a regular basis weren't around long enough to notice any irregularities. Had Russ been squirreling away the Chamber's funds to finance the new life he intended to start in California?

"As interim president, you can authorize an audit," Mark said.

Too bad Marshall was dead. As an accountant, he could have done it himself. Of course, as a protected witness, he wasn't supposed to practice his previous occupation. But maybe he would have made a few helpful suggestions.

Tricia pushed the thought aside. Marshall was gone and she was on her own. That is, if she agreed to take the position.

"How long do you think it would take to interview suitable candidates?" she asked.

"Our elections are usually held in November," Mark reminded her.

So, between six to eight weeks.

"I'll have to think about it." That meant consulting Angelica. Tricia had worked for the Chamber as a volunteer for nearly six months during the time Haven't Got a Clue was closed after the fire, and she had a good idea about how the operation worked, but Angelica had been deeply involved for two full years, and she'd completely turned it around by pure force of will. Tricia wasn't sure any of the current or former members would show that kind of commitment.

"Why would I want to take on this job?"

"I understand you worked as a volunteer for half a year. What's another two months?"

"My business was closed during that time."

"You have full-time help and this is your slow season," Mark said reasonably.

"No, it isn't. Have you seen the color of the leaves? As long as the weather holds, Stoneham will be inundated with tourists for the next three weeks."

Jameson merely glared at her.

Still, staying occupied would mean Tricia would have less time to think about Marshall.

But she stuck to her guns. "I'll give you my answer in a day or so."

"That would be satisfactory," Mark said.

Tricia opened her notebook and uncapped her pen. "So, what's the recruitment criteria?"

Mark glanced at his notes. "Those running need to make a firm time commitment. They should have full- or part-time help in their businesses, give a full two-year commitment, and have the financial chops to bring the Chamber back into solvency."

"Tricia ticks off all those boxes," Mary pointed out. "And why are you so adamant she couldn't do the job? Have you got something against strong women?"

Tricia tried not to smile at Mary's confidence in her abilities.

"Don't be ridiculous," Mark said.

"Then why don't we invite Tricia to run for Chamber president?" Terry asked.

"Look, we've already been over all that," Mark said. "Now, I've drawn up a list of names of possible candidates. Shall we discuss them?"

Dan Reed spoke up. "I'd like to present my proposed changes to the charter."

"Changes?" Tricia asked.

He turned a glare in her direction. "Yes. It's unfair that some Chamber members have more say in how it's run than others."

"It's one vote per business."

"Ah, but some of our members have more than one business."

"Such as?" Mary asked.

"Well, Nigela Ricita, for one. She owns half the village."

"And the other?" Tricia asked, already knowing the answer.

"Your sister."

"Angelica owns the Cookery and the day spa. Her manager speaks for the spa. She has a share in the Sheer Comfort Inn, but it's the innkeepers who speak for that business. Angelica speaks for the Cookery and Booked for Lunch with one vote. The same goes for NR Associates. And, I might add, each of these businesses pays separate dues. They all have different needs and aren't colluding for a power grab."

"I have to agree with Tricia," Mark said, which rather surprised her. "Our goal is to find a replacement for new leadership. You can present your ideas to him or her and the rest of the membership at our January meeting."

Dan was not pleased by the rebuke. He crossed his arms over his chest and sat glowering.

"Now, Mary, would you please pass out the list of possible candidates?"

Mary handed a stack of pages to Tricia, and she took one off the top and passed them on. She glanced at the names. Sure enough, her name wasn't listed.

Fine.

"Now, let's start the discussion with the top name on the list. What does everyone think about Leona Ferguson?"

Tricia left the warehouse at nine forty-five, and since the Sheer Comfort Inn was only a couple of blocks farther north on Main Street, she considered stopping in to see if Becca was there. But then she reconsidered. She didn't want to interrupt the innkeepers during the hustle and bustle of tidying up after the breakfast rush and getting ready for their next guests, so she waited until she returned to her office at Haven't Got a Clue before she dialed the inn's number from the vintage black phone that graced the cash desk. Three rings later, her call was answered.

"Sheer Comfort Inn. This is Marina. How may I help you?"

"Hi, Marina, it's Tricia Miles."

"Oh, Tricia. Hi. It's great to hear from you. We haven't spoken for months, ever since the Chamber moved to that dreadful warehouse and our meetings were suspended. I heard you're on the committee to look for a new president."

"Yes. We had our first meeting this morning."

"You weren't thinking of asking me, were you?" Marina sounded positively horrified at the notion.

"No, that's not why I'm calling. I understand that Becca Chandler is a guest at the inn."

"She was," Marina said, her tone going sour. "She called and canceled. Of course, we charged her the cancellation fee, but she was booked for a week. Things have been slow—we need the income." Well, Marina was assured a paycheck, but like nearly all the dedicated people Angelica hired, she was concerned for the health of the business.

"You'll be booked full for the next couple of weeks."

"Thank goodness," Marina agreed. "Leaf-peeping season is my favorite. That and Christmas. I love decorating for the holidays."

"Did Ms. Chandler say where she was staying?"

"No, just canceled."

"Okay, well, thanks."

"Good luck on your search for the next Chamber president."

"Thanks. Talk to you soon."

Tricia pressed the hook switch, waited a few seconds, and then let go and dialed Marshall's home number. Like her, he had a landline that was connected to the Armchair Tourist. He often picked up after hours so as not to lose a potential sale. Tricia didn't know if Becca had been given his cell phone and was pleased when the call was answered on the fourth ring.

"Hello?" Becca said apprehensively.

"Hi, it's Tricia Miles."

"Oh. This is a surprise."

"I wanted to apologize for ending our talk yesterday so abruptly."

"No need," Becca said simply.

"I know it's short notice, but I wondered if you were free for lunch?"

"How nice of you to ask. I'm dying to check out the Brookview Inn. Gene said it was his favorite eatery in the village."

And the most expensive, not that Tricia couldn't afford it. And it was more likely they could talk without an audience, especially if Tricia booked the private dining room.

"How does twelve thirty sound?"

"Perfect. I've got some errands to run. Give me directions and I'll meet you there," Becca said.

Tricia did.

"See you then," Tricia said.

As she hung up the phone, Tricia wondered just where Becca could be headed before their lunch date.

Leaving Haven't Got a Clue in Pixie's and Mr. Everett's care, Tricia drove to the Brookview Inn, which was already decked out with fall décor. And though she was right on time, her lunch partner was nowhere to be seen.

Tricia sat on one of the lobby's richly upholstered chairs to wait. And wait. She took the paperback she was reading from her purse and removed the bookmark, but soon found it too hard to concentrate and put the book away. After ten minutes, Tricia got up to pace. Five minutes later, she paused and glanced at the big clock on the wall of the Brookview Inn's lobby, the hands pointing to the Roman numerals for twelve forty-five. Becca was now fifteen minutes late. Tricia resumed her seat and wondered if she'd been stood up.

Once again, she pulled out her book and read for no more than a minute before looking over the top of her book to see a pair of legs before her.

"Hey, Tricia. Checking up on me?" asked Hank Curtis. Tricia had arranged for the former Army vet to interview as the Brookview's new manager. He'd be taking over for Antonio full-time in a matter of days. Talk about jumping into the fire.

"Not at all," Tricia said. "Just waiting for . . ." She paused. Becca certainly wasn't a friend. "A lunch date."

Hank looked surprised. No doubt he'd heard about Marshall and thought the idea of a date so soon after his death was crass.

"I'm meeting my friend Marshall's ex-wife, who's come to the village to settle his affairs."

Hank seemed relieved at the explanation. "Well, I hope you have a nice meal."

"Thanks."

"No doubt we'll be seeing a lot of each other in the future," Hank said.

Tricia wasn't sure how to react to that statement, then found that she didn't have to, for Becca finally breezed through the inn's front entrance. She saw Tricia, waved, and charged forward like the athlete she'd always been.

"Sorry I'm late," she apologized as Tricia rose from her seat.

Tricia managed a smile. "Perfectly fine. I hope you're hungry. The Brookview has a wonderful menu."

"I am," Becca remarked. She looked toward Hank. "And you are?"

Tricia spoke up. "This is my friend Hank Curtis. He's just started work managing the inn."

Becca nodded. "Nice to meet you."

"And you," he said, smiling.

The silence seemed to go on a little too long.

"Well, ladies, I hope you enjoy your lunches."

"Thanks, Hank."

"Nice meeting you," Becca said.

Hank nodded and turned back toward what had been Antonio's office.

"He's good-looking," Becca whispered, grinning.

"I hadn't noticed," Tricia said. "Shall we—?"

Becca turned to head toward the main dining room, but Tricia called her back.

"This way."

Becca raised an eyebrow but turned to follow.

"Welcome back to the inn, ladies," the receptionist said as they passed.

They met none of the staff as they walked down the corridor that led to the inn's private dining room. Once inside the room, Tricia pressed the switch on the wall to alert the staff that they had arrived, before shucking her jacket and taking her favorite wing-backed chair.

Becca stood behind the love seat and took in the room. "Nice. Did you ever have dinner here with Gene?"

"Uh, no. We had a favorite table in the main restaurant."

"Hmm," Becca muttered as she took in the rest of the elegant room. Was she disappointed by the décor or the fact that Tricia hadn't accorded the honor of dining in seclusion with Marshall? "So, what did you want to talk to me about?"

"Nothing in particular. I thought as you were going to be here for a few days you might need someone to help you navigate the area."

"I thought that's what GPS and Google Maps were for."

"There's nothing like having a personal guide," Tricia said.

Becca raised an eyebrow. "Are you offering that service?"

"Well, I do have a business to run, but I'd be happy to point you in the right direction for wherever you might need to go."

Becca nodded and finally sat on the love seat. "As it happens, I was able to find the Baker Funeral Home without any trouble. I've made arrangements for them to take care of Gene."

"I wondered," Tricia said.

"I'll need to hang around the village for a few days until I can pick up his ashes."

"What will you do with them?"

"Spread them at his favorite place."

"And where was that?"

Becca eyed Tricia for a long moment. "I'm not sure Gene would want you to know."

"Why not? He *did* ask me to marry him."

"And you didn't give him an answer."

Tricia said nothing.

Becca slouched against the love seat's back cushion, and

for a moment Tricia wondered if she was going to place her feet on the glass-topped coffee table.

Finally, Becca shrugged. "On the black sand of Hawaii's Panalu'u Beach."

Marshall had never mentioned Hawaii as a favorite destination, but then maybe that was because, as a protected witness, he wasn't supposed to talk about or visit former favorite haunts.

"Sounds beautiful."

"It's where we honeymooned."

Was it Tricia's imagination, or did Becca sound just a little possessive of her former husband? The one she'd left . . . and the one she didn't seem to be mourning.

A knock disturbed Tricia's musings and the door opened as the waitress entered with leather-clad folders containing the menu.

"Good afternoon, ladies," she said, and placed the folders on the coffee table. "I'm Sarah and I'll be taking care of you today. Would you like something to drink other than just water?"

"I'll have a glass of chardonnay," Tricia said.

"I'd like cucumber water with a lime slice, please," Becca said.

"I'm sorry," Sarah said, "but we don't serve cucumber water."

"It's quite easy to make," Becca said, her voice level.

Sarah, who'd served Tricia many times in the past, shot her a glance as though looking for guidance.

"Maybe the bartender knows how to make it."

"Uh, yes, I'll ask her. Would you care to look over the menu now?"

"We'll—"

"Yes," Becca said, and reached for one of the folders. It looked like it might be a short lunch.

Sarah rolled off the day's specials and then patiently waited while the women decided on their selections. Tricia ordered the broiled chicken and a small side salad, while Becca decided on the oysters appetizer and mixed greens.

Oysters . . . for her libido? The way she'd looked at Hank Curtis, anything was possible.

Sarah retrieved the folders and promised to soon return with their drinks. The door closed behind her and an uncomfortable silence fell over the room.

Tricia broke the quiet. "I was certainly surprised to learn that Marsh—er, Gene—was in the Witness Protection Program. He never let on to me."

"He knew what he was in for when he accepted a life of lies," Becca said with an edge to her voice.

"It doesn't sound like you approved."

Again Becca shrugged.

"You mentioned that Gene was lonely and contacted you. I've read that it could be fatal for a witness to step out of the shadows like that."

"It could have been. Gene contacted me after my accident."

"Yes, I read about it at the time." And refreshed her memory just hours earlier.

"Of course, at first he only sent a card. To tell you the truth, I was shocked to get it. I knew it could be dangerous for him. I didn't tell a soul and squirreled it away. But then I got another one and another one. I knew I shouldn't have kept them, but eventually, I was glad I did. At first the messages didn't seem to make sense—they were all rather cryptic. But I pieced together the clues and realized he was giving me a telephone number. I called it and he answered. After that, we kept in touch." She laughed. "It was all rather exciting. We'd buy cheap phones with limited airtime, speak once a month, ditch the phones, and do it all over again. It got so I looked forward to those calls. It was kind of like being a spy."

Or a drug dealer. Tricia had read about scenarios like that in one of the true-crime books Marshall had loaned her.

Becca sighed theatrically. "The thing was, we both knew it was stupid to stay in touch, but I was lonely, too. It got so I kind of regretted that we'd ever broken up. Once you're washed up you really find out who your friends are," Becca said bitterly. "My career, my sponsorships—all gone. But

I'm a strong woman and I've learned to take care of myself without a load of sycophants and hangers-on."

A knock on the door caused the women to look up. Sarah had arrived with their drinks and lunches. She set the plates on the table that overlooked the Brookview's front lawn and Tricia and Becca took their seats.

"Can I get you anything else?" Sarah asked.

"The check," Becca said. "I'll need to be leaving as soon as we're done with our meal."

Sarah nodded. "I'll be back in a few minutes."

Once the door had closed, Becca picked up her fork and continued with her recitation. "They say that opposites attract, and I guess it's true, but that doesn't mean a couple can live happily ever after together. That's where we were before Gene went underground."

"You were growing tired of each other?"

"Let's just say that we were spending more and more time apart. I was busy with my career and he was not one to step into the spotlight. My friends at the time weren't surprised when I told them we were splitting up. Marshall waited a year before he spilled what he knew to the feds. By then, my crowd had already forgotten him. And Martin wasn't such a big fish that the national news picked up on his trial."

"How well did you know Martin Bailey?"

"Well enough to stay away."

"But surely it was your connection to his wife that got Marshall—er, Gene—the job as his accountant."

She shook her head. "Gene was more than an accountant. He was also a top-notch financial adviser. Martin sought *him* out. It was Sandra who introduced us."

Why had Tricia assumed the opposite?

"What was the occasion?"

"None at all. It was a Sunday afternoon in late May and I was practicing on Sandra's home court when Gene came by with some papers for Martin to sign. They watched me practice and afterward we had a few drinks on the patio. I liked Gene. He was funny, he was smart, and he wasn't a sycophant—at least toward me. It was a refreshing change."

"Was he Martin's sycophant?"

Becca took a moment to think it over. "Hardly. He was straight up with him on his financial dealings."

"Then why would he work for such a despicable man?"

"For the money," Becca answered simply.

Marshall did have expensive tastes. The Mercedes, dining at the most expensive country club in Nashua, and the suits that never looked as though they'd come off the rack. Even so, he hadn't drawn all that much attention to himself during his time in Stoneham.

"Has Deputy Kirby updated you on the investigation?"

"Not today."

"Do you think Martin Bailey came after Gene as an act of revenge?"

"I hardly think so."

"And why's that?"

"Martin Bailey is dead. He died eight months ago."

Tricia's mouth dropped. And just how had she missed that little piece of information?

EIGHT

Tricia arrived at Angelica's apartment just after six that evening, feeling weary after the events of the day and knowing she would have to bring her sister up to date on everything.

She let herself in the Cookery. Sarge barked. She tossed him a biscuit. She helped Angelica with the treats and drinks before they settled into their usual spots in the living room. Was this to be her life from now on? Two single sisters relying on each other for sustenance and gossip? Well, not always gossip. And Tricia enjoyed spending her happy hour and dinner with her sister, which was why she and Marshall seldom went out in the evenings. She frowned. Boy, she'd been a cheap date—but then, he hadn't wanted to spend time with her at her Sunday family dinners.

"I want to know all about your date—especially since *we* didn't get to have lunch today."

"First let me tell you about Mark Jameson."

"I gather from your tone he's not all that pleasant."

"You've got that right." Tricia gave her sister a brief recap.

"You actually let the man talk to you like that?" Angelica asked, sounding disappointed.

"If nothing else, I was brought up to be polite at all times."

Angelica heaved a sigh. "You and me both. Why is it

when men are impolite, they're called strong leaders? When women are impolite, they're called the B-word."

Tricia had to agree.

"What do you think I should do?"

Angelica frowned. "Another B-word comes to mind: 'bolt.'"

"But that means walking away from your legacy."

"What legacy? That was destroyed when Russ Smith took over the job, although if Chauncey Porter had become president, it might have ended just as badly. I'm a pretty hard act to follow," Angelica said, and oddly enough, it didn't sound like bragging. "What do you want to do?"

Tricia shrugged. "The idea of getting the organization back on track does have a certain appeal, although the timing isn't ideal, what with leaf-peeping season here, but it would only be for a few weeks. I could probably chase people down before the business hours and Pixie and Mr. Everett can handle things at Haven't Got a Clue. I think I'd like to focus my efforts on winning back former members."

"But what can you promise them? If you aren't going to be the one in charge, you've got nothing to offer them except the *chance* things might turn around. Their membership fees could fall down a black hole with nothing to show for it. There are other, bigger Chambers in this part of the state they could join that could offer them a lot more—if only for networking opportunities."

Angelica had a point.

"So, what will you do?" Angelica asked.

"I think I'm going to go for it."

"Why? Do you have some kind of savior complex?"

"Maybe. You certainly do."

"Me?" Angelica asked, sounding puzzled.

"Look what you've done for this village. For people like Jake," the ex-felon chef at the Brookview Inn, "and Pixie and goodness knows how many others."

Angelica nodded. "Yes, I guess I have been a force for good."

Tricia scowled at her.

"Then there's only one thing for it. I will have to help you—that is, if you'll let me."

"Let you? I'll welcome you with open arms. But why now? I mean, you walked away from the job a year ago."

"Yes, well, that was before I hired so many amazing people to work in my companies. I feel cooped up since being saddled with this stupid boot. I'll be more mobile in the coming weeks. I just hope it'll be as much fun working with you again. We did make a fine team." Angelica's eyes widened. "You know, it occurs to me that with your vast managerial experience, you'd be a fine addition to Nigela Ricita Associates."

"No way!" Tricia said, raising a hand as though to fend off the suggestion.

"Why?"

"Running a vintage mystery bookstore was my life's dream. I'm not about to give it up."

"You can still do it as a side hustle," Angelica said dismissively.

"I don't want a side hustle. I want to be my own boss." She'd had a lot of authority while head of the nonprofit in Manhattan, but ultimately she'd had to answer to the board of directors.

Angelica shrugged. "Well, if you ever change your mind, the door is always open."

"Thank you." Though it pleased Tricia to know Angelica had that kind of faith in her, she was content to keep her work life as it was. At least for now.

"So, what else happened at the meeting?" Angelica asked, picking up her drink at last. Tricia did likewise.

"Dan Reed brought up the idea of drawing up a new charter with more checks and balances."

"After the Russ fiasco, that sounds prudent. What else?"

"It seems he doesn't want to allow the separate entities of Nigela Ricita Associates to have representation."

"Whyever not?" Angelica asked, looking puzzled.

"He thinks it should be one voice speaking for the entire company."

"No one ever thought that before."

"Well, *he* did and used you as the example."

"Me?"

"You do own the Cookery, Booked for Lunch, the day spa, and a share of the Sheer Comfort Inn."

"I may own them, but they're separate businesses with different needs and objectives. Besides, I don't run them all. I pay others to do that." Angelica scowled. "Dan's just being spiteful. He never got over my opening Booked for Lunch. And with the increase in crowds these past few years, I'm sure his income never dropped by more than a dime, if that."

Tricia was about to comment further when Angelica's cell phone rang. She looked at the number, her expression brightening. "Oh, it's Antonio." She stabbed the accept call icon and hit the speaker. "What's up, darling boy?"

"Mama, la nostra casa è in fiamme!"

Angelica sat bolt upright! "What?" she practically shrieked.

"What?" Tricia echoed.

"Where are you?" Angelica demanded.

"Nell'auto. Ginny è a casa. Ha chiamato i pompieri."

"What's going on?" Tricia asked, feeling frantic.

"Their house is on fire," Angelica whispered harshly before speaking into the phone once more. "We'll be there as soon as we can."

"Grazie!"

Angelica ended the call and struggled to her feet. "Ginny's already at the house. Get your coat—we're going!" Angelica said, hobbling toward the door and grabbing her jacket. "We'll meet them there."

"And do what?"

"Figure out our next step."

As she drove north, Tricia was glad they'd barely touched their drinks. The sky was darkening but an orange glow could be seen above the trees. The road in front of the driveway to the little cottage in the woods was choked with police cars and fire engines, lights flashing, while the yard was full of firefighters with swollen hoses trained on the house. Tricia parked her Lexus behind the last police car and the sisters stared at the terrible sight before them.

"It's fully engulfed," Tricia said, her voice filled with despair.

"We've got to find them," Angelica cried.

No doubt who "them" was: Antonio, Ginny, and little Sofia.

Tricia got out of the car and ran to the passenger side. Knowing the uneven terrain in front of the Wilson-Barbero homestead, she'd insisted on bringing Angelica's crutches. She retrieved them from the back seat and helped her sister out of the car.

A uniformed cop appeared before them. "You need to leave the area. We don't need rubberneckers."

"We are *family*," Angelica growled in as menacing a tone as Tricia had ever heard.

The young officer took a step back. "Last I saw, they were over there." He pointed to a copse of maples a little farther up the driveway.

"Thank you," Angelica said, and despite her booted foot and crutches, started off at a brisk pace that Tricia struggled to match.

Less than a minute later, they were reunited with their loved ones. Angelica clung to Antonio, both of them rapidly speaking Italian, while Tricia awkwardly embraced Ginny, with Sofia straddling her left hip.

"I'm so glad you're here," Ginny sobbed into Tricia's ear, nearly squashing Sofia between them.

"What happened?" Tricia asked, pulling back.

"I picked Sofia up at day care and came home to find the house in flames. I called nine one one and then Antonio. What could have happened for it to be burning so fiercely?"

"Have the firefighters told you anything?"

"They've been too busy fighting the fire," Ginny said, wiping a hand across her red, swollen eyes.

"Would you like to sit in my car, out of the smoke?"

"I'd prefer to stay, but I should get Sofia out of here. I don't want her to remember her home burning."

As the little girl wasn't yet two, Tricia doubted that was a possibility. Still, she hooked her arm around Ginny's and pulled her toward the road.

"I guess we won't be going to lunch tomorrow," Ginny lamented.

"Don't worry about it," Tricia assured her.

"What will we do? Everything we owned was in the house. Our clothes, our furniture. I don't even have a clean diaper for the baby."

"We'll get some," Tricia assured her.

Once she had Ginny and Sofia safely sitting in the back of her car, Tricia returned up the drive to wait with Angelica and Antonio, who'd been joined by one of the firefighters, whom Tricia recognized as Dan Farrar, the fire chief. They'd first met after the explosion that had destroyed the History Repeats Itself bookstore four years before. He gave Tricia a curt nod and headed back toward the house. The flames didn't seem as intense, but the smoke had grown noticeably thicker.

"We should move," Tricia advised, noting that Angelica leaned heavily on the crutches, her sore foot raised to take the pressure off. "Would you like to sit in the car with Ginny?"

Angelica shook her head, but then winced. "I probably should. Besides, we need to figure out where they're going to stay tonight."

"The Brookview has a few vacant rooms," Antonio said wearily.

"The Sheer Comfort Inn's suite will be much more comfortable. They had a cancellation, so it should be no problem. I'll call Marina to get the room ready for you."

Antonio nodded, leaned forward, and kissed Angelica's cheek.

The sisters started for the car while Antonio hung back to watch what was left of his home disintegrate.

Tricia made sure her sister could safely navigate to the car, and once they were out of Antonio's earshot Angelica said, "The fire chief said it looks like arson."

"Arson?" Tricia repeated, horrified.

"The fire was set in multiple locations."

"Who would have done such a terrible thing?"

"That's a very good question. I wish I knew the answer."

"Are you going to tell Ginny?"

Angelica shook her head. "It shouldn't come from either of us."

Tricia had just shut the passenger side door when another police cruiser pulled up across the road. Chief Baker exited the vehicle and Tricia hurried over to intercept him.

"I just heard," he said without greeting, and nodded toward the driveway.

"Grant, the fire chief told Antonio it looks like arson."

Baker looked pensive and shook his head as though to ask *What could he do about it?* Tricia had an idea.

"You *will* work with the fire department to figure out who did this and send them to jail."

"Of course. Our departments work together on these kinds of things all the time. My first question for you is, who's got it in for the Barberos?"

Tricia blinked, taken aback. "Nobody. They are the sweetest couple."

"Aw, come on, Tricia. Everybody's got some enemies."

"I don't."

Baker scowled. "I don't have enough fingers to count all the people who dislike you, starting with Doris Gleason."

He had a point. Tricia had helped put more than a few murderers behind bars.

"I certainly don't know of any," Tricia bluffed.

Baker looked skeptical. "Isn't it just a little bit funny how all this bad luck is suddenly being visited on your family?"

"My family?" Tricia questioned, playing dumb.

"Oh, come on, Trish. Just about everyone in the village knows that Antonio is Angelica's stepson."

Well, he had it partly right.

Tricia straightened, taken aback. "You think someone has it in for us?"

"You tell me," he said sourly. "Your boyfriend was killed,

you were nearly run down, and now your stepnephew's home has been set on fire. What do you think?"

Tricia chewed her lip. Had she been living in denial? The thought left her cold.

"Have there been any other arsons in the village or surrounding areas?" Tricia asked.

"No," Baker said emphatically.

Tricia thought about it but then shook her head. "Three incidents in less than a week is bad luck—not a vendetta."

"Oh, yeah? And what if something else happens? What will you tell me then—if you're in a state to speak?" Baker challenged.

What was he really asking? To be her protector?

"If anything else bad happens to me or anyone in my sphere, *you* will be the first to know."

"You promise?" He actually did sound worried.

"Yes." She needed to steer the conversation back to something less personal. "Have you heard from Deputy Kirby?"

Baker shook his head.

"Did you know Marshall's ex-wife has come to the village to wind up his affairs?"

Baker blinked. "That's rather quick, isn't it?"

"I thought so, too. She's staying at his apartment."

"You seem to know a lot about her."

"She came to visit me at the store—to check me out, I suppose."

"And her verdict?"

Tricia shrugged. "I have no idea. When I heard Marshall was a protected witness, I assumed his death was one of revenge, but Becca said the man he helped put in jail died back in February."

"So I understand. But there were more people in Bailey's organization that went to jail besides just him."

"Yes, but it took years before they could bring down the top man—and it was because of Marshall's testimony. It was a very brave thing to do."

"Hogwash." Baker practically spat. "He testified to save his own neck."

"If his death was a revenge hit, it hardly worked."

"The fact that he kept in touch with his ex-wife was a major red flag," Baker countered.

"And you think she led them directly to Marshall?"

"It could have been inadvertent. Her phone could have been tapped, her mail intercepted. There are a number of other different ways she would have outed him." But Baker didn't seem interested in elaborating on those possibilities.

He nodded toward the house that lay in ruins. "I need to talk to the fire chief."

"I'll be in my car with Angelica and Ginny—and out of this smoke." She'd probably have to wash all her clothes more than once to get rid of the stench.

"Thank you for coming," Tricia said quietly.

"It's my job," he reminded her.

Yes, it was.

NINE

 It was after eleven when Tricia and Angelica left the Sheer Comfort Inn. Earlier, Antonio had stayed with Sofia while the three women hit the big-box store on the highway, filling three carts with clothes, shoes, toys, diapers, and snack foods. Angelica had charged all the purchases while Ginny kept thanking her between bouts of tears.

Marina, at the inn, had rustled up some sandwiches and soft drinks for the group, but nobody felt much like eating. Once the family was settled, the sisters had headed for home.

"Now I wish I'd eaten one of those sandwiches," Angelica muttered as they approached the municipal parking lot.

"What did you have set for supper earlier?" Tricia asked as she pulled her car into her usual spot in the lot.

"Lasagna. Tommy made it. It's cooked, but it would take at least half an hour to reheat."

"We could nuke it?"

"No," Angelica said emphatically.

"What do you suggest?"

"Why don't we go to Booked for Lunch? There are cold cuts up the wazoo in the fridge, and every kind of bread on the planet."

"Every kind?" Tricia asked, giving her sister a quizzical look.

"Every kind that counts."

The sisters exited the car and headed for Angelica's retro café. Once inside, they inspected the big cooler in the kitchen and decided on what to have for their dinner. Ham and cheese on seeded rye with tomatoes and lettuce for Angelica, and tuna salad on whole wheat for Tricia. Angelica made cocoa while Tricia found an opened bag of potato chips and they sat down at one of the tables for their long-delayed dinner.

Angelica gazed at her sandwich wearily. "I feel heartsick."

"Me, too," Tricia admitted.

"Who would want to burn Ginny and Antonio's house down?"

"Grant thinks it's someone gunning for our family."

Angelica sat straighter. "Why would he think that?"

Tricia shrugged and plucked a chip from her plate. "Because two bad things have happened to our family in the space of two days."

"Ha! Marshall had nothing to do with our family. He only came to two of our family dinners—and one of them was Christmas."

"I'm just repeating what he said," Tricia remarked, and took a bite of her sandwich. As she chewed, she remembered she hadn't had a chance to catch her sister up on all the events of her day. She mentioned it.

"The private dining room?" Angelica asked, looking skeptical.

"I didn't want to be interrupted. As it was, Becca wasn't impressed and seemed eager to leave. And she was just a little bit rude to Sarah, the waitress." She explained about the cucumber water.

"There's no excuse for that. We try to accommodate people, but honestly . . ."

"Apparently the bartender was able to make what she wanted, although she didn't comment on it."

Angelica shrugged. "I have a meeting with Hank Curtis

tomorrow," she announced, smiling. "Goodness knows, it might be the only bright spot of my day. Would you mind driving me and we can have lunch there before my meeting at one? What do you say?"

And dining with Tricia *wouldn't* be a bright spot?

Tricia sighed. "Fine with me. I've got to eat somewhere. But not the private dining room."

"Agreed." Angelica stared into her cocoa. "Do you really think someone had it in for Ginny and Antonio?"

"I don't know. I sure hope not. But the fact is their home was destroyed. Some people do that kind of thing for kicks, but . . ." Tricia drew in a weary breath before continuing. "Grant said there hadn't been any other arsons in the village of late."

"That he knows of?" Angelica said.

"Yeah."

Angelica's expression was pensive. "How can we know we aren't being targeted?"

Tricia shrugged. "We have to keep up with what's going on in the village."

"And how do we do that?"

In years past, Angelica's employee Frannie Mae Armstrong could be depended on to report everything that went on in the village, but she was no longer in the mix of things. Pixie had a good idea of what was going on in the area but—to her credit—she was pretty much tight-lipped about it. Tricia wasn't sure she wanted Pixie to become Frannie's successor.

"We keep our eyes and ears open," Tricia said.

"Easy for you to say, you're not stuck at home ninety-nine percent of the day."

"You talk to your employees. Start asking more questions."

Angelica sighed. "Yes, I suppose I could. I'll just have to be very subtle."

"I have great confidence in your abilities," Tricia said, while she herself had the perfect cover—talking to former Chamber members. And she'd start first thing in the morning by calling Mary Fairchild and accepting the job.

With that decided, Tricia took a bite of her sandwich. Suddenly, she felt ravenous.

It was after midnight when Tricia arrived back in her apartment and received a thorough scolding from Miss Marple,
whose dinner had been delayed by at least four hours. Tricia
peeled off her smoky clothes, tossing them in the hamper,
and jumped into the shower. She had to wash her hair three
times before she was sure the reek was gone. By the time she
climbed into bed, Tricia felt exhausted but made sure to set
her alarm for seven. She had a lot to do that morning and
much of it needed to be accomplished before Haven't Got a
Clue opened.

   She checked her phone the next morning, but there were no
texts or missed calls from Ginny. Well, it *was* early. She would
contact her later in the day—after Ginny had had time to get
used to the idea of being homeless. She turned her thoughts to
other things—like dumping her smoky clothes into the washing machine and the Chamber recruitment project. As with
her hair, she figured she'd need to wash the clothes several
times to remove the odor. But she was glad for something to
do to kill a little time. She kept looking at the clock and it was
just after eight when Tricia allowed herself to call Mary Fairchild at home.

   "Goodness, I didn't expect to hear from you so soon," Mary
exclaimed. "You said you needed time to think about it."

   "Getting the Chamber back on its feet is important to me.
Do you have that list of people for me to contact?"

   "I can e-mail it to you."

   "Great. If you don't mind, I'd like to get started this morning. You know, talk to people before business hours."

   "Great idea."

   "Do we know when the next meeting will be?"

   "Sometime next week. I'll let you know as soon as I get
the word from Mark. By the way, what do you think of him?"
Mary asked.

   "He certainly has his opinions."

"Yes," Mary said, her voice flat, "he does."

"How did he get to be the head of the committee, anyway?" Tricia asked.

"Somebody needed to step up to the plate."

Did Mary think Tricia should have done so? After all, Russ Smith had been arrested only the week before. So much had happened in such a short period of time. It really was mind-boggling.

"I'll look forward to your e-mail," Tricia said as a bit of a reminder.

"Talk to you later," Mary said, and ended the call.

Tricia finished her coffee and she and Miss Marple headed down to Haven't Got a Clue to start their workday. It was Mr. Everett's day off, but unless there was a huge influx of customers, Tricia knew she and Pixie could handle whatever the day dished up.

The first thing Tricia did was fire up her computer. Mary hadn't yet sent the list of past Chamber members, so she filled the dumbwaiter with books to be shelved in the store above. She checked the computer again.

Nothing from Mary.

Tricia sent the little elevator up to the store, removed the boxes of books, and started filling the shelves. Ten minutes later she was back to check her computer.

Still no e-mail from Mary.

It was almost time to open the store when Tricia checked her e-mail on her phone to finally find Mary's list of names. She had just enough time to go to the office to print out the list before Pixie arrived for work.

"Hey, Tricia," Pixie called cheerfully.

"Good morning. My, you're in a good mood. I wish I could say the same."

Pixie's expression froze. "What's wrong now?"

Tricia explained what had happened to Ginny's little cottage in the woods.

"Oh, no! Those poor people."

"Yeah."

"Is there anything I can do to help?"

Tricia shrugged. "I'll let you know."

Pixie nodded, unbuttoning her coat. "What have you got there?"

"The list of former Chamber members who need to be sweet-talked into rejoining."

"You decided to join the committee?"

Tricia nodded.

Pixie pulled a face. "Good luck with that."

Tricia laughed. "If you don't mind, I'll go downstairs and make a couple of calls before the first of our customers arrives."

The door to the store opened, the little bell tinkling in response.

"You were saying?" Pixie said, smiling.

Tricia set her list aside and straightened. "Hi. Welcome to Haven't Got a Clue. How can we help you?"

TEN

Tricia was pleasantly surprised that a small but steady stream of customers had chosen that morning to visit the village. Pixie charmed an older man into buying half a dozen books by Nicholas Blake, and Tricia sold at least a dozen books by as many authors. If that kept up, the day looked to be a great success.

"Whew! What a great morning we're having," Pixie said.

"Before anyone else comes in, I have to ask a favor."

"Anything," Pixie agreed without even hearing it.

"Angelica has a business meeting at the Brookview Inn this afternoon. She needs a lift and asked me to have lunch with her there."

"I can go late. In fact, the NR roach coach is parked down the street. Why don't I whip out now and get a sandwich, that way I won't have to worry about eating out—and I'll probably save a few bucks, too. I really do need to start bringing my lunch more often. Eating out so often isn't good for my wallet or waistline."

"I hear you," Tricia said.

While Pixie was gone Tricia texted Angelica.

I'm ready to go anytime you are.

Tricia arranged to pick her sister up in the alley behind

the Cookery, and as soon as Pixie returned she hurried out the door to retrieve her car.

Angelica was ready as she pulled to a stop, waited for her sister to climb in, and off they went.

Tricia parked in the remaining handicapped spot, killed the engine, and hung Angelica's temporary handicapped parking permit from the post of her rearview mirror. Since the stairs at the back of the Brookview Inn were a lot easier for Angelica to navigate, Tricia helped her sister out of the car, handed her her cane that sported shabby-chic wild roses, and with Tricia by her side in case she stumbled, they went inside.

"Are you sure you don't want to have lunch in the private dining room?" Angelica asked.

"The restaurant is fine. Besides, the view is so pretty, even on a gloomy day."

Tricia matched her sister's pace as Angelica hobbled across the lobby toward the dining room.

"Welcome back," said Yvonne, the hostess. "How's the foot healing?" she asked Angelica, and indicated the ugly contraption where a shoe should have been.

"Not fast enough," Angelica groused. "Is our favorite table available?" she asked hopefully.

Yvonne shook her head. "I'm afraid someone got there before you, but there are still a few tables overlooking the brook where I could seat you."

"That'll do fine," Tricia said as Angelica shot her a perturbed look.

They followed Yvonne across the restaurant and Angelica took the seat facing south, while Yvonne placed the menus on the table. "Darlene will be with you shortly."

"Thank you," Tricia said.

Angelica struggled out of her jacket, picked up the ivory linen napkin from her setting, and then did a double take. "Hank Curtis is having lunch with a woman," she hissed.

Tricia craned her neck to look. "Good grief, it's Becca Dickson-Chandler."

"What's she doing having lunch with Hank? I saw him first."

Becca was at least a decade younger than Angelica. Famous and attractive, why wouldn't Hank want to share a meal with her? "You've met him once," Tricia reminded her sister.

Angelica frowned. "How did *she* get an invitation to lunch and I didn't?"

"Maybe she invited Hank."

Tricia looked over her shoulder to see Becca laughing. She certainly didn't look like she was grieving her dead ex.

Angelica heaved a dramatic sigh. "I'm so disappointed. Hank and I got on so well. We've spoken on the phone at least three times, you know."

"Part of his employment package was three meals a day. You can't deny him that."

"He's not supposed to treat strange women to an expensive lunch."

"When I had lunch with her, Becca had an appetizer and a plate of salad greens. I hardly think that's going to strain the inn's budget."

"He's still on probation," Angelica remarked.

"Are you going to remind him of that when you guys meet?"

Angelica glowered, her gaze sinking to her lap. "Probably not."

"Forget about her. We're here to enjoy a nice lunch and each other's company."

"Point taken," Angelica conceded.

Darlene approached the table. She'd been a waitress at the Brookview ever since Tricia had moved to the area, and probably long before that. "Good afternoon, ladies. Can I get you your usual martinis?"

Angelica shook her head. "Coffee, please."

Tricia raised an eyebrow at her beverage choice.

"I'm meeting with Hank at one," Angelica reminded her.

"And you?" Darlene asked, turning to Tricia.

"A pot of tea—made with boiling water, please."

Darlene smiled. "I know just how you like it. And what kind of tea?"

"English or Irish breakfast, if you have it."

Darlene nodded. "Would you like to order now?"

Angelica shook her head. "We'll be ready by the time you return."

Again Darlene nodded and pivoted.

Angelica continued to stare at the couple across the way.

"You're making a spectacle of yourself," Tricia hissed.

"I am not." Angelica's expression soured. "Okay, I am, too." She readjusted the napkin on her lap. "What could Becca Chandler possibly have to talk to Hank about? Didn't you say they just met?"

"I introduced them yesterday."

"But surely Hank only met Marshall that one time when you went to the homeless camp—that is, if that's what she wanted to talk about."

"That's right," Tricia agreed, remembering that day less than two weeks before. How drastically things had changed in so short a time.

"Then what else could they have to talk about?" Angelica reiterated.

"I don't know. Maybe she's going to throw a reception for Marshall's friends before she leaves the area."

"It would be a very small do. I mean, you're about the only one he was really friendly with."

And maybe that was why he seldom came to Angelica's little family dinners. As a protected witness, maybe he was warned about getting too friendly with others. It all made sense now.

Except . . . just days before his death, Marshall had taken Tricia on a picnic on land he said a friend owned, but he hadn't mentioned who that friend was. Only that it was to be a wedding venue next summer.

"What are you thinking?" Angelica asked.

Tricia quickly explained. "Do you think Karen at Nigela Ricita Realty could find out who owns that land?"

"If anyone can, it's Karen. She knows her stuff."

"I think I'll give her a call after lunch."

"Good. It'll give you something to do while I meet with Hank."

Darlene returned with their hot beverages and took their orders before disappearing in the direction of the kitchen.

Angelica's attention kept straying to the couple across the way.

"Are you going to stare at them the entire time we're here?" Tricia asked.

Angelica's head bowed. "Oh, all right. I'll be good—or at least I'll try."

"Thank you. Now, let's change the subject. Did you hear from Antonio this morning?"

Angelica sighed, looking profoundly sad. "Yes. They made it through the night, although just barely. None of them got much rest. Sofia was afraid to go to bed in a strange place and insisted on sleeping with them. That means Antonio and Ginny got little shut-eye. Taking her to day care this morning at least gave our little *bambina* a sense of continuity."

"I suppose it's too early for them to have made any concrete plans."

"Antonio was going to talk to their insurance company today. They'll probably get put up in an apartment. If only I hadn't sold that little house to Pixie, they could have moved in there temporarily."

Tricia shook her head. "It was too small—especially now that the weather is changing and they'll be stuck inside more. They'd all catch cabin fever in no time."

"And an apartment is better?"

"If it's got two bedrooms, it is."

Angelica shrugged. "If one were to look on the bright side, one might conclude that the fire was a blessing in disguise. It changed everything. Now they can build a new house with a larger footprint."

"But it'll take months for the insurance company to settle."

"That doesn't mean they have to wait for the check to get building. I want them in that rebuilt house before the new baby comes in the spring."

"That's a tall order."

Angelica frowned. "I've got the money. I can make it happen."

She did.

Darlene arrived with their orders. "Let me know if you need anything else."

The sisters nodded and picked up their forks. Neither of them spoke much as they ate. No doubt Angelica was preoccupied with interrogating Hank about Becca, while Tricia kept thinking about the picnic with Marshall. Who was the friend he spoke about?

She was determined to find out.

While Angelica met with Hank, Tricia sat in the lobby and reread the list of ex–Chamber members Mary had sent her earlier that day. They were a mix of shop owners and other service industry people. She even went so far as to stand on the big veranda in front of the inn to call the owner of the local garage, made a pitch for him to return to the Chamber, and then had to listen to him urge her to come in to have an oil change and her tires rotated. Well, she guessed she would probably hear similar pitches as she made her way through the list. Two calls later, and she got a message from Angelica. She was ready to leave. They met in the lobby and were quiet until they reached the back parking lot, where Angelica let loose.

"And then he had the audacity to say he enjoyed her company!" Angelica huffed as Tricia steered her car out of the parking lot and headed for Main Street.

Tricia couldn't say the same, but then Becca hadn't batted her eyelashes at her.

"I hope you didn't harp on their innocent little lunch during the whole time you spoke to Hank," Tricia said.

"I was the epitome of propriety. I must say, I'm not disappointed with his suggestions about sourcing produce for all of my eateries. We're going to save a bundle and still deliver top-quality fruits and veggies."

"Good."

"I spoke to several of the kitchen staff and they say Hank's firm but fair, and were impressed with his standards of cleanliness. Mind you, you could drop a piece of buttered bread and not tell if it fell side up or down. No matter what I think of his choice of lunch partner, I don't regret hiring him."

"Good," Tricia repeated, and braked as she approached the Cookery. "Do you need help getting in?"

"I'm fine," Angelica said. "See you after closing this evening?"

"Well, I haven't got a hot date, so I guess we're on."

"Very funny. See you later," Angelica said, and got out of the car.

Instead of heading directly to the municipal parking lot, Tricia drove down Main Street and parked by a tidy, if not charming, building. The big display window gave it a mid-century vibe not at all in keeping with the shops farther down the road. Since Kelly Real Estate had gone under, Nigela Ricita Realty had become the village's go-to place to buy or sell a home or commercial property.

Tricia had never been inside the office before and entered the compact space to the accompaniment of a loud buzzing that announced her arrival. Three desks lined one side of the long, narrow office, none of them manned at the time. Each desk housed a computer and stacks of file folders, looking messy and yet somehow conveying a sense of a successful business venture. The agents were probably out and about rustling up business or showing properties to prospective clients.

"Hello!" Tricia called.

Karen Johnson's pretty dark face popped into the doorway of the business's only office sporting a door. "Tricia. What are you doing here? Are you ready to buy a cozy little house or a property with a pool? I've got two that would be just perfect for you."

Tricia laughed. "Not when I've recently spent a bundle refurbishing my apartment."

Karen laughed and shrugged. "A girl can always dream. Come into my office and tell me what's on your mind."

Tricia crossed the outer office's commercial-grade carpet, stepped over the threshold, and took one of the client chairs in front of Karen's gilded French-style desk. Her office was quite different from the minimalist décor in the outer room, from the green pastel walls with their original art in baroque frames, to the sumptuous oriental area rug under her feet.

"I love what you've done with your workspace."

"It's not to everyone's taste, but it resonates with the girly side of my personality," Karen admitted.

How did the other agents feel about having to work in a more sterile environment? She'd have to ask Angelica about that.

"What can I do for you today?" Karen asked.

Tricia sighed. "I suppose you heard about what happened to my friend Marshall Cambridge."

Karen's gaze dropped to the top of her tidy desk. "Oh, yes. I'm so sorry for your loss."

"Thank you." Tricia sighed. "Just before he died, Marshall took me on a picnic to a beautiful piece of land at the north end of the village. It had a pond and a gazebo. I was wondering if you know the place."

"I sure do. I sold it myself."

"To whom?"

"Dr. Jameson. You know, the dentist who opened a practice across from the Brookview Inn about a year ago."

Tricia blinked. Mark Jameson had been Marshall's friend? "Uh, yes, we've met. Marshall said the owner was a friend who was going to open some kind of wedding operation."

"Yes. Louise Jameson, the doctor's wife, is a photographer. She recently rented a building near the horticultural society. She photographs a lot of weddings in their gardens. She's collaborating with Isabelle Garson, who owns a bridal shop in Nashua. The business should be up and running at full steam by April of next year."

"Wow. I had no idea."

"Were you impressed by the setting?" Karen asked.

"Yes, it was beautiful. We had a lovely picnic."

Karen's expression softened. "I'm glad you have a recent, happy memory of your man."

Tricia let out a breath. "So am I."

"Louise is not just a portrait photographer, she's quite well known and has done some fine-art stuff and shot architectural pictures for several coffee table books."

"It sounds like you know her well."

"Sure. We met in college when she was still Louise Griffin. She married Mark just as she was starting to get a name for herself." Tricia got the impression Karen didn't approve of her friend taking on her husband's moniker. How did she feel about the village's only dentist?

"Mark and I are on the committee to recruit a new president for the Chamber," Tricia offered.

Karen frowned. "Why aren't you running for the job? You know it inside and out."

Tricia chose her words carefully. "They're looking for some new blood."

"What's wrong with the old blood? That is, if you want the job."

Tricia shrugged. "I may step in for the interim, but come November . . ." She let the sentence slide.

"That's a pity," Karen said. "I think you'd be fantastic."

"Thanks. And since part of my committee duties is finding new members, can I ask if you know of anyone who's buying or leasing some of the empty commercial properties in the village?"

Karen looked thoughtful. "As a matter of fact, yes. A couple from Litchfield rented the front of forty-five Main Street for a shop. It's a sixteen-by-sixteen-foot space with a tiny bathroom—very inexpensive because of the size. They're beekeepers."

"That's interesting."

"They gave me a sample of their honey. It's delicious. They'll also be selling beeswax candles and royal jelly." Karen brushed the middle fingers of her left hand against her cheekbone. "Not a wrinkle in sight," she said of her nearly flawless skin. "And they say the medicinal uses are phenomenal, too."

Tricia would have to take her word on that. "Have they moved in?"

"They took possession over the weekend but I'm not sure if they're open for business yet."

"Maybe they'd like to join the Chamber. I'll have to visit them."

"Yes, give them a warm welcome. They only signed a year's lease and if they work out, my client would want them to sign for a much longer period when it comes up for renewal."

The buzzer sounded and a couple of voices could be heard from those who'd just entered the building—one of the associate real estate agents, no doubt, perhaps with a client.

"I'd better get going," Tricia said, and stood.

"I'm glad you stopped by. Perhaps we can get together sometime soon for coffee."

"I'd like that," Tricia said, and turned for the open doorway. Karen followed her.

"And if we rent or sell any other commercial spaces, I'll make sure to mention the Chamber."

"Thanks, Karen. You're a doll."

Karen laughed and again touched the flawless skin around her eyes. "And don't I know it!"

ELEVEN

Tricia dropped off her car at the municipal parking lot and headed for Haven't Got a Clue. As they'd had such a busy morning, Tricia was surprised to find the shop devoid of customers. And as it was Mr. Everett's day off, it was Pixie who was busy wielding the latter's lamb's-wool duster, making sure that everything was clean and tidy, while Tricia's cat sat nearby, watching her every move.

"I know I've been gone a terribly long time, but would you mind if I ran another quick errand?" Tricia asked.

"Not at all," Pixie said cheerfully. "Miss Marple and I are great companions."

As if to agree, Miss Marple said, *"Yow!"*

"I should be back in just ten or fifteen minutes."

"We'll be here. Oh, Ginny called. She asked if you would call her back when you get a chance."

"Sure. Thanks for relaying the message."

"No problem."

Tricia started off again, this time heading south. She passed All Heroes Comics and By Hook or By Book, looking for number forty-five. Since she'd last passed it, a cheerful red-and-honey-yellow sign had been erected over the entrance, declaring the BEE'S KNEES. Although a plastic CLOSED sign hung from the window, Tricia could see someone inside surrounded by cartons and unboxing their contents. She knocked on the plate glass. An older woman with graying hair turned and pointed to the sign. Tricia gestured for the woman to come forward, which she did.

"Sorry," the woman called, her voice muted. "We won't be open until next week."

"I'm from the Chamber of Commerce. Do you have a moment?"

The woman nodded and retracted the blade from her box cutter before opening the door.

Tricia hurried inside, the wooden floor creaking beneath her shoes. "Hi, I'm Tricia Miles. I own the mystery bookshop down the street and I'm a member of the Stoneham Chamber of Commerce. Have you thought about joining?"

"I'm Eileen Harvick. I've heard rumors about the disaster that's the local Chamber. Why would I want to join?"

"We're in the process of rebuilding and hope to have a new president installed by our November election." She looked around the small space, which, though cluttered with inventory, looked charming, reminiscent of the inside of a quaint Swiss chalet. "Your shop is adorable. I'd love to know about your products. I understand you and your husband are beekeepers."

"Yes, we are. We currently have six hives we care for at our property in Litchfield."

"Have you always been beekeepers?"

The woman smiled. "Heavens, no. I was a teacher in Merrimack for thirty years. I retired at the end of the school year—as did my husband. He's a former county sheriff's deputy."

Tricia had never run across a deputy named Harvick during her encounters with the Hillsborough County Sheriff's Department.

"How interesting. Is this your first commercial venture?"

"On our own, yes. But we've been selling our honey at the Happy Domestic for the past year, as well as our candles. The manager kept upping her orders, which gave us the courage to open our own retail establishment."

"Is your husband around?"

Eileen shook her head. "He's just gone home to fill up the back of the van with more product, but he should be back in a couple of hours."

"Perhaps I can come back when you're both here and give you my Chamber pitch."

"That sounds fine," Eileen agreed.

"And I wonder," Tricia said, straining to look around Eileen, "if I might buy some of your royal jelly. I understand it has wonderful medicinal properties."

"Yes, it does."

"My sister recently had foot surgery and would love for it to heal in a jiffy."

Eileen laughed. "It's good stuff, but it's not a miracle cure—although some of my customers might dispute it. If nothing else, it should help minimize the scarring. We sell a topical cream as well as dietary supplements we get from a national supplier."

"Could I buy a container for her?"

Eileen turned and reached for one of the smallest jars, as well as a brochure. "Why don't you take her this as a gift from Larry and me. If she likes it, she can come back after we open and buy the larger size."

"That's very generous of you. Thank you." Tricia stowed the jar and leaflet in her purse. "I'm a bit of an amateur baker. Once you're open, I'll be back and buy one or more of your specialty honeys."

"Thanks. We'd appreciate it. We're having a soft opening on Tuesday if you'd like to drop by then."

"Okay. I'll be sure to stop in."

"I'll look forward to it," Eileen said, and walked Tricia to the door.

Tricia waved good-bye and was about to head back to Haven't Got a Clue when she remembered she was supposed to call Ginny. Pulling out her phone, she tapped the contacts list and in seconds heard the phone ring.

"Hey, Tricia," Ginny answered wearily. "Thanks for getting back to me so quickly."

"How are you guys making out?" Tricia asked as she walked.

"Okay, I guess. It's all so surreal. You have a home you

love and—poof—it's suddenly gone. I don't know what to do with myself and have been rattling around the suite for the past hour or so. Maybe I should have gone in to work today, but I knew I'd be useless."

"If there's anything I can do to help, just ask. Pixie and Mr. Everett want to help, too," Tricia said, and slowed her pace to a crawl.

"That's why I wanted to talk to you. I'm really bummed that we missed lunch this week."

"Me, too. I ended up taking Angelica to the Brookview today for a meeting with Hank Curtis."

"She's kind of sweet on him," Ginny said with a half-hearted laugh.

"The feeling may not be mutual."

"That's too bad. Maybe you could tell me all about it tomorrow. We need a lot of stuff to replace what we lost. Antonio's going to take care of Sofia, and my morning mission is to hit the big-box stores along the highway and stock up on more clothes and baby stuff, but even more, I need a friendly face to talk to. Could we have lunch at Booked for Lunch around twelve thirty? I don't want to wait until our Sunday family dinner. I think I'd just end up bawling—and nobody needs that, least of all me."

"Of course," Tricia said, her heart aching for Ginny.

"Okay," Ginny said, suddenly sounding more cheerful. "See you tomorrow."

"Right on the dot," Tricia promised.

Ginny ended the call.

Tricia arrived at Haven't Got a Clue feeling more than a little down. She tucked her phone back into her purse before entering.

Pixie had given up dusting and sat in the reader's nook, holding a book while Miss Marple sat primly on her lap, purring loudly. "Welcome back, Tricia," Pixie said, and made to get up, but Tricia waved her to sit, unwilling to upset her cat. She settled on the opposite chair. "Did you speak to Ginny?"

"Yes. She's very upset, and who can blame her under the circumstances," Tricia said.

Pixie nodded. "Yeah, we spoke for a few minutes and she cried. It broke my heart," she said, getting misty-eyed herself. "I wish there was something I could do to help."

"I'm sure the best thing you can do is to give her a big hug the next time you see her."

She swallowed and nodded once more. "I will."

Tricia unbuttoned her coat and looked around the shop, which appeared pristine. Even the carpet had been vacuumed. Pixie had been very busy before she'd taken a reading break.

The shop door opened, letting in several customers. Miss Marple jumped off Pixie's lap and the females of Haven't Got a Clue all went back to work.

By the time closing rolled around, Tricia was ready to sit down for a change. They'd had a superior day of sales, which was good news for her bottom line, but she was pooped.

After saying good night to Pixie, Tricia headed for the Cookery, entered, and headed for Angelica's apartment, welcoming the sound of Sarge's joyful barking. Was there anything so heartwarming as the bliss conveyed by a canine who was ecstatic by your very presence? As Tricia entered Angelica's apartment, Sarge sailed into the air and Tricia caught his little wiggling body, and as she seldom did, let him lavish her face with doggy kisses, planting more than one of her own on the top of his fluffy white head.

"Leave poor Tricia alone," Angelica ordered, but that only made Tricia hold the little dog tighter. She welcomed his love and admiration. So did her soul.

With one last kiss, she set the dog down and made a leap for the crystal biscuit jar Angelica kept on her kitchen island. She tossed Sarge a biscuit and he happily snatched it up and headed straight for his doggy bed.

"What treats do you have for me?" Tricia asked, hoping she didn't sound desperate.

"Just cheese and crackers, I'm afraid. I hope you don't mind *brie en croûte*."

Hell no.

Tricia removed her jacket, settling it on the back of one of the island stools. "What a day," she practically groaned.

"What happened now?" Angelica asked, pulling the pastry-covered cheese from the oven and setting it on a platter before surrounding it with butter crackers.

"The low point? Talking to Ginny."

"Oh, dear," Angelica commiserated. "Yes, I spoke to her, too. Three times this afternoon. That poor child is at her wit's end." She shook her head. "Come, get the drinks ready, and let's go sit in the living room and compare notes on the day."

As she'd done the night before, Tricia assembled the drinks and brought them and the cheese platter on a tray, setting them on the coffee table. The sisters took their regular seats, Tricia collapsing against the back of her upholstered chair. "I'm mentally exhausted."

"What happened after you dropped me off after lunch?" Angelica asked.

"Too much."

"Did you visit Karen at the realty office today?"

"I did indeed. And you'll never guess who owns that piece of land where Marshall took me for the picnic a couple of weeks ago."

"You're right. I'll never guess. So, tell me," Angelica said, and plunged a knife into the still-steaming cheese round.

"Dr. Mark Jameson, DDS."

Angelica scowled, spreading cheese onto a cracker. "Really?"

Tricia nodded. "It seems his wife is partnering up with someone from Nashua for weddings."

"Is she a coordinator or something?" Angelica said, and took a bite.

"A photographer." Tricia sat straighter and fixed her own cracker.

"That's interesting. Are they going to let her into the Chamber if he's already a member, or will they be considered one entity like I am?"

"I'm sure that's a big part of why he stuck up for you. But I've got a question for you."

"Anything, dear sister," Angelica said, picking up her stemmed glass.

"Why does Karen Johnson have such a sumptuous office and the rest of the stiffs in the realty office have to work in a place that looks like the DMV?"

"Oh?" Angelica looked perplexed, but then shrugged. "I guess I hadn't noticed. I can't say I've been in the office since I signed the paperwork to sell the house to Pixie. How glamorous *is* Karen's office?"

"Like something out of a French château. Gilded furniture, original art on the walls—it's absolutely gorgeous."

Angelica looked thoughtful. "She e-mailed Nigela asking if she could decorate her office. I never thought she'd go over the top. None of it was paid for with company funds. She painted the room herself and furnished it. I thought it was a great savings."

"I'm sure it was, but the outer office just isn't all that welcoming—for the employees or the clients."

Angelica smiled, looking almost gleeful. "Well, I'll have to do something about that. That'll be almost as much fun as picking out furnishings for Antonio and Ginny."

Trust Angelica to find the silver lining in a gray cloud.

"I'm sure the part-timers will thank you for it."

"Oh, not me. Nigela. She's a dream to work for."

"If you say so."

"Anything else happen today?" Angelica asked.

"Did you know there's a new business opening next week? It's called the Bee's Knees."

"Yes. Brittney over at the Happy Domestic was despondent when they said they'd be withdrawing their products. She's looking at different suppliers for candles, but will forgo the honey."

"That's generous of you."

Angelica shrugged. "I want to support *every* new venture in the village."

"They also sell royal jelly."

"What's that?"

"Bee food. Worker bees feed it to the hive's queen. It's supposed to be good stuff. Karen swears it has taken away her facial wrinkles."

Angelica looked skeptical. "She doesn't need it. She already has flawless skin."

"Ah, but what if that's what *gave* her the wrinkle-free skin?"

Again, Angelica shrugged.

"As a matter of fact, Eileen Harvick, the owner, gave me a sample jar. I told her about your surgery and she thought it might help work against scarring." Tricia got up, rummaged through the pocket of her jacket, and returned, tossing the jar to her sister before taking her seat once more. "Let me know what you think."

"I certainly will. Did you get any honey while you were at it? Theirs is really good stuff."

Tricia shook her head. "But I promised I'd buy some during their soft opening. Maybe you'd like to go with me on Tuesday."

"Maybe. But if I don't, perhaps you could get me a large jar of their wildflower honey. That's my favorite."

"Will do." Tricia sipped her drink. "There's another reason I want to go, as well. Eileen's husband is a former Hillsborough County deputy."

"So? He won't know any more about Marshall's death than you do."

Tricia sighed. "That's true. But, it never hurts to ask. And speaking of Marshall, something he said keeps sticking in my mind."

"What's that?" Angelica asked.

"He said a friend of his owned the property where we had that picnic. Since it's Mark Jameson, shouldn't he have offered his condolences to me at the Chamber recruitment meeting the other day?"

"Not if he's the SOB everybody seems to think he is."

Tricia mulled the idea over again. "What if it wasn't Mark who was his friend? What if it was his wife, Louise?"

Angelica looked thoughtful. "It's a possibility, I suppose."

"What if they were *more* than friends?" Tricia suggested.

"You mean lovers? While he was dating you?" Angelica asked, aghast.

"Well, Marshall was here in Stoneham for almost a year before we met and we weren't exactly dating. We were friends with benefits." Which was why his marriage proposal had been such a surprise. "What if he had the same arrangement with Louise as he had with me?"

Angelica's eyes widened. "Maybe you should get checked for an STD."

Tricia scowled at her sister. "It's just nasty speculation on my part—especially without any evidence at all. I was thinking I might seek out Louise's studio on my morning walk. It's supposed to be across from the Stoneham Horticultural Society."

Angelica shook her head. "What are you going to ask the woman? *Hey, were you and my guy bonking behind my back?*"

"What if he was bonking *me* behind *her* back? If I didn't know about her, maybe she didn't know about me. And if they were intimate, it could have happened and been over before Marshall met me."

"It seems like everybody around here is getting bonked but me," Angelica muttered.

"You said you were taking a break from relationships."

"That was until I met Hank Curtis, but now it looks like he's more interested in Becca than a shot with me," she said bitterly.

As far as Tricia knew, Hank hadn't loaded Cupid's bow with Angelica as a target. She didn't bother saying so.

"That doesn't explain how Marshall got permission to take you to the pond for a picnic," Angelica said.

"Who says he had permission? He knew about the place and he took me there. It was deserted. Probably nobody even knew we'd visited."

Angelica shrugged and sighed. "What excuse will you use to meet Louise? You can hardly say you want to book her for a wedding."

"No, but I could book her for a family portrait."

Angelica brightened. "That's a marvelous idea. We don't have a professional one, though goodness knows we had the opportunity when we were on the *Celtic Lady*. We should have Grace and Mr. Everett join us, too. I wonder if I should get a professional photo taken of Sarge, too." At the sound of his name, the little dog perked up his ears and cocked his head, looking incredibly cute. "You ought to get a nice photo of Miss Marple, too."

"I don't know that Louise would even welcome doing pet photos. I think it takes a special skill. Karen said the studio was small. I don't know if she can accommodate a crowd like us."

"If she's a portrait photographer, she's got a backdrop just waiting to be used," Angelica advised.

"You're probably right. If I can't stop in, I might give her a call to see what she offers."

"Good idea."

"I'll take my walk a little later than usual in case she doesn't open until ten."

"She may be open by appointment only."

"I'll take the risk," Tricia said. "I'll text Mr. Everett and warn him he might have to open my store tomorrow."

"He's such a sweetheart, I'm sure he won't mind," Angelica said.

"So, what's on the menu tonight?" Tricia asked.

"Since we both had such a heavy lunch, I asked Tommy at the café to make us a salad. How does that sound?"

Tricia helped herself to another cracker gooey with brie. "Great."

"Even better for me. I don't have to reheat it."

They chatted about the real estate's office décor, Tricia's calls to Chamber members, and Angelica's ideas for Ginny and Antonio's new-and-improved home. But Tricia's thoughts kept returning to Louise Jameson and what she might have meant to Marshall.

She wasn't sure she really wanted to know.

TWELVE

It seemed as though the sun had taken a vacation as Tricia woke up to yet another morning of gloomy skies. At least the weather app on her phone told her the good news that the afternoon would bring intermittent sunshine, which would definitely be welcome.

After dressing in wool slacks, a turtleneck, and the Aran sweater she'd bought in Ireland the month before, Tricia started off on her morning walk, grateful she'd dressed warmly. She hadn't gone far before she was surprised to see the flashing OPEN sign behind the big glass window at the *Stoneham Weekly News*. Peering through the glass, she saw Patti Perkins sitting at her desk behind the reception counter and waved before entering. "You guys are already up and running again?"

Patti grinned. "You bet. Although we won't be putting out an edition for another week or two. We've got to beef up our advertising first—get some money coming in. Mr. Barbero—Antonio"—she corrected herself—"says that although we're a branch of Nigela Ricita Associates, we have to pull our own weight. We can't do that without advertisers."

"Then let me be the first to buy an ad."

"Thanks, Tricia. The *SWN* team all thank you."

"When will Ginger be back at work?"

"Starting Monday. She'll hit the phone and make some personal visits to our former advertisers, while Antonio does some schmoozing with clients he dealt with when he worked at the Brookview Inn."

"Is he working today?" Ginny had mentioned he'd be watching Sofia.

Patti shook her head. "He was supposed to have coffee with a graphic designer who's done work for the big boss's event planner"—which would be Ginny—"but it's been postponed until Monday. Isn't it terrible what happened to his house?"

"Yes, it is," Tricia agreed.

"I can't wait to see the new masthead. Both Ginger and I are going to be trained on a couple of graphics programs so that our ads won't look so amateurish."

"I can't believe Antonio would use such a description."

Patti giggled. "He didn't, but I can read between the lines."

"How do you feel about that?"

"Ecstatic. I've worked here for the better part of a decade and the only training I ever received was from Russ—if that's what you could call it. I'm going to take some bookkeeping classes, too. Ginger's excited that she might get to work full-time."

"That's great. I'm so happy to hear that things are about to improve."

"It's been a tough couple of weeks, but it seems like it was all just a bad dream."

Tricia wished she could feel the same way.

"Now, let's talk about that ad," Patti said eagerly.

Though Tricia had never been a fan of the local weekly rag, she was determined to do her part to make Antonio's dream job pay off for him. She hadn't had an opportunity to talk to him about his role in the Nigela Ricita Associates empire, but taking care of the *Stoneham Weekly News* had to be quite a comedown. She wondered if she ought to bring up the subject the next day when the family got together for their weekly dinner.

Tricia made her usual circuit around the village but made one detour. She passed the Stoneham Horticultural Society, which took up most of the block, and sure enough, a small building across the street housed the Jameson Photography Studio. It was just after ten when she stepped up to the shop's front windows, where white lace sheers gave the interior some semblance of privacy, but Tricia could see that the lights were on inside and she decided to pop in to check it—and its proprietress—out. A little bell rang as she opened the door.

"Be right there," called a female voice from the back of the building.

Tricia closed the door and looked around what must have once been the front parlor of the vintage shotgun house. Several roll-down screens were suspended from the ceiling. Carpet-covered benches of varying heights could probably seat four or five, and a shelving unit held hats, scarves, silk florals, and other props. Framed portraits of brides and grooms silhouetted by a setting sun graced the walls, while an antique oak lectern held a massive book of photographs—apparently a showcase for the owner's work. The room wasn't big, and Tricia's makeshift family numbered seven in all. Could they all squeeze into the space, or would it be better to have the photograph taken at Angelica's place?

A woman, who Tricia assumed was Louise Jameson, emerged from the back room with a large mug of steaming coffee in hand. She was blonde, lithe, and attractive, maybe five or more years younger than Tricia, with a simple gold band covering the ring finger of her left hand. "Hi. Can I help you?" she asked.

"I'm Tricia Miles."

At the sound of her name, Louise's eyes widened. "Oh."

Tricia waited, but when Louise didn't elaborate, she started again. "I own the mystery bookshop up on Main Street."

"How . . . how nice."

"Are you Louise? I understand you take group portraits."

"Among other subjects," Louise said rather evasively.

"My sister and our family would like to have a group shot made. Is this something you'd be interested in doing?"

"I'm always interested in taking photos—the more the merrier," she said, and gave a nervous laugh. "When did you want to schedule it?"

"I'd need to discuss it with our family, but I was hoping it could be on a weekend when most of us don't have to work."

Louise shook her head. "I don't usually work in the studio on weekends, but I'm sure we could arrange something. Would you have another date in mind?"

Tricia shook her head. "I was just walking by when I saw your sign and thought I'd pop in and talk to you and maybe get your rates."

"How did you hear about me?" Louise asked, her tone colored with suspicion.

"Karen Johnson at NR Realty. She told me about your studio. I had no idea we even had a photographer here in Stoneham."

"Then I sure need to get out more," Louise joked half-heartedly.

"Is this your main studio?"

"Uh, I have another room in the back, but most of my portraits are taken right here."

Tricia nodded. "Do you have a rate sheet?"

Louise placed her coffee cup on her prop shelf and reached for a brochure housed in a tall, rectangular crystal vase. She handed the trifold leaflet to Tricia. "My number's on the last panel. You can call during business hours to make an appointment. If I'm out on an assignment, voice mail will pick up or my assistant can schedule a sitting."

"Fine. Oh, and there are seven in our family—the youngest is a toddler."

"Young or old, it doesn't matter to me," Louise said.

"That's good to know. Do you only do portraits here, or will you come to one of our homes?"

"I prefer my studio. I've got the proper lighting. After all,

I don't use a cell phone for my work," Louise said rather defensively.

Tricia wasn't sure how to react to that statement, so she said nothing. Instead, she forced a smile. "Great. We'll be in touch next week. Thanks for speaking with me."

"Anytime," Louise said brightly, but her eyes belied her words.

Tricia's visit had rattled her. If nothing else, she would need to speak to Louise about Marshall at another time. But for now, she would have to be patient.

"I'll look forward to your call," Louise said.

With a smile and a wave, Tricia exited the studio.

As she retraced her steps, heading toward Main Street, Tricia again wondered if Louise and Marshall could have been lovers. He liked accomplished women—if she could include herself in that description—and by the looks of the photos she'd seen in the studio, Louise had photographic chops. But if she was mourning Marshall's loss, she sure didn't show it.

And you've been accused of the same thing, Tricia reminded herself.

But she *did* mourn him. What she felt was deep, and painful, but quite confusing as well.

Somehow, Tricia had a feeling it would take some time to get over Marshall Cambridge.

THIRTEEN

 It was close to ten thirty when Tricia entered Haven't Got a Clue, where the heavenly aroma of coffee permeated the air.

"Good morning, Ms. Miles," Mr. Everett greeted her from the front cash desk. Before him stood a mug filled with the fresh brew and an open book. Miss Marple was curled in a ball beside it.

"It sure smells good in here." A shiver shook her and Tricia rubbed her hands together. "Doesn't it feel colder than it should be for this time of year?"

"The weatherman says it should be in the low sixties by three this afternoon."

"I'll take your word for it," Tricia said, and headed for the beverage station. "What are you reading today?"

"Rex Stout's *Champagne for One*."

Tricia nodded. "I haven't read that in a while. I'll have to do so again—and soon." She chose a mug from the shelf under the coffeemaker. "Thanks for opening the store this morning. I'm afraid I've got another favor to ask of you."

"I'm always willing to do whatever I can do to help," Mr. Everett offered her.

"I'm having lunch with Ginny today."

"On Saturday?" he asked, surprised.

"Did you hear about the fire?"

Mr. Everett nodded. "We spoke yesterday. She was quite upset. I asked if she needed anything, but she assured me that she, Antonio, and Sofia were well taken care of. Grace was particularly upset to hear the news. She went and visited Ginny at the inn."

"I'm sure Ginny appreciated her concern."

"We think of her as the granddaughter neither of us ever had."

Tricia nodded.

"Yes. She specifically asked and I didn't want to disappoint her. We're set to meet at twelve thirty at Booked for Lunch. She wants to talk. I have a feeling she means vent over what happened to their lives since the fire."

"We're at a loss as to what we can do to help."

"To paraphrase the Beatles, all they need is love."

"That we can give them," he said, which was a rare admission from the deeply private man.

"I might be more than an hour. What will you do about your lunch hour?"

"There are several options along Main Street. I'm sure I can find something for sustenance once you return."

"I could bring you a sandwich or whatever you want from the café. That is, if you wouldn't mind eating in the office downstairs," she said, and filled one of the ceramic mugs from the shelf under the station.

"Mind? I'd enjoy it. It would give me a chance to catch up on my reading."

Tricia allowed her staff to read anytime there weren't customers in the store, so his glee at the offer was hardly a perk. But Mr. Everett's eyes sparkled with delight at the prospect and she didn't contradict him.

"Great."

The shop door opened and an older man and woman entered, decked out in matching rainwear.

"Good morning," Mr. Everett greeted them, "and welcome

to Haven't Got a Clue. Please let either Ms. Miles or myself know if you have any questions or would like a recommendation."

"Thanks," the woman said as she and her companion ventured deeper into the store. "We'll have a look and let you know."

Tricia set her coffee cup on the table beside the beverage station and chose some jaunty music to brighten up the dark morning. In no time, she was tapping her foot in time with the beat and trying, but not succeeding, to banish troubling thoughts from her mind. It would take more than caffeine and the Clancy Brothers to do that.

As Tricia had promised, she arrived at Booked for Lunch exactly at twelve thirty, but to her surprise, Ginny had actually arrived early. "I think this must be a first," Tricia said brightly.

At the sound of her voice, Ginny looked up, her eyes brimming with tears, and then leapt to her feet to give Tricia an all-encompassing hug, hanging on tightly. Tricia patted her back, holding on for long seconds before pulling back.

"Are you okay?"

"I've been better," Ginny said honestly, and braved a smile. The women took their seats. "Thank you so much for coming," she said, her voice tight with emotion.

Ginny already had a cup of half-drunk coffee sitting in front of her. She let out a weary sigh. "Ever since the fire, I've found it really hard to concentrate."

Tricia offered her a sympathetic smile. "Losing just about everything you own will do that to a person."

"Not that the big boss"—their code phrase for Angelica under her Nigela Ricita name—"will pressure me to return to work, but I want to be back at my desk on Monday. I need some semblance of order in my life. But I'm also reevaluating everything about *that* life. Antonio and I have been putting too much of our energy and time into our work lives. We've got a great daughter and we're going to have another baby in the spring. I love my job, but I love Sofia more. I wasn't thrilled when I found out I was pregnant again"—just weeks before—"but now I see it as a blessing. I need my family. My husband, my children, and you guys, too, of course."

"I'm glad to hear you say that."

"I feel like I need to hold you, Angelica, Grace, and Mr. Everett tightly and try and keep you all safe."

"You can't do that. Nobody can," Tricia advised.

"I know . . . but I can't stop thinking about how fragile life is. You know that . . . losing Christopher and now Marshall."

Boy, did she ever. But those losses didn't have equal value. She'd known Christopher for fifteen years—had been married to him for a decade—and Marshall for a little over a year. Still, it would take time to get over Marshall's loss, too. If nothing else, he'd been her friend. And though rationally she knew why he hadn't told her his true history, she'd always feel a little hurt that Marshall probably would never have told her the truth about his past.

And yet, if they'd married, would he still have kept Becca in his life? Had she been the one he'd wanted but gave up for what he'd deemed a greater good, or was Baker right when he'd said Marshall had turned state's evidence only to save his own neck? She'd probably never know.

"Yeah," Tricia admitted.

"I'm a horrible person," Ginny said with regret. "The minute I heard what happened to Marshall, I should have done more than just send you a text."

"Don't worry about it," Tricia said. In fact, she hadn't even noticed. What did that say about her level of grief? Should she be offended? Actually, she wasn't. Because the outside world had no clue about how close she was or wasn't to Marshall. As Angelica had pointed out, Tricia didn't even need the fingers on one hand to count the times Marshall had attended the Sunday family dinners. And despite her affection for Ginny, she wasn't about to share the depth of her feelings about her loss.

Tricia decided to change the subject.

"I was surprised—really, shocked—when Angelica told me that Antonio wanted to take over the *Stoneham Weekly News*."

"No more than me," Ginny admitted. "But we talked it over in depth. He's not giving up as much command of Nigela Ricita Associates as you might think. He loves the idea of directing a newspaper—rinky-dink as it might be—but he intends to offload a lot of the day-to-day responsibilities to the women who've been keeping it alive despite Russ Smith's bad management."

Tricia smiled. "I'm glad to hear that. I spoke with Patti Perkins this morning, and she and Ginger are ecstatic that they'll be able to contribute more to the paper."

"And finally get paid according to their abilities," Ginny added. "Antonio intends to write one big story a week while monitoring other NR Associates projects as well, but hopefully he should also have more downtime, too. We'll need that once the new baby comes." Ginny gave herself a shake. "We should probably order lunch. I wish I had more of an appetite."

"You're eating for two now," Tricia teased.

Ginny almost laughed. "Yeah, I guess I am."

"Why don't we live dangerously and start with dessert?" Tricia suggested.

"I happened to notice there was a Boston cream pie under the cake dome on the counter," Ginny said with a nod in that direction.

"I'll bet Tommy made it this morning. He's a pretty darn good pastry chef."

Ginny nodded thoughtfully. "I suppose I could wash it down with a chocolate milkshake—a small one. I don't want to get *too* crazy."

"And I could go for a vanilla one myself," Tricia admitted. She looked up and signaled Molly, the waitress, who started toward them, already peeling back the last page from her order pad.

"What can I get you ladies?"

"A terrible indulgence in every way," Tricia said.

"Isn't that the best kind?" Molly asked with a laugh.

"You bet," Tricia said, giving Ginny a heartfelt smile. Ginny nodded.

As Molly walked away, Tricia turned back to Ginny. "Angelica sees your rebuilding plans as a blank canvas. How would you fill it?"

Ginny actually smiled. "Well, now that you mention it . . ."

FOURTEEN

 Tricia and Mr. Everett spent a pleasant afternoon together made better still by an influx of customers who'd traveled to southern New Hampshire in search of pretty fall colors and had stumbled across such a quaint little village. They gushed about their visits to other merchants along Main Street and of their pleasure at discovering such a gem of a place.

Listening to them made Tricia feel proud of her adopted home and the small part she played to make it appealing. Better still, she was happy to hear the effusive praise for Angelica's contributions under her own name and that of her Nigela Ricita brand that had transformed the tired little village of used bookstores into the travel destination it had become—and in such a short span of time.

Inspired by those testimonials, Tricia was determined to look for sparks of joy in what had become such a dark time.

As they began preparations to close for the day, Tricia turned to Mr. Everett. "I'm in charge of dessert for our family dinner tomorrow. Is there anything you'd like me to make?"

Mr. Everett's gaze dipped. "When I was a small boy, my favorite fall treat was apple crisp. My mother made it often from the apples that grew in our own backyard. Such happy,

happy memories," he said with a wistful smile. "Would that be something the others might enjoy?"

Tricia smiled. "I'm betting everyone will. I'll need to get some apples, but I've got everything else I need to make it."

"May I contribute the apples?"

"Of course. Then it would be *our* contribution to dinner."

He nodded, satisfied. "Your sister is so generous she rarely lets us pitch in."

"Would you like to do more?"

"We would."

"Then I'll mention it to her."

"Please don't let her think we're ungrateful," Mr. Everett clarified.

"Not at all. What would you like to bring next week?"

Mr. Everett looked thoughtful. "I could make the dessert."

"What would you make?"

Mr. Everett flashed a smile. "A surprise."

Tricia positively grinned. "Go for it!"

That evening, after yet another exuberant greeting from Sarge, the first thing Tricia noticed upon entering Angelica's apartment was that she was wearing pink-sequined sneakers. "Congratulations on the fancy new footwear."

"Thank you, thank you," Angelica said lightly, and held out the foot that the day before had been encased in a heavy, ugly boot. "They were delivered this afternoon. Do you like them?"

"They bring me joy," she said, and laughed.

"À la Marie Kondo?"

"Sort of. But instead of judging things for joy, I'm going to look for the good."

"Oh, so a combination of Marie and Pollyanna?"

"It beats being miserable."

Angelica smiled. "I got a pair for Sofia, too. I thought we'd look like twins." Angelica frowned. "I wonder if I should have gotten a pair for Ginny, too. She could use a smile."

"Why don't you ask her tomorrow?"

"Good idea."

"I take it your foot feels okay to wear something other than that clunky boot?"

"They might be pushing it," Angelica admitted, "but they've done wonders for my spirit. Now help me with the snacks and drinks so I can get off my feet and sit on my butt."

Tricia hung up her jacket and collected the glasses and the evening's treat, which was some kind of white dip with pretzels.

"What have we here?" Tricia asked.

"Beer dip."

Tricia wrinkled her nose. She really wasn't much of a beer drinker. Neither was her sister. She said so.

"But Tommy at the café is. He made it for us. It couldn't be easier, either. Cream cheese, beer, salad dressing mix, and cheese. Taste it. You're going to love it."

Tricia picked up a pretzel, dipped it lightly into the bowl, and took a bite. "Whoa! That is good."

"Let's sit down and pig out," Angelica said with a giggle.

Tricia brought out their snack and drinks and they sat in their usual spots in the living room, with Angelica taking the chaise end of the sectional and elevating her feet. She gave them a wiggle. "My foot might not be one hundred percent back to normal, but I'm ready to get back to living a *real* life," Angelica proclaimed.

"Are you actually allowed to walk in those shoes?"

"Allowed—yes. Encouraged . . . eh, that's debatable. But I can get along with crutches or the knee scooter, and from now on I intend to be a lot more active. I want to heal—and I don't want to lose my mobility. So if I take it carefully, I should be able to start getting out more."

"That's great."

"And remember, I promised to help with your Chamber mission."

"I've called a couple of people. The committee is supposed to meet again sometime next week," Tricia said. "Since physically canvassing past members isn't in the cards for you, would you be up to making a few phone calls?"

"I've never been afraid of a telephone," Angelica said self-assuredly.

"Great. I'll e-mail you the half of my list of people I never want to speak to again."

"Who are they?" Angelica asked, and picked up a pretzel, taking a deep swipe of the dip.

"The members who didn't vote for me to be Chamber president."

Angelica nodded. "Good idea. What else happened to-day? Tell all, because I'm bored silly."

While they sipped their drinks and sampled the dip, Tricia gave her sister a brief recap of each of her adventures, but Angelica wasn't satisfied and peppered her with questions.

"Instead of Antonio, I think maybe you should be in charge of the paper."

"Manage it, definitely. Write for it?" She shook her head. "My specialty is writing recipes—not mediocre ad copy." She sighed. Angelica's writing career had been on hold for so long, Tricia doubted she'd ever get another cookbook contract. Well, there was always self-publishing, but she also knew that cook-books didn't translate all that well when it came to electronic editions. Angelica's publisher had arranged for wonderful photography to accompany each of her recipes, which she wasn't sure her sister could handle on her own.

As though channeling Tricia's thoughts on photography, Angelica said, "Tell me more about Louise Jameson's studio. Is she any good?"

"From the samples I saw on display, yes. And her studio is very cute, albeit small."

"What did she seem like as a person?"

Tricia thought about it for a moment. "Guarded. Of course, I was dying to ask her how she knew Marshall, but I didn't want to blow it. I'll have to take my time—get to know her a little bit better—before I can ask her any difficult questions."

"Well, laying some silver across her palm could help grease the wheels."

"More like letting her swipe my credit card," Tricia re-marked. She took a sip of her martini before changing the subject. "I told Mr. Everett I was making dessert for tomorrow night's dinner and he suggested apple crisp."

"What a great idea," Angelica said, and took another hit of beer dip.

"*And* he had a request."

"Oh?"

"Yes, that you let him and Grace contribute to our dinners in some way."

"Oh, but that's not necessary."

"They would *like* to," Tricia stressed. "If you don't mind, Mr. Everett would like to bring next week's dessert."

Angelica looked thoughtful. "He *is* a wonderful baker."

"There, then it's all settled."

Angelica nodded.

"I'm looking forward to you being able to climb the steps to my apartment so I can host you for happy hour and dinner. It's been more than a month since I did. I know exactly how Mr. Everett and Grace feel by not being able to reciprocate your generosity."

"Well, when you put it that way, I guess I can understand."

Tricia nodded. "Now, with that settled, what's for supper?"

FIFTEEN

When Tricia returned to Haven't Got a Clue that evening, she found a bag of apples sitting on the cash desk along with a note from Mr. Everett.

I stopped at the grocery store. I didn't want you to have to wait until tomorrow to receive the apples to prepare the crisp.

Your Friend,
Wm. E.

Tricia smiled. Friend? Mr. Everett was far more than a friend and employee to her and the rest of their little family.

She carried the bag up to her apartment and started peeling the fruit, humming tunelessly as she worked. Making dessert was one of the joys she was determined to find every day.

She decided not to bake the crisp, but to put it in the oven when she got to Angelica's the next day. There was nothing like the spicy aroma of dessert baking to get the old taste buds going.

And, taking Mr. Everett's cue, Tricia examined her bookshelves and came up with another Rex Stout favorite for her evening's reading pleasure: *Too Many Clients*. After finishing it, she drifted off to dreamland.

After the second good night's sleep since Marshall's death, Tricia headed downstairs to pick up the newspaper, once again lamenting that the print edition came out only on Sundays. Okay, so she was a dinosaur, but as much as she enjoyed the convenience of an e-reader, she still enjoyed reading the printed word—selling hardcovers and paperbacks was her bread and butter, after all.

As she poured her first cup of coffee of the day, she scanned the headlines before opening the front section. At the lower right was a two-paragraph story about the body of a man found by hikers in the woods near Rindge, some twenty-plus miles from Stoneham. Foul play was suspected.

Tricia let out a breath. Someone she knew here in Stoneham had mentioned growing up in that little town west of Milford, but she couldn't for the life of her remember who it was. There seemed to be foul play happening all over southern New Hampshire. The mystery reader in her wondered what kind of mayhem had been involved. With brief reports such as she'd read, sadly, she'd probably never find out.

Find some joy, she told herself, and skipped to the comics page. But before she could catch up on the antics of the Cobb family, the landline rang. These days, she didn't receive many calls on that number outside of store hours but decided to set the paper aside and answer the phone anyway.

"Hello."

"Hey, Tricia, it's me, Becca."

"Hi," Tricia said cautiously. "What can I do for you?"

"I need to play."

Tricia scowled. "Play?"

"Yes. I may be retired from professional tennis, but I need to keep up my game and I need to practice. Are there any tennis courts in the vicinity?"

Tricia thought about it. Sure, at the local nudist camp, and some private courts in a couple of backyards. And then there was . . . "There are courts at Stoneham High School, but they're not nearly the quality you're used to."

"Honey, I learned to play tennis on a weed-filled patch of asphalt in Hoboken when I was the size of a firecracker and just as explosive. As long as I can lob a ball over a net, I'll be good to go. Do you have any connection with the school?"

Tricia thought about it. She'd been a contender in the Great Booktown Bake-Off that was held at the school back in the summer. She was acquainted with a former teacher at the school, but other than that she had no real connection with the local school district.

"Give me a day or so and let me see what I can do."

"Thanks. A day without tennis is like a day without—"

"Sunshine?" Tricia supplied.

"Not exactly," Becca said. "You have to understand, since I was ten years old, tennis has been my life."

It made sense that she would miss practice, let alone the game—and why she was willing to give up her marriage to keep playing. "I'll see what I can do."

"Do you know anyone who'd be willing to play with me? Someone I won't automatically slaughter." She laughed.

Tricia didn't.

"If my sister hadn't recently undergone foot surgery, she might have been a candidate. She was heavily into the game until she had a repetitive motion injury." That sounded pretty much true.

"That's too bad. I don't know what I'd do if I couldn't play. That's why I have an indoor court on my property."

It occurred to Tricia that Becca probably had a lot more money than Angelica—and that was saying something. And if so, why was she spending time winding up Marshall's piddly affairs? Couldn't she just pay someone to do that? After all, as far as Tricia knew, he lived comfortably, but not extravagantly. Then again, everything he'd told her was a lie. Had he escaped his old life with money to spare? Had he gotten a settlement from Becca? If asked, would Becca answer honestly or just tell her she was out of line?

"Are you still there?" Becca asked.

"Yes, sorry."

"Have you ever played?"

"It's been a long time since I picked up a racket. I don't think I could keep up with you."

"If nothing else, you could just lob balls and I could return them. I could get a couple dozen balls at the sporting goods store up on the highway."

"Why not rent a machine for that?"

"I've already tried," Becca said, sounding bored.

"Okay, let me find out if I can finagle a court first, then we'll talk about the rest."

Becca let out a breath. "All right. Call me when you know something."

"Will do."

"Thanks."

Tricia hung up the phone. She didn't mind helping out someone in need. And she had, after all, offered to help Becca any way she could. But finding her a tennis court? She thought about it for a moment and remembered she did know someone who might be able to help. And he would be arriving for work in less than three hours.

There was no point in opening Haven't Got a Clue sooner than noon on a Sunday—especially during non-peak traffic. To keep busy, Tricia gave her apartment another thorough cleaning and had just enough time to shower and change before the magic hour arrived. But when she went down to her store, she saw Mr. Everett had already arrived and was busy with his beloved lamb's-wool duster.

"You're here early," Tricia said by way of a greeting.

Mr. Everett smiled. "I consider myself lucky to have such a wonderful job with such good coworkers. Many people my age can't find meaningful work."

Tricia nodded at the validity of that statement. So many employers wanted younger workers so they could pay them less, but Tricia had found just the opposite with the people who worked for her. Not only did Mr. Everett and Pixie always show up on time, they almost never asked for time off or called in sick for the odd "mental health" day. It was worth paying them more than minimum wage and giving them benefits, as well.

"Thank you so much for the apples. It was so sweet of you to deliver them last evening."

"It was my pleasure."

"The crisp is ready to go into Angelica's oven and we can eat it piping hot with vanilla ice cream."

The old man's eyes practically sparkled with pleasure.

Tricia remembered her telephone call from earlier that morning. "Mr. Everett, you used to be on the Stoneham School Board. Do you think you could help me get permission for Becca Dickson-Chandler to practice on their tennis courts while she's here in Stoneham?"

"I'd be happy to put out some feelers, although I would hate to do so on a Sunday."

"Tomorrow would be fine."

"Very well. I'll make some calls and get back to you then."

"Thanks. You're a dear."

Mr. Everett's head dipped and his cheeks turned pink.

"Well now, what kind of trouble can we get into today?" Tricia asked.

Before he could answer, the bell over the door rang and Tricia looked up to see Grant Baker enter the shop. He was dressed in uniform, which seemed strange for a Sunday, and glanced around the shop, as though looking to see if there were customers present. "Morning," he called.

"Just about afternoon, actually," Tricia said.

Mr. Everett merely nodded. As though sensing the chief wasn't interested in buying a vintage mystery, Mr. Everett turned to his boss. "Ms. Miles, unless you need me right now, I'll be down in the office updating the inventory."

"Thank you, Mr. Everett."

He nodded and headed for the back of the store. Tricia and Baker watched until he'd rounded the wall for the stairs.

Baker stepped forward. "It's the first time in a long time I've seen you alone in your shop."

"The day's young," she said with a shrug. "What can I do for you?"

Baker moseyed up to the glass display case that doubled as the cash desk. "It looks like we're alone."

As if to contradict that statement, Miss Marple jumped up on the counter and plopped down in front of them, telling Baker, "*Yow!*"

"Are you here on official business?" Tricia asked, eyeing his police service cap. She wasn't in the mood for a personal conversation—if that's what he had in mind.

"We think we've found the pickup truck that killed Cambridge—Chandler—whatever his real name was," he added dismissively.

Tricia's heart jumped. "Where?"

"It was dumped in Hunter's Creek at the edge of the village. There was no sign of the driver. And, of course, the feds confiscated it before the state lab could get its hands on it," he said bitterly.

"What happens next?"

Baker shrugged. "They'll try to lift some prints, but my guess is the vehicle was wiped clean before it was abandoned. We're dealing with a pro here." He shook his head and swore under his breath. "But don't worry. I'll solve this."

Would he? It seemed to Tricia that she'd been better at his job than he'd been—not that she would ever voice that opinion. And she wasn't sure she wanted to poke around too much on this one. Whoever had been driving that truck had tried to run her down, too.

She wouldn't find joy in being the state's latest murder statistic.

"Thanks for sharing this with me. It brings me hope that Marshall's killer will soon be brought to justice."

He raised a hand. "Fingers crossed." He cleared his throat. "There was one other thing I wanted to ask you about."

"Oh?"

He looked into her eyes. "Tricia, do you ever see us getting back together?"

Tricia looked into Baker's mesmerizing eyes. She could see flecks of gold in his green irises, but then she had to remind herself that the attraction to them had always been based on her feelings for her ex-husband, Christopher. She'd told Christopher there was no way they would ever be reconciled—and, with his death, that pronouncement became reality. But had she really meant it? More than a year after his death she still found herself mourning his loss, missing him every day. Had he been the one true love of her life?

"I'm sorry, Grant, but no. With my romantic track record, I'm beginning to think that maybe being single is what I was meant to be all along. There are worse things in life."

"Are you sure?" he asked, and for a moment she thought the macho man before her might actually cry.

"Pretty sure." *At least about you*, she mentally added.

Baker nodded, swallowing.

"But that doesn't mean we can't be friends," she offered because, for a time, Baker *had* been an important part of her life.

"Like you and Marshall were?" he asked, sounding hopeful.

"Friends with benefits?" she asked.

He nodded.

She shook her head. "Just friends."

Baker nodded—she thought with sad acceptance. "So be it." He straightened. And cleared his throat, becoming all business once again. "Do you want me to keep you informed on anything I hear about Chandler's death?"

"Yes, of course! I need that kind of closure."

"Well, then, I guess I'd better get going. I've got lots of paperwork to attend to."

"On a Sunday?"

"They pay me a salary—not by the hour," he reminded her.

She nodded and in a moment of sentimentality reached out to touch his arm. "Thanks for stopping by. I really appreciate you keeping me apprised of the case."

Baker shrugged and patted her hand. "All in a day's work."

He turned and headed for the door. Tricia watched him go, feeling sad for what had been—and could never be again.

SIXTEEN

After collecting her unbaked dessert, Tricia switched off her shop's lights, set the security system, and locked the door, then she and Mr. Everett headed next door. June had waited for them to arrive and bid them good night before taking off for the day, leaving Tricia to lock up.

"Looks like we're the first to arrive once again," she told Mr. Everett.

"Punctual as ever," he agreed, and followed her to the back of the shop and the stairs for Angelica's apartment, where the heavenly aromas of roast chicken, garlic, and lemon greeted them.

As usual, Sarge was over the moon to see them, and they made a big fuss of the little dog only to have the scenario repeat when the others arrived.

"Help yourselves to drinks and hors d'oeuvres," Angelica called as she helped Sofia off with her coat, but the little girl was far more interested in her nonna's sparkling sneakers.

"Would you like a pair, too?" she asked.

Sofia nodded enthusiastically, and Angelica asked Antonio to pass her the wrapped package that sat on her computer desk.

"You're spoiling her," Ginny warned.

"If you'd like a pair, I'd be happy to spoil you, too! Just tell me your size."

"Really?" Ginny asked, delighted. After all, because of the fire, she might possess only the shoes on her feet.

"Of course."

"Then, yes, please," she said as her daughter tore into the pink-and-purple princess paper.

"I think I'd like a pair as well. I wonder if they come in blue," Grace said.

"They do. Would you let me buy you a pair as well?"

"That's terribly generous of you, Angelica."

"Give me your size, too."

"What about Tricia?" Antonio asked. "Shouldn't she have a pair as well?"

Tricia's eyes widened. Did she really want to make that kind of a fashion statement? Would rejecting the idea make her sound like a party pooper?

Find that spark of joy, she reminded herself.

"Do they come in black?"

"They sure do." Angelica rubbed her hands with delight. "Isn't this exciting. We'll practically be quintuplets."

"Mr. Everett, do you feel left out? Because I certainly do," Antonio quipped.

"They come in men's sizes, too," Angelica offered.

Antonio froze, his eyes widening in horror. "Uh, *no grazie*," he demurred, and everyone had a laugh. It felt *good* to laugh.

"Does everyone have a drink?" Angelica asked as she tied the laces on Sofia's new footwear. "Ginny and Mr. E, I made a pitcher of virgin piña coladas for you. I hope you'll like it."

"Dear lady, I like everything you make for us."

"Thank you, Mr. Everett."

He turned to his wife. "Would you like a glass of wine, dear?"

"Yes, please."

Since Angelica was busy being a loving grandmother, Tricia played hostess, grateful to be of use. Once everyone was seated with a drink and the big bowl of guacamole and chips was within reach, Tricia sat down next to Grace.

"I feel like it's been ages since we had an opportunity to talk," Grace said. "How are you doing?" she asked sincerely.

Tricia sighed. "Every day it gets a little easier. Well, not easier . . . just that I'm getting used to the new normal."

Grace nodded.

"It's a good thing I have the store and my new Chamber project to work on."

"Yes, William told me you were on the recruitment committee. How's that going?"

"Slowly," Tricia hedged. "My main assignment is to sweet-talk former members into rejoining the organization."

"I don't envy you the task. Russ Smith turned a lot of people off with his reckless management."

"He sure did."

"I understand Mark Jameson is in charge of the committee," Grace said.

"Do you know him?"

Grace shook her head. "I was told he's a dentist and a bit full of himself," Grace said. "Linda"—her secretary at the Everett Charitable Foundation—"went to him to have a filling replaced. She thinks he comes on a little too strong."

"In what way?"

"She thought he was verbally abusive to his staff. Telling one of them she was stupid when she made a mistake, instead of using it as a teaching moment."

Not everyone was a good teacher. Tricia knew it often took two or three attempts to acquire a new skill. It didn't help with someone breathing down one's neck looking for perfection on the first try.

"She decided not to stay with the practice," Grace added, and sipped her wine.

Sofia was enjoying her new sneakers, squealing with happiness and racing around the living room with Sarge in hot pursuit.

"Antonio, you ought to take some pictures or make a video of this," Ginny said, nodding in her daughter's direction.

"Good idea," he said, and pulled his phone out of his pocket.

"Speaking of photos," Angelica said, "Tricia's met the new local photographer. Wouldn't it be wonderful if we all went to her studio and had a family portrait taken?"

Her question was met with several blank stares.

"You don't like the idea?" she asked, sounding hurt.

"Uh, no—it sounds wonderful," Ginny said, her voice just a little wobbly. Everything seemed to make her teary these days.

Tricia glanced at Grace and Mr. Everett, who seemed unsure if they, too, were included in the invitation.

"We'll have to coordinate our schedules so that we can all meet at the photography studio where Ms. Jameson prefers to work. It might have to be a weekday appointment as she reserves Saturdays for weddings and Pixie works at the day spa, so Haven't Got a Clue wouldn't have coverage."

"Weekdays might be hard," Ginny said.

"I'm sure your boss would be more than happy to give you a few hours off," Tricia said.

"She'd be an absolute shrew if she wouldn't," Angelica said, and winked.

"Grace, can you easily rearrange your schedule?" Tricia asked.

Grace's smile was beatific. "Absolutely."

"Great, then it's all settled," Angelica said happily. "Tricia, would you try and arrange it soon?"

"I'll make it a priority," she promised.

"Oh, dear. We're running low on chips. Tricia, would you be a dear and get some more from the kitchen?"

"Sure thing." She rose from her seat, picked up the nearly empty bowl, and turned to leave the room.

"Antonio, would you mind refilling everyone's glasses?"

"But of course," he said, and followed Tricia into the kitchen.

Tricia removed the clip from the bag of king-sized tortilla chips and shook out enough to fill the bowl. Antonio cleared his throat, capturing her attention.

"I was very sorry to hear of your friend's death. I apologize for not mentioning it sooner."

"Thank you," Tricia said. "Congratulations on taking over the *Stoneham Weekly News*."

"It is a dream come true, although just a little one." He held up a hand with this thumb and index finger just about an inch apart and laughed.

"What are your plans for the paper?" Tricia asked.

"To make a profit," he said succinctly. "I understand you've already bought an ad."

"And plan to do so on a regular basis."

"You are too kind."

"Will you boost the editorial content?"

"That is my plan."

"Will you run a story on Marshall's death?"

He shrugged. "It will be old news by the time we print next week, but I will make sure mention is made of his passing. Patti has suggested we start running death notices. Would you like to compose one for him?"

Tricia hesitated. She wasn't sure how much of what she knew about Marshall's life she should share. Should she keep his past life a secret? Mention Becca as his ex-wife? Maybe she wouldn't want to be outed. She'd have to ask her the next time they spoke. "Yes, I'll pull something together," she promised.

The rest of the evening was filled with fun and laughter. Even Ginny managed a few smiles as Sofia tested out her new shoes with some innovative dancing moves.

Tricia almost forgot she was supposed to be grieving.

SEVENTEEN

It was still dark when Tricia awoke the next morning. The clocks would be turned back in a few weeks, and the nights would close in far too early. Fall in New Hampshire. Tricia turned up the heat and got ready for her day.

With a cup of coffee in hand, Tricia turned on her laptop and impatiently waited for it to boot up so she could click the bookmark and scan the headlines of the online edition of the *Nashua Telegraph*. Civil unrest, climate change, and an unstable Dow average seemed to be the topics that dominated the news that morning, all things she had no personal control over. And it seemed that local news was getting harder and harder to find. More and more, she had to rely on the TV stations in nearby cities that uploaded stories to the worldwide net since her own village had only a weekly rag that concentrated more on ads than actual news. It probably wouldn't change under its new leadership, either.

Remembering the short article she'd read the day before in the Sunday print edition, Tricia used keywords to Google about the body found in Rindge two days before. The man had been identified as one Joshua Greenwell, a forty-six-year-old white male well known to local law enforcement.

What did that mean? Was he a habitual criminal who'd

crossed paths with cops both local and county or statewide? The cause of death was pending autopsy results, but she remembered the original story—short as it was—mentioned the Sheriff's Department was looking at it as suspicious and that foul play was suspected.

She shrugged and clicked on another bookmark. October had its brilliantly warm, sunny days and just as many cool, gloomy weeks. Every day was a crapshoot and Tricia made it her business each morning to check online to see what she could expect for the day. Cool, cloudy, but only a ten percent chance of rain. She'd take it.

After checking her social media pages and posting fall-themed pictures of Haven't Got a Clue, Tricia fell into the sinkhole of time wasted on such sites. When she glanced up at the clock she was horrified to see that her store would open in just fifteen minutes.

Tricia headed downstairs to get the beverage station up and going, wishing she'd thought to make a batch of cookies the evening before. Her customers would just have to accept the coffee, tea, or cocoa she provided.

Before she could measure the ground beans, the phone rang. Even though the store wasn't due to open for another fifteen minutes, she picked up the vintage phone's heavy receiver. "Haven't Got a Clue. This is Tricia."

"Ms. Miles." It was Mr. Everett. "Good news. I was able to reach my acquaintance on the current school board and received permission for Ms. Dickson-Chandler to use their tennis court this afternoon."

"That's great."

"She may use it any time after five o'clock. He did ask if she would be willing to sign autographs, but I discouraged that idea. However, if she would like to do so on another day, I would be happy to pass that along."

"I'll ask her and let you know. And please thank your . . ." She hesitated. If Mr. Everett hadn't called the person he'd spoken to a friend, should she? "Your contact for me and Becca."

"I shall do that. And I'll see you tomorrow when I come in to work."

"As always, I'll look forward to that."

"Good-bye, Ms. Miles."

"Good-bye, Mr. Everett."

She hung up the phone and then called Becca on Marshall's landline once more.

"Hey, Becca."

"Tricia, did you find me somewhere to play?"

"Yes. The local high school says you can play any time after five this evening."

"Terrific. I've already got a couple dozen tennis balls. I was whacking them against the back of the building, until Gene's neighbor came out and asked me to stop when one of them ricocheted and hit their back door, nearly breaking the glass."

Oops. It must have been Tommy over at Booked for Lunch.

"Will you meet me there? I've got an extra racket."

"Uh . . ." She hadn't planned on it, but then had more questions to ask of the former tennis star. "Sure. Do you know where the school is?"

"I've passed it at least six times."

"The court is located behind the school. You can access it from the side street."

"Great."

"I've got a question for you," Tricia said.

"Shoot."

"The local newspaper is planning to run a short piece on Marshall's death next week."

"Oh." She sounded less than thrilled.

"Would you like to be mentioned?"

"No. Have them only speak about his days here in Stoneham, would you?"

"Okay."

"Thank you. Anything else?" Becca asked.

"Not right now."

"Fine. I'll see you at five. And thanks," Becca said, and ended the call.

Tricia hung up the phone just as Pixie arrived for work wearing her long khaki raincoat and a sour expression.

"Good morning," Tricia greeted her.

"What's so good about it," Pixie mumbled, hurrying past her boss and fleeing to the back of the store to hang up her coat. When she returned, she hadn't cheered up one iota.

"Is something wrong?" Tricia asked, and, to her surprise, Pixie burst into tears.

"Oh, Pixie, what's wrong?" Tricia asked, gathering her friend in a hug.

"I lost my tooth!" she cried, pulled back, and opened her mouth enough so that Tricia could see the gold canine crown was indeed missing, and all that was left was some kind of metal post.

"What happened?"

"Oh, Fred"—her husband—"brought home some toffee apples last night as a treat."

Oh, boy. Tricia knew how this story was going to end.

"I took a bite and—out it came. It wasn't even loose or anything."

"Then you've still got it?"

Pixie nodded.

"Can it be cemented back in?"

"Well, it could—if my dentist hadn't left on a two-week vacation to the Ozarks."

Now, that was a destination Tricia had never considered, although she'd heard it was nice. "He's got family there," Pixie recounted. "What am I going to do?"

"Well, there is that dentist here in the village: Dr. Jameson."

"Yeah, I've heard about him," Pixie muttered.

"Oh?"

"Yeah. That not only is he expensive, but he's mean to his staff, too." Which corroborated what Grace had told Tricia the evening before. "He's only been open a little over a year and already he's gone through three receptionists and two hygienists."

Tricia could believe the part about the man being mean to his staff. He sure hadn't shown her much—any?—respect during the Chamber recruitment meeting. "Why don't you give the office a call and see if they can at least cement the crown back in until your dentist returns and can fix it permanently."

"I guess I could," Pixie reluctantly agreed. "I can't bear the idea of looking like a hillbilly for two weeks. You know how much I pride myself on looking my best."

Tricia could agree with that statement, at least in spirit. Pixie did look good in vintage skirts, blouses, and dresses. But were Tricia to make a decision on a crown, it wouldn't be a gold one. But somehow Pixie managed to pull it off, and Tricia reminded herself that when people saw it for the first time they often smiled.

"I'll go downstairs and call from the office," Pixie said.

"And while you do that, I'll get the coffee going."

Tricia filled the coffeepots with water and made two pots of java: decaf and high-test. Both pots were dripping steadily when Pixie returned.

"They can fit me in at eleven. Will that be a problem?"

That was fast. "Of course not."

"Apparently they had a cancellation," Pixie explained, wringing her hands.

Convenient.

"Would you like a cup of coffee?"

Pixie shook her head. "I brushed my teeth before I left the house. I don't want to go in there with coffee breath."

"Well, it'll be here when you return."

"Are you doing anything special for lunch?"

"Just meeting Angelica—as usual."

Pixie nodded just as the door opened and a customer walked in. Pixie clasped a hand over her mouth before greeting the woman. "Mm mame im Mimmi. Mm I melp moo?"

The woman looked taken aback. "What are you saying?"

Tricia stepped up. "Welcome to Haven't Got a Clue. I'm Tricia. Please let me know if I can be of any help."

"I'm looking for a book to finish off my Ross Macdonald collection. Would you have a copy of *The Way Some People Die*?"

Pixie nodded vigorously.

"Uh, yes, we do," Tricia said. "Would you follow us?"

Pixie homed in on the book like a hound on the trail of a fox, handed it to the woman, and then stepped back. She looked it over and nodded. "I'll take it."

"May I take it to the register while you keep browsing?" Tricia offered.

"Yeah. Thanks."

Tricia smiled and took possession of the book. "Let me know if you need any other assistance."

"I'll do that, thanks."

Tricia started for the cash desk with Pixie following in her wake.

"Thanks for taking over," Pixie whispered. "Jeez, I sure hope that dentist can glue my tooth back in."

"I'll cross my fingers for you," Tricia promised.

It was always a joy when Haven't Got a Clue could welcome visitors, and while there wasn't a rush that morning, there was a steady stream of one or two people in the shop for most of the morning. Even without Pixie, Tricia could handle the customers, ringing up the sales and anticipating a few weeks of steady income. In between customers, she made calls to several of the former Chamber members she hadn't been able to track down in person and wasn't surprised when she received their voice mails. Like her, they all worked during business hours. She left messages, telling each they could reach her on her cell phone at any time, and hoped they'd return her calls. If they didn't, she at least had done her duty.

Pixie texted that she would return to the shop after her lunch break and got back to Haven't Got a Clue just before two o'clock. Unfortunately, her sour expression had returned. "I'm sorry I'm so late."

"How did it go?" Tricia asked cautiously.

"When I made the appointment, they said they had a cancellation."

"And they didn't?"

"There were no other cars parked out front, and I didn't

see any other patients, but I ended up sitting in the waiting room for almost half an hour before I got in to see the doc. And then they made me have X-rays, and then hold a wire while they shocked the tooth to see if it was dead, which it wasn't. They didn't tell me I was supposed to let go of it if I felt a jolt. So there I sat like a dummy getting shock therapy."

"What?"

"I know—I know!" Pixie cried. "I told you that dentist was expensive. He charged me two hundred and fifty bucks just to glue the crown back on—and then he says he can't guarantee the work!"

"Wow."

"He told me not to eat anything hot, or anything cold, or anything hard, or sticky. I figure that leaves mashed potatoes and baby food. I guess that's okay, though, since I had to empty our checking account to pay for it and won't be going food shopping for a while."

For a moment, Tricia thought Pixie might burst into tears again. She knew that buying Angelica's little house had put Pixie and Fred in a tight financial spot, but she didn't realize things were that dire.

"Hey, your birthday is coming up soon. Why don't I reimburse you for the cement job as a gift?"

"Oh, Tricia. I couldn't ask you to do that. You already overpay me."

Apparently not nearly enough.

"I insist."

Pixie lowered her gaze, looking embarrassed. "That's really nice of you. If we didn't need food on the table for the next couple of weeks, I'd say no. But even if it's just mashed potatoes for me, Fred's gotta eat. Thank you."

"You're welcome. I'll write a check out and when I get back from lunch, you can run to the bank to deposit it in your account."

"You're the best boss in the world."

No, she wasn't—but she tried to treat her employees fairly.

"Now, I've got just enough time to write the check, and then I'll be off for my lunch with Angelica."

Tricia hurried downstairs to her basement office, wrote out a personal check, and returned to the store up above. Waving a quick good-bye, Tricia flew out the door and headed for Booked for Lunch.

Angelica hadn't yet arrived but as Tricia was about to head to their reserved table in the back of the café, she spotted Claire Rawlings, who was seated at the table by the front window. Claire owned Tails and Tales, a shop dedicated to serving the needs of Stoneham's pets, selling books, toys, and treats. She'd taken over the original Chamber of Commerce offices, which had once been home to a company that built log cabins—and had used its rustic décor as a backdrop for her own decorating scheme.

"Hey, Claire. It's been a while since I've seen you. How have you been?" Tricia asked.

Claire turned somber. "Not as well as I'd hoped."

"Oh, I'm sorry to hear that."

"Yeah, well, it is what it is," she said bitterly. "These lulls in business between seasons are killing me."

"I'm sorry to hear that. I'm part of the committee to recruit a replacement for the Chamber of Commerce president. Part of that mandate is to ask former members to trust us to nominate a candidate who'll commit to work hard to rebuild the Chamber and get us all more promotion in this part of the state."

"Are you running?" Claire asked.

"I've been asked not to."

"Whyever not? I voted for you last time. And Russ Smith proved he was incapable of replacing your sister."

"Thank you so much for saying so."

"What would you think if I voted for you as a write-in candidate?"

Tricia laughed. "Flattered."

Claire nodded. "I suppose condolences are in order."

Suppose? Tricia waited for her to continue.

"On the death of your friend Marshall Cambridge."

"Oh, thank you," Tricia said politely.

"I'm sorry, but I never did like the man," Claire muttered.

"Why not?"

"Because when he first came to Stoneham, he owned that horrible little porn shop on the edge of the village."

Tricia hadn't been enamored with the idea of the sleazy shop called Vamps. But Marshall's primary interest was the true-crime section it maintained. Considering what she now knew about his past, it all made sense. And it seemed Marshall got out of the business just in time. The new owner couldn't make a go of it and the business folded within two months of purchase. The big FOR SALE OR LEASE sign had already faded and the building on the edge of the village looked unkempt and abandoned.

"Scuttlebutt around the village is that he was part of the government's Witness Protection Program. Was he a racketeer?" Claire asked hungrily.

Tricia gaped. Who had spilled the beans on Marshall's past? "Uh, not to my knowledge," Tricia said, feeling unnerved and pressed upon. "He was a kind and decent man."

"Not if he was a turncoat looking to save his own neck after working for a felon."

Tricia wasn't sure how to respond to that accusation, so she ignored the jibe. "So, would you consider rejoining the Chamber?"

Claire frowned. "It's an extra expenditure, but if bringing in new blood will also bring in more tourist dollars, I guess I could be persuaded."

"Great. We'll keep you informed." Tricia nodded toward the uneaten half of a BLT that sat on the plate before Claire. "It was nice to see you again," she said, and gave a smile and a nod of acknowledgment before proceeding to her table, taking the side that kept her back to the rest of the café. She wasn't in the mood to accept any more less-than-genuine expressions of condolence that afternoon.

It wasn't long before Angelica arrived. She had ditched the crutches and hobbled in with a cane. She wasn't wearing her sparkling footwear, however, and had on a pair of brown flats. Perhaps the sequins were just for special occasions.

"Sorry I'm late," she apologized, set her cane against the wall, and scooted into her seat across from Tricia.

"It's all right. I'm not sure I have much of an appetite anyway."

"Tell your big sisti all about it," Angelica encouraged, but before Tricia could speak, Molly, the waitress, swooped over to take their orders. Once she'd left, Tricia explained.

"On my way to the table, I stopped to pitch rejoining the Chamber to Claire Rawlings."

"Yes, I saw her on my way in." Angelica shook her head. "I haven't been in to buy some of her homemade doggy bones for Sarge since I had my surgery."

"Apparently she could use the business."

"I'll send June over to get some this afternoon. What did Claire have to say?"

"That she didn't like Marshall."

"Why would she say that?"

"Because he owned Vamps."

"Oh," Angelica muttered, as though that explained everything. "Is she going to rejoin?"

"Maybe. She said she'd do a write-in vote for me."

Angelica brightened. "What a marvelous idea."

"Who says I want the job?"

"Who says you don't?"

"Me."

"Not very adamantly," Angelica quipped.

"She also mentioned Marshall being in the Witness Protection Program. How could she have found out about that? I haven't told anyone but you."

"Well, I certainly didn't tell anyone. Do you think it could have been anyone in the Stoneham Police Department? Surely by now they all know, being as it's such a small force."

Maybe. Tricia wondered if she should ask Baker. But then, she really needed to stop calling him whenever she had a question. Even though she'd told him she wanted them to remain friends, it wasn't really true.

"What else has got you down?" Angelica asked.

Tricia sighed. "Pixie lost her gold tooth to a toffee apple. And her dentist is on vacation."

"Oh, how awful."

"She went to see Mark Jameson and he charged her an arm and a leg to cement it back in."

"Poor Pixie."

Tricia waved a hand in the air. "I took care of it."

"Aw, you're a good boss."

Tricia gave her sister a smile. "I learned from one of the best."

"You're only saying that because it's true," Angelica said, and laughed. "Anything else happen today?"

"Not yet, but later this afternoon I'm going over to the high school to lob tennis balls at Becca Dickson-Chandler."

"What?"

"She needs to practice."

"Well, you certainly aren't up to her level."

"Like I didn't know that. But she asked me to hit some balls across the net for her to return. I can certainly do that."

"Are you sure you want to? It's only been four months since you broke your arm."

Tricia frowned. "I hadn't thought of that," she said, and rubbed her forearm. It had been a compound fracture and Tricia had undergone surgery to fix the break, which had been repaired with a rod and screws. "What am I going to tell her?"

"That you've got a stand-in."

'Who?"

"Well, me, of course."

"You can't even put weight on your foot for a full minute, how are you going to whack a dozen tennis balls across a net?"

"Hopefully, with a racket."

"I'm serious," Tricia said.

"So am I. My knee scooter has a stop on it. That'll keep me in place."

"Yes, but in order to throw the ball in the air and then hit it, you'll have to throw your upper body into it. That'll send you butt over teakettle."

Angelica scowled and then sighed. "I guess you're right." She glanced at the big clock with the circle of pink neon around it and looked thoughtful. "We have two hours and forty-five minutes. I will figure something out."

Molly arrived with their sandwiches and soup, setting the dishes on the table before them.

"You wouldn't happen to know anyone around here who's any good at tennis would you, Molly?"

The waitress shrugged. "Now? No. But my daughter used to play doubles on the Stoneham High tennis team."

"Would she be available to play this afternoon?" Tricia asked.

Molly shook her head. "She moved to Boston. There are more IT jobs there than here in little old Stoneham."

Tricia's heart sank.

"What about her other teammates? Do any of them still live in the area?"

"Oh, sure. Ginny Wilson, for one."

"Our Ginny Wilson?" Tricia asked.

"The one and only. I'm surprised you didn't already know that. She was good, but she missed out on a scholarship. If you need a partner, why don't you ask her?"

"I've got her on speed dial!" Angelica said, taking out her phone.

"Thanks, Molly," Tricia said, and the waitress gave her a nod before turning to check on her other customers.

Tricia put a hand on Angelica's arm to stop her from calling. "We can't ask Ginny to play against Becca. She's pregnant."

"So? That doesn't mean she's an invalid. For your information, Serena Williams won her twenty-third Grand Slam title at the Australian Open while pregnant."

"Yes, but she's a trained athlete."

"Ginny isn't going to play Becca. You said it yourself, she just wants someone to lob tennis balls in her direction."

Tricia picked up her half grilled cheese sandwich and shook her head. "I doubt she'd do it. I mean, she's so dedicated to her job, she felt guilty for taking just one day off after the fire."

"She won't if I ask her to do it."

"She'd do it *because* you asked her to do it."

"Do you think Ginny would turn *you* down?"

"Yes, if it takes her away from her work—and I wouldn't want to give her that opportunity."

"She only works until five. She could leave a few minutes early."

"What about Sofia? Someone's got to get her at day care."

"Antonio can do that."

Tricia bit into her sandwich, savagely chewing, while Angelica sampled her tomato and roasted red pepper soup. They didn't speak for a minute or two until Angelica broke the quiet. "Well, are you going to call her?"

Tricia swallowed a spoonful of soup, her frown returning. "The minute I get back to Haven't Got a Clue."

EIGHTEEN

The store was empty of customers and Pixie had left to go to the bank to cash Tricia's check when Tricia pulled out her cell phone and tapped Ginny's number on her contacts screen. *Answer, answer, answer,* she mentally begged as it continued to ring. Just before it would have gone to voice mail, Ginny spoke. "Hi, Tricia. What's up?"

"Hey, Ginny. How are things going?"

"I love the structure of being back at work. The suite at the Sheer Comfort Inn is beautiful, but it's just not home. I miss my own bed. I miss my beautiful yard. I miss my favorite coffee cups."

Hearing the sadness that tinged Ginny's voice was heartbreaking.

"But you didn't call to hear me complain."

"You're not complaining. And even if you were, no one would blame you. Have you heard from the fire chief today?"

"No. They're still investigating. It could take months until they figure out what happened. All we know is that someone deliberately destroyed our home—our lives."

"But you're safe and you can rebuild."

"Yes. We *are* safe." She didn't seem all that thrilled about the rebuilding aspect. "What can I do for you?" Ginny offered.

"Well, actually, I was wondering how you felt about tennis."

"Tennis?"

"Yes. I didn't want to bring it up yesterday, but it seems Marshall was well acquainted with Becca Dickson-Chandler."

"Oh my God—are you kidding me?" Ginny asked, suddenly sounding like her old enthusiastic self.

"No. In fact, she's here in Stoneham to tie up his affairs and she asked if I would be willing to help her find a place to practice."

"And?"

"And she's going to meet me at the Stoneham High tennis courts at five."

"Can I come? Can I meet her?" Ginny asked excitedly.

"Well, actually, I was hoping you'd be willing to do just a little bit more."

"Like what, like what?"

"Would you be willing to hit some tennis balls in her direction? Of course, she'd love someone to play against, but there's nobody around here in her league. I was going to do it myself until Angelica questioned whether that would be a good idea—"

"Not after breaking your arm back in June," Ginny agreed. "I'd be absolutely thrilled to help her out."

"You'd have to leave work a little early."

"I'll be out of here in a flash for an opportunity to meet one of the country's greatest tennis players."

Tricia smiled. "I was hoping you'd say that."

As the afternoon progressed, Tricia had a change of heart. Was she willing to risk Ginny's health and that of her unborn baby to placate Marshall's ex-wife? And all because she selfishly wanted to wheedle more information from the woman about the man she thought she'd known? And to what end? Nothing she learned about Marshall would bring him back. And perhaps those answers would only confuse and upset her more.

Angelica's Serena Williams defense didn't cut it for Tricia. Serena was a trained athlete. For the most part, Ginny led a sedentary life, spending her weekdays behind a desk. She did chase a toddler on weekends, but then again all Ginny had to do was toss tennis balls in the air and give them a whack.

Paranoia doesn't suit you, Tricia told herself. Still . . .

Although Stoneham High was only a few blocks from Haven't Got a Clue, Tricia drove herself and Angelica, parking in the rear of the building closest to the tennis courts. They'd brought along what Angelica called "necessary supplies" of bottled water in a small cooler, a couple of hand towels, and Angelica's old tennis racket—just in case—and a folding chair.

A few students jogged the dirt track around the athletic field, but as Mr. Everett had mentioned, there were no gawkers hanging out at the courts.

"I can't help but worry," Tricia muttered as she handed her sister her crutches.

"Maybe you should just go home and I'll catch a ride back with Ginny."

"I can hardly do that when I'm the one who set this up for Becca."

By the time Tricia had removed the chair from the trunk of her car and set it up for Angelica on the side of the court, Ginny had arrived. She was dressed in work clothes consisting of a pink blouse, black slacks, and a matching sweater, plus a pair of brand-new, white track shoes that looked like they'd just escaped from the box.

"Wow—I'm surprised I got here before Ms. Dickson-Chandler."

"Oh, call her Becca," Angelica advised.

"Excuse me, but *you* haven't even been introduced to her yet," Tricia chided her sister, who merely rolled her eyes.

No sooner had she finished her admonishment than a charcoal gray Dodge Caravan pulled into the lot. Becca got out of the car. She wore a blue tracksuit and a ball cap emblazoned with the United States Tennis Association logo. She reached in and brought out a duffel bag. "Tennis anyone?" she called, and laughed. She walked over to where the others were stationed at the side of the court, setting her stuff down on the ground.

"Wow, a minivan?" Tricia asked, surprised by Becca's

choice. She'd been expecting something more in the way of a Porsche or Lamborghini. She laughed. "You look just like a soccer mom."

"And I suppose you drive a Rolls Phantom?" Becca barked.

"Hardly. Becca, this is my sister, Angelica."

"Nice to meet you," Becca said, and shook Angelica's hand.

"And this is my niece, Ginny. She's going to be the one helping out today."

Becca looked at Tricia quizzically.

"As my sister reminded me earlier, I broke my arm earlier this summer and I really don't want to put a strain on it."

"Totally understandable." Becca turned to Ginny. "Nice to meet you."

"I've been a fan of yours since I was a kid," Ginny said excitedly as she shook Becca's hand. "I even had a poster of you up on my bedroom wall."

Don't gush, don't gush, Tricia silently implored.

"Played tennis, did you?" Becca asked with just a hint of derision in her voice.

"A little bit," Ginny said modestly.

"Well, let's see what you can do." Becca emptied the duffel, which contained several cans of tennis balls that turned out to be Day-Glo pink, as well as her racket. She removed her sweat jacket and tied it around her waist. "Would you get the balls ready, Tricia?"

"Sure thing."

Tricia opened the cans while Ginny hefted Angelica's racket, checking to see that it wasn't warped. "It's in good shape."

"I had it restrung just last year."

"Planning on playing again?" Ginny asked.

"One never knows," Angelica said, and sighed.

Ginny handed her sweater to Angelica while Tricia set the balls in the middle of the court. Ginny moved to stand by her. "All you have to do is just hit the balls in Becca's direction," Tricia told her.

Ginny nodded.

"Anytime you're ready," Becca called from center court.

Tricia retreated to the sidelines.

Ginny picked up one of the pink balls and bounced it for a few seconds before she tossed it into the air and slammed it with amazing power. Becca returned the shot with equal force, sending it sailing to the far side of the court.

Ginny picked up the next ball, bounced it, whacked it, and Becca hit it hard, sending it to the opposite side of the court. On the next volley, Ginny dived to return it, Becca hit it back—not once, not twice, but three times before the tennis pro passed her.

Little Ginny, the eighteen-year-old who had not won a tennis scholarship because "she wasn't good enough" could hold her own against a world champion. Okay, Becca was past her prime, but Ginny could still hit a tennis ball.

Ginny, who had only a high school education, had risen from retail clerk to marketing executive in only four years. And why? Because she'd been given a chance. Angelica had seen a kernel of greatness in Ginny—had given her the opportunity to manage the Happy Domestic. And after Ginny's marriage to Antonio, Angelica had elevated her to manage the NR Associates Marketing Department. It wasn't just nepotism, Ginny had the smarts, the vision, and the skill to pull that off. And now she was giving a tennis world champion a run for her money.

"Woo-hoo!" Tricia called as Ginny dived to return yet another savage backhand shot.

"Who is this ringer?" Becca yelled in Tricia's direction.

"My niece!" Tricia called with enthusiasm.

Ginny and Becca ended up batting balls back and forth for almost an hour while Angelica's phone captured some of the action. This was something Ginny could not only tell her children about in the future, but she'd be able to show them, too.

Becca did not jump over the net, but she looked satisfied as she approached her opponent.

"You gave me a great workout, Ginny. You're a very talented *amateur*," Becca said. It was supposed to be a compliment, but it didn't come out sounding that way.

"Thanks," a smiling Ginny said, still breathing hard, her

face beaded with sweat, apparently missing Becca's derisive tone. "And to think, I haven't played for at least five years—well, a real game, anyway. I work out several times a week with Wii tennis, and I knock balls off the brick wall in my backyard."

Becca scowled, looking just the teeniest bit angry.

"It's like riding a bike," Angelica quipped, and handed Ginny a towel.

"Would you be willing to do it again tomorrow?" Becca asked.

Ginny wiped her brow and gave Tricia a sly grin before turning to Becca. "Sure. As long as the weather holds I could probably carve an hour out of my day."

"Great. We'll meet here again tomorrow evening—same time?"

"Can do," Ginny agreed.

"Thanks for arranging this, Tricia," Becca said. "I'll be in touch." She picked up the balls, stuffing them into her storage bag, and headed for her car.

Angelica handed Ginny a bottle of water. "Are you okay?" she asked, concerned.

"Okay? I'm fantastic. You have no idea what a gift Tricia has given me at a time when I've lost so much."

"I'm betting you're going to be sore tomorrow," Tricia said.

"And I've got that lovely soaker tub waiting for me at the suite at the Sheer Comfort Inn. I intend to luxuriate in it once Sofia nods off."

"I'm so proud of you," Angelica said, and drew Ginny into a hug.

"Me, too," Tricia said, but her smile was short-lived.

Her motivation for agreeing to set up this tennis date had been to find out more about the investigation into Marshall's death and the life he'd left behind. Unfortunately, she hadn't had the opportunity to ask Becca one question.

NINETEEN

 Angelica was in high spirits as they drove back to the municipal parking lot. So much so that one might have thought *she* was the one who'd played triumphantly on the tennis court. Tricia listened, but she didn't take it all in. She had other things on her mind.

Angelica unlocked the door to the Cookery and the sisters trundled up the stairs to her apartment. After a warm welcome from Sarge, they took off their coats and headed for the kitchen, where Angelica already had a pitcher of happy hour cocktails waiting.

"We're not too much later than usual," she said as she pulled a tray of something wrapped in plastic from the fridge and turned on the oven.

"Are we in a hurry?" Tricia asked.

"Not a bit."

"What have you got there?"

Angelica set the tray on the island. "Mushrooms wrapped in bacon and covered in barbecue sauce. It's something Tommy threw together for us. They only take ten or fifteen minutes to bake. It should taste fabulous."

"I'll bet."

"Oh, did you have a chance to call Louise Jameson to set up our family portrait?"

Tricia winced. "Rats! With everything that went on today, I completely forgot."

Angelica did not look pleased, but she didn't berate her sister, either. "Perhaps you'll remember tomorrow," she said pointedly.

"I will *definitely* call her tomorrow."

"What were you doing that took up all your time?"

"You mean besides running my store and arranging things for Becca?"

Angelica nodded and put the tray of appetizers in the oven.

"I called the last of the people on my Chamber list to try to talk them into rejoining."

"How'd that go?"

"Nobody returned my calls—so far," she amended. As if on cue, Tricia's phone rang. She glanced at the number and, recognizing the name, answered. "Hey, Billie, thanks for returning my call."

Billie Hanson was the manager of the Bank of Stoneham. Tricia had dealt with her for business transactions on a number of occasions since she'd arrived in town nearly seven years before. It was said that Billie was named after Billie Burke, the actress who played Glinda the Good Witch of the North in *The Wizard of Oz*. Not that she looked like that icon of the silver screen. She didn't have long, frizzy red hair, nor was she tall. In fact, Billie, short and squat, reminded Tricia of a fireplug. As she always wore slacks, Tricia couldn't imagine her ever dressing in a glittering pink gown, but then these days Tricia rarely wore a dress of any kind, either.

"So the Chamber is going to regroup now that Russ Smith is in jail," Billie said.

"That's the plan," Tricia replied as Angelica started gathering plates and glasses and setting them on the island. Tricia wandered into the living room to pitch her speech, but she could tell by the chilly silence at the other end of the line that Billie wasn't impressed.

"Why don't they just ask you to step in to run the organization? The members, myself included, should have rioted months ago to toss Russ out on his keister and let you run the show."

"So many members fled, there was no one who felt able to confront him. But now that Russ is out of the picture, it's been decided that a new face should breathe life into the Chamber."

"It's too bad Angelica couldn't come back. She left pretty big shoes to fill."

But in the future, they wouldn't be stilettos.

"Once Russ cut out the networking opportunities, there was no reason to rejoin. Making connections was the whole point of joining in the first place," Billie lamented.

"I completely agree," Tricia said.

"Who else is on the recruitment committee?" Billie asked.

Tricia reeled off the members' names.

"And you say Dr. Jameson is the head of the committee?" Billie repeated. "I wouldn't have thought he'd have the time."

"Why's that?"

"I heard he's set to open another office in Merrimack to test the waters to see if he'd do better there than his practice here in Stoneham is doing. He lives here in the village, and it's said he's thinking about running for a seat on the Board of Selectmen next year. And that's not all."

"Oh?" Tricia asked, welcoming more information.

"Yeah. He's never banked with us so I feel as though I can talk about it," Billie said, which wasn't like her. She really must dislike the man to go on so. "Rumor has it he's also putting up the money for his wife's wedding destination partnership."

So, despite her appearance of self-sufficiency, Louise's photography business wasn't strong enough to carry her new venture.

Interesting.

"So, will you give the Chamber another try?" Tricia asked.

Billie didn't speak for long seconds. "You're asking the bank to cough up another year's membership fee on just the chance the organization can be saved."

"I'm taking that leap of faith and so are other former members. The situation can't improve unless we work together and give it a chance."

"Well, if you put it that way, I guess I could, too. I mean, it is a deduction."

"That's the spirit," Tricia encouraged her.

"Shall I write you a check and put it in the mail tomorrow?"

"We're going to have an audit done. Depending on what we find, we may even open a new account. Either I or someone else on the committee will be in contact with you about our plans."

"I'd prefer to deal with either you or Mary. I don't trust Dr. Jameson. In fact, if he was running for the group's presidency, there's no way I'd rejoin."

Tricia frowned. How many others would feel the same way?

"Thanks, Billie. The revamped Chamber will be in touch." Tricia said good-bye and ended the call. She returned to the kitchen and set her phone on the island.

"Will Billie return to the Chamber?" Angelica asked from her perch on one of the stools.

"Yes, although with trepidation. She wishes you'd return to lead the organization."

"Well, I *did* do an excellent job. Unfortunately, I wasn't able to set the tone for how to keep it afloat. Of course, if not for Russ throwing his hat into the ring, you would have won the election and the Chamber would still be thriving."

That was about as good a compliment as Tricia was likely to receive.

"It turns out people don't like Dr. Mark Jameson," Tricia offered.

"Am I supposed to be surprised by that statement?" Angelica asked.

Tricia shook her head. "But when you hear the same story from more than one source, it gets to be more than a mere rumor. And Billie spilled some gossip concerning Dr. Jameson and his wife."

"Really? I've never known Billie to gossip."

"Me, either, which is telling." Tricia related what the bank manager told her.

"If I were to be a negative person," Angelica began, "I might see why Louise and Marshall parted ways."

"What do you mean?"

"If—and we still don't know if she and Marshall had a thing going—but *if* she wanted her husband to underwrite her wedding venue, she might have dumped Marshall to see the project come to fruition."

"We still have nothing but supposition to tie her to Marshall."

"Yet," Angelica said.

The scenario Angelica kept pushing meant one quite disturbing reality: that Marshall had been bedding two women. He'd asked Tricia to marry him. Did that mean he'd asked Louise first and she'd declined so he'd asked Tricia while intending to keep Louise in his life?

Tricia's opinion of Marshall was diminishing by the day.

One thing she kept forgetting was that Marshall himself wasn't the paragon she'd thought. Of necessity, nearly everything he'd told her was a lie—the biggest of which was that by aiding and abetting his boss, Martin Bailey, in criminal activity, he was just as much a felon.

"Trish?" Angelica asked, shaking her sister from her reverie. "Are you ready for the cocktail hour or do you want to wait for the mushrooms to come out of the oven?"

"Let's pour those martinis now. It's been a long, long day," Tricia said.

She did the honors, and instead of relocating to the living room, they stayed in the kitchen.

"How did you make out with the list of former members I gave you?" Tricia asked.

"It was a hard sell," Angelica admitted. "As you indicated, they are not your cheerleaders, but I reminded them of the progress the Chamber made after Bob Kelly's defeat—never mentioning my part in that transformation, of course—and expressing my conviction that the organization can quickly rebound."

"You are amazing," Tricia said.

Angelica positively grinned. "Now, what's on tap for tomorrow?"

"There's the soft opening of that new shop, the Bee's Knees. Do you still want to come with me?"

"You bet. I've been rubbing that royal jelly on my incision and I swear it's already healing a lot faster. I want to get more and start rubbing it on my—"

"Crow's-feet?" Tricia asked.

"Laugh lines," Angelica corrected Tricia. "Will you buy anything?"

"Besides honey, I might be persuaded to buy some of that royal jelly—just as an experiment, you understand."

"Uh-huh," Angelica said, and sipped her martini. "What time do you want to go?"

"Mr. Everett and Pixie are both working tomorrow so I can afford to be away from the shop for a while longer. How about right after lunch?"

"Perfect."

Once again, it was still dark when Tricia awoke the next morning, but the forecast called for sunny skies if not warmer temperatures later that early October day. That was fine. Tricia enjoyed sweater weather, and boy did she own a lot of them.

Although the shop wasn't due to open for nearly half an hour, Tricia slipped Louise Jameson's business card into her slacks pocket and she and Miss Marple headed downstairs to get ready for the day. She even went so far as to unlock the door and turn the sign hanging there to OPEN in case any customers showed up early. Even so, she was surprised a few minutes later when the little bell over the door rang to announce a visitor. It wasn't a customer, however, but Chief Baker.

"Do you have a minute to talk?" he asked.

"I'm making a fresh pot of coffee. Would you like a cup?"

Baker shook his head and Tricia continued to set up the beverage station. "What's on your mind?"

"There's been a development in the Cambridge case."

Tricia's heart skipped a beat and she pivoted to face the chief. "Did the marshals find out who ran him down?"

"They think so."

"Did they arrest him?"

Baker shook his head. "He's dead."

Tricia's breath caught in her throat. "Suicide?"

Baker shook his head. "It was made to look like it, but the local PD says no."

"They've got jurisdiction?" Tricia asked.

Baker nodded.

"Then Marshall *was* murdered."

"It looks like it. That was their big lead. They're doing an extensive background check and will share that information with my department all in good time."

"Then we may never know what his motive was?" Tricia asked with bitterness.

Baker shrugged. "It was probably one of Bailey's associates—or a family member—who hired him to make the hit. That kind of thing happens all the time."

It did in fiction, at least.

Tricia shook her head—guilt, dread, and despair vying for prominence within her. "Poor Marshall."

"Yeah," Baker agreed sadly.

"What was the dead man's name?"

"Joshua Greenwell."

Tricia's eyes widened. "I read online that he'd been found dead in Rindge. What was his connection to Marshall?"

"None that I can see. He was just some punk."

"Do you think he killed for thrills?"

Baker shrugged. "It wouldn't be the first time it's happened. Maybe that's why he came after you, too."

"I'm glad to know that he won't be making a return visit. How did they know it was him who was driving the stolen pickup?"

"A partial fingerprint was found on the dash."

"What was the cause of death?"

"Gunshot."

It seemed like half the people in the state owned guns. No lead there.

The bell over the door rang once again as Mr. Everett arrived for work. "Good morning, Ms. Miles." He nodded in the local top cop's direction. "Chief Baker." His tone couldn't be called icy; cordial, maybe, but Tricia knew Mr. Everett was not Baker's fan, probably because he'd caused Tricia so much heartache in the past. Tricia was over it; Mr. Everett held a grudge for her. He headed for the back of the shop to hang up his jacket.

Baker hadn't missed the chilly reception. He cleared his throat. "I better get back to work."

"Thanks for stopping by with the news."

"You're welcome," he said. He touched the brim of his hat. "Talk to you later."

Tricia watched as he left the store. Mr. Everett approached, tying his apron. "What news did the chief bring?"

"They found the person who killed Marshall."

"That's good news, then," he said.

"Not entirely. The man turned up dead. The report I read online said he died under suspicious circumstances." Tricia looked thoughtful. "Do you know anyone here in the village who came from Rindge?" She explained why she'd asked.

"I daresay a dozen or more," Mr. Everett said thoughtfully.

"Would I know them?"

"Possibly." He recited several names, but none of them rang a bell. "How would you like me to start the day?" Mr. Everett asked, changing the subject.

"How about with a nice cup of coffee? I'm sorry I don't have any cookies."

"Coffee is fine."

The door to the shop opened and Pixie had arrived for the day.

"Oh, you're just in time," Tricia said. "I have a wonderful story to share with you two concerning Ginny."

Mr. Everett's eyes lit up. He looked upon Ginny as a stand-in granddaughter. "Oh?"

After Pixie hung up her coat, the three of them gathered around the beverage station and Tricia relayed the story with great enthusiasm and it played well to her willing audience. But the daily coffee klatch was cut short thanks to the unexpected arrival of a Granite State tour bus that parked down by the municipal lot. It was all hands on deck for the rush of customers. Pixie and Mr. Everett manned the cash desk as Tricia wandered around the store suggesting books and helping customers find requested titles.

It wasn't until nearly noon when Tricia finally had an opportunity to phone Louise Jameson.

"Jameson Photography. This is Louise."

"Hi, Louise. It's Tricia Miles. We spoke on Saturday about a possible family photo shoot."

"Ah, yes. Let me grab my appointment book. I've had a cancellation for Thursday afternoon. It's a two-hour block. That should be enough time."

"Wow. That's much sooner than I expected. But I'm sure I can rally the troops. What time?"

"Two thirty to four thirty."

"Just about perfect. I'll contact the rest of the family just to make sure they can all get away from their jobs and confirm it with you."

"Great. I'll see you all on Thursday."

"Bye."

Tricia ended the call. Now all she had to do was call all the parties involved to verify their availability. And, she wondered, how was she going to bring up the subject of Marshall Cambridge?

She'd have to figure that out—and soon.

TWENTY

As per their usual routine, Tricia and Angelica met at Booked for Lunch for their afternoon repast. Tricia caught her sister up on what she'd learned that morning about the suspect in Marshall's murder, and the upcoming photo shoot.

"Thursday? Wow, that's fast. I'll need to hit the day spa that morning to get my hair and nails done. Shall I make an appointment for you, too? We can go together!" Angelica said.

"Yes, please."

"What are you going to wear?"

Tricia shrugged. "Probably a sweater set."

"Oh, no," Angelica admonished. "You must have something nicer than *that*."

Tricia wasn't much of a clothes horse. "I guess I could wear a suit."

Angelica cringed. "It's too bad we aren't the same size. I've got so many fabulous outfits."

"What will you wear?"

Angelica looked thoughtful. "It's going to be a tough decision. I'll let you know on Thursday."

The breeze was stiff, but the sun was warm on their faces that afternoon as Tricia and Angelica left Booked for Lunch and made their way down Main Street.

"I sure hope Mr. Harvick is in," Tricia said. "I want to ask him about the man who apparently killed Marshall."

"Who says he knows anything about the guy?" Angelica countered.

"He *was* a county deputy."

"So are a lot of other people. He couldn't possibly know every petty crook who crossed the county jail's threshold."

"You never know," Tricia quipped as they crossed the street at the corner. She'd come prepared with brochures and had rehearsed her Chamber pitch. She figured if she faltered that Angelica could back her up. The Chamber had been the epitome of efficiency under her leadership. It was definitely a hard sell now that it no longer lived up to those standards.

There were no empty parking spaces in front of the Bee's Knees, and it seemed the shop was near to bursting with first-time customers. A harried but happy-looking Eileen stood behind the register ringing up sales while a man stood in front of the big shelf in back that was no longer filled with honey, no doubt thanks to the tour bus that had stopped by earlier in the day, giving his own sales pitch to willing listeners. The Miles sisters moved closer to take in what was obviously a well-rehearsed speech. Harvick told of the health benefits of his bees' honey and the long-burning times of their hand-dipped candles. They were pretty and smelled wonderful. Tricia was determined to buy a box or two of them, as well.

Harvick helped the customers make their choices and directed them to the cash register. Finally, it was Tricia's time to be served.

"Hi, I'm Tricia Miles from Haven't Got a Clue mystery bookstore up the street, and this is my sister, Angelica. She owns the Cookery. We came to not only patronize your store but talk to you about joining the Stoneham Chamber of Commerce."

"Oh, yeah, I've heard about it," he muttered just as sourly as his wife had done days before.

"I hope you'll give us a chance to explain," Angelica said.

Harvick shrugged. "Go for it."

Tricia stood by in wonder as Angelica charmed the man. By the time she finished her spiel, he was ready to write out a check.

"That won't be necessary today. We'll be in contact to let you know about our next group meeting where you'll hear all about our plans for the future," Angelica finished enthusiastically.

"Sounds good to me. Now, what is it I can get you ladies?"

"Which of your honeys do you recommend for baking?" Tricia asked.

"Well, we have several," Harvick said, and gave them a detailed description of each. Angelica bought one of each, while Tricia eyed the rest of the items on sale. The variety of their stock was far greater than she would have thought. She selected a jar of honey, some honey mustard, a medium jar of the royal jelly, and several tubes of lip balm made with beeswax, intending to give them to her employees and perhaps Ginny and Grace.

"I understand you're a retired sheriff's deputy," Tricia said casually.

Harvick nodded. "Twenty-five years with the department," he said proudly.

"Did you ever run into a suspect by the name of Joshua Greenwell?" Tricia asked innocently.

"Oh, yeah," Harvick said with a knowing nod. "A petty little thief we called the Snitch."

"He was a tattletale?" Angelica inquired.

"In spades. Sometimes whatever he had to sell was worth the price of putting up with him, but usually he just ratted out people he thought had stiffed him as a way to get even."

"Did you know he was found dead a couple of days ago?"

Harvick crossed his arms across his chest. "I heard. I didn't shed any tears."

No, Tricia supposed a hardened law enforcement officer wouldn't. But Harvick was now a civilian. Did he hold a grudge?

"They say it was murder trying to look like a suicide," Tricia said.

"Oh, yeah? Who says that?"

"Everyone," Tricia said evasively. She didn't want to let on that she'd spoken to Baker about the man's death.

Harvick shrugged. "It was bound to happen eventually. You don't turn on just about everyone you know without someone deciding they've had enough and fixing the problem—permanently."

"Do you know our chief of police, Grant Baker?" Angelica asked.

Harvick's expression was bland. "I worked with him for years before he became a detective with the Sheriff's Department. That's when he became super serious and you couldn't share a joke without him nailing you with those cold green eyes."

Cold? Tricia had never thought of Baker's eyes as cold. Stern sometimes, and mesmerizing quite often—but never cold. Was this a case of petty jealousy? Baker had retired from the Sheriff's Department with full benefits. He now had a lucrative job with a steady income. Did Harvick have an inkling of how precarious the financial life of a shop owner could be? If not, the day's good sales shouldn't be expected on a regular basis. On a good week during prime tourist season, Stoneham drew thousands of visitors. The rest of the time . . . perhaps a score.

"Can I help you with anything else?" Harvick asked.

"I think I'm done shopping," Angelica said. "I need to get back to work."

"Me, too," Tricia said.

Harvick produced a basket, packed it, and carried it to the register, where Eileen waited.

"Don't be a stranger," he said.

"Thanks. We won't," Angelica promised as Harvick headed to the back of the shop and disappeared behind the door marked PRIVATE.

Eileen packed their purchases into two flat-bottomed shopping bags. "There you go. And thanks for supporting us on our soft opening day."

"We'll be back," Tricia promised, and the sisters exited

the store. "So, what do you think about the Bee's Knees?" she asked.

"It's very cute. They've got good products. I hope they do well."

"Me, too."

"What was that line you fed Mr. Harvick about *everyone* knowing that Greenwell character was murdered?"

"Okay, maybe not *everyone*, but it *was* a suspicious death."

"And when will you find out for sure?" Angelica asked.

Tricia shrugged. "Only time will tell."

Tricia ducked out of Haven't Got a Clue early that evening to catch the last of Becca and Ginny's tennis practice. They were just finishing up as Tricia parked her car behind the school. This time, only Ginny's car occupied another parking space.

Ginny had brought her own racket—which had survived the fire thanks to being stored in the garage—water, and towels, and that day she was properly dressed for a workout. She uncapped her water bottle and took a slug.

"You drove?" Tricia asked after greeting both women.

Ginny nodded. "I knew someone was staying in Marshall's apartment. I didn't realize it was Becca." NR Associates Marketing Department was located on the floor above Booked for Lunch, with Marshall's apartment being located on the third floor.

"I told her about my close friendship with, uh, Marshall, and that I'd been called in to help settle his estate," Becca explained.

"We ran into each other in the stairwell this morning when I was coming to work and she was heading to the Bookshelf Diner for breakfast."

Marshall had a small but well-stocked gourmet kitchen. Did Becca prefer restaurant food or did she just dislike cooking for herself? To be fair, Tricia had once felt the same way. She watched as the women packed up their gear.

"Here's an idea," Tricia said. "Why don't I drive Becca back to Marshall's apartment? That way you can get back to your family, Ginny."

The offer would save Ginny only a minute or so since the Sheer Comfort Inn wasn't far from the heart of the village. But she gave Tricia a knowing look and nodded. "Thanks, Tricia. I'll see you for lunch on Thursday."

"You bet," Tricia said.

"Same time tomorrow?" Becca asked Ginny.

"I'll look forward to it." Ginny gave Becca and Tricia a smile before heading to her car. They watched as Ginny drove away. Tricia was the first to speak.

"So, Ginny's working out as an exercise buddy?" Tricia asked.

"Yeah," Becca said halfheartedly. "She's better than nothing."

A flash of anger coursed through Tricia. Becca was no longer a world champion. That Ginny could hold her own against Becca said a lot about how far Becca's ability had deteriorated since her accident. Tricia bit her tongue. She wasn't cruel enough to point that out.

"I kind of hoped you'd show up today," Becca said diffidently. She reached into her duffel bag and removed the little velvet box Tricia had seen the night of Marshall's death. "I thought you might like to have this." She handed Tricia the fuzzy cube.

Tricia pulled back the hinged lid and stared at the diamond solitaire engagement ring. It wasn't that much different from the one Christopher had given her more than fifteen years before, albeit at least a carat smaller. "It's very pretty."

"Do you want it?" Becca pressed.

Tricia shook her head and handed it back. "I suppose you'll sell it."

Becca shrugged. "Probably. I already have one that looks exactly the same. It's worth at least a grand," she said off-handedly. She closed the lid and eyed Tricia. "Do you have a key to Gene's apartment?"

Again, Tricia shook her head. She hadn't given him a key to her place, either.

"Did you know Gene had a gun?" Becca asked.

"No. Why?"

"It's missing." Hence, the question about Tricia having a key.

"I suppose he had one for protection. Just in case." As a protected witness, he had to be living on the edge, wondering if one of Martin Bailey's lackeys might find him and try to eliminate him.

"Yeah. Of course, he wasn't expecting to be run down in the street. If he'd been carrying the gun on the night he died, I doubt he'd have had an opportunity to use it."

"What kind of gun was it?" Tricia asked.

"A nine millimeter Glock."

Tricia knew that the handgun was one of the most popular sold in the US. "I suppose Gene told you where he kept it."

"In a safe bolted to the floor in the closet."

Tricia had never poked around in his closet, just as she'd never expected Marshall to root around in hers. "Did the apartment look like it had been searched when you got there?"

"Gene was a very tidy man," Becca said, which Tricia could attest to as well. "The apartment was not. I assume that the feds or the local cops searched it after his death, although I don't know why they should."

"You could ask Deputy Marshal Kirby."

Becca scowled. "I'd get more information from a turnip. The thing is . . . as far as the feds are concerned, their job is done. The second Gene died, he was out of the program. I'm surprised they bothered to inform you." She looked thoughtful. "As you never heard from Kirby again, I'm assuming they figured you weren't of any importance."

It wouldn't be the first time someone thought that way, Tricia considered bitterly. That said, she had other questions to ask. "What do you know about Gene's relationship with Louise Jameson?"

Becca raised a quizzical eyebrow. "So, you know about her?"

"It's guesswork on my part, but I assume Gene and she were lovers at some point."

"Oh, yeah," Becca confirmed.

Tricia felt a slow burn rise within her. "Why did they break up?"

"Who said they did?" Becca asked blankly.

Tricia blinked, taken aback. "Well, Marshall *did* ask me to marry him."

"He liked being married. Louise wasn't interested—at least in marrying him. Let's face it; a respectable dentist has a lot more cachet—and a bigger bank account—than the former owner of a crappy little porn shop."

Tricia tried to digest that little nugget of information. "But Marshall was a lot nicer person than Mark Jameson appears to be."

"Who says nice has anything to do with it?" Becca asked.

"What are you saying?"

"That Gene couldn't give Louise the financial security her dentist husband could."

"And he told you that?"

"Of course. We had no secrets."

And Marshall—Gene—had plenty of secrets he'd kept from Tricia. The more she learned of them, the harder she judged him.

"Have you met Louise?" Tricia asked.

"No, and I don't care to, either." She glanced at Tricia's car. "Are you ready to go?"

"Yeah." Tricia was more than ready to be shed of the great Becca Dickson-Chandler. In fact, if she never spoke to the woman again, it would be too soon.

She wondered if she'd soon feel the same way about Louise Jameson.

"He asked her to marry him first?" Angelica asked, sounding offended.

The sky outside Angelica's second-floor window was beginning to darken as Tricia held the chilled stemmed glass tightly and sighed. "Yeah."

"Well, that wasn't very nice."

"Tell me about it."

"I'm sorry he treated you so poorly. But then . . ."

Tricia glared at her sister. Not many of the men in Tricia's life had treated her very well, from her first real love, Harrison Tyler, to her ex-husband, Christopher, to Russ Smith, Grant Baker, and lastly Marshall. She didn't need her sister to remind her of that fact.

Tricia sighed. Maybe it was time to just call it quits on guys altogether since she obviously couldn't pick a good one. But then, she rarely pursued anyone—she was usually the one being pursued.

"Let's talk about something else," Tricia suggested.

"Such as?"

"As long as I'm griping about people, I'll spill on Becca, too."

"What's she done now?"

"She disparaged Ginny."

Angelica's mouth dropped open. She caught herself and shut it once again. "In what way?" she asked angrily.

"Intimating that she's not a very good tennis partner."

Angelica's eyes widened. "She ought to be grateful she's got *anyone* to practice with."

"I agree."

"Don't you dare tell Ginny," Angelica admonished, got up from the chaise, and began to hobble around the room.

"I hadn't planned to. And shouldn't you stay off that foot? It looks a little swollen."

"I've been trying to build up my stamina," Angelica admitted. "But I'm just so angry at Becca for Ginny's sake, I could bite her."

"She'd probably bite back—with poisonous fangs."

"No doubt."

Angelica limped another circuit around the room before returning to the chaise. She picked up her drink and took a healthy slug.

"Did you get any work done today?" Tricia asked.

Angelica nodded. "I had a phone conference with Trevor, the architect working on the plans for Ginny's and Antonio's house. He assessed what's left of the building with a structural engineer and they decided it's a total loss."

"I'm sure the insurance company thinks the same thing."

"But this gives us plenty of room to start from scratch. Ginny is determined to stay on that property, and I don't blame her. All those trees and the lot is almost an acre in size. It's just gorgeous, especially now when the leaves are so pretty. And to think they'll be missing all that."

"They'll be back in their new home next fall."

"It seems like forever right now, but it's doable. And they'll probably be stuck in some crummy little apartment for Christmas. My heart aches for them."

"When will you all meet with the architect?"

"Hopefully next week. He's got other clients. I'm just glad we called him in before the fire happened. At least we're on his schedule."

"I guess that's their silver lining," Tricia suggested.

"You bet."

Silver lining . . . the term was tantamount to a joke when the family had lost everything they owned. They'd spent the previous Christmas celebration at Angelica's apartment, but Tricia knew Ginny wanted to establish her family's own traditions. Maybe the following year—with a newer, bigger home—the Barberos could host some of their makeshift family's holidays.

It was with a pang of regret that Tricia realized she would always be on the sidelines of such events. She and Christopher had been too involved with their careers to plan a family . . . and then it was too late.

It was what it was. Sometimes it hurt . . . but more often, Tricia had very few regrets.

Yeah. It was what it was.

She remembered her goal of finding tidbits of joy in every day. "So, what are we having for dinner?"

Angelica grinned.

TWENTY-ONE

Sometimes Tricia managed to avoid an excess of drama in her life for months at a time. Those times seemed to be coming at shorter and shorter intervals. But it was apparent when Pixie arrived for work the next morning dressed in black that she was suffering from more than just the blues. Mr. Everett turning up with a bag of bagels caused her spirits to plummet even more.

"I don't dare have one," Pixie lamented. "I've been eating a lot of oatmeal and soup. I'm afraid to even eat a cracker in case my tooth cracks off again. I had a friend who had a bridge. She bit into a soft cookie and all her front teeth were gone." She shuddered. "I don't want that happening to me."

Tricia wasn't about to point out that the bridge had probably been cracked before she'd taken a bite of the cookie.

"I'm sorry," Mr. Everett apologized. "It was thoughtless of me to forget about your situation."

"No, no!" Pixie assured him. "You're the sweetest person in the whole world and I'm just a fraidycat. I'm sure I could chew it on the other side of my mouth."

"I will not be offended in the least if you decline to eat one. Perhaps you could take it home to Fred."

"Thank you, Mr. Everett. I'll do that."

Poor Pixie needed a pick-me-up. Tricia gazed around the store and knew just how to raise her spirits.

"You know, I was thinking. With the good weather and wonderful fall colors, we've already seen an uptick in customers. Perhaps we should do a bit more decorating to make Haven't Got a Clue even more welcoming to our guests. You know, play up the fact that we're an autumn destination. What do you think?"

Pixie's eyes widened in delight. Of course, the month before, Tricia had had to restrain Pixie from adding faux leaves, pumpkins, and dried corn shocks until they threatened to take over the entire retail space. Tricia's idea of decorating had always been "less is more," whereas Pixie's was "more is more is more" and then some.

"What were you thinking about?" Pixie asked cautiously. Tricia had apparently dashed her hopes far too often.

"I don't know. Why don't you head downstairs, grab the fall decorations tote, put it in the dumbwaiter, bring it up, and we'll go through it again to see what seems appropriate."

"Sure thing," Pixie said, and practically raced for the stairs to the basement office and storeroom. Mr. Everett followed her and waited at the top of the stairs.

While Pixie was gone, Tricia cleared the stacks of books and magazines that littered the big square coffee table in the reader's nook, setting them temporarily on the floor. Of course, her actions immediately drew Miss Marple's attention. The little cat liked to supervise any and all work that went on in the store—that is, of course, unless she was napping. She had her priorities, after all.

Between them, Pixie and Mr. Everett carried the large blue plastic tote through the store and plunked it on the table. Pixie removed the lid and pulled out a long orange, yellow, and gold-leaf garland. Weeks earlier, Tricia had nixed its use, but now she let Pixie decide where to hang it.

"How about above and around the washroom door? It'll be in the back—not at all intrusive," she said almost defensively.

"That sounds lovely," Tricia agreed.

The door to the shop opened, the bell overhead ringing cheerfully, letting in a female customer dressed in a black ski jacket, knit cap, jeans, thigh-high black leather boots, and wearing sunglasses.

"Hi. Welcome to Haven't Got a Clue. I'm the owner, Tricia. Let me know if you need any help." The young woman gave Tricia a salute and ventured farther into the store.

Tricia spoke to her employees. "Pixie, why don't you and Mr. Everett hang the garland while I take care of the store. We'll figure out what else we want to use when you're done with that."

"Sure thing," Pixie said.

Tricia turned her attention to the stack of books customers the day before had decided not to buy. She picked up three of the books, intending to return them to the bookshelves. As she approached the Agatha Christie collection, she noticed her customer wasn't browsing the shelves. Instead, she was on her phone, texting. Had she come into the store just to warm up? But then, dressed like that, she should have been more than warm enough on that sunny, early October morning.

Tricia reshelved the books and saw that, armed with pushpins, Pixie was balanced on the second rung of the step stool, hanging the garland. Smiling, Tricia returned to the cash desk to retrieve the rest of the unwanted books when one slipped off the counter to land on the floor behind the display case. With a sigh, she rounded the cash desk to pick it up.

It was then that the roar of what Tricia immediately identified as a motorcycle boomed out on Main Street. Tricia glanced out Haven't Got a Clue's big display window to see a biker, clad in black leathers and a full-head helmet, stop in front of her store. The rider threw back his left arm and lobbed something in the direction of her shop. Tricia instinctively ducked as the big glass display window shattered into what seemed like a million pieces, sending potentially lethal shards like shrapnel into the store.

Tricia heard a yell from her customer and lifted her head to see the first few letters of the bike's license plate as the powerful bike took off north.

At the sound of the crash, Miss Marple skedaddled in the direction of the back of the store. Pixie and Mr. Everett came running past her as Tricia scooted around the counter and her customer made a beeline for the exit. "I'm getting out of here," she hollered, wrenched open the door, and let it bang shut behind her.

"What happened?" Pixie demanded.

Tricia looked down to see the brick that had landed just inches from the cash desk. If it had been six inches to the left, it could have destroyed the display case and severely injured Tricia.

Mr. Everett bent down to pick it up, but Tricia raised her voice to stop him. "Don't touch it! There might be fingerprints."

Mr. Everett straightened. "We should call the police."

"We should call the emergency enclosure people," Pixie piped up. "Man, it's gonna be dark in here until we can get the window replaced."

The last time the window had been broken—during the fire—it had been nearly six months until it and the shop's front facade had been repaired.

Tricia didn't bother with the vintage phone on the cash desk—there was too much glass on and surrounding it—and pulled her cell phone from her slacks pocket, tapping in 911. "I want to report vandalism!"

It was Mr. Everett who captured a distraught Miss Marple, calmed her, and returned her to Tricia's apartment. Pixie was on the phone to the enclosure repair company while a gale blew through the aperture and an agitated Tricia scanned the street for the sight of a police SUV.

June from the Cookery came by to ask if everyone was all right, as did Terry from the All Heroes comic-book store, and both melted away when Chief Baker showed up on foot to take the police report. And as usual, upon his arrival, Pixie became scarce, disappearing into the basement office. She always did that when law enforcement appeared on Tricia's doorstep.

Baker eyed the gaping hole.

"Thanks for coming, Grant, but you don't have to personally show up every time I have a problem," Tricia said.

He shrugged. "I was the only one available. Of course, if you'd like me to leave," he said, his voice hardening, "I'm sure one of my officers could be here in four or five hours."

"No, let's get this over with," Tricia said affably, not wishing to aggravate him, despite his sarcasm.

Baker asked the usual questions, filling in a form on a clipboard he'd brought along. "Was there anyone else in the store at the time of the incident?"

"Yes. A woman came in. Now that I think of it, she seemed rather suspicious."

"In what way?"

"Most of my customers are older. They come in looking for our vintage mysteries. The woman appeared to be about thirty and she wasn't really browsing the bookshelves. I thought maybe she'd just come in to get out of the cold, because she had her phone out and was texting."

"And then the biker threw the brick through the window?"

"Yes, not long after."

"Can you give me a description of this dynamic duo?" Baker asked sarcastically.

Tricia told him what they looked like. "I didn't see the entire license plate on the bike, but I got the first three letters: ZBR."

Baker scowled and shook his head. "It doesn't make sense. What idiot commits such an act in front of witnesses and in broad daylight?"

"A thrill seeker. Or a fool," Tricia suggested.

"You got that right," Baker said.

"So, you think they *were* working together?" Tricia asked.

Baker shrugged. "It's possible. Could you identify the woman if you saw her again?"

Tricia sighed. "Probably not. I mean, she had her hair tucked under her hat and wore sunglasses. I only got to see the lower portion of her face. When a customer comes in, I don't immediately commit their features to memory in case I have to pick them out of a lineup."

"The shades should have warned you something was amiss," Baker said, almost accusingly.

"Plenty of people walk in here during the summer wearing them," Tricia pointed out.

"But don't they usually take them off once inside?" he countered.

Tricia didn't bother answering.

Baker decided he didn't need to interview Mr. Everett or Pixie, as they had been at the back of the shop when the incident occurred. He did pull out his cell phone and take a few pictures, as did Tricia—Baker chronicling the evidence for the crime report, whereas Tricia needed pictures to forward to her insurance company.

Baker withdrew a pair of latex gloves from his pocket and deposited the brick into a paper evidence bag. "I'll send this to the state forensic lab for fingerprints, but don't get your hopes up. It's not likely anything will come of it."

"Why do you say that?"

"Think about it. It was a coordinated effort. The woman came in, texted her guy to let him know the coast was clear, and he struck. She disappeared. I wouldn't be surprised if they'd done this same hit-and-run deal before."

"But why target me?"

Baker shrugged. "A one-in-a-million chance."

Tricia wasn't sure she believed him. As he'd mentioned after the fire at Ginny and Antonio's home, she and her loved ones seemed to be experiencing a period of unsettling events.

Why was more than one someone deliberately trying to make her life miserable?

Tricia changed the subject. "Did you get a look at the autopsy report for Joshua Greenwell? Was there gunpowder on his hands?"

"No."

So, Greenwell's death had now been officially deemed murder. "Did they determine what kind of gun killed him?"

"What is this, an interrogation?" Baker asked.

"You know I'm interested in such things," Tricia insisted.

"Now you're just being ghoulish. It's not your best trait." Tricia ignored the insult.

"It was a Glock. There. Are you happy?" Baker asked tartly.

"That's interesting."

"It's actually a pretty common handgun. In fact, it's one of the most popular guns on the market here in the US."

Which she already knew, proving the point, since Marshall had owned the same weapon. And it was missing. And now Tricia felt uncomfortable because . . .

She gave herself a mental shake. She didn't want to go there.

"What else can you tell me?"

"I really shouldn't be telling you anything," Baker said, crossing his arms over his chest.

Ah, but he wanted to get back into her good graces. Just how much should she push him?

"What happens now?" Tricia asked.

He shrugged. "We keep investigating. Someone somewhere knows what went down."

"The killer, obviously. But he—or she—isn't likely to volunteer that information."

"We've been poking around and have a few leads I'm not at liberty to share with you," Baker said.

"About Marshall's previous lovers?"

Baker's eyes narrowed. "You know about that?"

"I'm assuming you learned about it the same way I did— from Becca Chandler."

Baker frowned. "Yeah."

"Well, please make that clear to the parties involved," Tricia said, not wanting to name names in case he was fishing. "I had no intention of outing Marshall's former lover."

"And why's that?"

"Because it's none of my business who he was with before we got together."

"That's very noble of you," Baker stated. "It seems to me that anyone with an ounce of curiosity would want to know all the juicy details. And you, of all people, have more curiosity than ninety-nine percent of the population."

Was he baiting her? It seemed as though he was, and she was not about to take that bait.

"Are we done?" Tricia asked.

"You let me know we were done last Monday night," Baker said, his voice flat.

Tricia shook her head. "We were done two years ago, and we both moved on. I have no idea why you'd have thought my feelings would have changed in the interim."

"I made a mistake."

Not his first, either.

Baker gathered up the evidence and his clipboard. "I'll be in touch."

"Thank you for coming," Tricia said as almost an afterthought.

Would he finally get the message she wasn't and would never be interested in him again?

She sure hoped so.

With Baker off the premises, Tricia called for Pixie to come back to the shop to help her clean up the glass.

As Tricia picked up the jagged chunks, Pixie hauled out the vacuum cleaner.

It was going to be a long, long day.

TWENTY-TWO

An agitated Angelica called not long after Baker's retreat, demanding answers, which, of course, Tricia didn't have. She assured her sister she'd tell all later. "But we may have to cancel our lunch. I'm waiting for the emergency closure team to arrive. Mr. Everett and Pixie will need to go to lunch, and I honestly don't want them getting chilled, although Mr. E can work down in the office for the rest of the day if he wishes to stay."

"I don't want you getting chilled, either. Why don't you close up for the day?"

Tricia sighed. It was probably a good idea. Customers weren't likely to shop in a store that doubled as an icebox. "I'll think about it."

"Let me know about lunch later. If you can't make it, I can open a can of tuna. But you will come for dinner, won't you?"

"You bet. Talk to you later."

Tricia spent the next hour or so pondering why anyone would want to target her or her store.

At the top of her list of suspects: Bob Kelly. He was serving a twenty-five-year-to-life jail sentence for murder—and he blamed her for his situation. Ha! Killing a man in cold blood—in front of a myriad of witnesses—had put him behind bars, not Tricia. Although, she was the state's star witness. The jury had taken only an hour to convict him. Still, Bob had convinced someone to target Tricia. That that person was now also in jail for the accidental death of another should have put Bob's vengeful ideas to rest, but sometimes Tricia would wake in the night with thoughts that someone else might again seek revenge on Kelly's behalf. Before his arrest, Bob had had many friends in Stoneham. People who felt they owed their success to him for reviving the village by establishing it as Booktown.

And what about Marshall's death? Tricia still strongly believed his killer could have come after him as an act of revenge on behalf of Martin Bailey.

Both villains who'd menaced her had been strangers. Joshua Greenwell and now the man-and-woman team who'd taken out her window. Had both of them been for hire?

Tricia pulled out her phone and did a little Internet research. After ten minutes, she had the information she needed. But she still had questions. After her conversation with Baker earlier that morning, Tricia didn't want to ask his opinion. But there was someone else she could ask.

Since Tricia was already wearing her coat, she grabbed her purse and phone. "I'm going to run a quick errand. I shouldn't be gone long," Tricia said. "Call me if the closure team shows up, will you?"

"Sure thing," Pixie called from the back of the store, where she and Mr. Everett were at least out of the wind.

Tricia hurried south down Main Street and entered Stoneham's newest shop once again.

"Welcome back to the Bee's Knees. What can I help you with today?"

"Hello, Mr. Harvick. I wonder if I might bend your ear for a minute or two."

"Call me Larry."

"Thanks, Larry. I have a question about police procedures I was hoping you could answer."

Harvick shrugged. "Shoot."

Tricia winced. Just what she suspected might have happened.

"My store suffered vandalism this morning."

"Yeah, I went to the bank earlier and couldn't miss that gaping hole where your front window used to be."

"I Googled the MO," Tricia said, noting Harvick's skeptical expression at her nomenclature, "and found there've been a number of these hit-and-run brick-wielding attacks in southern New Hampshire over the past few months. It's almost as though it's a vandalism-for-hire type of crime. Had you ever run into anything like that during your time with the Sheriff's Department?"

He nodded. "More than once. Usually, they're protection rackets. A pay-up-or-we'll-break-your-legs kind of thing. Either that or for insurance fraud. I hadn't heard of this specific crime, but I wouldn't put it past someone to offer such a service. These are interesting times we live in."

A little too interesting for Tricia.

"How would someone go about advertising such a service?"

Harvick shrugged. "Word of mouth. Same as if you were looking for any kind of vandalism. Of course, if I were you, I'd be wondering who's targeting you and why."

"It's been on my mind. My niece's home was also targeted. Arson."

Harvick shook his head. "I'm assuming you've reported all this to the police?"

"Yes."

"And why are you asking me about it instead of Chief Baker?"

"Let's just say he and I don't always get along."

"Uh-huh." Harvick had probably heard about Tricia's reputation as the village jinx—and how unlucky she was when it came to love, too. News spread quickly in a small village.

"Is there anything else I can help you with?" Harvick asked.

Tricia looked around the tiny shop before deciding to buy a few more tubes of lip balm. After all, you can never have too much—not that she'd be kissing anyone anytime soon.

At that moment, she was okay with that.

As she passed By Hook or By Book, she heard a pounding on the window and saw Mary get up from her chair behind the cash desk, casting what looked like a crocheted baby blanket aside and running for the door.

"I'm so glad I caught you," Mary said, just a little breathless.

"What's up?"

"Mark has called a meeting of the Chamber recruitment committee for eight o'clock tomorrow morning. Sorry it's such short notice, but you know how he is."

Tricia refrained from rolling her eyes.

"Can you make it?" Mary asked.

"Sure."

"Great. I'll see you then," Mary said, and hurried back into her shop, and Tricia continued walking.

The others on the committee must have spoken to all the candidates. Tricia would send texts to all those who hadn't returned her calls. If they didn't respond, then it was a sure bet they weren't interested in rejoining the Chamber. No doubt they'd wait until whoever was elected the next president instilled a reasonable level of confidence in the Chamber and those who'd stuck with it. She couldn't really blame them. If she hadn't been an integral part of the operation during the time her store was closed, she'd have no faith in the organization, either.

When she returned to Haven't Got a Clue, Tricia sent Mr. Everett home for the day, not willing to risk him catching a cold, but Pixie insisted on staying. A few curious customers dared to enter the shop but were chased away as soon as the emergency enclosure team arrived, setting up sawhorses, noisy Skilsaws, and a compressor for their nail guns.

An hour later, the store was secured, and Pixie had made

a DON'T MIND OUR MESS sign on the computer to hang on the
store's glass door. Tricia had borrowed several lamps from
her apartment, and while the lighting was a little more than
subdued, it was also kind of cozy with so much incandescent
light. Ginny wouldn't have approved, as every time she arrived at Tricia's apartment she would lecture her to replace
the bulbs with halogen or some other more efficient lighting.
Yeah, she really should do that . . . but she found that incandescent lighting was warmer. Either that or she was just
stubborn.

Pixie ducked across the street to get some take-out sandwiches and the soup of the day from Booked for Lunch and
they hunkered down to eat.

"Are we going to open tomorrow?" Pixie asked.

Tricia sighed. "I don't know. I guess we'll see how the rest
of the afternoon goes. I sure don't want to lose customers—
not at such an important time of the year—but we don't look
very inviting right now."

"Did you get an estimate on when the window can be replaced?"

"I think I might do an Angelica and just pay for it up front
and hope the insurance company writes me a check fairly
soon. I'll call the guys who replaced it last time and see if
they can come tomorrow to at least give us an estimate."

Pixie nodded and carefully took a bite of her club sandwich, chewing on the left side of her mouth and washing the
food down with a gulp of coffee.

The door opened and both women looked up hopefully,
but it was only Antonio.

"Dear Tricia, what on earth happened to your store?"

Tricia sighed. "It's a long story."

Antonio joined them at the reader's nook, taking the seat
next to Tricia. "I have time to listen."

Tricia noticed that Antonio was carrying a steno pad. Was
she to be the top story for his first edition of the *Stoneham
Weekly News*?

Tricia told him everything she knew, including her theory
about who had vandalized her store earlier in the day, but

leaving out the fact that she suspected Joshua Greenwell may have targeted Marshall and perhaps also torched Antonio's home. She wondered if she should send him to speak with Larry Harvick. Yes, perhaps she would.

Antonio listened, jotting down a few notes as she spoke. "It certainly is very worrisome," he told her after she'd finished.

"What other stories will you be covering in your first issue? The opening of the Bee's Knees perhaps?"

"Ah, yes. Patti suggested we cover that as well. Perhaps I can convince them to advertise with us."

"Give them front-page coverage on their opening and I'm sure they will. Starting out so late in the season, they'll need all the locals to know they're open for business. They have wonderful gift items—great for the holidays."

"Are you sure they haven't hired you to promote their store?" Antonio asked with a grin.

Tricia laughed. "I just want to see them succeed."

"As do we all. And what of the recruitment committee for the Chamber of Commerce?"

"I'm on it," she confirmed. "In fact, we're having our second meeting tomorrow morning. Are you going to cover that?"

"*Sì*. I have an appointment to speak to Mark Jameson this very afternoon. It seems he's had a cancellation in his dental office."

Pixie gave Tricia a sidelong glance and a smug smile.

"From what I've heard, that seems to happen quite a bit," Tricia said.

Antonio shrugged, wearing a poker face. Would he prove his journalistic prowess and probe into the reasons for the patients who fled Jameson's practice?

Only time would tell.

"Have you had an opportunity to write the short death notice for your friend?" Antonio asked.

Tricia cringed. She'd forgotten all about it. "I'll try to get it to you before Friday."

Antonio nodded. "Very good." He glanced at the clock on

the wall. "I will let you ladies finish your lunch in peace. And I will see you on Sunday," he told Tricia.

"I haven't missed one of our Sunday dinners yet," Tricia said, smiling.

Antonio gave them a wave and headed for the door. After he was gone, Pixie plucked a potato chip from the snack bag on the table and sighed. "Ginny sure is lucky to have a swell guy like that."

"Yes, she is," Tricia agreed. "But you've got a great guy, too."

Pixie grinned. "I sure do. Once you reach our age, love ain't that easy to find."

Was she referring to Fred and herself or her and Tricia? Pixie had at least a decade on Tricia.

The door opened, letting in a potential customer, and Tricia leapt to her feet. "Welcome to Haven't Got a Clue. Let me know if you need any help finding a book."

The woman nodded.

Tricia picked up the remnants of her lunch and retreated to the cash desk, with Pixie's observation about love still stuck in her mind. Lately, she'd begun to think she was better off alone. At that moment, she wasn't at all sure.

TWENTY-THREE

Tricia didn't spend much time at Angelica's apartment that evening. She felt restless and anxious about the photo shoot with Louise Jameson the next day, knowing she was going to confront the woman about her tryst with Marshall. Or she could just ignore what Becca had told her—humiliated her, really. And even before that, she'd probably clash heads with Louise's husband, who, like more than a few people in the village, had taken a dislike to Tricia without really knowing her.

She awoke the next morning feeling as though she lurked under a dark cloud, despite the clear blue sky that greeted her once the sun was up.

Tricia arrived at the drafty warehouse that housed the makeshift offices of the Stoneham Chamber of Commerce precisely at eight o'clock, walking in with Mary Fairchild.

"So, what do you think our fearless leader will have to say?" Mary muttered.

"Who knows," Tricia said.

They entered the building and took their seats on the cold, plastic folding chairs. Nobody had shucked their coats, as the temperature inside matched what was outside—forty-something degrees.

With no niceties like fresh-brewed coffee to warm those

in attendance nor a box of local pastries, Tricia was glad she'd eaten an early breakfast of an egg-white omelet with frozen peppers—but no onions—she'd thawed in the microwave. No chance of bad breath that way.

Mark Jameson stood at the head of the table and called the meeting to order. "Thanks for being here, everyone. I'm pleased to say that Leona Ferguson has graciously agreed to run for the presidency of the Chamber. But as several of you have pointed out, she needs an opponent. Therefore, I have decided to run against her."

"Wait a minute," Mary called out. "You didn't tell us *you* were interested in running for Chamber president. Shouldn't we choose from the other candidates we've vetted?"

"And who are they?" Mark asked.

"You tell us! You took that process on yourself," Mary said, her voice rising.

"Believe me, I tried to convince others to step up to the plate and no one was interested."

"So, what about Tricia?" Terry McDonald asked. "The vote was split within a very close margin during last year's election. You're relatively new to the Chamber. How many of our current members even know your name?"

"I have a reputation here in the village," Mark said gravely.

Yeah, and as far as Tricia knew, it wasn't all that good.

"What do you think, Dan?"

The Bookshelf Diner's owner gave a sidelong glance at Tricia and smirked. "I'm fine with you running for Chamber president, Mark."

Tricia ignored him. "I'm very flattered you want me to run, Mare and Terry, but it was agreed at our last meeting that I wouldn't." Not that she'd really been consulted. "Let's move on, shall we?"

The corners of Mark's mouth quirked up. "Fine. Now, we'll campaign until the second Thursday in November and then hold a vote. What's our budget look like, Mary?"

"Nothing."

"I've spoken with the Chamber's accountant and he's agreed we should call in an outside party for the audit."

"How are we going to pay for it?" Mary asked.

"With future earnings."

"How long can we run on a deficit?" Terry asked.

"Not long," Jameson muttered. "But I've spoken with law enforcement and they are going to look into Russ Smith's finances. It's doubtful we can recover what he's taken, but we're sure going to try."

Who did he mean by *law enforcement*? Chief Baker or the county district attorney's office? Tricia didn't bother to ask.

"Did everyone call or drop in on the former members on their lists?" Jameson asked.

Nods and a yes or two answered his query.

"And Tricia?" Why did he keep eyeing her so critically?

"I stopped into a number of stores or left messages for everyone on my list, and even one that wasn't. The Bee's Knees opened just yesterday."

"Were they interested in joining?" Mary asked.

Tricia shrugged. "Perhaps there's a lot of distrust after the way Russ vandalized the Chamber."

"We need to reestablish a permanent meeting place. Everyone loved going to the Brookview for the breakfast meetings," Mary said.

"With no budget?" Terry asked.

"Would you care to host a meeting at your diner, Dan?" Mark asked.

"No, I would not. I don't have a party room big enough, and I'm not about to foot the bill for coffee and Danish for a bunch of freeloaders."

"Potential members," Tricia reminded him.

"Until they cough up their membership dues, they're freeloaders," Dan stated.

"Tricia, you're friendly with Antonio Barbero. Couldn't you get us a freebie or at least a discounted price at the Brookview Inn?" Mary asked, sounding hopeful.

Tricia shrugged. "Antonio no longer manages the inn. He's taken over the *Stoneham Weekly News*."

Mary pursed her lips, looking annoyed.

"But I can reach out to NR Associates, who own the inn,

and ask what they could do for the Chamber. They've been very good to us in the past," Tricia reminded them all.

"Fine. You do that," Jameson said condescendingly, and she bristled at his tone. "In the meantime, we're stuck with this warehouse until at least January, but we need to look for something a little less industrial."

"And how are we going to do that without money?" Dan asked.

Mark turned to Tricia again. "Got any contacts at NR Realty?"

Tricia sighed. Did they really expect Angelica, or at least her alter ego, to cough up for *everything* the Chamber needed? "I will ask. That's all I can do. I spoke with their manager, Karen, just the other day, and she's said she'll endorse the Chamber to her prospective clients."

"So, she expects to rejoin?" Dan asked.

"None of the NR Associates businesses ever left the Chamber," Tricia said bluntly.

"That's all well and good," Jameson said, "but we need to woo those who *have* left."

How perfectly ungrateful of the man! If Tricia were a different person, she wouldn't even speak the Chamber's name to Angelica or anyone in her network of businesses.

Jameson blathered on about potential future plans, while Tricia spent the time counting the days until she could be free of her frustrating volunteer job—*and* Mark Jameson.

No sooner had Tricia returned to Haven't Got a Clue than it was time for her to join Angelica to what their father had always called *get beautified* when their mother had her weekly appointment at the local hair salon.

Tricia met Angelica outside the Cookery. "Are you ready for this?"

"More than," Angelica said.

"Are you sure you want to walk to the day spa? I can get the car and—"

But Angelica held up a hand to cut off her sister. "No. I

need to exercise my foot if it's going to recover. If it swells up later today, I'll just employ RICE. Rest, ice, compression, and elevation are my best friends."

Tricia admired her sister's tenacity but worried she might be pushing her healing foot too far too soon.

It took them almost ten minutes to walk the two blocks to the day spa. Once there, Tricia and Angelica were greeted by Booked for Beauty's manager, Randy Ellison. At other times when the sisters had jointly arrived at the day spa, Randy would personally do Angelica's hair while Tricia was open to accepting anyone who was working that day to take care of her tresses. Every one of the stylists was a skilled hairdresser, and so far she had no complaints.

"I was surprised at your sudden appointment," Randy said as he draped a black plastic cape around Angelica's neck and shoulders, while Marlene did the same to Tricia.

"We're going to get our pictures taken this afternoon— our whole little adopted family group," Angelica gushed.

"That's nice," Randy said blandly.

"We're booked this afternoon at Louise Jameson's photography studio. Do you know her?" Tricia asked. She seemed to be asking that question of everyone.

"The local photographer?" Randy asked, his expression souring as he spritzed Angelica's hair with water.

Tricia nodded.

"Please hold still," Marlene told her.

"Oh, sorry," Tricia said, going rigid.

"Mrs. Jameson dropped by earlier this summer looking to make a deal with the salon," Randy commented. He did not sound happy.

"What kind of deal?" Angelica asked. She owned the day spa, but Randy ran the operation. He evidently didn't convey to his boss everything that went on in the salon.

Randy snipped a lock of hair at the base of Angelica's neck. "She said she was partnering to open a wedding venue somewhere north of the village and she wanted a deal providing brides with a discounted hair-and-makeup package."

"That sounds reasonable," Angelica said.

"Not with the discount she was asking for—fifty percent, with a ten percent kickback going to her business for bringing in the trade!"

"And you didn't go for it?" Tricia asked.

"Girl, I need to keep the lights on, you know."

From what Angelica had told her, so far Randy was doing a great job—and the business was doing well under his management.

"What kind of discount would you have given them?" Angelica asked.

"Twenty—with no kickback. It should be up to the lady to build that into her price packages. And honestly, I can get more locals through the door with a ten percent coupon. That nice woman Ginger at the *Stoneham Weekly News* is going to take care of everything. The first one will go in next week's issue."

Evidently, Angelica hadn't known that fact, either, but it brought a smile to her face. Naturally, she wanted Antonio's new venture to succeed, but Tricia knew she wasn't about to browbeat anyone—even those who worked for her—into supporting him, either.

One of the other stylists brought her client back to the chair next to Tricia's. The woman's hair was wrapped in a black towel, as she'd just returned from the hair-washing station in the back of the salon.

"So, what time is your sitting?" Randy asked Angelica.

"Two thirty. I'm glad it's not windy today. I wouldn't want my blowout to be for nothing."

"Are you getting a business portrait done?"

"I haven't decided, but that's a good idea."

"We could hang it here in the salon." Randy struck a pose, indicating a space on the wall near his employee-of-the-month display, which showed snapshots of the day spa's stylists. He laughed. "We could hang a plaque that says 'our founder.'"

Angelica seemed to mull it over and shrugged. "Why not?"

"Are you going to the photography studio over on Cedar Avenue?" the woman in the chair next to Tricia asked.

"We're both going," Tricia said as Marlene snipped to trim the layers in her hair. "Have you been there?"

"No, but my sister has." The woman frowned.

"Didn't she like her work?" Angelica asked.

"Oh, she liked the pictures. It was her radical ideas that put her off."

"What do you mean?" Tricia asked.

The woman shook her head. "Children. I heard that photographer and her dentist husband don't like them. Can you even trust someone who doesn't like or want kids?"

Tricia knew plenty of women who'd never had children, herself included. But she'd had a career and her childbearing years had slipped away in the interim. And then she'd been divorced. She'd never considered single parenthood, though she knew at least three of her former coworkers who'd grown tired of waiting for Mr. Right and jumped into motherhood via adoption or in vitro fertilization.

"Don't *want* or *can't* have children?" Tricia asked.

It was apparent from the woman's expression that she hadn't considered the latter possibility. "Well, now that you mention it . . . I don't know."

Then you shouldn't spread such a negative suspicion, Tricia thought, wishing she could educate the woman, but then she might be looked at with even more negativity.

"Well, I'm looking forward to having my portrait taken," Angelica said.

"Me, too," Tricia echoed, although not as enthusiastically.

The woman sniffed and turned her head away.

"So," Randy said, his voice light, as though to ignore the dark turn the conversation had taken. "What about those Patriots?"

"Football?" Angelica asked, appalled.

"Okay, then, who's read the latest edition of *Vogue*, and what did you think?"

No one answered. The canned music, which Tricia was sure none of the customers enjoyed, played on.

Was the woman beside her the only person in the village who held a grudge—however misplaced—against Louise Jameson?

Maybe Tricia would find out later that afternoon.

TWENTY-FOUR

Because the makeshift Miles-Barbero-Everett family was to assemble later that afternoon for the photo shoot, Tricia and Ginny postponed their usual Thursday lunch to the next day—*if* Ginny could get away. Since Angelica was used to eating alone on Thursdays, Tricia retreated to her own apartment and made a salad out of the odds and ends she had on hand and ate it while checking her store's e-mails. Her online reputation was growing as *the* place in the New England states to find vintage mysteries. Pixie was a big part of that. Since she'd arrived on the scene, her love of tag and estate sales had been a big source of keeping Tricia's store supplied with the vintage mysteries that kept the business afloat. Pixie didn't ask for anything but the price she paid for the books she purchased, knowing her salary depended on Haven't Got a Clue being well stocked at all times. But such sales became fewer as autumn edged closer to winter. Soon Tricia would have to start scouring the Internet for more vintage tomes.

After loading her lunch plate into the dishwasher, Tricia grabbed her jacket and purse and headed out the door. It was such a beautiful fall day, that instead of driving, she decided to walk the three blocks to Louise Jameson's photography studio.

The bell over the door rang cheerfully as Tricia entered.

Louise looked up from a camera on a tripod. "Hello, Tricia. I'm almost ready for you and your family. I need to finish a few chores out back."

"That's okay. I'll just look at some of your work, if I may."

"Sure."

Louise ducked out back and Tricia strolled around the studio, studying the photographer's work. She heard Louise speaking with what sounded like another woman as Tricia studied the portraits on display in greater detail. After looking at several of the large wedding photos she concentrated on one detail . . . the copyright. Instead of Louise's name, all the display photos were marked *Mark Jameson Enterprises*.

That was odd. Did that mean that Louise didn't actually *own* the copyright for any of her work? Had she and her husband entered into a financial agreement with some kind of tax incentive in mind?

A rattle at the door caused Tricia to turn and see that the rest of the Miles-Barbero-Everett gang had shown up in two cars, minutes apart, parking on the street outside the studio, everyone dressed in their Sunday best and ready for their portraits to be taken.

A young woman Tricia had never seen entered the studio. She couldn't have been more than twenty, with straight brown hair that was held in check by a thin white elastic headband, and dressed in a black turtleneck and jeans. "Hello, I'm Kristin. I'm Louise's assistant and I'll be helping you choose just the right photo package for your family."

Kristin was well versed in the services the studio sold, and it took more than half an hour of negotiating terms before the photographer actually entered the studio to take the pictures.

"Hello. I'm Louise Jameson. Thank you for choosing me to be your family photographer. Now, let's get started."

Louise suggested seating arrangements and props, and took pictures with the enthusiasm expected of a Fashion Week pro. The group shots came first, followed by family separations, and finally individual portraits for those who wanted them. After what the woman in the day spa had said about Louise and children, Tricia was sure she was wrong. Louise was great at coaxing smiles out of Sofia and had her laughing throughout the shoot.

As Louise had predicted, the whole ordeal had taken just about two hours. Tricia let everyone else have their photos taken, being the last in line. By prearrangement, Angelica caught a ride back home with Antonio and Ginny while Tricia lagged behind. She had a number of questions for Mrs. Jameson.

"Tilt your chin to the left. That's right. Now to the right. Good—good." Louise snapped photo after photo as Tricia wondered who, if anyone, would want a professional portrait of her. Maybe she could use it for promotional purposes, but she couldn't think when. She didn't even have a boyfriend to give a wallet-sized print to. Then again, she'd have proof sheets e-mailed to her by the next day and only have to pay for the photos she selected.

"That's a wrap," Louise called, sounding pleased, and held out the small screen on her digital camera to flip through and show Tricia several of the shots she'd taken.

"They look great."

Louise smiled. "I'm glad you like them. If you'd like any of the photos to be corrected, though, that will be an additional cost."

"Corrected?"

"Photoshopped."

Photoshopped pictures? Did Louise think her current clients were that vain? Okay, maybe Angelica would go for a little smoothing around the neck, but Tricia felt grounded in reality. Like it or not, she wasn't getting any younger.

Louise began to pack up her equipment, but Tricia wasn't in a hurry to leave. It was time to push for some answers.

"I understand you knew my friend Marshall Chandler."

Louise visibly straightened, her expression guarded. "We were acquainted."

"He died last week. A hit-and-run accident. I assume you were aware of that."

"I heard," Louise said succinctly, her features rigid as though she was desperately trying to hold her emotions in check.

"A couple of weeks ago, he took me on a picnic on a beautiful piece of property just north of the village, telling me it's a soon-to-be wedding venue."

Louise merely stared at Tricia.

"He said a friend of his owned the venue. I've heard that friend was you."

Still Louise said nothing.

"It's a beautiful property."

Louise swallowed. "Thank you."

Tricia nodded. "Funny, he never told me that the two of you were such good friends. How did you meet?"

"Uh, through the local Chamber of Commerce."

Unless she'd joined in the past few months, Tricia knew Louise's words were a bald-faced lie. Due to her volunteer work for the Chamber, Tricia had an intimate knowledge of the Chamber's membership list. Did Louise even know Tricia was on the recruitment committee with her husband?

"Did you know Marshall's ex-wife was in town?"

"Ex-wife?" Louise asked, startled. "I—he told me she was dead. An accident."

"She did have a serious accident, but she recovered. This was after their divorce."

"But Marshall told me . . ." Louise didn't finish the sentence. Obviously, Marshall had shared his false history with her, too. "What's she doing here?"

"Ostensibly to wind up his affairs."

"That was quick, wasn't it?"

"Time waits for no one," Tricia said.

Louise sighed. "Look, I don't know what you want from me. I'm sad Marshall died, but we were really just acquaintances."

"That's not what his ex said."

Louise's eyes widened. "She . . . what?"

"Apparently, she and Marshall spoke often. She knew all about your affair—and the fact that he asked you to leave your husband."

Louise's mouth dropped open and she quickly looked to see that her assistant wasn't within listening distance. "Keep your voice down," she hissed.

Tricia stepped closer to the door, with Louise following, her eyes wide, fear shadowing them.

"Becca quite bluntly told me that it was you he wanted to be with, but as you'd rejected the notion, he'd settle for me."

Louise's lips quirked into the ghost of a smile. "That couldn't have been easy to hear."

Aha! Acknowledgment . . . but the fact brought Tricia no joy.

"It didn't matter. I had no intention of saying yes."

"Poor Marshall," Louise said blithely.

"Yes. It seems nobody loved him enough to be a lifelong partner. Not his ex-wife, not you, or me, either."

"What do you propose to do with what you learned about Marshall and me?"

"Nothing," Tricia said honestly. "But you should know that your husband and I are on the Chamber of Commerce recruitment committee for a new president."

Now Louise looked downright scared, probably knowing she'd not only been caught in at least one lie but also that her husband might find out about her tryst with Marshall.

"I have no intention of saying anything to Mark. It's not my business, but I thought you should know."

Louise's eyes narrowed. "Why did you come here? To taunt me?"

"No, we honestly wanted our portraits taken. You do good work."

"Get out," Louise said.

Tricia grabbed up her coat from the rack near the wall and left the studio.

She had a feeling she wasn't going to get her photographic package.

Tricia walked back to Haven't Got a Clue, grateful for the brisk air. It helped clear her head of the junk that was beginning to accumulate. As she turned onto Main Street, she could see a Granite State tour bus parked near the village's municipal lot, and the sidewalk was crowded with people. She hoped her store would be just as full.

Mr. Everett had not returned to the shop after the picture-taking session, and Pixie was holding the fort, but Tricia quickly stowed her jacket behind the cash desk and jumped in to help take care of the customers who were lined up. Tricia looked at the clock and saw it was nearing five. The customers were already getting antsy, worried they might miss the bus, but between them, Tricia and Pixie cleared the line in less than ten minutes. Finally, the door closed behind the last of them.

"Whew!" Pixie cried. "That was intense. But I loved every second of it. It's such a challenge during peak times when it's just the two of us."

"I'm sorry I didn't get back sooner. It was such a pretty day I wanted to walk—and then I spent a few minutes after our session speaking to the photographer. I should have—"

But Pixie held up a hand to interrupt Tricia. "I thrive under this kind of pressure, so don't apologize."

It was true, Pixie loved dealing with the customers, she was efficient, and just as knowledgeable as Tricia when it came to current and vintage mysteries.

"How do you think we did today?"

"Enough to pay the day's rent."

Since Tricia owned the building outright, that wasn't a concern.

"How did the picture-taking go?" Pixie asked.

"Well. We got to see a few of the photos, but she'll be sending us electronic proofs via e-mail, probably by tomorrow."

"Oh, I can't wait to see them. Did Mr. Everett wear a nice tie?"

Tricia stifled a grin. "Yes, he did. But I won't tell you which one, because you'll want to be surprised."

"Maybe he can show me tomorrow."

"I wouldn't be surprised."

Pixie surveyed the shop. "Goodness, look at the mess those customers left. There are books piled everywhere."

It took the two women nearly an hour to tidy the store and get it ready for the next day's onslaught of customers.

Since they'd had no shoppers since those on the bus had departed, Tricia decided to close the shop five minutes early. She and Pixie donned their coats and locked up.

"See you tomorrow!" Pixie called, and headed up the sidewalk, and Tricia entered the Cookery.

"You're just in time," June called cheerfully, shrugging into the sleeves of her jacket. "I'm ready to call it a day."

"I'll lock up," Tricia said, and said good-bye. A minute later, she was inside Angelica's apartment. Much as she enjoyed their happy hours above the Cookery, Tricia would be glad when her sister's foot healed enough that they could share some of those hours after work at her place. She'd paid a lot of money to transform her apartment and it seemed she rarely got to spend time in her lovely living room. About the only time she spent in her kitchen was when she made cookies for her staff and customers. She mentioned as much to Angelica.

"Give me another week and we'll try it."

"Only if you think you're up to it."

"Thanks to that royal jelly, my incision is healing nicely." Angelica assembled crackers and slices of sharp cheddar on a plate while Tricia poured their drinks. "So, what did you think of our photography session?"

"It went well," Tricia said.

"I hope the e-mail with my proofs comes tomorrow. I can't wait to have beautiful pictures of Antonio, Ginny, and Sofia scattered around my apartment."

"What about my picture?"

"Oh, yeah, you, too," Angelica said almost dismissively, and picked up the plate of crackers. "Did you learn anything interesting after the rest of us left the studio?"

Tricia carried the tray of drinks into the living room. "Definitely. And it's official," she announced. "Louise and Marshall *did* have an affair."

"I can't say I'm surprised," Angelica said, taking her usual seat. "How did she take the news that you knew about their tryst?"

"Not well. I suspect I may be out the cost of my portrait package."

"You could always file a complaint with the Chamber of Commerce, although with her husband currently active in its ranks, it could get awkward when you explain the circumstances."

"Speaking of Mark Jameson, before you got to the photo studio, I noticed that all Louise's big portraits were copyrighted Mark Jameson Enterprises. What do you make of that?"

Angelica looked thoughtful. "Maybe he's one of those male chauvinist pigs who can't bear for his wife to have autonomy. Or maybe it's just a shrewd business move to consolidate their assets, although I think I saw that Dr. Jameson has the initials LLC after his name on the sign in front of his practice. As a dentist, he could be sued for malpractice, and being a limited liability company would save his personal or other business assets."

"Then how about the word 'enterprises'? Do you think they're just grouping Louise's studio in with the wedding venue as one company?"

"It sounds reasonable. He probably hired a good attorney to draw up his contracts and file his incorporation papers."

"Somehow, it all seems fishy to me."

"Do you think he knew about Louise's affair with Marshall and wanted to punish her—to keep her under his thumb?"

"Who says her relationship with Marshall was the first time she strayed?" Tricia remarked.

"Once a cheater, always a cheater. That's been my experience with men," Angelica said sourly.

"Not every man cheats. Christopher never cheated on me," Tricia said. "And I don't believe he was in a relationship during the time we were apart, either."

"Why not?"

"He told me so."

"And you believed him?"

"If nothing else, I don't think he ever lied to me."

"Such a paragon of virtue," Angelica said flippantly.

"Well, you thought so after he saved your life."

"Yes," Angelica admitted contritely. "And I'm sorry. Except for his poor judgment in leaving you, he was a man of character. I'll forever be sorry that he's gone."

As would Tricia. But that didn't mean they would have gotten back together again, either.

"What else did you learn?" Angelica asked.

Tricia shrugged. "Nothing much. But Louise seems to think I'm going to rat her out to Mark."

Angelica raised an eyebrow. "And will you?"

"No. It's not my business. Marshall is dead and gone. Well, until Becca scatters his ashes in Hawaii, that is."

"Why Hawaii?"

Tricia explained.

"Well, you didn't want them anyway, did you?" Angelica asked.

"No. That would be creepy."

"Would you have said that about Grandmother's ashes?" Angelica asked.

No, Tricia wouldn't. That's because she loved her late grandmother unconditionally. But she deserved that kind of devotion. Tricia wasn't at all sure Marshall did—from anyone.

Was it telling that she felt guilty just thinking that thought?

TWENTY-FIVE

 No sooner did Tricia return home from dinner than her phone rang. She looked at the caller ID and answered. "Hi, Becca."

"Do you have a minute to talk?" Becca asked.

"Sure. What's on your mind?" Tricia asked as she opened a cupboard door and removed a can of cat food. It was just about Miss Marple's dinnertime.

"I wondered what your take would be on me running the Armchair Tourist?"

"Why would you want to do that?" Tricia asked, taken aback.

"Well, I'm obviously not going to be making the rounds touring with the senior tennis league," Becca deadpanned.

Tricia took out a clean cat bowl. "I thought you said you didn't want to be stuck in some crappy little town. East Podunk, I think you mentioned."

"That was when I had the world at my command," Becca remarked.

"And you don't miss those days?" Tricia asked, switching the phone to speaker mode and setting it on the counter.

"Of course I do, but I'm also a realist. According to Gene, his shop made money. I was a great tennis champ, but not anymore. My endorsements dried up. I have to live, but I don't want to hang out at malls and tennis clubs signing photos taken twenty years ago. What kind of pathetic creature do you think I am?"

"You mentioned it, not me," Tricia defended herself while Miss Marple danced around her feet, eager for her supper.

Becca exhaled a breath. "Sorry. I'm a little touchy on that subject."

And how.

"But you haven't answered my question," Becca insisted.

Tricia put down the bowl of food and reached for the water bowl. "What do you know about retail?"

"Absolutely nothing. But Gene had an assistant and he'd given her quite a bit of responsibility. I figured I might be more of a behind-the-scenes manager while she handles the day-to-day affairs. Hank told me about the elusive Nigela Ricita and how she's almost single-handedly saved the village." Bob Kelly got the original credit for that. NR Associates just built on that success—and had done a fantastic job. "It sounds like someone else could come in and do even more of the same in this part of the state."

Tricia filled the bowl with fresh water and set it down. "What kind of niche business would you bring in?" Tricia asked.

"I don't know. I haven't given it a lot of thought. I'd have to talk to some people. Maybe join the Chamber of Commerce and talk to a few people on the Board of Selectmen."

"Yes, you could do that."

"So, what do you think?" Becca pressed.

"Start off slowly. See how hard it is to keep a business afloat during the months when Stoneham isn't a tourist attraction. That's the real test."

Becca sighed. "That does seem like prudent advice."

"That's the only kind I have to offer. But while you wait, do your homework. Find that niche product or service that locals and the tourist trade will support. Have you thought about giving tennis lessons?"

"Never! No one could afford that kind of expertise."

"What about starting a tennis club? You could hire the past and present high school stars to teach the basics."

"Oh, please."

"Didn't you say you started out on a crummy asphalt court?"

Becca sighed. "Yes, I did." She was quiet for a moment. "I guess I've become a snob."

"Well, the locals won't like that. You need to be nice to people."

"I'm never not nice."

"Becca!"

"Okay, sometimes I'm a little snarky. I often think I've earned it."

Tricia let out an exasperated breath before continuing. "There's something else you need to think about."

"What's that?"

"How do you explain that Marshall—and that's how everyone around here knew him—was married to you? All anyone has to do is look you up on Wikipedia to find out you've only been married once, and the man's name wasn't Marshall Cambridge."

"Oh, dear. And I've already introduced myself as his exwife—but only a few times."

"A few too many times," Tricia said.

Becca sighed. "I'll have to concoct some story."

"Do you still have any PR contacts from your old life?"

"Maybe," Becca said, drawing out the word.

"Give them a call and see what you can do in the way of damage control."

"I could just say it was none of their business."

"And if the press noses around? If nothing else, you *are* still considered a tennis celebrity."

"Crap!" Becca barked. "I'd better hang up and start making some other calls. We'll talk again soon," she promised, and ended the conversation.

Tricia shook her head, considering their talk. The one thing Becca hadn't mentioned was what Marshall's employee thought of working for the Armchair Tourist's new owner.

Tricia decided she'd investigate that first thing the next morning.

Tricia's phone rang just before eight o'clock the next day, and she was pleased to see it was from the window contractor.

"We're in the area and we'll be at your store around nine. Is that okay?"

Tricia let out a breath. That put her plan to visit the Armchair Tourist on hold for a few hours. Still, Ava wouldn't be around to open until close to ten anyway. "Sure. It's so dark in the shop, we'll be glad to have daylight once again."

After hanging up the phone, Tricia decided to dress warmly. The forecast called for another day of sunshine, but the high was predicted to be only in the midfifties. Tricia was glad she'd had her photo taken the day before. She decided she'd wear a cap and knew that by noon she'd be suffering from a bad case of hat head.

Miss Marple was not happy to be left behind when Tricia closed the door to her apartment. But at least the cat would be warm and safe until the window replacement was complete.

It was Mr. Everett's day off, so Tricia texted Pixie to tell her what to expect and asked if she minded stopping at the Coffee Bean to pick up a dozen doughnuts for the installation crew, not wanting to leave the store in case they arrived and she was nowhere to be found.

Sure thing!

The workmen arrived not ten minutes later and immediately set to work. They'd already removed the plywood that covered the aperture when Pixie arrived for work dressed in her big, moth-eaten full-length fur coat, with a matching hat sitting jauntily on top of her head. It wasn't a look Tricia wanted to emulate, but she had to admit the style complemented the covers of some of the vintage mysteries that lined her shelves.

Tricia made a couple of pots of coffee and tried to keep warm by walking up and down the length of the store, while

Pixie sat in the reader's nook in perfect comfort. After an hour of drafty air wafting in, Pixie's coat began to look downright chic.

If tourists were wandering Stoneham's main drag, Tricia never saw them. And she was beginning to sweat about her lunch with Ginny when her phone pinged.

Sorry to cancel lunch, but Antonio and I have to meet with the insurance adjuster. See you on Sunday.

Much as she looked forward to those lunches with her niece by marriage, Tricia was glad not to feel quite so rushed. She quickly texted her sister to act as a stand-in.

You bet! See you at the café, Angelica answered.

After hours of futzing around, the men had the new window in place and even put a coat of primer on the raw wood around the frame.

"Thanks for the doughnuts and coffee!" the guys called as they finished packing up their gear and drove off.

By then, it was Pixie's lunch hour—in fact, she was an hour late.

Tricia turned up the heat and was starting to feel antsy about ever getting a chance to take care of her own agenda.

While Pixie was gone, Tricia waited on a couple of customers interested in filling out their collections and sold seven Ellery Queen novels and four by Josephine Tey. Not bad, considering they'd had no traffic the entire morning.

When Pixie arrived back from lunch, Tricia scooted out the door to seek out Ava and see what she thought about Becca taking the reins of the Armchair Tourist.

Tricia entered the store, which was bereft of customers, and found Ava standing at the counter with a laptop before her.

She looked up. "Oh, hi, Tricia. What brings you here today?"

"I came to see how you're doing."

Ava shrugged. "Okay. Marshall's life didn't go on, but mine does. And so does my job here. In fact, I've been given more duties."

"What do you mean?"

"Marshall saved a lot of the ephemera from Vamps." The

porn shop Marshall had run at the edge of the village. "He was selling it off piecemeal on eBay and Etsy. Becca gave me the passwords and asked me to keep those shops alive . . . at least until they find out Marshall is dead. Then we'll probably have to set up new shops. But we can name them something similar and, hopefully, his clientele will still find us."

Marshall had never mentioned online sales, at least not to Tricia, and she said as much.

"Oh, sure. That was a big part of our income. When the stacks of magazines and prints run out . . . well, I'm not sure we can survive through the winter. Although . . . just last month, I set up a way to sell the products we carry directly on the Internet with a buy button on our website. Marshall thought buying in bulk and undercutting certain other websites might draw in customers."

Marshall had had it all figured out.

"How do you like the idea of working with Becca?" Tricia asked.

Ava's mouth curved downward. "Not so much."

"How come?"

The young woman scowled. "She seems kind of . . . money hungry."

"What do you mean?"

Again Ava shrugged. "I don't know. Maybe I'm being too critical, but Marshall loved his pinup girl prints. He wanted to sell them to people who would love them as much as he did. Becca couldn't care less."

Tricia had to admit, some of those pinup pictures from the 1940s had captured her heart, too. The women depicted could have been stand-ins for the characters in so many of the vintage mysteries she loved and sold. Of course, many of those books had been written by misogynist men, but there were quite a few women who wrote during those times, too. Women like Dame Agatha Christie, Dorothy L. Sayers, Margery Allingham, Josephine Tey, and Ngaio Marsh, to name a few.

"I must admit, I've found Becca to be a bit brusque," Tricia admitted.

"That's putting it mildly," Ava grated.

"But do you think you can work with her in the long-term?"

Ava shrugged. "We'll see. I like this job, and because Marshall gave me a lot of responsibility, I've learned a lot. But if this one goes sour, there are other jobs out there and I now have more skills if I have to sell myself to a potential employer."

"Is there anything else he kept from Vamps you can sell to keep the business afloat?"

Ava shrugged. "Just the old true-crime magazines and books. I guess he had a self-storage unit on the edge of town. Becca said she was going to go and have a look. I hope I don't have to take pictures and sell all that stuff, too. Some of the photos in those books are positively gruesome." Tricia had read more than her fair share of them, and the crimes reported were often grisly. She didn't envy Ava taking on that task. Had Marshall been attracted by that kind of reading material because of his own criminal past?

Curiosity nibbled at Tricia's mind. She sure would like to see what else Marshall had squirreled away in that storage unit. She wondered if she could convince Becca to let her go with her when she inspected it.

There was only one way to find out. By asking.

Tricia glanced at her watch. She had just enough time to call Becca before she was to meet with Angelica for lunch.

"I'd better get going. Good luck with all your new duties."

"Thanks," Ava said.

Tricia left the shop and walked next door to Booked for Lunch, but instead of going in, she pulled out her phone and made her call.

"Hey, Becca. I was just talking to Ava at the Armchair Tourist. She says Marshall—er, Gene—had a storage unit on the edge of town."

"Apparently."

"Have you had a chance to open it?"

"I was going to do that this afternoon before I meet Ginny for practice. Why?"

"I'm curious. Can I tag along with you?"

"I guess." She paused. "If there's anything of value, maybe you can help me load up my car. I'll want to empty the thing before the next month's rent comes due."

"Great. Text me when you're ready to go and I'll make myself available."

"You got it."

The call ended.

Tricia couldn't imagine what else Marshall could have stashed in the unit. She'd thought he'd parted with all his inventory when he'd sold Vamps, but it looked like he'd let go of only the worst of the pornographic material. Were those books and magazines now moldering in his former shop or had the person who'd bought the business sold them in liquidation? She really didn't know or care. But somehow Tricia felt strongly that Marshall's storage unit would hold something her friend with benefits would have wanted to keep secret.

What that was, Tricia had no idea.

TWENTY-SIX

Angelica was already waiting in their reserved booth when Tricia arrived at Booked for Lunch just five minutes late.

"There you are, I was beginning to worry."

"Sorry. The guys fixed my window this morning—"

"So I saw. It'll look as good as new once the paint is finished. If the weather holds, maybe Mr. Everett can do that tomorrow."

"Good idea. I'll ask if he'd be interested. Otherwise, I can do it myself while he holds the fort. Anyway, I spoke to Ava at the Armchair Tourist." They ordered, and Tricia gave her sister the rundown, but Angelica seemed antsy, wanting instead to talk about the proofs she'd received from Louise Jameson. While she spoke, Tricia pulled out her phone and checked her e-mail. As she suspected, she hadn't received hers. If they didn't show up that afternoon, she'd give Louise a couple of days before inquiring. She was already prepared for an excuse such as *Oh, I accidentally deleted them*. Until then, she'd give Louise the benefit of the doubt.

They were just finishing their meal when Tricia's phone pinged. She looked at it and shoved it back in her purse. "I've got to go."

"Go where?"

"To the self-storage units near the highway."

"For what?" Angelica asked, confused.

"I'll tell you all about it after closing tonight. Thanks for lunch! See you then."

Tricia grabbed her coat and practically flew out the door.

She met Becca in the municipal parking lot, standing beside her vehicle and dressed in purple sweats. She jerked a thumb toward the passenger seat. "Get in."

Tricia did as she was told. As soon as the women had buckled their seat belts, Becca started the engine and drove out of the lot.

"So, what have you been up to?" Tricia asked.

"Packing up Gene's duds for the Clothes Closet. Someone at the diner told me about it. I'm sure not going to be wearing his suits, and I figured someone else could. It's too bad Gene was so short. Some of those suits were tailor-made. Hank Curtis would have looked great in them."

Yeah, if he hadn't been at least five inches taller than Marshall.

"Have you seen Hank lately?"

"Not since we had lunch the other day. I've been busy."

So she had.

Tricia changed the subject. "Checking out this storage unit is kind of like going on a treasure hunt, isn't it?"

"So far I haven't found any gold doubloons or fabulous jewels among the rest of the stuff our guy collected during the past eight years, so I'm not all that hopeful."

Our guy? Did Becca include Louise Jameson in that equation? Should she tell Becca about her conversation with Louise? Probably not.

"Any updates from law enforcement about the person who ran Marsh—er, Gene—down?" Tricia asked.

"Not a peep. I wasn't all that enamored with Deputy Kirby, who didn't seem all that interested in investigating Gene's death, and your Chief Baker seems just as bored by the subject."

"I'm sure that's not true," Tricia said. "I've known Grant Baker for five years and he's a dedicated public servant."

"If you say so," Becca quipped. She braked as they approached the self-storage facility on the edge of the village. She plucked a plastic keycard from the pull-out drawer that housed two beverage-restraint devices and a slot for odd change, pushed the auto window opener, and thrust the card into the reader. The ten-foot-tall black metal gates opened and Becca slowly steered down the asphalt drive flanked with buildings that housed up to twenty units per side.

"What are we looking for?" Tricia asked.

"Unit four twenty-six."

Becca made a left at the end of the row and they scanned the numbers attached to the aluminum garage doors until they reached the proper one.

"This is it," Becca said, moved the gear shift to park, and killed the engine.

The women got out of the van and stepped in front of the corrugated metal garage door that hid Marshall's treasures from view.

"I'm surprised you haven't checked this unit out before now," Tricia said.

"I didn't know about it until this morning. I found the key just sitting on the floor of Gene's bedroom. I'm surprised I hadn't stepped on it before then."

Becca reached into the pocket of her jacket and pulled out a separate key on a ring that said *Stoneham Self-Storage*. She poked it into the padlock that sealed the door and turned it. Removing the lock, she stuck it in her pocket. "Will you give me a hand pulling up this door?"

"Sure."

The women reached down and grabbed the handles, hauling the big door up.

The inside was dark, but not dark enough to keep them from identifying what lay just inside on the cold concrete floor.

A body.

Of Mark Jameson, DDS.

TWENTY-SEVEN

 The color drained from Becca's face as she turned to face Tricia. "Boy, you really *are* the village jinx."

"I am not!" Tricia asserted. She looked down at the body, feeling more than a little disheartened. "Maybe there's a chance he's still alive," she said, trying to be optimistic.

Becca stepped back. "Like hell, but you can check if you want. I'm not touching a dead body."

Tricia crouched down and placed her fingers against the dentist's neck. The flesh was cold to the touch. He'd been dead for hours, although thanks to the cool fall temps—and to her relief—he still smelled as fresh as a daisy. She straightened and shook her head.

"Well, this really screws up my day," Becca grated. "Do you know this guy?"

Tricia nodded. "We're on the recruitment committee for a new president for the local Chamber of Commerce. He's Louise Jameson's husband."

"Holy crap," Becca cursed.

Tricia took out her cell phone, tapping in the code to awaken it.

"Wait, what are you doing?" Becca asked, sounding panicked.

"I'm going to report this to the police."

"Can't we just . . . leave?"

Tricia looked at the woman in disbelief. "No!"

"Give me one good reason!" Becca demanded.

Tricia pointed to the camera mounted on the building across the way.

Becca sighed. "I guess that is a good reason."

"Better yet, the video footage will identify the killer."

"You knew this guy, right? Who'd want to kill him?"

Oh, nobody really. Just his wife; Pixie—for being overcharged to have her tooth cemented; and half the Chamber's recruitment committee. And goodness knew how many others Jameson had alienated in his fortysomething years on the planet.

"Let's just say there might have been a line of people with at least some kind of grudge."

Becca scrutinized Tricia's face, her eyes narrowing. "Gene told me that whenever you found a body, Chief Baker almost always suspected you."

"You've got that right." Tricia tapped 911 on her keypad. She wasn't looking forward to the ensuing conversation. Whenever she called, the dispatcher gave her a hard time—as though she was to blame for every little unsavory incident that occurred in the village.

She wasn't wrong.

Less than five minutes later, the first police SUV arrived with lights flashing and siren screaming—as did the second and third. Crime must have been slow for such a rapid and noisy arrival of the entire force's fleet of vehicles. Baker wasn't far behind, but at least he didn't employ the earsplitting alarm.

While the other cops stood around talking among themselves, Baker exited his SUV, slapping his service cap on his head as he approached. He glared at Tricia. "Why in God's name is it always *you*?"

Becca glibly waved. "Us."

Baker sighed and stepped over to take a look at the body. "Anybody know who this guy is?"

"It's the village dentist, Mark Jameson," Officer Henderson volunteered, not sounding pleased. "He told me my kid needs orthodontia. She's seven. She doesn't even have all her permanent teeth yet."

Maybe Officer Henderson would have liked to rub out the good dentist, too.

Baker turned back to Tricia. "And how do you know him?"

"The Chamber of Commerce." She didn't bother to go into the details but knew he'd press her on that sooner or later.

"And how about you?" he asked Becca.

"I never laid eyes on this guy in my life—or his."

"What are you doing here?" Baker asked Tricia.

"Helping Becca. This is Marshall's storage unit. We came to look at what's in here and decide what to do with it."

"Did Chandler even know Jameson?"

"Beats me," Becca said.

"He may have met him at a Chamber event. I didn't even meet him until last week," Tricia said.

Baker didn't look convinced, which was typical, and another reason Tricia would never have married the man. He always suspected her of killing someone.

"Look, Chief, I only found the key to this unit this morning. That must mean someone else has a key as well," Becca suggested.

"I didn't know he had the unit until this afternoon," Tricia piped up. "Marshall's assistant, Ava, told me about it."

"Don't tell me. You called Ms. Chandler here to ask if you could nose around in it."

"I welcomed the opportunity of assistance," Becca cut in, which was probably the nicest thing she'd said about Tricia so far.

"If nothing else, the fact that there are cameras all around the site should lead you right to whoever it was who stuffed Mark's body into this unit," Tricia said.

Baker nodded toward Henderson. "Go to the office and see if they can bring up the video." The chief was probably disappointed he wasn't going to be able to pin this crime on Tricia, either.

Henderson nodded, turned, and jogged toward the office, near the front gates.

"Has the ME been called?" Baker asked.

"We were waiting for you," Officer Reynolds said.

Baker shook his head and looked like he was about to disparage his subordinate but Becca interrupted before he could do so.

"Just how long is this going to take?" she asked bluntly.

"As long as it takes," Baker practically barked at her.

"Well, I'm getting cold. Come on, Tricia, let's go sit in my van."

For once, Baker didn't argue. Tricia squelched a smile and impishly considered sticking her tongue out at the chief. She followed Becca to the van and got in.

Becca slammed her door. "I can see why you wouldn't want to marry that guy. What a jerk."

How did Becca know Baker had even asked? Maybe she assumed he'd asked her years before when they'd been an item. Tricia wasn't about to educate Becca on the subject. More likely, it was Marshall who'd told her. He seemed to have shared everything about his life here in Stoneham with the woman.

"You certainly know how to handle him."

Becca waved a hand in dismissal. "To me, he's just another line-judge bully. I've known that type since my first tennis match. Give guys like him a little power and their testosterone soars."

Tricia wasn't able to stifle a smile. She was beginning to like Becca Chandler.

The shadows were lengthening by the time the state lab guys and medical examiner had arrived and after Chief Baker had peppered Tricia and Becca with more questions before he'd let them leave the self-storage facility. They'd have to make formal statements, but that could wait until the next day or Monday.

"What are your plans for the evening?" Tricia asked Becca as she drove back to the municipal parking lot.

"I got some boxes from the liquor store in Milford. I've got a date with a bottle of wine and a big roll of packing tape. I intend to get as much done as I can tonight. Why?"

Tricia shrugged. She'd thought about inviting Becca to share happy hour with her and Angelica but quickly nixed that idea. She wouldn't be able to talk freely about the day's experiences if she had an audience.

"Are you still considering staying here in Stoneham after what happened today?" Tricia asked instead.

"I don't know. It seems like there's a lot of death and mayhem going on. I'm surprised Gene wanted to stay in a place like this."

"Stoneham once claimed the title of the safest village in the state."

"Good luck trying to get that back," Becca muttered.

Becca pulled into the lot, parked the van, and the women got out. They walked across the lot to the sidewalk that flanked the street, which was devoid of traffic—both foot and vehicular, as all the shops along it had closed some twenty minutes before.

"Thanks for letting me pick your brain for the past few hours," Becca said.

"There wasn't much else to do while we waited until the chief said we could leave."

Becca nodded.

Tricia paused when they arrived at the Cookery. The interior was darkened, as was Haven't Got a Clue's. After sending her a text earlier in the afternoon, good old Pixie had closed the shop once again.

"I'll let you know what I decide—about staying here in Stoneham," Becca said.

"Okay. I'm sorry the village hasn't shown you its good side. It really is a very pretty and relatively safe place to live."

Becca gave Tricia a sidelong glance. "If you say so."

"Have a good night," Tricia said, and Becca waved as she continued down the sidewalk.

Tricia let herself into the Cookery and made for the back of the shop and to the door marked PRIVATE, and the evening ritual began with a hearty welcome from Sarge, the distribution of dog biscuits, and a greeting from Angelica.

"My, but you're late tonight," she said. "I was afraid the stem glasses might shatter, as they've been in the fridge so long."

Unlikely.

"So, what kept you so late? Did you get an influx of customers right at the end of the day?" Angelica asked as she retrieved the martini pitcher from the fridge.

Tricia sighed and sank onto one of the island's stools. "No. I've been at the self-storage unit since I left you after lunch."

"That was hours ago!"

"Tell me about it."

"So, what did Marshall have stashed in his unit? More smut?"

"As a matter of fact, we found Mark Jameson's dead body."

"What?" Angelica cried, and pivoted.

Tricia explained while Angelica dumped some pretzel sticks into a bowl and scooped out some of the Bee's Knees honey mustard from a jar, placing it into a small bowl.

"Wow. You *have* had a day. My biggest accomplishment was making a sub for our supper."

"I haven't had a sub in ages."

"Neither have I. I thought it might be fun."

"Provolone or Swiss cheese?" Tricia asked.

"Swiss, of course!"

Tricia picked up the tray of drinks and snacks and took them into the living room, while Angelica zoomed along behind her with her little knee scooter and settled on the chaise end of the sectional. "I'm sorry to hear Mark is dead. His passing will no doubt hold up receiving our photo packages."

"Ange, how can you think about such a thing at a time like this?"

Angelica held her hands out in submission. "I have so little to look forward to being stuck here at home. I almost wish I hadn't gone through with the foot surgery. If I'd known how long it was going to hurt and heal, I might've held off for another couple of years."

Tricia passed out the drinks and sat back in her chair. "What a day," she lamented, taking a gulp of her martini.

"What did you and Becca talk about for all those hours you had to wait?" Angelica asked, and picked up a pretzel, dipping it into the mustard.

"She's thinking of staying in Stoneham and running the Armchair Tourist."

"Really? I wouldn't have thought she'd have the temperament for it—or want to, for that matter."

"Me, either, but it sounds like she isn't as financially set as one would think of a former star tennis player. And I wasn't about to ask for details."

"No, that probably wouldn't have been well received. Do you think Becca could be a success at running a business?"

Tricia shrugged. "I don't know. She's kind of brusque. Ava isn't sure she wants to stay under Becca's leadership. It's all just supposition at this point. I suspect Becca will find retail boring after a week or two and move on. But I sure enjoyed the way she handled Grant this afternoon. Maybe I should learn to be more brusque."

Angelica shook her head in disapproval and took a sip of her drink. "So, who do you think killed Mark?"

"I have no idea. But let's face it, he wasn't a very nice man."

"Well, maybe now that he's gone you can run for the Chamber presidency."

"No way."

"But you'd be so good at the job—and good for the village."

"Mary and Terry think so. Dan and Mark were adamant that I wouldn't be the one running."

"The heck with them. Male chauvinist pigs," Angelica added under her breath.

Tricia stared into her drink.

"What else is wrong?" Angelica asked.

"I feel awful about Mark. And Becca was right. If she didn't kill him—and why would she?—someone else had to have had another key to the padlock on that storage unit."

"It has to be Louise."

"Maybe. I suspect it'll come out that Mark was holding the copyright of her work over her head to keep her from . . . doing something."

"Maybe leaving him," Angelica remarked.

"Maybe."

"But that's not all that's bothering you, is it?" Angelica prompted.

Tricia leaned forward and grabbed a pretzel stick, gouging out some of the honey mustard and eating it. "The thing is . . ." she began. She wasn't sure she could say the words out loud. But then, during the past couple of years, she and Angelica had had fewer secrets between them. "It really bothers me that I let myself be conned by Marshall. He was charming."

"Most con men are."

"Yes, but he was also a felon. Most who enter the Witness Protection Program are only there because they're really bad people. If nothing else, he was a cheat."

Angelica eyed her sister. "That's not all that's got you irked."

Tricia sighed. "I'm really cheesed that Marshall only asked me to marry him after Louise turned him down. . . ."

"Oh, Trish, you're not still torturing yourself over that."

"I know! I keep reminding myself that I wasn't about to accept his proposal, anyway."

"Probably because you instinctively knew it would never work out."

"Definitely. If there was ever a rebound relationship that was doomed from the start, it was Marshall and me," Tricia said.

"Don't look at it that way," Angelica scolded. "Now, admit it. You were perfectly fine with the way things were. And the fact that Marshall asked you to marry him definitely screwed up everything."

"I hate to admit it, but you're right."

"Of course I am," Angelica stated. She sighed. "What is it you really want, Tricia?"

"Peace and quiet," she blurted without thinking. "I don't want to have to worry about pleasing anyone else. I've gotten to the point where all I want is to please myself."

"Well, it's about time," Angelica said. "Don't let anyone—even me—tell you how to live. Goodness knows I'd never have married four times if I'd only paid attention to what I really wanted."

"And what was that?"

Angelica swallowed, and her mouth trembled. When she spoke, her voice cracked. "To be Antonio's mother. It took far, far too long before I made it happen. I kept thinking—I need a man in my life. Well, being with Bob Kelly finally proved me wrong. The only man I need in my life right now is Antonio . . . and hopefully a new grandson."

"You wouldn't want another granddaughter?"

"Of course I would. It would just be nice to have one of each. You know, to carry on the family name."

"The Miles name stops with us," Tricia muttered.

"And maybe that's not such a bad thing," Angelica groused. "But we'll leave a proud legacy, and I can't say that of Daddy."

Another con man Tricia had loved . . . still did. But the less said about the sisters' parents, the better.

Tricia polished off the rest of her drink. "I'm starved. Let's have our sub with our next drink. It's too bad we don't have a bag of potato chips."

"Who says we don't?" Angelica said.

Tricia smiled.

Her evening was looking just a little bit brighter.

TWENTY-EIGHT

Tricia woke up to a gloomy day, which was destined to have a detrimental effect on sales in her shop. Leaf peepers were deterred by gray skies, wet weather, and the muted colors as the saturated leaves dropped from the branches in droves and stuck to the roads as though with glue. The one bright spot was that she'd get to spend the day with Mr. Everett while Pixie worked her magic on the locals with her acrylic nail designs at Booked for Beauty.

After showering and dressing, Tricia headed down to Haven't Got a Clue to make sure the shop was ready for any customers who braved the inclement weather. She was about to start the coffee when her cell phone rang. It was Becca calling.

"Hi, Becca. Long time, no hear from," Tricia said, her mood buoyant despite the outside conditions.

"What do you know about some joker named Barbero?" she asked angrily.

Uh-oh.

"Uh, he's a friend. He's just taken over the *Stoneham Weekly News*, in fact. Why?"

"Because he just accosted me in the Bookshelf Diner."

"Accosted you? That doesn't sound like Antonio."

"Yeah, well, there I was eating my egg-white omelet and

he came up to my table. I figured he might be a fan or someone wanting an autograph. Instead, he said he was writing an obit for that pitiful little rag Gene almost stuck me with and he said he'd heard about me from his wife. Who the hell is that?"

Tricia cringed. She'd dragged her feet on writing Marshall's death notice and had promised to have it to Antonio the day before. But it had slipped her mind with everything else she'd gone through since the night Marshall had been killed. And her growing annoyance with the dead man had caused what positive feelings she had for him to dissipate. "Uh, his wife? That would be Ginny," she answered sheepishly.

"Did you have her rat on me?"

"What do you mean 'rat'? Half the village knows you're here and who you were—uh, are," Tricia quickly amended. "What was he asking you about?"

"He wanted to know how I could be Marshall's ex-wife when my Wikipedia entry lists Gene Chandler as my ex-husband. He wanted to know when Marshall and I were married."

Tricia's head drooped. "I did warn you just the other night that it was bound to come out. What did you tell him?"

"That it was none of his damn business! But he kept pestering me with questions and wouldn't take no for an answer."

Tricia sighed. "He is a journalist, and that's what journalists do."

Becca snorted a laugh. "Oh, please!"

"No, really. Antonio took journalism in college."

"What college? Hokey Pokey University?" Becca retorted.

"I'm not exactly sure. But his stepmother told me about his degree."

"And who's that?"

"Nigela Ricita."

Becca was quiet for a moment. She knew Nigela's outstanding reputation in the village and that she owned or rented a good deal of the properties or businesses in the area.

"Isn't everything about this whole village all just a little incestuous?"

"'Nepotism' might be a better word," Tricia corrected, "but only because the people Nigela hires have the qualifications for the jobs they hold."

Good grief. Was keeping Angelica's secret as bad as the truths Marshall kept from her? But then, Angelica wasn't a felon. Her motivations were all altruistic—or at least the majority of them were.

"I thought you were supposed to be writing Gene's obit for the paper—and not mentioning anything about his past," Becca accused.

Tricia cringed. Yes, she had said she would do it.

"Look, I'm sorry you're upset, but what do you want me to do about it?"

"Tell that man to *never* bother me again!"

"By the time the story comes out, Marshall will have been dead nearly three weeks," Tricia pointed out. "Even Mark Jameson's death will be a week old by then."

"Yes, but what if some of the bigger news outlets pick up the story?"

That really would be a coup for Antonio, unlikely as it was to happen.

"I don't think you should worry about it."

"Says you, who has never been the subject of such bad press."

Not to the extent Becca had experienced. But Russ Smith had printed a number of unflattering stories about Tricia in the *Stoneham Weekly News* that were just as searchable on the World Wide Web.

"So, you won't help your friend?"

Tricia blinked in confusion. "Friend?"

"Me!" Becca wailed so loud Tricia had to back the phone away from her ear.

Friendly enemy, possibly. *Acquaintance* was probably the most charitable term Tricia could think of.

"I'll . . . I'll speak to him," Tricia said. "But I can't make any promises. The content of the *Stoneham Weekly News* is up to its editor, and that's Antonio. And you know that once a reporter gets his or her teeth in a story, they're as tenacious as a terrier."

"Don't I know it. I've had more bad press than I care to remember."

Tricia idly wondered if, thanks to her interest in tennis, Angelica would remember. Of course, all Tricia had to do was hit the Internet and do a little research and all those tales would be available in a split second. But she'd ask her sister just the same.

"I'd better go," Becca said. "I only hope I can get Chief Baker to let me back into Gene's storage unit. I'm not paying that company another dime to hold on to whatever junk he collected."

They'd been able to see only piles of stacked cartons with no idea what was in any of them. Knowing Marshall, he'd probably made an inventory. Heaven only knew where it would be. Most likely on his personal or store computer. Did Becca have access to his passwords? Probably not. Tricia didn't bother to mention it.

"Talk to you later," she said.

"Sure thing."

Tricia set her phone down. She supposed she could take a few minutes to pop over to the newspaper that morning. It opened at eight. She still had more than an hour to kill before Haven't Got a Clue opened.

Grabbing her jacket, Tricia left her store and started north up the sidewalk. Crossing the street at the light, she made her way up Main Street. Booked for Beauty was packed with customers getting cuts and color jobs, and as she looked in the big display window, Tricia could see Pixie at her nail station busy working on a twentysomething's manicure. She happened to look up and waved cheerfully. Tricia waved back. Pixie gave her a quick thumbs-up and went back to work, and Tricia continued on to the *Stoneham Weekly News*.

As expected, Patti was behind the counter, sitting before a computer screen, but Ginger was nowhere to be found. Tricia pushed through the door and an annoying buzzer sounded. She much preferred the tinkle of the little bell that rang when her shop door opened.

Patti looked up. "Hey, Tricia, what brings you here today? Ready to place another ad?"

"I was hoping I might speak to Antonio. Is he in?"

The door to the inner sanctum opened and a smiling Antonio entered the reception area. "Tricia! I thought I heard a familiar voice." He waved his hand in a grand gesture. "Welcome to my new home."

Tricia winced at the description. As far as she knew, the Barbero family was still hunkered down in the suite at the Sheer Comfort Inn and might be for weeks.

"Won't you come in and sit?" Antonio invited her.

"I'd love to," Tricia said, and sidled around the counter to go back to Antonio's office.

The décor had changed since Russ Smith's departure. For one thing, it was tidy and the desktop was clear of clutter, and all evidence of the destruction Russ's son, Russell, had inflicted had been erased. The room still needed a fresh coat of paint, but Antonio would probably take care of that in due time.

Tricia took the guest chair and gave Antonio a smile. "How did you like your first full week working on the *Stoneham Weekly News*?"

Antonio leaned back into the chair and grinned. "*Magnifico!* This is what I was born to do."

"I'm so glad you're getting to finally fulfill your life's dream. I'm sorry I didn't get back to you with the paragraph on Marshall's death. I could tinker with it tonight and get it to you by tomorrow morning."

"It is not necessary. I have been working on it," Antonio said, sounding confident. Perhaps a little *too* confident.

"Um, yes. So I heard. In fact, I got a call from Becca Chandler this morning and she was more than a little upset that you tracked her down at the Bookshelf Diner. In fact, she said you accosted her."

Antonio frowned. "Do you believe I am *capable* of accosting a lady?"

"No, of course not. That was *her* perception. But I'm asking you to please drop an in-depth article on Marshall."

"Tricia, there appears to be a *much* bigger story here," Antonio insisted.

She sighed. "But there's no good end to it."

"You say that, but how do you know it?" Antonio persisted, his voice rising just a bit.

"Because I'm privy to most of that story," she admitted, deliberately lowering her voice.

"But not *all*," he said.

"No."

Antonio suddenly stood and straightened to his full—towering—height and shook his head. "I will not drop this. I have my journalistic reputation to uphold."

Tricia's eyes widened. A reputation to uphold? Antonio didn't even have a single issue of that nasty little rag under his belt. Tricia had never been fond of the village's weekly newspaper, and now her negative feelings toward it were only intensifying.

"Will you tell me what you know about Marshall—if that was his name?" Antonio asked bluntly.

"Becca asked me not to."

"So, your loyalty is to a complete stranger instead of your own blood?" Antonio accused.

"No," Tricia said, growing frustrated. "But I gave her my word. That's a solemn oath. I hope you understand that."

"No, I do not. In Italia, family is everything," Antonio insisted. "Those who turn against their family are"—he seemed to struggle to find the right word—"traitors!"

"What are you saying?" Tricia asked, her insides tightening.

"Rejecting that connection is tantamount to blasphemy."

Tricia didn't agree, but it was apparent that trying to convince him of her argument was fruitless.

"I guess we'll just have to agree to disagree."

"That I will not do," he said adamantly. Why was he so angry? "I think you should leave now, Tricia."

"Antonio," she protested.

He pointed toward the door, his face twisted with fury.

For a moment, Tricia just stared at him. Then she got up, opened the door, and walked out of the office.

"See you later, Tricia," Patti called cheerfully, but Tricia didn't acknowledge her salutation as she exited the building.

She walked away, feeling shaken. She'd never exchanged a cross word with Antonio in the four years since they'd first met. She found herself walking slowly back toward her store, still unsure what had transpired between them and wondering how they were ever going to get past that awkward moment.

Perhaps Angelica would have some words of comfort to offer her that afternoon when they met for lunch.

At least, Tricia sure hoped she would.

TWENTY-NINE

As always, Mr. Everett arrived for work just a little early, and as cheerful as ever. Tricia put on a brave face, greeting him in kind, but her nerves were still shot. Now all she had to do was get through the day without letting it bother her . . . too much.

Once they'd shared their usual cup of coffee, Mr. Everett picked up his lamb's-wool duster and started his workday. Meanwhile, Tricia checked online for news of updates on Mark Jameson's death. Other than a brief paragraph from one of the TV news websites, there was no further information. Tricia scowled and considered her encounter with Baker the day before. She was grateful it had been Becca and not she who had tested his patience. She wanted so badly to pick Baker's brain and wring him for information, but what excuse could she make?

She thought about it for a few moments before she pulled out her cell phone and called the chief.

"What is it now, Tricia," Baker answered, sounding bored.

"I was wondering if you wanted me to come in this afternoon to make my official statement."

"We're shorthanded. It can wait until Monday morning."

"Oh. Okay. Did you learn anything from the video from the storage unit's camera system?"

"Nope. The system was down. It looks like sabotage."

"What?"

"Yeah, they've had a number of units broken into of late. The system went down Wednesday evening and hadn't yet been repaired."

"How convenient," Tricia said.

"Very," Baker agreed. "These break-ins are sometimes an inside job, but the manager said he hadn't had any employee problems. Could've been kids just trying to find some stuff to pawn."

"Chief," someone called out from a distance. "We've got the warrant."

"Is that for Marshall's or Mark's killer?" Tricia asked, suddenly alert.

"I've gotta go," Baker said without answering. "We'll talk soon." Without a good-bye, Baker ended the call.

Tricia stared at her now-silent phone. Had Baker just gotten the warrant to make an arrest for the two murders? She'd find out—but not quickly enough.

She wondered how Louise had taken her husband's death. Was she distraught or relieved? Would she now be free to own her work, or had Jameson set up his business so that she'd never gain control of her rightful intellectual property? As his wife, it was likely she'd inherit his entire estate . . . unless he'd set things up to exclude her. Louise hadn't given Tricia the impression she was in a loving relationship, but she had rebuffed Marshall in favor of staying with her dentist husband. It sure sounded unpalatable to Tricia.

Another tour bus, filled to the brim with tourists, arrived, and Tricia and Mr. Everett easily handled the shoppers who crowded into the store. Tricia heard her phone ping but was too busy ringing up sales to check her message until a midday lull when Mr. Everett had gone to lunch.

Very busy, can't meet at BFL, said Angelica's terse text.

Tricia didn't have time to reply since the door to the shop opened, letting in another three customers, one of whom asked for immediate assistance. She'd just have to ask Angelica about the rift with Antonio at happy hour after closing.

When Mr. Everett returned, Tricia headed to her apartment, opened a can of soup, and made herself a quick lunch. She'd barely managed to finish when Mr. Everett called to ask for assistance. My, how Tricia loved leaf-peeping season and the crowds of tourists who descended on the village.

Considering they'd had several buses earlier in the week, with good sales, Saturday had been the best day and Tricia felt considerably cheered. She and Mr. Everett got the store ready for the next day's sales before grabbing their coats to leave.

"Have you decided what you're going to bring to our family dinner for dessert tomorrow?" Tricia asked.

"Since last week you consulted me for a favorite, I thought I might ask the same of you."

"How thoughtful of you." Tricia chewed her lip and thought about it. "How about a pie?"

"What kind?"

"Anything."

Mr. Everett nodded sagely. "I thought I might like to try to make a pumpkin pie. From scratch. Grace picked up a cooking pumpkin at the store the other day for just such an experiment."

"Then it sounds like it was meant to be."

"Would you like whipped or ice cream with that?" Mr. Everett asked.

"Why don't you surprise me?"

Mr. Everett nodded, trying to suppress a smile. "I shall do so."

Tricia locked the door and the two of them started off. "See you tomorrow!" Tricia said as they parted in front of the Cookery. June had already left for the day and so Tricia let herself into Angelica's shop and headed for the upstairs apartment.

When Sarge enthusiastically greeted Tricia as she entered, Angelica was quick to reprimand him. "Hush! Go to your bed, Sarge," she said sternly.

The little dog was used to being told to quiet down, but Tricia had never heard her sister say the words quite so sternly. Sarge looked at her with wide, frightened brown eyes and almost seemed to cringe, but he was too well trained to disobey a direct order and padded over to his bed, where he immediately hunkered down, looking completely demoralized.

Tricia stepped up to the counter to get a couple of biscuits from the lead crystal jar on the counter when Angelica spoke again. "No."

Tricia blinked. "No what?"

"Don't give Sarge any biscuits. He's being punished."

"For what? For greeting me like he has hundreds of times before?"

Angelica didn't answer.

Tricia studied her sister's ultra-rigid posture and the taut lines around her mouth. "What's wrong, Ange? Can I help?"

"Of course you can help," Angelica snapped. "I got a very disturbing call from Antonio earlier today. You should tell him everything you know about Marshall and his background. You should have done that when you visited him this morning. What's wrong is you giving your loyalty to a complete stranger instead of Antonio."

Tricia had had nearly a dozen conversations with Becca since she'd arrived more than a week before. "She's no longer a complete stranger."

"Becca is not a nice woman," Angelica remarked. "You've said so yourself. And she showed her true colors when she disparaged Ginny, who was doing *you* a favor by practicing with her on the tennis court."

"Becca has her faults," Tricia conceded, "but she asked me not to talk about Marshall to others—and especially not the press. I promised her I wouldn't."

"You told me," Angelica countered.

"And it was in confidence. Are you going to betray that trust?"

Angelica pursed her lips and said nothing.

A prickly feeling along her spine caused Tricia to shudder. Was it a sense of déjà vu? When they were younger, she and Angelica had never gotten along. Tricia always wondered if it was because Angelica had had to share the lime-light of their parents' affections with the interloper five years her junior. But then, it was apparent that their mother doted on Angelica and merely tolerated Tricia, for reasons she had only recently become aware of.

"Angelica, please answer my question," Tricia implored.

Long moments passed before Angelica answered. "I haven't decided."

Tricia swallowed hard. It had taken nearly seven years for the sisters to build a close, loving relationship that was cemented by trust. Suddenly it felt like an earthquake had just shaken away all that they'd built.

Tricia wasn't sure what to say next, but she wasn't about to issue an ultimatum.

The sisters stood staring at each other for long moments.

Tricia forced a smile and softened her voice. "Why don't we pour a couple of martinis and talk about this more?"

Angelica remained as rigid as a statue. "I didn't make any."

"Oh, well, I could—"

"I don't think so," Angelica said curtly.

"Don't think what?"

"That we need to have a drink. In fact, I'm beginning to think we drink far too much."

Maybe that was true. But happy hour had become a part of their lives—the best part, where the sisters could let down their hair and discuss their lives. And if they drank only tea, it would still be the best part of Tricia's day.

"Why are you so upset with me?"

"Upset? I'm not upset," Angelica said tartly.

"Then why are you speaking to me in that tone?"

"What tone?" Angelica asked, and Tricia knew from experience that this was no time to try to reason with her sister.

"Maybe I should come back tomorrow."

"I don't think so," Angelica said once again.

"Excuse me?"

"I said, I don't think you should come for dinner tomorrow, either."

"How about Monday?" Tricia asked. Now she was getting irked.

Angelica just glared at her.

Tricia was glad she hadn't taken off her coat. She turned, headed toward the door of the apartment, and closed it behind her.

Never had she heard such a hollow sound.

THIRTY

Tricia spent a rather lonely evening restlessly pacing her apartment. She thought what she and her sister shared had become an unbreakable bond. Now . . . she doubted every confidence they'd shared, the times when she had depended on her sister to build her up when she'd been down.

She'd come to depend on her sister's opinions and advice. And what shocked her most was that Angelica, who had leaned toward fairness, had suddenly reversed her stance and seemed hell-bent on defending Antonio no matter what. Then again, just the evening before, Angelica had declared that all she'd wanted most of her adult life was to be a mother to the child she'd given up at such an early age. But was she now taking that desire to an unhealthy—at least for Tricia—degree?

And she'd cried. Cried because there were times when Angelica had defended her—especially the year before when they'd met their parents for lunch in Bermuda. Angelica had stood up to their formidable mother and had pleaded Tricia's case, even if Tricia had wanted to crawl under the table and hide.

If her sister would reject her for abiding by her sense of morality, then what they had shared had been a sham all along.

That hurt. More than hurt, it was devastating.

The only thing Tricia could think of to soothe her soul was to bake, and even that had been a gift from Angelica. Tricia had finally been able to channel that part of her grandmother's soul, but if it hadn't been for Angelica, Tricia was sure she never would have embraced that calling.

And it was, yet again, thumbprint cookies she made, because Mr. Everett would be working the next day. They were his favorites, and he was one of her favorite people. If he gave her even the slightest of smiles because of them, it would make her day.

Tricia wasn't much of a TV viewer, preferring to get her news from *USA Today* and the *Nashua Telegraph*'s online editions, but that evening she turned on one of the Nashua TV station's news programs for background noise as the cookies cooled. It was then she heard the news.

"An arrest has been made in two murders that occurred in the past two weeks in Stoneham. Louise Jameson has been charged with the deaths of her husband, local dentist Mark Jameson, and Marshall Cambridge, owner of the Armchair Tourist," the dark-haired female anchor reported. "We have few details at this time, but will keep you posted as the story develops."

Tricia found herself standing before her TV with her mouth gaping.

Louise Jameson arrested? It didn't make sense—at least in Marshall's case. What could her motive be? She'd turned him down—not the other way round. She'd chosen her marriage to Mark over Marshall. If Mark held the copyright on her photos, she had at least expected him to bankroll her wedding venue project. It was possible he'd pulled out of that agreement and she could have killed him in a fit of rage, but Tricia hadn't gotten the impression Louise was a killer.

Then again, she hadn't thought Frannie Armstrong capable of killing, or Henry Dawson. Much as she disliked Bob Kelly, she was shocked that even he had committed murder. Did she tend to look for the best in people instead of their worst traits?

Tricia listened to the weather report before turning off the set. She didn't want to hear any more disturbing news.

After the cookies had cooled and were safely ensconced in a plastic container, Tricia fed Miss Marple and took to her bed to read . . . not that she took in even one tenth of the words she scanned. Her mind kept going back to the hurtful conversation with Angelica. Okay, she could see why Angelica would side with Antonio—her only child, and one she couldn't (or rather, wouldn't) acknowledge to the world at large as her own—but it hurt just the same.

And Tricia had never known Antonio to be anything but strong. That during his first foray into journalism he'd resorted to squealing to his mother about his encounter with Tricia was not an indication of any kind of journalistic integrity. If he couldn't see that, then he had no business trying to establish himself as a member of that profession.

Eventually, Tricia drifted off to sleep, but disturbing dreams of being hounded and judged kept visiting her in the night.

She awoke in the dark and way too early.

It would be a very long day.

Haven't Got a Clue didn't open until noon on Sundays, which gave Tricia way too long with time on her hands and not much to think about except the rift with her sister and the possibility that Louise Jameson might have killed Marshall and her husband.

Tricia set off for her usual walk but ended up traveling far beyond her customary route. By the time she returned to her shop, it was nearly twelve and she estimated she'd covered ten miles, making her glad she always wore sensible shoes.

Grace dropped off Mr. Everett five minutes before Haven't Got a Clue's opening and he entered the shop with his home-made pie in hand. "Good morning, Ms. Miles."

"Good morning," Tricia said, forcing some cheer she didn't feel into her voice. "Looks like your pie came out beautifully."

Mr. Everett peeled back the plastic wrap to reveal that instead of crimping the bottom crust, he had cut out tiny maple leaves for the edge, each perfectly brown with a shiny egg-wash glaze.

"I think it turned out well," he said, which was unusual, as he seldom accepted praise, let alone gave it to himself. "I hope the rest of our friends will enjoy it."

One thing was for sure, Tricia wasn't going to get a slice. She wasn't about to voice that fact.

"Could you store it in your refrigerator until this evening? I wouldn't want it to spoil."

"Of course."

As he was about to hand the pie over, Tricia's cell phone rang. She looked at the screen and saw it was Becca calling. "I'd better take this," she said, and answered the call. "Hi, Becca, can you hold on for a minute? I've got to take something from the shop up to my apartment."

"Fine," Becca said testily.

Tricia stuck the phone in her slacks pocket and took the pie. "I'll be back down in a few minutes," she told Mr. Everett, who nodded. They headed for the back of the shop, where Mr. Everett hung up his coat and Tricia climbed the stairs to her home. She placed the pie in the fridge and retrieved her phone.

"What's up?" she asked Becca.

"I wondered what you thought of Louise Jameson's arrest."

Tricia sighed. "I don't know what to think."

"I've got a theory."

"Do tell," Tricia said, and leaned against her kitchen island.

"I think she killed them both."

"Based on what?"

"Gene told me she was bitter that her husband wove her business into his scheme to tie whatever profits she made from her studio into his financial empire—same with the wedding venue."

So Tricia hadn't been the only one to notice it.

"But why would she want to kill Gene, her lover?"

"I haven't exactly figured that out," Becca admitted. "I really don't know much about the bitch." Her description of Louise could be applied to herself. "Maybe she was jealous of you."

Ha!

"The cops are sure a man named Joshua Greenwell was at the wheel of the truck that killed Gene."

"Who she *could* have hired," Becca pointed out. "The cops must have found a connection or else they wouldn't have arrested her."

Tricia wasn't so sure.

After a good day of sales, it was time to close Haven't Got a Clue. Tricia hadn't mentioned the rift among her, Angelica, and Antonio, and she'd been dreading having to tell Mr. Everett that there was a change of plans for that evening. He so looked forward to the whole makeshift family being together, and it wasn't going to happen on that day.

At 4:59, Mr. Everett grabbed his coat from a peg at the back of the store. "And we're off to have another wonderful evening with our little family," he said gleefully.

"Uh, not tonight, I'm afraid," Tricia said, and forced a grin. "I have a lot of paperwork I need to catch up on and if I don't scour the Internet for some deals, we'll be low on stock during the holiday crunch."

Mr. Everett frowned. "But surely you can take an hour or so for camaraderie and a wonderful meal."

Tricia's throat constricted even as she forced yet another smile. "Not tonight," she reiterated.

"But I made the pumpkin pie especially for you," he insisted.

"Don't worry about it."

"But what will you have for your dinner?"

"I have plenty of food in my larder," she lied. She hadn't hit the grocery store in almost two weeks. The milk in her fridge was on the cusp of souring. She might have to—

shudder!—resort to adding some of the nondairy whitener she kept in the beverage station for her store's customers.

"Does your sister know you won't be attending dinner?" Mr. Everett asked.

"Oh, yes," Tricia answered blithely. "We discussed it." No lie there.

"Well, all right, then," Mr. Everett said, but still looked doubtful. "Shall I save you a piece of pie?"

Tricia patted her stomach. "I could stand to lose a few pounds, but I know everyone else will enjoy it. You can tell me how much on Tuesday."

Mr. Everett studied Tricia's face and she could tell he wasn't accepting her obvious line of bull. "Well, if you say so," he reluctantly said.

Tricia forced a smile. "Now, go and have a wonderful time. And I'll see you on Tuesday."

Mr. Everett took possession of his beautiful pie and nodded. "I will see you then."

Smiling, Tricia watched him go. When the door closed behind him, she let out a sigh, looked around her empty store, and fought the urge to cry.

THIRTY-ONE

 That evening, Tricia moped around her apartment, wondering what the family was having for dinner. Wondering how the conversation was evolving and how Angelica had explained her absence.

Tricia scrambled a couple of eggs, drank a mug of cocoa, and went to bed early with a good book. It was times like that she noticed how deadly quiet her apartment was. She didn't feel comfortable calling anyone to vent her frustration. She counted Angelica and Ginny as her closest friends. Pixie was a good listener, but although Tricia was quite fond of her, their relationship just wasn't the same.

After a fitful night of sleep, morning eventually arrived, and Tricia dragged herself out of bed, forcing herself to go through her usual routine. Instead of her accustomed route, she power walked other streets, trying not to think about what was eating at her mind and emotions.

Back at Haven't Got a Clue, she put some change in the till, made coffee, and stared at the clock, daring it to be opening time.

Pixie arrived five minutes early, in high spirits. That day she'd donned what Tricia thought of as her Katharine Hepburn outfit. A black, long-sleeved blouse, high-waisted tan slacks, and her hair in a topknot.

"We're going to have a wonderful day!" Pixie declared as she poured herself a cup of coffee at the beverage station.

"We sure will," Tricia said, forcing cheer she did not feel into her voice.

The little bell over the door rang and the women turned, expecting their first customers of the day. Instead, it was a sad-faced Mr. Everett who entered Haven't Got a Clue.

"Mr. E, what are you doing here on your day off? Come to hang out?" Pixie asked brightly.

"Er, no. I came to see Ms. Miles," he said sheepishly, and looked down at a business-sized envelope he held in his hands.

Tricia stepped closer. "Is everything all right?"

"Er, well, no." The old man hesitated. "I missed you last night at . . ." But then Mr. Everett didn't finish the sentence.

"I missed you, too," Tricia said.

Mr. Everett looked to be on the verge of tears. He thrust the envelope he held toward her. "It's with great sorrow that I must tender my immediate resignation."

Tricia blinked. "What?"

"It's not what I would wish to do under other circumstances, but you see, Grace . . ." But then he didn't elaborate.

Tricia understood only too well.

Grace had no other family. The Miles-Barberos had accepted her and Mr. Everett into their family. Little Sofia thought of Grace as her other nonna. If Grace had to choose sides, and obviously she had, she would choose the warm embrace of Antonio, Ginny, and—most of all—that golden child all of them loved so much.

Tricia fingered the envelope and nodded slowly. "I understand. But I want you to know that you will always be my friend. And if you ever wish to come back to Haven't Got a Clue, I will welcome you with open arms."

Mr. Everett's eyes brimmed with tears. He swallowed several times and nodded. But then he turned and headed for the door, closing it behind him without a backward glance.

Pixie let out a breath that was almost a sob. "I don't get it. What's going on? Why . . . ?" But then she couldn't seem to finish the sentence.

"It seems I'm caught in the middle of a family feud," Tricia said simply. "And unfortunately I'm on the losing side."

"But why?"

Tricia shrugged, and it took a few long hard moments before she could speak again. "These things happen."

"But not to you guys. You're special."

Not anymore, Tricia thought sadly. *Not anymore.*

Tricia braved a smile. "I'm sure things will straighten out in a day or two," she said, although she wasn't at all convinced.

As lunchtime approached, Tricia realized she didn't have much in the way of groceries. No way was she going to cross the street to go to Booked for Lunch, and she noticed that Pixie had patronized the Bookshelf Diner for her midday meal.

Instead, she decided to head to the grocery store in Milford. She'd stock her cupboards and hunker down. If nothing else, Miss Marple would be pleased to have her cat mom home during her midday and evening meals. And perhaps things would be ironed out and maybe in a few weeks she could slide back into her evenings with Angelica.

Except . . . how could she? Tricia now knew where she stood. Without saying it aloud, Angelica's meaning hadn't been lost: When push came to shove, she had her *own* family. She really didn't need Tricia.

Tricia's cell phone rang. She looked at the caller ID and frowned. Now what did Chief Baker want?

"Hello, Grant," she said, feeling weary.

"Hi, Tricia. I'm calling to give you an update on the brick-throwing motorcyclist."

"Did you catch him—and her?" she asked eagerly.

"Not exactly."

"What does that mean?"

"It seems they had an accident."

The muscles in her arms tensed. "Go on."

"They must have hit a greasy patch on the highway. A motorist with a flat tire saw the bike down in a gully. He called nine one one and . . . Well, it must have been instantaneous."

"Are you sure it was the right couple?"

"The license plate was ZBR3. There was a partial print on that brick thrown through your window. We'll have proof positive once the state lab confirms it belonged to the male victim."

"What was his name?"

"Tyler Holden."

"And the woman?"

"Ashley Emery."

The names meant nothing to Tricia.

"Are you okay?" Baker asked. "You sound kind of down."

A shudder ran through her. "Angelica and I had a little tiff. It'll all blow over in a couple of days."

"Does that mean you're free for dinner tonight?"

Tricia frowned, glad Baker couldn't see her sour expression. The guy just wouldn't give up! She kept her voice neutral. "Sorry, but I already have plans." Yeah, to sit alone at her kitchen island and eat a sandwich or something even less interesting. And why was she being so careful with his feelings, anyway? She should have just said *No!*

"Well, if you need a sounding board, I'm available," Baker offered.

"Thank you," she said, if only to be polite. "Would you keep me posted on any other developments?"

"Sure."

"Have a good evening," Tricia said.

"You, too."

Tricia ended the call. She sat staring at the phone. So, the man who lobbed a brick through her window and the woman who'd texted him were now both dead. The man who'd run down Marshall and had possibly torched Ginny and Antonio's home was also dead.

What did they have in common?

That they'd made attacks on the Miles-Barbero families. They appeared to be petty criminals.

That they had probably been paid to wreak havoc, and

now they were dead. One had been murdered. Was the accident that killed the biker and his girlfriend a premeditated murder?

Whoever had hired them had also silenced them . . . or had them silenced—and permanently.

The shop door opened and several women entered. Tricia immediately brightened. "Welcome to Haven't Got a Clue. I'm the owner, Tricia. Let me know if you need any help."

The women smiled and dispersed to begin browsing.

Tricia gave herself a little shake and gazed out the window, where she could just see the sign for Booked for Lunch. It reminded her that she needed to get a shopping list together. She grabbed a scrap piece of paper and began to make notes.

Still, the thought of that trio of felons lying dead in a morgue was still stuck in her mind.

Her phone pinged. She glanced at the screen. It was a text from Ginny. *Are we still on for lunch?*

Tricia cringed. Their weekly lunch had been postponed twice.

Why don't we just wait until Thursday? Tricia texted back.

She expected an immediate text back, but instead, her phone rang: Ginny.

"Hey," Tricia said, keeping her voice low so as not to disturb her customers.

"Why weren't you at our Sunday dinner last night?" Ginny demanded.

Tricia hesitated before answering. Should she tell the truth, or would that make the situation that much worse? She took a chance. "Uh . . . I was asked not to come."

"By whom?" Ginny demanded.

"Angelica."

"What? Why?"

"I really don't want to go into it."

"Why not?"

"Because . . . because it's all rather silly. At least, it should be."

"Does this have anything to do with Antonio and that

miserable excuse of a newspaper they acquired?" Ginny asked, her voice tightening.

"Well, sort of."

"I knew it. I knew that rotten excuse for a fish wrapper had to be the cause."

"What do you mean?"

"Ever since Antonio came up with the idea of running that birdcage liner, he's been obsessed with becoming the next Clark Kent."

"Have you heard from Becca?"

"Not since she canceled our practice on Friday. I was going to text her this morning to see if we're going to play."

"She may not answer your message."

"Why not?"

"Because Antonio badgered her about Marshall's death and details about his past—and hers. Angelica's in his court because . . . well, I don't have to tell you why, but Becca also . . ." Tricia let the sentence trail. She wasn't about to reveal how Becca had disparaged Ginny.

"She said I was a lousy player and beneath her skill level."

"Well, sort of."

Ginny let out a dismissive breath. "She's told me that since the second day we played. If I'm such a slouch, why did she keep asking me to come back?"

Ginny had a point.

"You're not offended."

"Ha! How many years did I work in retail? Nobody can insult me and take me down unless I let them. Becca's a blowhard, but she's also taught me a lot in the past week on how to improve my game. After the new baby arrives, I'm going to join a tennis league and get back into it. I can't tell you how much I've missed playing."

"I'm glad something good has come out of this whole messy situation."

"But not for you," Ginny said bluntly. "I knew something was up last night when Antonio and Angelica kept looking at each other every time your name was mentioned."

"That's not the only collateral damage. Mr. Everett quit this morning."

"What?" Ginny practically wailed.

"I have a feeling Grace made him do it. This is just supposition on my part, but I'm guessing she sensed there was a rift and if he continued working for me it could alter things. If it appeared they were choosing sides, she might be afraid that you and Antonio could keep them from seeing Sofia and . . . well . . ." But Tricia couldn't go on.

"Good grief," Ginny said, sounding exhausted. She let out an exasperated breath. "I refuse to let that Russ Smith–tainted ad rag unhinge our lives."

"Ginny, please don't do anything to—"

"Oh, you better believe I'm going to do something. I will not stand for any kind of bullying. Not from Antonio or Angelica. And they are going to hear from me. I will not let my daughter think that kind of behavior is acceptable. Not from her nonna and especially not from her father," Ginny said fervently.

She is woman, hear her roar, Tricia thought with the smallest hint of a smile.

"I need to nip this behavior in the bud," Ginny declared. "And right now. Talk to you later."

The call ended.

One of the women customers ambled up to the cash desk. "Excuse me, but there are so many wonderful books here, I'm having a hard time making a choice. Can you give me a recommendation?"

Tricia's insides felt wobbly after two jarring conversations in a row but somehow she managed a smile. "I'd be delighted."

The shop was devoid of customers when, less than an hour later, Ginny marched into Haven't Got a Clue with a humble-looking Antonio and Angelica following in her wake. Because of their hangdog expressions, Tricia was surprised Ginny hadn't dragged them in by their ears.

"Hi, Pixie. Would you excuse us for a few minutes?" Ginny asked, her voice as sweet as could be.

Pixie shot Tricia a glance before answering, "Uh, sure. I've got some work down in the office I can do."

"Thank you."

Tricia had a feeling Pixie would hang out at the top of the stairs and listen to every word that was said, but she also knew Pixie wouldn't breathe whatever she heard to another soul. At least she was pretty sure she wouldn't.

Once Pixie was out of sight, Ginny turned, arms akimbo, and glared at the guilty parties. "Well, what do you have to say for yourselves?"

Antonio's gaze was fixed on the carpet. "I . . . I am sorry I was unreasonable. When you said we should agree to disagree, I should not have protested. I behaved like a child."

"And you, Angelica," Ginny prompted sternly.

Angelica's fingers tightened on the handle of her cane. In her other hand was the shopping bag she'd received at the Bee's Knees. "I'm sorry, too, Tricia. I was only trying to be supportive of—"

"I know," Tricia said. "I accept your apologies and thank you for coming."

"I brought you a peace offering."

"You didn't have to do that."

"Well, they're not my size."

Angelica offered Tricia the bag. She took it and peeked inside to see a shoebox. Slipping the top off, she nudged the tissue paper and smiled: black sequined sneakers.

"Thank you."

Suddenly Angelica lunged forward with tears in her eyes and grabbed Tricia in an awkward hug. "I'm sorry, Trish. I'm so sorry," she whispered in Tricia's ear between sobs.

Tricia patted her back. "Hey, it's okay."

Angelica pulled back.

"Now, why don't you three sit over there in the reader's nook and talk things through," Ginny suggested. "I still have to speak to Grace and Mr. Everett and straighten things out with them before I can pick Sofia up at day care."

The three of them nodded solemnly and watched as Ginny flounced out the door.

Tricia offered the others a shy smile. "I guess we'd better do as she asked."

"Yes, or else I will be in the cur house." He meant *doghouse*, but Tricia got the gist.

They all took a seat in the reader's nook and looked at one another self-consciously. "Well?" Tricia asked.

"I should explain why I was so stubborn on Saturday," Antonio began. He looked at Angelica, who nodded, as though to encourage him. "When I met Ms. Chandler on Saturday morning, there was something very familiar about her face."

"Well, she was a world-renowned tennis player," Tricia pointed out.

Antonio shook his head. "That is not it. I know nothing about her past career. I knew I had seen her at the Brookview Inn . . . and not that long ago."

Tricia's eyes widened. "But she told me she'd never been to Stoneham before last week."

"As she told me, as well," Antonio said.

Tricia sat back in her chair and Miss Marple ambled up and jumped into her lap, purring. She turned around three times before she settled down. "You know, when Becca came into the shop the day I met her, she showed me some pictures she'd said Marshall had sent her of Stoneham."

"What kind of pictures?"

"Of the Armchair Tourist and the *Stoneham Weekly News*. I didn't realize it until just now that those pictures showed the mums in the urns in front of each of the Main Street merchants. Marshall couldn't have sent them to her because they were planted the morning *after* he died."

Antonio nodded. "Ms. Chandler has not been entirely truthful on several fronts. It seems she stayed at the Brookview Inn for two nights during last year's holiday season."

Tricia felt her mouth drop as she petted her cat. But then she remembered something else. "That makes sense. The other day when I had lunch with Becca at the Brookview, Cindy at the front desk said 'Welcome back, ladies.' It wouldn't have occurred to me that Becca had been there before—especially as she told me she was looking forward to visiting the inn for the first time."

"Why would she tell so many lies?" Angelica asked.

Tricia felt a slow burn rise up her neck. "Who knows? Maybe Marshall didn't want her to be seen coming out of his apartment."

"Do you think they were hooking up?" Angelica asked.

"At this point, I wouldn't put anything past Marshall," Tricia said bitterly. "But it also kind of puts the whole revenge plot to rest."

"What do you mean?" Antonio asked.

"The idea behind the Witness Protection Program is that the person entering it risks his—or her—life by contacting people from their past. Marshall contacted Becca after her accident and they kept in touch for years. Despite that, no one came after Marshall until last week. That tells me no one was watching Becca all that closely—especially if she had met Marshall right here in Stoneham last year."

"But from what you said, Becca was in the village at least a day before she visited you," Angelica said. "Could she have been in the area for a day or so before Marshall was killed, and if so, why?"

"Would you feel comfortable asking Ms. Chandler?" Antonio asked. "Or do you think it's too dangerous?"

That he was concerned for her safety warmed Tricia's heart. "I don't know," she answered honestly. "I've been iffy when it came to trusting Becca. Now I feel absolutely terrified. We can't let Ginny practice with her anymore."

"As she has already agreed to pick up Sofia, I think she is safe tonight, but I will tell her of our conversation as soon as I see her this evening."

"The less we truck with that woman, the better," Angelica agreed. "We should go straight to Chief Baker and report all these anomalies."

"I'm not so sure," Tricia said.

"That would steal my scoop," Antonio said, sounding hurt.

Tricia couldn't help but smile. Ginny may have been right about Antonio's Clark Kent fixation. "We need more proof that Becca's up to something nefarious before we talk to the chief."

"And what about Louise Jameson being arrested for her husband's death?" Angelica asked.

"She was released this morning after posting bail," Antonio reported. "I went to her studio to speak with her, but her assistant said the studio would be closed for the foreseeable future."

"And I still don't have my proofs," Tricia muttered.

"It still doesn't make sense to me that she was arrested at all," Angelica said. "Okay, I can see she might *want* to kill her husband—he wasn't a very nice man. But Marshall? What for? Apparently, he wanted *her* and she rejected *him*. Where's the motive?"

"Then it seems more likely Ms. Chandler would have killed Marshall," Antonio said.

"I'm still not clear on what her motive could be," Angelica said.

"Lots of times there really *is* no motive," Tricia pointed out. "I mean, didn't we just go through that with Susan Morris's murder? It was a crime of passion—or at least unreasonable anger."

Angelica looked pensive. "When Ginny suggested we talk and compare notes, I was pretty sure we'd come to some kind of consensus. Now I feel confused and more than a little frightened," Angelica admitted.

"I do not think you should be alone the next time you speak to Ms. Chandler," Antonio told Tricia. "Please promise me you will call me to escort you should you confront her."

"She's already taken a dislike to you," Tricia pointed out. "It seems to me that I shouldn't talk to her in person from now on. When I do, I'll make sure it's by phone."

"That makes me feel a little better—but not by much," Angelica remarked.

"I'd like to speak to both Becca *and* Louise. I think they're both credible suspects for masterminding at least one murder each," Tricia said.

"Are you sure you don't want to talk about all this to Chief Baker?" Angelica asked.

Tricia shook her head. "I'm keeping my distance from him until I have something concrete to report. You know he always questions my motives. It's the prime reason we broke up in the first place."

Angelica nodded and her bottom lip quivered once again. "I . . . I'm so sorry I bit your head off on Saturday. I was—"

Tricia held up a hand. "We never have to speak of it again. We're sisters and no one and nothing can come between us again." She waited, half afraid her sister might not agree.

Angelica nodded. "Never again."

A surge of affection for her sister rushed through Tricia, but all too soon it faded. She glanced at Antonio. "Today was your deadline to put the next issue to bed. Did you print anything about Marshall?"

Antonio shook his head. "My instinct is to wait. We are printing a death notice, but we don't yet have the full story behind Marshall Cambridge's life. What about your promise to Ms. Chandler?"

"I did my duty to her. I asked you not to delve into Marshall's past. If you choose to pursue the story, I can't stop you."

"Yes, but now *you* are invested in trying to discover the truth," Antonio pointed out.

Tricia nodded, albeit reluctantly. "I have more information than I had on Saturday morning. I no longer feel a loyalty to that promise, to Becca—and sadly, even to Marshall. It's a bitter pill to swallow when you've been lied to on multiple fronts."

"I am sorry," Antonio apologized.

"What are you going to do next?" Angelica asked.

Tricia sighed. "I want to speak to Louise Jameson, and fairly soon."

"Good luck pinning Mrs. Jameson down," Antonio said.

Tricia pursed her lips. "I'm going to call her now." She pulled out her cell phone and tapped Louise's name on her contacts list. The phone rang and rang, only to be picked up by voice mail. She decided to leave a message.

"This is Tricia Miles. I'd like to speak to Ms. Jameson about the proofs from my photo shoot last Thursday. I haven't yet received them." She gave her e-mail address. "I might also be able to help her with her current legal problem. Please have her call me." She left both her cell and landline numbers and ended the call.

"Do you really think she'll contact you?" Angelica asked.

"There's not much else I can do at this point. If she's gone into hiding—and who could blame her?—she may even have left the village, although I'm sure law enforcement has told her how far she can go without being considered a flight risk."

"Her bail was set at a hundred thousand dollars," Antonio said.

"Maybe she has more financial latitude than you imagined," Angelica suggested.

"Maybe. Or maybe her attorney helped her arrange bail. Either way, I don't suppose it matters. She's out of the pokey—at least for now."

"Was that a bluff—your telling her you could help with her legal problem?"

"Partly."

"What will you tell her?"

"Right now? I have no idea."

THIRTY-TWO

Tricia decided to wear her new sequined sneakers to Angelica's that evening for happy hour and dinner. They didn't have as much support as she would have liked, but they *did* look cute and gave her an emotional boost. After what she'd endured the previous few days, she really needed that.

No mention was made of Marshall, Becca, or Louise, and Tricia was perfectly fine with that. Instead, Angelica spoke of other things.

"Earlier today, I paid a visit to the NR Realty office. You were right. Karen did a wonderful job decorating her office, but it made the rest of the place look like the DMV."

"What are you going to do about it?"

"Paint, for one thing. New carpet. Buy some art for the walls and add some separators so that the staff has at least some privacy. And I think I might get a white-noise generator so that conversations won't be echoing around the room. I'm sure the clients would appreciate that as well."

"Does Karen know you're Nigela?"

"I don't know. I went as myself, saying I was asked to have a look and suggest solutions."

"What did Karen think about the proposed changes?"

"She seemed okay with it. One of the agents came in and when she heard why I was there, was thrilled."

"Then you'll have more happy employees."

"I'm afraid they haven't been very happy. The agent told me she'd been thinking of going to work for a realty office in Milford. She's done well for the company. I would have hated to lose her over something as mundane as crappy office décor."

"How soon can the changes be implemented?" Tricia asked, enjoying her first martini in three days.

"I've already contacted the design firm that worked on the Brookview. They're going to give me some preliminary sketches and cost estimates before the end of the week."

"That's great."

Angelica looked down at her untouched drink. "I feel bad about what happened on Saturday—" she began.

"Didn't I say we never had to mention it again?"

"Yes, but . . . I can't believe I treated you so poorly. That's not me—or at least, that's not who I ever want to be again."

"Let's drop it," Tricia said, exasperated.

"No," Angelica insisted. "We *need* to talk about it."

"You wanted to protect Antonio. But he's a grown man. He doesn't need his mama to run interference for him. If he's going to be a journalist, he needs to grow a thicker skin."

Angelica nodded. "Exactly. And we both know that the *Stoneham Weekly News* isn't ever likely to print any earth-shattering news, but he would like to have a little fun with it."

"I thought it was funny the way Ginny described it as an 'ad rag.'"

Angelica shrugged. "I don't suppose it'll ever be much more than that. But Antonio can play journalist while he oversees the bulk of the NR Associates portfolio. And without the Brookview Inn to worry about, he should have more time to spend with his family in the future."

"Including you?"

"Exactly."

Tricia wasn't about to ask where she landed in that family

dynamic. She decided to change the subject. "So, what treat have you concocted for our supper?"

"Nothing fancy, I'm afraid. Good old comfort food. Tommy made us a chicken pot pie and provided a salad and some rolls."

"I'm all for comfort food," Tricia said, because, as it was, she was sure she'd feel more than a little discomfort the next time she spoke with Becca Chandler, and she wondered if she'd even have an opportunity to talk to Louise Jameson.

Discomfort was putting it mildly. But she also felt compelled to find out the truth about the relationship each woman had had with Marshall, because it was now obvious to her that the man had loved both of those women more than he'd loved her. That he found them inaccessible and had decided to settle for her was even more demeaning.

One thing was for certain, Tricia no longer had any warm feelings for the stranger she'd known as Marshall Cambridge.

Tricia awoke early on Tuesday morning. It had been two weeks since Marshall's death. She wasn't sure why she was still counting the days, but she probably would do so until whoever had planned his death was brought to justice.

Was it justice he deserved? He'd avoided the scales of justice—saving his own neck—when he'd testified against Martin Bailey. Was it karma that had brought him down?

Tricia didn't really believe in karma, although sometimes she wished she did.

Tricia took off on her usual early-morning walk on that brisk October morning and meandered the streets of the village until she found herself on Cedar Avenue. Like Main Street, it had a back alley running parallel to it. She decided to hike down the alley to see if there were signs of life behind the Louise Jameson Photography Studio. Some of the houses had small parking pads, and the photography studio was one of them. A late-model Audi was parked there.

Although it wasn't even eight o'clock, Tricia approached

the building and knocked on the door. When no one answered after thirty seconds, she knocked again. And after another thirty seconds . . .

The curtain on the window next to the door moved. Tricia waved to the building's occupant. For all she knew, it might have been Louise's assistant, Kristin. The curtain was pulled back once more. Tricia pondered knocking a fourth time, when she heard the sound of a chain being drawn back and the dead bolt being thrown before the door was wrenched open.

"Boy, you don't give up easily, do you?" a scowling Louise accused.

"Can we talk?" Tricia asked cautiously.

Louise turned away. She didn't slam the door in Tricia's face, so Tricia entered the small dated kitchen, which looked like it hadn't been updated since the 1940s, and smelled like fresh-brewed coffee. Louise was clad in a flowing silk robe decorated in large fuchsia flowers. Her hair hung around her shoulders and looked like it could use a good brushing. It was her haunted eyes that struck Tricia. She looked like a woman in mourning, but was it for Marshall or Mark?

"What is it you want—besides your proofs?" Louise asked as she grabbed a mug from the counter, cupping it with both hands.

"Then you got my message."

"Yeah. What kind of help can you offer me with my 'legal problems,' or was that just a line to get me to talk to you?"

"On paper, you make a good suspect for your husband's death—but for Marshall? I don't think so."

Louise leaned against the old-fashioned counter. "And why's that?"

"Because you weren't a spurned lover. If anyone was spurned, it was Marshall."

"Any other theories?"

"I suppose Mark could have been responsible for Marshall's death. But I also got the feeling he didn't like to get his hands dirty."

"You've got that right."

"He could have hired Joshua Greenwell, the man suspected of being the hit-and-run driver who killed Marshall."

"But Mark didn't even know about Marshall. If he had, he would have used it against me."

"Are you sure he didn't? Or has your work always been copyrighted Mark Jameson Enterprises?"

"It has since the day after we returned from our honeymoon," Louise said bitterly.

So, Tricia was at least right on that account.

"And what about now? Now that Mark's dead, do you *own* Mark Jameson Enterprises?"

"It's complicated—just like everything Mark set his mind to. It's all so convoluted I'm not even sure I can access the funds to pay my lawyer's retainer—and it's a whopper."

"Has law enforcement decided the copyright problem was the motive you might have had for killing Mark?"

"Partially." She gave a mirthless laugh. "It turns out that while I was cheating on Mark, he was cheating on me."

Tricia hadn't considered that scenario. "Did you know?"

"Hell, no! But I haven't been back to the house since he died. I have no interest in ever again sleeping in our former marital bed." She looked around the shabby kitchen, but it wasn't with disdain. "I've been working on getting the apartment over the shop in shape to sublet. I had hoped to lease it after the holidays. Instead, I might just stay here and put the house up for sale. If I can get decent money for it, I'd at least be able to pay my legal bills."

Tricia eyed the shabby space. Old though it might be, it was not decrepit. Instead, it oozed vintage charm, much like the robe Louise wore. It wouldn't be a horrible place if she had to downsize her life.

"I suppose the chief believes you had a key to Marshall's storage unit."

"I didn't even know he *had* one. And if I did, and if I murdered my husband, why would I stash his body at the storage facility? I had a unit there for about six months before I moved my equipment into this place. I'd been using our garage, which wasn't at all comfortable for me or my clients during the winter and the worst of summer. And Mark was sick of parking his car in the driveway. He *let* me rent this place."

Magnanimous of him, Tricia thought.

"How did Baker find out about you and Marshall?" Tricia asked.

"I don't think he had a clue until after I was arrested."

Yes. When it came to murder, the spouse was always first on the list of suspects.

"You said you might be able to help me with my legal problems," Louise reminded Tricia.

Tricia chose her words carefully. "I tend to believe you more than I believe Marshall's ex-wife. I've caught her in a couple of lies."

"I sure hope you'll make that clear to Chief Baker *and* the Hillsborough County district attorney's office," Louise declared.

"Under ordinary circumstances, I'd speak with Chief Baker, but now isn't a good time. Although it does occur to me that I do know someone else who might get me an in with the DA's office."

"But what can you tell them? That you have a gut instinct I'm not a killer?"

"That they ought to look a little harder to find a viable suspect. I've got to think your lawyer thinks the charges are trumped up."

"He does. But that doesn't stop crooked cops and prosecutors from railroading people to prison."

"Chief Baker has never struck me as a crooked cop. In a hurry to make an arrest, maybe; but he's also admitted mistakes when he's made them." Like the many times he'd suspected Tricia of being a criminal only to have to eat crow.

"I'd appreciate anything you can do on my behalf," Louise said sincerely. "And I'll make sure to send your proofs today. I may not be taking on new clients right now, but I sure need to collect money for those jobs that're still in the pipeline. It might be all I have to live on until I can get a judge to give me control of my share of our assets."

"My sister will be very glad to hear that. She's eager to have prints made of the family."

Louise nodded.

Tricia pitied the poor woman. New Hampshire was not a community-property state. If Mark had tied up Louise's photography copyrights, what other nasty little surprises was she going to find out once she'd hired an accountant to try and unravel the mess?

Right then, Tricia felt pretty good about being a single woman who controlled her own destiny.

She was pretty sure she'd never marry again. That said, she wasn't about to commit to saying never. One never knew what the future held.

THIRTY-THREE

Tricia returned to Haven't Got a Clue in plenty of time before opening. To her surprise, Pixie had already arrived, had set up the beverage station for the day, and was busy with the lamb's-wool duster. "I figured with Mr. E gone, you might need me more than ever," she said sadly.

Tricia nodded. "We'll just have to make out as best we can. I can call a temp agency to see if they can send someone to help me on the weekends, at least until we can find someone permanent. I know how much you love working at the day spa on Saturdays and spending your Sundays with Fred."

"I wouldn't want to have to give either of them up—but I could do it until we find someone."

"Thank you," Tricia said. Of course, she could run the store on her own . . . but not during the Christmas rush, which was only weeks away.

Tricia's phone pinged. She pulled it from her jacket pocket and looked at the name of the person who sent the message: Becca. She ignored it. "I'm going to hang up my coat, then pour myself a cup of coffee. Would you join me?"

Pixie laughed. "Is there room for both of us in one mug?"

Tricia rolled her eyes. "Very funny."

"Made you smile."

"Only a little," Tricia admitted.

By the time she returned to grab a cup at the beverage station, the door to the shop opened and Mr. Everett stepped inside, his shoulders drooping, looking like he'd lost his best friend.

"Mr. Everett. We didn't expect to see you here today," Tricia said.

Pixie joined Tricia as Mr. Everett stepped forward. "Good morning. I . . . that is, Grace and I spoke to Ginny yesterday afternoon. It was rather an embarrassing conversation."

And Tricia had no doubt he wasn't about to reveal the gist of that discussion. She waited for him to continue.

"Ginny assured us that nothing will ever come between us that we can't discuss. She promised we would always be in Sofia's life."

Tricia hadn't been wrong about that, either. Still, she didn't comment.

Mr. Everett lowered his gaze to the floor and fiddled with the buttons on his coat. "I was wondering if I might rescind my resignation. I would truly miss working for you, Ms. Miles, and with Pixie."

Instead of answering, Tricia walked over to the display case and retrieved the envelope Mr. Everett had given her the day before. She returned to the beverage station and handed the envelope to him. "I would be very pleased to have you back with us. You're an integral part of Haven't Got a Clue."

"That's right," Pixie chimed in. "We'd miss you terribly."

Mr. Everett dared to look up and there were tears in his eyes. He wasn't one for great shows of affection, so Tricia restrained herself from hugging him.

"Why don't you hang up your coat and we'll all gather in the reader's nook for our first cup of coffee of the day."

"That sounds like a fine idea," Mr. Everett agreed.

As he started for the back of the store, Pixie gave Tricia a big toothy grin and a thumbs-up.

Tricia's phone pinged. She took it out, glanced at the screen to see Becca had texted her, and once again ignored it. This time Pixie didn't comment. Back in her pocket went the phone.

"Well, let's see what kind of trouble we can get into today," Tricia said with a smile.

Tuesdays were always the slowest day of the week for retail, or at least it seemed so to Tricia, but that day, with sunny skies and the leaves practically shimmering, the stiff breeze blew in a lot of customers looking to add to their book collections or buying early holiday gifts. Tricia and her staff were kept busy making recommendations, restocking the shelves, and grinning until their cheeks ached. Pixie and Mr. Everett went to lunch at Booked for Lunch, and Tricia joined Angelica there after they returned. She filled her sister in on the conversation she'd had with Louise—and Mr. Everett's return—before returning for the final few hours of the day.

Her cell phone rang three times during the afternoon—each of the calls from Becca, which she ignored. But finally, when there was a lull in the store's foot traffic, it was with reluctance that Tricia retreated to her office, picked up her phone, and tapped Becca's number from her contacts list.

"What's going on?" Becca demanded without even saying hello. "Suddenly Ginny is ghosting me and you took hours to get back to me."

Tricia wasn't sure how to reply to that statement. Her mind whirled before she answered. "I'm a bit concerned that you haven't been totally honest with me about certain things."

"Such as what?" Becca asked.

"Well, for one thing, that you arrived in Stoneham before Gene died."

Becca didn't immediately reply. "Who says?"

"The pictures on your phone, for one. They were taken *after* Gene's death, but before you supposedly showed up in Stoneham."

"How do you know that?"

"I saw the flowers in them being planted the morning *after* he died."

"Oh."

"Is that all you have to say?"

"Gene was right. You're one sharp cookie."

The last thing Tricia wanted to be described as was a *cookie*.

"What else?" Becca asked.

"You implied that you'd never set foot in Stoneham before you arrived two weeks ago, but the receptionist at the Brookview recognized you when we went there for lunch. Antonio went back through the reservations and found you'd stayed at the inn for two nights last year over the holidays."

Becca sighed. "Okay, so I'd visited Gene back then. He stood me up to go to *your* Christmas dinner."

Yeah, one of the few times he'd attended Tricia's family affairs. "But he left that gathering early. It all makes sense now."

"It's not like we were sneaking around or anything," Becca said defensively.

"Then what do you call it?"

Again Becca sighed. "Okay, we *were* sneaking around."

"And what about Louise?"

"What about her?"

"I don't know about you, but I don't think she killed Gene."

"How about her husband?"

"If I'd been married to the jerk, *I* might have killed him. But for some reason, as much as she might have had motive, I don't think she did."

"Is that a decision made from proof or a gut feeling?"

"The latter," Tricia admitted.

"And what are you going to do about it?"

"Speak to a former sheriff's deputy."

"Former? And what can he do?"

"Probably nothing, but it seems awfully convenient that Louise was arrested for both murders when the Sheriff's Department seems to think Gene's death was a murder for hire."

"I thought Baker was in charge of the investigation," Becca said.

"Not when the man they think did the killing was found dead in another jurisdiction."

"How interesting," Becca said. "And you think one of Martin Bailey's friends or employees hired him?"

"I don't think so. If it was you who drew one of Bailey's associates to Gene, it most likely would have been the first time you spoke to him, let alone when you came to Stoneham last December."

"It was dangerous and stupid and I'm sorry I ever contacted him. Poor Gene might be alive today if I hadn't."

"But you did it anyway," Tricia said, and didn't soften her tone. "And why were you in the area the day he died?"

Becca sighed. "It was our wedding anniversary," she said, her voice filled with sadness. "I was lonely. I was unhappy. It was damned selfish of me, but I also thought I should try to talk him out of asking you to marry him."

"And why was that?"

"Because he didn't love you."

The words should have hurt, but they no longer held that kind of power.

"Were you hoping to get back together with him?" Tricia asked.

Becca let out a long breath. "Yeah. It was a stupid idea, but with Marty gone, and since we'd seen each other several times since my accident, I thought—hoped—we could make it work."

"And why do you want to move here to Stoneham, or was that just a passing fancy?"

"No, I'd kind of like to stay here. Not in that apartment on Main Street—it's not at all my taste. The lease runs out in a few months. I might stay until it does and if I like the area, look for something more to my liking. I saw a real estate office farther down on Main Street. Can you recommend it?"

"Yes. The woman in charge is Karen Johnson, but you could work with any of the agents. They're all good." Tricia still had more questions. "What about that storage unit? Have you had a chance to go through it?"

"To tell you the truth, I've been avoiding it. I really should go through it so I won't have to pay the rent on it for November. What gets me is that I never saw that key on the floor of

Gene's bedroom. I'd been walking through it for days. It didn't just fall from the sky."

"Do you think it was planted?"

"I don't know. But there are an awful lot of fishy things going on, so why not? His keys were in law enforcement's hands for a day or so after his death. Before they were given to me."

"But you had a key to his apartment, otherwise you wouldn't have canceled your reservation at the Sheer Comfort Inn so quickly."

"Yeah, I had a key."

"Gene gave it to you?"

"I . . . sort of copied it when I was here for Christmas last year."

So, she'd had her sights on a reconciliation even back then. And when Marshall had left Tricia's holiday celebration, had he gone back to his apartment to bed Becca?

Tricia didn't want to know. She thought of what Becca had told her just moments before.

"You can't possibly think Deputy Kirby or Chief Baker planted those keys in Marshall's apartment."

"Gene's apartment," Becca clarified. "Why not? Maybe one of them was hoping to pin it on me."

"But Kirby dropped out of the investigation pretty quickly."

"Then maybe it was *your* Chief Baker."

He wasn't Tricia's chief. Still, the suggestion made Tricia feel uncomfortable.

There was no way Baker could have known Marshall intended to ask Tricia to marry him. It had been a shock to her. Becca and Ava knew his intentions, but Marshall wasn't close to anyone else in the village. What if Baker had seen Marshall as an impediment to him getting back together with Tricia? Could he have decided to eliminate his rival?

Tricia gave herself a shake. The whole idea was absurd. Except . . . Larry Harvick said everyone in the Sheriff's Department knew Joshua Greenwell, which meant Baker did, too. Would he have known the brick-throwing motorcyclist, too?

Greenwell's body had been found in Rindge. Was Baker the person she knew who'd grown up there?

"Hey, are you still there?" Becca asked.

"Yeah. I was just thinking about—" But did she want to say the words aloud? Could Grant Baker have been responsible for Marshall's death? And another four people's as well?

No, that wasn't possible. It *couldn't* be possible. Grant Baker was a good cop. Tricia had never seen him diverge from the straight and narrow. Not ever.

"I . . . I'll have to get back to you later," Tricia told Becca.

"You've just figured out who had Gene killed, didn't you?"

"I don't know. I have my suspicions. I . . . I need to do some research. I'll get back to you."

"Tricia, wait!"

But Tricia ended the call. Setting the phone aside, she tapped the computer's keyboard to awaken it and brought up a new browser window. She Googled Baker's name and came up with a number of entries. She scrolled through each one, skimming the text until she found what she wanted. Someone had scanned and uploaded a copy of the article Russ Smith had written when Baker had taken the job of Stoneham police chief. One sentence fragment immediately jumped out at her: *Baker, originally from Rindge, Cheshire County . . .*

Tricia sat back in her chair, her stomach doing a somersault.

Her phone rang. She glanced at the screen and saw it was Becca calling back. She ignored it and focused her attention on what she thought she knew.

No. No. No! It just didn't make sense. Why would a man who'd dedicated his life to the law have made such a dramatic and sinister change of heart?

Because of you, Tricia's inner voice taunted.

That didn't make sense. She'd made it clear to Baker—many, *many* times—that there was no future for them.

But just weeks before, he'd jilted his fiancée and then abruptly asked Tricia to marry him.

She sat back in her chair to ponder everything she knew about Marshall's death.

He'd been killed by a third party. That someone had apparently also targeted Tricia, but nothing had come of that. Still, her family had been attacked, too, in the form of arson, only for the alleged perpetrator to be found dead a few days later—and in an area of the state Grant Baker knew well.

But as Tricia thought about it, she realized she'd been targeted again when the guy on the motorcycle tossed a brick through her shop window. She'd been able to give the first few letters of his license plate and the next thing you know he and his accomplice had ended up dead on the side of the highway. How convenient was that for whoever hired them?

What didn't make sense was Mark Jameson's death. Had he been killed as an excuse to frame Louise Jameson for Marshall's death? Was the idea behind that crime that Jameson found out about Louise's affair with Marshall, they argued, and she killed him either in a fit of rage or in self-defense?

Becca had a key to Marshall's apartment, and it was days later she'd been given Marshall's personal effects—including his set of keys to his home and business. What if copies of them had been made? What if someone—oh, the heck with it, Tricia decided to just pin the crime on Baker—had gone back to the apartment to plant the key to the lock on Marshall's storage unit to make sure Becca would find it? Her movements had been pretty easy to follow. She took most of her meals at the Bookshelf Diner. If Baker had staked her out, he could have easily followed her movements.

It could *have happened that way*, Tricia told herself.

And all because Baker wanted her?

She kept rejecting him. Might that cause him to finally turn on her?

A shiver ran through her. *Uh-oh.*

Tricia's phone pinged. Again, it was Becca. *Tricia, don't ignore me!*

She did.

Tricia glanced at the time at the bottom-right of her computer screen. She still had an hour before all the shops on Main Street closed their doors for the day. She knew of only one person who might give credence to her theory, not that she was going to spill what she thought she knew. But this someone might have the key as to why Grant Baker would abandon his principles.

That person was Larry Harvick.

THIRTY-FOUR

Tricia didn't even bother putting on her coat. She scooted past Pixie and Mr. Everett and practically ran down Main Street toward the Bee's Knees. Luckily for her, the shop was empty and Eileen and her husband were busy restocking the shelves for the next day's customers.

"Hi, Tricia. What's up?" Larry Harvick called, hefting a box filled with jars of honey.

"I was wondering if you had a few minutes to speak to me."

"What about?"

Tricia glanced at Eileen, who immediately got the hint.

"Uh, I'll go open those boxes of candles. Be back in a minute." She left the shop, disappearing behind the door marked PRIVATE.

Harvick set the box down and straightened. "So?"

"The other day you made a comment that really stuck in my mind."

"What was that?"

"About Grant Baker's eyes. You called them 'cold.'"

Harvick nodded. "You mean you never noticed?"

"No," she answered honestly. "I got the feeling you didn't really like him and I wondered why."

"Whether I like him or not is immaterial."

"I assume you were judging him personally and not his work ethic."

"Yeah. I never liked the guy. I thought he had a mean streak."

"What do you mean?"

"He was always a little rough with the suspects when making arrests. He doesn't do much of that himself these days, I guess, what with being the *chief* and all."

Tricia had never known Baker to be physically abusive. He hadn't been a particularly generous lover, but they had enjoyed some pleasant intimate moments. When he wasn't suspecting her of murder, they'd been cozy together plenty of times. Was that something he could turn on and off like a switch?

"Did you think he was an honest cop?"

"You mean did I think he'd take a bribe or something?"

"Not exactly."

"What is it you want me to say?" Harvick asked.

Tricia chewed her lower lip and contemplated just blurting out her suspicions, but the truth was she had absolutely nothing in the way of proof to back up what she was thinking. A gut feeling wasn't enough to slander someone who was respected in the community.

"I understand you've undergone a recent loss," Harvick said, changing the subject.

Tricia nodded.

"And that someone close to you lost her home to arson."

Again Tricia nodded. News sure got around.

"And just the other day you had your shop window destroyed. I'd say you are either having a bad string of luck . . . or someone is out to get you."

Tricia stood rock still, her nails digging into the palms of both hands.

"Do you think Baker is behind these acts of violence?" Harvick asked.

"Personally?" she asked, her voice squeaking.

Harvick nodded.

Tricia found it hard to meet the former deputy's gaze. "I know he didn't throw that rock through my window. I caught a partial license plate number on the guy's bike. They found the man and his accomplice dead in a gully off the highway. It looked like they'd been forced off the road."

"And the guy who allegedly killed your boyfriend was found shot in the woods near Rindge," Harvick said, his voice neutral.

"Yes," Tricia whispered. "The chief grew up in that area. He knows it well. And Joshua Greenwell was shot with a Glock. Marshall, my"—she hesitated—"boyfriend, his Glock went missing."

Harvick let out a breath, crossed his arms over his chest, and gave her a long, hard look. "What do you intend to do about all this?"

"I . . . I don't know."

"If you want my advice, you should consult an attorney. And whatever you do, don't allow yourself to be alone with a man you suspect of murder."

"I didn't say I suspect Chief Baker of murder."

"No. You didn't have to."

His words sent a chill through Tricia.

Until then, she hadn't felt afraid.

The wind had picked up and it felt like Tricia had to slog up the street to get back to her store—or was it that she was so filled with dread that it just seemed that way?

No customers had arrived during her short visit down the road. Pixie was behind the cash desk and Mr. Everett was tidying up the reader's nook when she pushed through the door. The little bell over it rang cheerfully, but at that moment she found the sound resoundingly irritating.

"Are you okay?" Pixie asked.

"What do you mean?"

"You look like you've seen a ghost."

Tricia gave a shudder and waved her hand dismissively. "It was pretty cold out there. I should have worn a coat."

Mr. Everett came forward. "Would you like me to make you some cocoa? That would warm you up fast."

"No, thank you, but it's kind of you to offer."

"Did your errand go well?" Pixie asked.

"Fine," Tricia answered succinctly.

The three of them looked at one another for a long moment.

"Um, I need to make a phone call. I'll just head down to the office to make it and be right back."

"Sure," Pixie said, giving Mr. Everett a curious look.

Tricia gave them a smile—definitely forced—and hurried to her office. She'd never bothered to add her attorney's number to the contacts list on her cell phone, so she had to look it up. But when she made her call, the phone rang and rang until voice mail kicked in. "You have reached the office of Roger Livingston. Our hours of operation are—"

Tricia listened and then tapped the end call icon, frowning as she glanced at the clock. Sure enough, it was well after five o'clock. Why couldn't lawyers keep the same hours as shopkeepers? But then, they arrived at work earlier. Luckily, Tricia was an early riser, and she would call the lawyer's office first thing in the morning.

But morning was a long, long way off.

Tricia heaved a sigh, feeling overwhelmed. Somehow, she had to get through the next fourteen hours. To do that, she needed to isolate herself. To stay safe. And that meant she needed to lie low and protect Angelica, too.

Tricia picked up the phone and called her sister.

"Where are you?" Angelica asked.

"Home." She crossed her fingers as though to negate the lie she was about to tell. "I'm sorry, but I won't be coming over this evening. My stomach is upset." Well, that wasn't far from the truth. Her stomach had been tied in knots ever since she'd spoken to Larry Harvick.

"Would you like me to come over and sit with you?"

"Oh, no. I don't want you to climb stairs any more than you have to. By this time of the day, your foot is usually swollen."

"Yes, but I can put my feet up just as easily in your apartment as in mine."

"I don't think so. I'm just going to curl up with a good book and maybe open a can of soup later—if I feel up to it," she added for effect.

"Well, if you say so," Angelica said sadly. "I've already been alone two evenings in the last week. I don't want it to become a habit."

"Hopefully I'll feel better tomorrow and we can go back to our usual routine."

"Okay," Angelica said reluctantly. "Feel better."

"I'll talk to you tomorrow."

"Yes, call me in the morning to let me know how you are."

"I will. Bye now."

"Bye."

Tricia hung up the phone.

The sky would soon be darkening. Her first concern was to secure her store and make sure her employees were safe. She decided to close the shop and send Pixie and Mr. Everett home. She'd decide how to proceed after speaking with her attorney in the morning.

Tricia arrived back in the shop and, as hoped, found no customers. "Let's call it a day," she said, flashing a smile.

"But we've still got another forty-five minutes to go," Pixie protested.

"It doesn't look like we'll be getting any more customers—"

But before she could finish the sentence, the door opened and a man and woman entered. "Oh, good, you're still open," the woman said.

Pixie took care of them while Tricia stood behind the counter and fidgeted, her gaze glued to the clock.

The couple stayed until the bitter end, pleasing Pixie with their more-than-a-hundred-dollar sale. Once they were on their way, Tricia pulled down the front display window's blind. "That's it for today."

Pixie gave Mr. Everett yet another curious look, but she went to the back of the shop, grabbed their coats, and the pair headed out the door.

"See you tomorrow," Tricia called as she locked up. A shiver ran up her spine as she darkened the lights. She'd need to do the same in her apartment. It was then she wished she'd gone for light-darkening shades on the second floor of her home, and not just in her bedroom suite.

With the shop secure, Tricia locked the door leading to her apartment, and she and Miss Marple headed up the stairs. Tricia threw the dead bolt behind her, turned, leaned against the door, and heaved a sigh of relief. Next up, she closed the curtains. She waited until that was done before turning on her lights.

Tricia decided against making a drink or pouring herself a glass of wine. She was probably being paranoid, but she wanted her wits about her . . . just in case. Instead, she made herself a mug of hot chocolate and was rummaging around in the cupboard looking for something other than cat food for her dinner, when her cell phone rang. Tricia glanced at the screen and saw it was Grant Baker calling. No way did she want to speak to the man she suspected of being responsible for the deaths of five people.

She ignored it. Sure, she always had an excuse she could use for not answering. She'd left the phone in her purse and didn't hear the ringtone because it was in another room. It was on charge down in the shop. But Baker was well aware of her cell phone habits. He knew she kept it nearby in case Angelica would call or text.

The phone pinged.

It was Baker.

I see your lights are on. No dinner with Angelica tonight?
Tricia's blood ran cold.

Want to share a sub or a pizza?
No! She didn't.

Why was he even contacting her? She'd made it clear—way *too* many times—that she wasn't interested.

Tricia had been stalked before by Russ Smith. That Stoneham's chief of police now seemed obsessed with her was even more frightening. Where was she supposed to go for help? And what if she mentioned what she suspected to other law enforcement agents? How many bad cops had been protected from investigation, let alone prosecution, because of the Blue Code of Honor?

Before Stoneham had hired its own police force, they'd been under the jurisdiction of the Hillsborough County Sheriff's Department. Sheriff Adams had been reelected and the two times the women had met they'd clashed. Tricia doubted the sheriff would give her theories a hearing, let alone act on them. And Baker had been one of her most-trusted deputies. No, she didn't think she could count on any help from the Sheriff's Department.

What about Deputy Marshal Kirby? Becca said that the man had washed his hands of investigating Marshall's death. He'd seemed to be a dedicated agent of the federal government. How willing—or able—would he be to get involved in a local investigation?

The phone pinged again.

TRICIA ARE YOU THERE?

The fact that the message had now been typed in all caps was all the more frightening.

Tricia wasn't sure what to do, so she paced. Not in the living room. Yes, the drapes were drawn, but she wasn't willing to cast even the hint of a shadow against them.

Instead, she climbed the stairs to her bedroom suite, leaving it in darkness as she crept toward the windows that overlooked Main Street. She peeked out the side of one of them, but the shadows between the streetlamps would give excellent cover to anyone who had a bead on her building.

She couldn't call 911 to report her fears because Baker was likely to show up to personally investigate.

The locks were formidable, and the barrier to the back alley had been fortified after the break-in the previous month, but her shop's front door was glass, and just as vulnerable as the display window the brick-wielding biker had breached.

Tricia descended the stairs to the second floor of the building and continued to pace. Miss Marple jumped up onto one of the kitchen island stools to watch her go to and fro between the stove, refrigerator, and sink.

Tricia's phone pinged again.

TRICIA WHY AREN'T YOU ANSWERING ME? Baker's text demanded.

Tricia paced faster.

"*Yow!*" Miss Marple said, as though expecting an explanation for Tricia's odd behavior.

"I don't know what to do," Tricia told her cat.

Seconds later the security alarm down in the store went off. Tricia looked around her home, but there was nothing she could use as a weapon. And then her gaze caught the block of oak that housed her kitchen's knife collection. She could use any one of them as protection, but she knew that Baker possessed far more physical strength than she did. Odds were he might be able to turn such a tool against her.

As abruptly as it came on, the alarm went silent.

When they'd parted, Baker had given Tricia back her key—or at least a key. He'd made duplicates of Marshall's keys. Why hadn't she suspected he had one or more of hers as well? And he knew how to operate the shop's security system. He'd armed and disarmed it many times during the times they'd been together.

Tricia stood rock still. What should she do now?

"Tricia!"

It was Baker's muffled voice coming from the shop below.

"Come down here, will you? I need to speak to you."

Harvick's warning came to mind: "*Whatever you do, don't allow yourself to be alone with a man you suspect of murder.*"

Tricia crept to the door of her apartment, testing the handle to make sure it was locked. She checked the dead bolt as well.

"What do you want?" she called.

"To talk. I promise—that's all I want to do."

"I'm sorry," Tricia hollered, "but I no longer trust you."

The truth was, the seed of doubt was planted days before when Harvick mentioned Baker's cold green eyes.

"I don't blame you. But I swear, I only want to talk—to explain."

Tricia bit her lip. Several years ago, she would have trusted the man with her life. Now she suspected him of taking *five* other lives.

Tricia thought back to her time with Baker. They had made love together. She had cried on his shoulder—and more than once. He had brought her flowers, her favorite pizza, and wine. Could she trust him one last time?

Against her better judgment, Tricia pulled back the bolt, turned the handle's lock, and opened the door a crack. She looked down the lighted stairwell, which had been plunged into darkness not too long before, and saw Baker standing at the bottom. He was out of uniform, wearing jeans, a sweater, and a light jacket, still looking impeccable.

"Come on," he said, his voice soft and calm, and raised a hand, palm up in encouragement. Tricia took a step forward, but quickly closed the door behind her to keep Miss Marple in the apartment. She had no idea what she was walking into, but felt the need to protect her cat from harm.

Why was she being so cavalier with her own life?

Tricia advanced another few steps, pausing halfway down. "Start talking," she said.

"I saw you go into the Bee's Knees earlier."

Stalking! her mind screamed. She backed up a step.

"You spoke to Larry Harvick. I get it. You figured everything out and you needed a sounding board," Baker said.

Tricia said nothing, afraid to even move. If she had to, she could scramble back into the apartment and slam the door. But Baker was in good physical shape. He could probably kick the door in. She could barricade herself in her bedroom suite—and call who? If she called 911, would the Stoneham police force act against their leader?

Baker shook his head and leaned against the wall. His jacket pocket caught on the banister and Tricia saw the open holster and the gun that rested inside it. She could tell it wasn't his service weapon. She'd watched him clean it how many times?

Marshall's gun had gone missing. Joshua Greenwell had been shot with a Glock. Was it Marshall's gun in that holster?

Baker laughed mirthlessly. "I shouldn't have underestimated you. You were always one step ahead of me, my love."

Tricia cringed at his last two words. She hadn't been his love for years. Standing stoically, she still said nothing. She didn't want to ask any questions. She decided to just listen.

He began again. "Everything went wrong, right from the moment you told me you wouldn't marry me," he said bitterly. "That idiot Greenwell was just supposed to *scare* Cambridge—not *kill* him."

"And why did he come after me?" Tricia demanded. "Did you want me frightened as well?"

"No!" Baker protested. "Not at all. When I learned he'd done that, I was so angry, I nearly killed him that night," Baker remarked. "But at least he didn't hit you, too."

"And why did he burn Antonio and Ginny's house nearly to the ground? Was that to spite me, too?"

Baker brandished a crooked smile. "That wasn't in the original plan," he admitted. "Josh was just supposed to scare them, too. But he got carried away. That's when I knew I had to take him out."

Tricia cringed. *Take him out?* "How did you justify that?"

"The guy got high on hurting people. That wasn't what I paid him for. He became a liability."

"So you killed him and buried him in a shallow grave in the woods near Rindge."

Baker's expression darkened. "I hadn't planned on some hiker's dog digging up the bastard."

Although she'd suspected as much, it took a few moments for Tricia to digest his murder confession. "And the biker and his girlfriend?"

Baker's frown deepened. "You weren't supposed to see the motorcycle's license plate. Once it was part of the official documentation, Tyler and his girlfriend had to be silenced as well. They were just petty thugs for hire," he said contemptuously, as though the couple had had no people in their lives who had loved and would miss them. Okay, they weren't the cream of society and should have languished in jail for their misdeeds, but they didn't deserve to die for such a petty crime, either.

"And what about Mark Jameson? What offense did he incur that warranted your wrath?"

"During the course of my investigation, I found that his wife was cheating on him with *your* lover. That really pissed me off."

"So, you killed him as an act of revenge?" Tricia asked, confused.

Baker shook his head. "She was the perfect patsy. But more than that, that dentist bastard was determined to cheat you out of running for and winning the Chamber of Commerce presidency."

"What?" Tricia asked, appalled.

"You *should* have won last year. If that jerk Russ Smith hadn't thrown his hat in the ring, you would have won. The misogyny in this village is ridiculous."

Yes, and Baker had been guilty of it on more than one occasion, too, so his explanation rang hollow.

"What makes you think I want to be Chamber president?"

Baker frowned. "Come on, Tricia. Angelica set you up to be her successor. And you wanted it, too."

Maybe . . . but Tricia shook her head. "No, *you* wanted to plant suspicion on Louise Jameson as being in a love triangle. Yes, she did have an affair with Marshall, but she knew her financial security lay with her husband. She wasn't about to risk that for mere sex."

"It was a gamble I was willing to take."

Tricia shook her head. "Oh, Grant. How could you be so cruel? And why would you think I would want to be with anyone who could do such despicable things?"

"I'm not despicable . . . or at least I wasn't until the past few weeks. I messed up, Tricia. I really did. I lost everything I ever stood for and believed because of you."

Tricia's ire grew exponentially. "You stupid, selfish man. Don't you dare blame your weakness on me. Whatever choices you've made, they weren't based on my input."

Before he could retort, Baker's head turned sharply, and he looked toward the front of the store.

"Tricia?" Angelica called.

Baker's hand flew to the gun on his hip and he stepped away from the stairs.

"Angelica!" Tricia hollered. "Get out! Go home. Now!"

"What do you want?" Baker shouted.

Tricia took two steps down and paused. She could hear Angelica speaking, but couldn't make out the words.

"Ange!" Tricia hollered, and hurried down the rest of the stairs and entered the shop.

Baker stood before Angelica, hand still on the butt of the gun.

"Trish, what's going on?" Angelica called.

"What are you doing here?" Tricia demanded.

"I brought you some soup from Booked for Lunch." She held out a large foam container with a plastic lid.

"You better leave," Baker told Angelica sternly. "Now!"

Angelica's puzzled expression instantly turned dark as her gaze took in Baker's hand and the gun in the opened holster. "Have you threatened my sister?" she demanded.

"Ange, no!" Tricia shouted. "Grant!"

For a split second, Baker's attention was drawn away from the woman in front of him. But then Angelica lunged forward, yanked the lid off the soup, and threw it at him.

Baker let out a howl as the scalding liquid splashed onto his shirt and hand. He pivoted and rushed toward Tricia. She quickly sidestepped him as he crashed into the big steel barrier that led to the alley. But instead of coming after her, he fumbled to unlock the door.

Angelica advanced and Tricia intercepted her, grabbing her by the coat and hauling her back toward the front of the store. But before they got there, she felt a blast of cold air as Baker finally got the back door open and escaped into the alley.

"What's going on?" Angelica demanded.

"He broke into my store. He—" But she never got to finish the sentence as a single gunshot splintered the night.

Tricia and Angelica looked at each other for a split second and then rushed toward the door to the alley. Despite her bum foot, Angelica somehow made it there before Tricia. She wrenched it open, gasped, then threw out an arm to bar her sister from exiting. "Don't look!"

"What do you mean?"

Angelica pushed Tricia away from the door and slammed it shut. "Call nine one one. Now!" she commanded.

"What happened?" Tricia demanded, a new and terrible fear crawling through her.

Angelica shuddered and pressed the palms of her hands against her eyes as though to blot out what she'd seen. "He blew his face off."

THIRTY-FIVE

 Although it was well past eleven in the morning, the CLOSED sign hung on Haven't Got a Clue's door and the lights were darkened.

Tricia had spent the rest of the terrible evening before speaking to police officers and sheriff's deputies, counting and recounting the events leading up to Grant Baker's suicide. But no matter how many times she told the tale, it was still hard to believe he was dead—and that he'd taken his own life.

Poor Angelica had been a basket case. But then, she had seen the aftermath of that one fatal shot. After way too many repetitions of the evening's events, Tricia had finally called Antonio and asked him to take Angelica home and put her to bed, although Tricia was sure her sister would have a hard time sleeping after what she'd seen, and Tricia was grateful Angelica had sheltered her from that terrible sight. She owed her sister for sparing her that. But Tricia hadn't slept well, either. She'd ended up on her couch, the TV on, while insipid holiday movies played through the night. Christmas was over two months away, but that didn't seem to matter. She dozed fitfully, with Miss Marple pressed to her side, her quiet purr like a balm on Tricia's soul.

When morning arrived, Tricia texted Pixie, told her what had happened, and closed the shop for the day. She'd still pay her employees, but she knew she couldn't face the public . . .

not just yet. And maybe after this traumatic event, she would take a short leave of absence. Martha's Vineyard was a few hours' drive and a ferry ride away. There'd be no bustle of tourists, and she could probably rent a house or maybe stay at one of the hotels for a few days or a week. She could leave Haven't Got a Clue in Pixie's more-than-capable hands and give herself at least a few days to heal.

She'd think about it.

With her store closed, Tricia spent the morning puttering around her shop, not accomplishing much because she couldn't really concentrate, but trying to keep busy nonetheless. When her cell phone rang, she glanced at the screen and saw the number belonged to the Sheriff's Department. "Hello?"

"Ms. Miles? This is Sheriff Wendy Adams of the Hillsborough County Sheriff's Department. Would you have a few moments to speak with me?"

"Of course."

"May I come to your store?"

"When?"

"Now. I'm standing outside your door."

Sure enough, Tricia looked up to see a figure standing before the door. She hurried over to it and let her guest in, turning on the lights as the sheriff entered.

Tricia hadn't spoken with Adams in over four years, so she was more than a little surprised to see her. "Won't you sit down?" she asked, directing the sheriff to the reader's nook.

Adams took a seat there and removed her service cap, setting it on the coffee table.

"Ms. Miles," Adams began, "I'm very sorry you've been thrust into this terrible situation."

Tricia had never liked the sheriff because of her abrupt manner and acid tongue, but the years seemed to have tamed those tendencies.

"Why has your department taken over the investigation?" Tricia asked.

"The Stoneham Police Department has no detective division. Chief Baker was its only real investigator."

"And what have you found out?"

"I spoke with former deputy Harvick and he corroborated that you spoke with him yesterday about your suspicions on the recent deaths in the area."

Tricia didn't have the patience to listen. "Why did Grant kill himself outside my door last night?"

"It wasn't a spur-of-the-moment decision," Adams said.

Tricia's mouth dropped open. "What?"

"Chief Baker left a detailed accounting of his actions during the past several weeks, taking full responsibility. Apparently, he couldn't live with what he'd done. He showed up on your doorstep because he hoped to spend one last evening with you."

"Then what? He would have shot himself in front of me?" Tricia asked, anguished.

Adams shook her head. "No. He planned to return to the place where he'd dumped Greenwell's body."

That wasn't a much better solution. Then some hapless hiker would have found him and been just as distraught as Angelica had been after seeing his lifeless corpse.

"The gun he used . . . it wasn't his own, was it?" Tricia asked.

Adams shook her head. "It was registered to Marshall Cambridge."

As she'd suspected, Baker *had* taken it when he'd searched Marshall's apartment.

"I believe it may have been used to kill Joshua Greenwell, too," Tricia said.

"We're having it tested, but Chief Baker confessed he did use it for that purpose. He'd originally planned to dispose of the gun, but as the incidents mounted, he apparently changed his mind."

The deaths of five people were being described as mere incidents?

"What happens now?" Tricia asked.

"It's pretty much an open-and-shut case. We tie up the loose ends and go about our business," Adams said succinctly.

As though Grant Baker had never lived.

Tricia was pretty sure business as usual was going to be pretty hard to replicate in the coming weeks.

Adams stood and reached out a hand to touch Tricia's shoulder. "I know you once had feelings for Chief Baker. I'm sorry it had to end this way."

"Thank you." What more could she say? She stood and walked Adams to the door. "Good-bye, Sheriff Adams."

"Good-bye, Ms. Miles."

Tricia closed the door behind the sheriff and headed back to her seat in the reader's nook. She was about to sit down when the little hinged brass flap marked LETTERS on her door opened and the daily mail was dropped inside. Tricia turned to retrieve the stack of envelopes. It consisted of bills, the usual junk mail, but one letter was addressed to her with no return address, although the handwriting was hauntingly familiar.

She tore open the envelope and sat down to read the letter.

Dear Tricia,

If you're reading this, I'm now dead. Hopefully you will have heard about it from some other source and so this letter won't be a shock.

I just wanted to let you know how much I love you. I had to break off my engagement with Diana because she was no match for you.

I think I've loved you since the moment I met you and was too stupid and pigheaded to see that having you by my side would mean more than my career aspirations. Christopher realized it too late, and so did Russ Smith, and, I'm sure, Marshall Cambridge, too. I've left instructions but wanted to let you know that I've taken care of both you and Mandy.

His ex-wife.

Above all, I want you to be happy. Find someone to love who will truly appreciate you, because I sure failed you.

All my love,
Grant

Tricia wiped a tear from her eye and set the letter on the coffee table.

Love? she thought bitterly. The man hadn't known the meaning of the word. If he had, he would never have put her through the terrible shades of negativity that now burdened her soul.

So, he'd taken care of her in his will. She guessed he hadn't noticed that she was perfectly capable of taking care of herself. She didn't want his money, but she knew of plenty of charities who could benefit from such a gift.

Clearing her throat, Tricia retrieved the letter and stuffed it back into its envelope. Then she picked up her phone, tapped her contacts list, and made a call.

"Hi, Ange. It's me, your sister. How would you like to take a magical mystery vacation?"

"I can be packed in twenty minutes."

THIRTY-SIX

Although Thanksgiving was still a week away, the Brookview Inn was already decorated for Christmas, with a twelve-foot faux fir tree in the center of the lobby, laden with sparkling gold ornaments and twinkling white lights.

Members of the Stoneham Chamber of Commerce had filed in almost an hour earlier and enjoyed the inn's spectacular continental breakfast, which included six different pastries, coffee, tea, cocoa, and juices, all courtesy of Nigela Ricita Associates. Leona Ferguson and Terry McDonald had been drafted to run for Chamber president, and the ballots had already been passed out, the voting completed, and collected once again. Mary Fairchild and Dan Reed had retreated to the back of the room to tabulate the votes. As much as Tricia liked Leona, she thought Terry seemed to have better managerial skills. He would need them to pull the Chamber out of its financial hole.

The preceding weeks had been quiet, which was fine with Tricia. But life had gone on in the village, despite the events of October. Becca had taken up part-time residence in the village, splitting her time in a condo she'd rented in Milford and her home outside of Boston. Ava had become her biggest fan, and she seemed to be getting the hang of running a retail establishment. She'd even joined the Chamber.

Tricia glanced across the room to see that Louise Jameson sat at one of the tables for eight and right beside Becca. It seemed the women had become quite friendly. They'd invited Tricia to several of their coffee klatches, but so far she'd turned them down. She just wasn't up to socializing. Not quite yet. From what she'd heard, Louise was trying to untangle the financial cat's cradle her husband had left behind, but rumor had it she'd be successful in getting to copyright her work in her own name. That was one triumph for her.

Ginny and Antonio sat on the other side of the table with Angelica between them. They'd been in animated conversation about the architect's plans they'd received just the evening before, spreading out the drawings on the table and debating the pros and cons. It looked like Ginny would be the outright winner of that discussion. The original house and property had, after all, been hers.

Tricia and Angelica had not gone to Martha's Vineyard, but they had traveled to New York, where they'd had tea at the Ritz-Carlton, watched a couple of Broadway shows, and even visited Tiffany's. It didn't change what had happened, but it was a welcome respite. And by the time their week of vacation had ended, they were ready to face life in their adopted hometown once again.

Mary had taken Mark Jameson's place as the de facto head of the Chamber but had confided to Tricia that "I wouldn't want this job on a permanent basis," and was eager to hand off the responsibility to either Terry or Leona. She and Dan moved to stand at the front of the dining room, with Mary moving behind the lectern. Neither of them looked happy. Mary called the meeting to order.

"We seem to have a problem," she began, and adjusted the reading glasses perched on her nose. In one hand she held a piece of paper which she consulted. "It seems we have a tie."

"Oh, no," Tricia groaned. The voting the year before had been so close, and now they had a tie!

"How could that happen?" Leona called out.

"We have fifty-two members and forty-eight of us voted today."

"How do we break the tie? Do we vote again?" Terry asked.

"Well, that all depends if the write-in candidates agree to serve."

"Write-in candidates?" Leona asked.

"Who are they?" Terry asked.

Tricia felt her whole body sag with dread.

"Angelica and Tricia Miles. They both received twenty votes each!"

"I propose they both serve," hollered Claire Rawlings from Tails and Tales.

"I second that," called Billie Hanson from the Bank of Stoneham.

Mary sighed. "Tricia, Angelica—what do you say?"

Tricia glared at her sister, who shrugged—but then grinned.

Tricia stood and gave a weary sigh. "We accept."

RECIPES

Tricia's Apple Crisp

INGREDIENTS
4 medium tart cooking apples, sliced (4 cups)
¾ cup packed brown sugar
½ cup all-purpose flour
½ cup quick-cooking or old-fashioned oats
⅓ cup butter, softened
¾ teaspoon ground cinnamon
¾ teaspoon ground nutmeg
Whipped cream or ice cream, optional

Preheat the oven to 375°F (190°C, Gas Mark 5). Grease the bottom and sides of an 8-inch-square pan. Spread the apples in the pan. In a medium bowl, stir together the sugar, flour, oats, butter, and spices until well mixed; sprinkle over the apples. Bake about 30 minutes, or until the topping is golden brown and the apples are tender. Serve warm with whipped cream or ice cream if desired.

Yield: 6 servings

TOMMY'S BEER DIP

INGREDIENTS
2 packages (8 ounces each) cream cheese, softened
⅓ cup any kind of beer or nonalcoholic beer
1 envelope ranch salad dressing mix
2 cups shredded cheddar cheese (mild or sharp)
Pretzels

In a large bowl, beat the cream cheese, beer, and dressing mix until smooth. Stir in the cheddar cheese. Serve with pretzels.

Yield: 3½ cups

GARLIC CHEESE DIP

INGREDIENTS
8 ounces cream cheese, room temperature
½ cup mayonnaise
1 cup sour cream
4 heads garlic, roasted
½ teaspoon garlic salt
2 cups freshly shredded mozzarella cheese
½ cup freshly shredded Parmesan cheese
¼ cup fresh minced parsley, plus some for garnish
*   (or 1 to 2 tablespoons, dried)*
Toasted bread crostini or crackers

Preheat the oven to 350°F (180°C, Gas Mark 4). Grease a small baking dish with nonstick cooking spray. In a medium-sized bowl, beat the cream cheese, mayonnaise, and sour cream with an electric mixer until smooth. Stir in the roasted garlic and garlic salt, then stir in the cheeses and parsley. Pour into a small baking dish. Bake for 20 to 30 minutes, or until the edges are golden brown and the cheeses are melted and bubbly. Garnish with fresh minced parsley and serve with crackers or toasted bread for dipping.

Yield: approximately 3 cups

ACKNOWLEDGMENTS

My thanks go to my friend and fellow author Shirley Hailstock, who is a font of wonderful information and advice that she gladly shares. Patricia Winton is my go-to gal when it comes to making sure I don't botch writing the Italian language. (Google Translate can do only so much, so thanks, Patricia!) Thank you, too, to my readers Elaine Batterby, Jenne Turner, and Jill Kerns, for other info salted into this novel. And as always, thank you to members of the Lorraine Train for their help and support: Mary Ann Borer, Amy Connolly, Linda Kuzminczuk, Debbie Lyon, Kim Templeton, and Pam Priest.

The recipes included in this book were tested in Fahrenheit.

Turn the page for a taste of the next
entertaining Booktown Mystery

CLAUSE OF DEATH

Available in hardcover from Berkley Prime
Crime in June 2022!

Tricia Miles glanced over the notes she'd jotted down the previous evening in anticipation of that morning's Stoneham Chamber of Commerce meeting. How things had changed for the Chamber in just six months.

The previous October, the organization had been on the brink of insolvency, housed in a drafty warehouse unsuitable for its members to meet in, and was hemorrhaging warm, dues-paying bodies by the day. And then came the election, with an outcome no one had anticipated. The two candidates hadn't received enough votes to win, but two write-in non-contenders were tied. And that's how Tricia and her sister, Angelica, were now copresidents of the Chamber.

It was true that membership hadn't bounced back quite as fast as the sisters had hoped, but thanks to the generosity of their colleagues, they had obtained office space, a free meeting space, and office supplies. They could manage for the rest of the year, when it was hoped dues would once again float the Chamber's financial boat.

Tricia and Angelia had worked together during Angelica's tenure as the organization's leader, when Tricia had volunteered while her vintage mystery bookstore, Haven't Got a Clue, was closed due to a fire. At that time, and under Angelica's leadership, the Chamber had thrived. Tricia was to be her heiress apparent but lost the vote by a mere three votes when Russ Smith had thrown his hat into the ring. When the elected leader had died of a heart attack, it was deemed Russ was the victor. He spent the next ten months on a quest to destroy the organization and would have succeeded if he hadn't been arrested for murder, with a charge of embezzlement of the Chamber's assets thrown in for good measure. When he eventually came to trial, he was destined to spend many years, if not the rest of his life, as a guest of the New Hampshire penal system.

The Brookview Inn, which was owned by Nigela Ricita (known to only a few as Angelica herself), had graciously allowed the chamber to meet for the rest of the year with no fee. Chamber members did have to cough up ten bucks each to cover the cost of their continental breakfasts, but those who had bothered to check would have found that the cost to guests was actually twenty percent more. Perhaps not a bargain, but the meetings so far had been pretty well attended. Clearly, the members saw the benefit of the Miles sisters' leadership.

Angelica gave Tricia a nudge. "Hadn't you better start the meeting? The members will be eager to get back to their shops to start the workday."

"You're right."

Tricia got up from her seat and walked to the front of the restaurant, tested the microphone, and gave one last glance at her notes before speaking. "Welcome, everyone," she began, and waited for the voices to die down and the members present to give her their full attention.

"Before we start, let me remind you there are still plenty of the Brookview's marvelous pastries left, as well as hot coffee and juices, so feel free to enjoy them." She paused. "First on today's agenda are the summer flowers for Main Street. Once again, Nigela Ricita Associates has graciously agreed to provide them, as well as plants for the urns in front of the Main Street merchants' stores."

A polite ripple of applause met that statement.

"Next, we have a guest who's looking to open a new business here in Stoneham." Tricia nodded toward the table closest to the podium. "Mr. Rick Lavoy."

A man of about forty, dressed in a dark gray sports jacket, a light gray shirt, and Dockers, stood. "Thanks for the welcome," he said to a polite smattering of applause.

"Why don't you tell us about your ideas for your new enterprise," Tricia said.

Lavoy turned to face the room. "My partners and I own a craft brewery in Nashua and we're looking for a property here in Stoneham to open a tasting room."

"To build or rent?" came a male voice from the back of the room.

"To rent, at first. If we're successful, we might like to build here in the village or close to the highway."

"Tell us more," Tricia encouraged him.

"We'd be open during regular hours all summer long and cut our hours during the off-season, probably only open on weekends."

Eli Meier, a not-so-longtime member of the Chamber, stood, waving a hand for recognition. He owned the Inner Light bookstore, two doors down from Tricia's shop. When she first arrived in Stoneham, his store stocked books on religion and spirituality, but of late, it had begun to carry more books on a variety of conspiracy theories, from lizardlike aliens about to take over the world to dark politics and beyond. Eli had seemed to transform as well, from being a mild-mannered gentleman to a paranoid individual who'd read too many of his own stocked items.

Tricia heaved a sigh and nodded in his direction.

Eli turned to Rick. "You *do* know Stoneham is known as *Booktown*, not beer-guzzling town." A nervous spate of murmuring rumbled through the room.

"Stoneham is a tourist destination," Tricia said. "Books drive the interest, but a diversity of businesses will bring in more than just book lovers. The more we have to offer, the greater our tourism reach. It's a win-win situation."

"For cretins," Eli scoffed. "Do we want a lot of low-class beer swillers in our midst?"

Rick cleared his throat loudly. "Excuse me, but our clientele are connoisseurs and we've done the market research to confirm it. They're also high-order readers; that's why we decided to establish a tasting room here in Stoneham. It was a no-brainer because your demographic audience is ours as well."

"I find that hard to believe," Eli jeered. "Stoneham was meant to resemble that fabled town in Wales, Hay-on-Wye. A *real* book town. *That's* what we should be striving to attain."

Well, yeah, except *that* village was steeped in history, with Tudor buildings and old-world charm. The village of Stoneham was old by American standards, but not nearly as old as those in Europe. Most of the buildings in Stoneham had been built in the early days of the twentieth century, and were, in most cases, merely dated. Most, but not all, were in good repair. That said, Hay-on-Wye's current claim to fame had only come about during the 1960s. Stoneham's rebirth was less than a decade old, but its moniker of *Booktown* had made it a reading destination in a lot shorter time.

Tricia directed her attention to Lavoy. "Are you working with NR Realty to locate a suitable property?" she asked.

"Ms. Johnson is showing me a possibility in an hour or so."

"We wish you good luck," Tricia said, and then encouraged Rick to join the chapter.

Rick threw a sour glance in Eli's direction but nodded anyway.

"Next up—" Tricia began.

"I'd like to make a motion!" came a voice from the back of the room. Again, Eli stood, waving a hand for recognition.

"And that is?" Tricia asked, and sighed yet again. Eli had been making a pest of himself for months.

"That the Chamber stop encouraging non-book-related businesses from opening up on Main Street. Us bookstore owners are being squeezed out."

Tricia shot her sister an annoyed glance. This wasn't the first time Eli had harangued them on the subject.

Dan Reed stood. "I second that motion." Dan owned the Bookshelf Diner and had a long-standing grudge against Angelica for daring to open her retro café, Booked for Lunch, which served one meal a day, just doors down from his full-service diner that was open from six o'clock in the morning until nine at night. It seemed to Tricia that he, too, lived to cause trouble at the Chamber meetings just to irritate the copresidents.

"I third it," came a voice from the left side of the room. Though she'd been one of the original booksellers recruited to Booktown nearly eight years before, Betty Barnes, from Barney's Book Barn, Stoneham's children's bookstore, was new to the Chamber. Did Betty even understand parliamentary procedures where there was no thirding of a motion?

Tricia took a breath, determined to keep her cool. Ignoring Dan and Betty, Tricia addressed her comments toward Eli.

"Eli, you know the Chamber has no power to stop businesses from renting space on Main Street. In fact, it helps the entire village when all the storefronts are occupied. As of now, there are three empty establishments on the east side of Main Street, including the one next to your own shop, and only one on the other."

"Well, then it should be up to you—as head of the chamber—to recruit new *used* bookstores to the village. That's what Bob Kelly did!"

A rumble of agreement went around the room, but not everyone was in Eli's court.

Larry Harvick stood. "Are you saying I'm not welcome in Stoneham?" he challenged Eli. Harvick was a former county sheriff's deputy and had opened the Bee's Knees, a gift shop that featured products from his hives. They also carried other bee-related items, including books. They were new volumes, whereas most of the booksellers stocked mostly used books with some new stock. Eli also carried some newly published books, so what was he squawking about?

"Our village is known as Booktown, not bee town," Eli challenged.

"Yes, but we've always had other businesses," Tricia pointed out. "Like Leona Ferguson's shop, which sells new and vintage dishware."

Leona leapt to her feet. "I was one of the first businesses to take a chance on Bob Kelly's little experiment here in Stoneham," she said indignantly. "He certainly welcomed me with open arms."

"That's only because you rented one of *his* empty buildings," Eli replied with a sneer in his voice.

"Well, I now *own* the building," Leona countered, "and I'm staying put." She turned on Dan Reed. "And why would you second the motion? You don't even sell books."

"Maybe not, but I have the word 'book' in my business name and my restaurant is decorated with old books that customers are free to buy if they wish. They're all priced for sale."

"And covered in years' worth of diner grease," Leona muttered loud enough for some to hear and giggle over.

"Now, now," Tricia chided. "As you know, the old warehouse where the Chamber was briefly located has been razed. There's room for several more storefronts—including bookstores."

"Yeah, and who bought the lots?" Eli demanded. "And what businesses are going to go in them?"

Again, Tricia sighed. "A limited liability company bought the property only hours after it went on the market. We don't know who owns it or what their plans are for the land."

"So it's not Nigela Ricita Associates?" Mary Fairchild asked from the table closest to the podium. "Everybody figured that since she already owned half the village that it was *her* who was going to develop it."

She would have liked to, Tricia thought, but didn't share that information with Mary.

"Well, the least you can do is recruit more bookstores— just like Bob Kelly did!" Eli practically shouted at Tricia.

Oh, yeah, saintly Bob Kelly, who'd started the Chamber and recruited the businesses for his own enrichment. He'd bought up most of Main Street for a song and advertised for booksellers who'd relocated and paid him rent. At that moment, Bob was languishing in state prison with a very long sentence for murder. Tricia had to bite her tongue not to bring up that last little piece of history.

Angelica raised her hand and Tricia acknowledged her. "Eli, perhaps you'd like to form a committee to investigate the recruitment of more bookstores," she said sweetly. "Dan, maybe you'd like to be the first member to join Eli on such a recruitment effort."

Dan glowered at her.

"I second that motion!" Mary called.

"It wasn't presented as a motion," Eli growled at her. "And I don't have time to spend on a stupid committee."

"You didn't think it was stupid when you suggested it," Harvick commented sourly.

"Why don't we table this discussion for another time," Tricia said, hoping to regain control of the meeting.

"I second that motion!" Terry McDonald of All Heroes Comics called. He gave Tricia a smile and what could only be described as a cheeky thumbs-up.

"That wasn't a motion, either!" Eli complained.

"I move that we end the meeting," Leona called out.

"I second that," Mary agreed.

Tricia had no gavel—and should have rectified that problem long before then—and called, "So moved." She let out a breath. She'd barely touched on her list of things to bring up before the assemblage. She gave her sister a sour look, but Angelica merely shrugged. She'd have to face the group and preside over the next meeting. Good luck to her!

"Well, that went splendidly," Angelica said, and threw a look over her left shoulder to see the members get up from their seats, some heading for the pastry table to fill their pockets and purses with paper napkin–covered mini Danish, croissants, and donuts. Well, better that than for them to be thrown away.

"So, honestly—how do you think the meeting went?" Tricia asked.

"Not nearly as contentious as I thought, which means we'd better have a lot of good news to share next time."

"And how do we accomplish that?"

"Miracles *do* happen," Angelica said, and rose from her seat. "It's time to thank the waitstaff and kitchen staff. As always, they've gone above and beyond the call of duty to provide us with a lovely breakfast."

But as the sisters made their way toward the kitchen's swinging door, Eli stepped out in front of them, stopping them in their tracks. "You didn't have to cut me off," he complained to Tricia.

She stood her ground. "If you recall, it was Leona Ferguson and Mary Fairchild who moved to end the meeting."

"Probably from a signal from you."

Tricia wasn't going to argue with the man. "If you'll excuse us."

"Excuse? Never. And mark my words, we *will* be discussing the lack of new booksellers at the next meeting."

Tricia smiled sweetly. "I'll be sure to add it to the agenda."

Eli muttered an oath and pivoted, nearly running into the inn's manager, Hank Curtis.

"Whoa!" Hank called. "Everything okay here?"

Eli growled something unintelligible and shoved Hank aside, striding toward the exit. They watched him leave. "Was there a problem?" Hank asked.

Tricia shook her head. "Mr. Meier was a little upset by the abrupt end to the meeting."

"We were on our way to thank the staff for the lovely breakfast they provided," Angelica said, and batted her eyelashes. She seemed to think she had a chance at a relationship with Hank, but so far he'd resisted all her attempts at engagement.

"Were you able to sit in on much of the meeting?" Tricia asked.

Hank shook his head. "Too busy."

"But isn't it in the inn's best interest to know what's going on within the Chamber in case it could pertain to the inn?" Angelica asked.

"I get most of what I need from the Chamber bulletin."

Tricia beamed. *She* was in charge of the monthly newsletter. "I'm glad you find it useful."

Hank looked at his watch. "We've got a lunch meeting that begins in about ninety minutes. I'd better make sure we'll be ready. I'll convey your thanks to the staff." He gave them a curt nod. "I'm sure I'll see you soon, ladies," he said, and left them.

Angelica watched him go and heaved a great sigh.

"You have too much on your plate right now to enter into a relationship," Tricia reminded her sister.

"Who says I need a relationship? But I wouldn't mind a little romp in the hay once in a while."

Tricia glared at Angelica.

She gave a shake. "You're right. Besides all my business ventures, I've got a new grandbaby arriving soon, too."

Someone cleared his throat, and Tricia turned to face Rick Lavoy.

"Mr. Lavoy—?"

"Call me Rick."

"Rick. You must have a terrible impression of our organization. I'm so sorry you weren't greeted with more enthusiasm. My copresident and I"—Tricia waved a hand in Angelica's general direction—"think your tasting room would be an enormous asset to the village."

"There's always a couple of crabs in every group. I can assure you that everyone at my table was welcoming and seemed quite interested in my establishing a tasting room here in the village. I've already spoken with the manager at the Dog-Eared Page, who expressed an interest in selling several of our draft beers. I still think Stoneham would be a good fit. And to keep in the Booktown spirit, we plan to stock a variety of books on the subject. They may be more focused on current titles, but then the village is known as Booktown, not necessarily *used* Booktown."

"That's true." Tricia's specialty at Haven't Got a Clue was vintage mysteries, but they were getting harder and harder to find. Her stock and trade were still used books, but she sold many new books by current authors, and still hosted author signings as well.

"Perhaps we could do lunch sometime to discuss the matter further," Rick suggested. "I know my wife would love to pick your brains. She does most of the marketing for us. It was she who suggested we investigate locating the tasting room here."

"We'd love to meet her," Angelica said. She handed Rick a business card. "Feel free to give us a call so we can arrange it."

Rick pocketed the card. "I'll do that. Nice meeting you ladies, and hope to see you again soon."

They watched him go and Angelica sighed.

"Sorry, he's married," Tricia teased.

Angelica sighed again. "All the good ones are."

The sisters headed for the inn's back entrance. "Maybe we should give Eli's suggestion some real thought. How does one recruit booksellers to Stoneham, anyhow?" Angelica asked. It hadn't been a problem under her Chamber leadership.

"The same way Bob Kelly did. Place ads in magazines. That's how I found out about the place. I called him, we chatted, and then I came to visit."

"But as I recall, at the time the place was pretty much dead," Angelica said as they started down the steps to the parking lot.

"It was. But Bob had a glib tongue and darned if he wasn't right. Look at where Booktown is now."

"We're bustling all right," Angelica said, taking out her key fob and unlocking her car doors. "But I refuse to give Bob all the credit." Especially since it was Angelica who'd invested the most capital to bring prosperity back to the village. They got in the car.

"I still want to know who bought the warehouse site and what they plan to do with it."

Tricia fastened her seat belt. Angelica did likewise. "I thought Antonio"—Angelica's son—"was looking into it?"

Angelica backed the car out of the parking space. "He keeps coming up against brick walls. It looks like a shell company is guarding the true ownership."

Tricia gave a stifled laugh. "That term always sounds sinister to me. Like someone is trying to hide something."

"Was that remark directed at me?" Angelica asked, sounding miffed.

"Well, your shell company *is* Nigela Ricita Associates. You *are* hiding your identity behind the name."

"I had a very good reason for doing that."

"Which you never told me," Tricia said.

Angelica's gaze was fixed on the road. "If you must know, it was so Daddy wouldn't find out about it. He'd just want a little loan—or *five*."

Yes, their grifter of a father had borrowed money (and never repaid it) from people who were now his ex-friends. Their mother controlled the finances and kept their father on a short leash. If she hadn't, he'd probably be in jail for the next ten to twenty years.

"But I think you're right," Angelica said as they approached the municipal parking lot on Main Street. "I can't help but think that whoever bought that lot did it deliberately to keep me from purchasing it."

Tricia laughed. "Now you're starting to sound like Eli with his conspiracy theories."

"Sometimes," Angelica said, her voice deadly, "conspiracy theories are based on fact."

Angelica parked her car in the village's municipal lot and the sisters got out, starting off for the sidewalk that lined Main Street.

"I've got to go to the bank," Tricia said.

Angelica looked appalled. "Do you mean to say you had yesterday's receipts in your purse this whole time?"

"Of course."

"But what if you'd been mugged? What if someone got into your purse while you were getting a coffee refill at the inn?"

"It's not high tourist season, so it's not a huge sum, as we haven't exactly been inundated with customers."

Angelica shook her head disapprovingly. "You be careful," she warned. "Heaven only knows who you might run into."

"You worry too much. I'll be fine. I'll see you tonight. It's my turn to host happy hour."

"What are we having for dinner?"

"It's a surprise." Yes, it was, because Tricia had to hit the grocery store in Milford to get *something*, or else they'd be dining on stale crackers and canned pâté cat food.

"See you later."

Angelica gave a wave and Tricia headed for the sidewalk and the village's only stoplight. She crossed the road and covered the two-block distance in five minutes. As she hit the first step of three in front of the bank's granite edifice, a tall, good-looking man, probably in his midforties, a little beefy, with a close-cropped ginger beard, came barreling out and nearly knocked her over.

"I'm terribly sorry," he said, his voice carrying the hint of an Irish lilt. Tricia's memory flashed and her breath caught in her throat.

"Ian? Ian McDonald?"

"Tricia Miles? Is it really you?" he asked, and laughed.

The two had met two years before aboard the *Celtic Lady* cruise ship. Tricia had found the door to a cabin open. When she'd reported it, Ian had arrived. He'd been the ship's security officer, and had ended up investigating the death of one of the authors on the cruise.

"What are you doing here in Stoneham?" Tricia asked.

"I'm staying with my cousin, Terry."

"Terry McDonald from All Heroes Comics is your cousin?" Tricia asked, aghast.

"That's right. We both spit in a tube for one of those ancestry DNA searches, found we were second cousins, and here I am."

"That's amazing," Tricia said, a little overwhelmed by the revelation.

"I knew you lived in New England, but I had no idea it was Stoneham. It truly is a small world," Ian said, his grin wide.

"In fact, I own the mystery bookstore right next to Terry's shop. It's called Haven't Got a Clue."

"Its facade is charming. I'm a huge Sherlock Holmes fan.

You've done a great job replicating the front of his home. I planned on stopping in either later today or tomorrow."

"You're welcome anytime."

Ian glanced at his watch. "Much as I'd love to catch up with you right now, I'm afraid I've got an important errand to run. I promise to come visit you in the next day or so. Perhaps we could go to dinner?"

"That would be nice," Tricia said, a warm glow coursing through her.

Ian flashed another winning smile and clasped her hand. "I'll be in touch." He gave it a tighter squeeze and then let go, giving her another smile and a brief wave before he headed north up Main Street.

Tricia watched him for a few moments before she heaved a heavy sigh and continued into the bank.

After making her deposit, Tricia turned south to go back to her store. Was it unusual that second cousins crossed vast expanses of ocean just to meet? Back on the ship, Ian had told her that he spent most of his limited vacation time with his sister and her family in Ireland. As Tricia walked, she idly wondered how long Ian would be staying in the village. Because of the nature of his job, it couldn't be for more than a few days. She had to admit, she'd been intrigued with the dashing ship's officer. And though he'd made it clear there was no fraternizing with the cruise passengers, now that they were both off the ship . . .

Stop it, she commanded. Thanks to her unhappy past, she was done with men—with the whole concept of romance. She'd heard the locals whisper. She *was* unlucky in love and everyone in the village knew it. Some had even taken to calling her the Black Widow, since it seemed every man she was involved with met some terrible, if not fatal, end.

To be the Black Widow *and* the village jinx was too much to take. Still, tight-lipped, she strode toward her store with her head held high.

Tricia thought back to what Ian had said: he had an important errand to run. Here in Stoneham? He'd just left the bank. What else could be called important? A visit to the post office or the liquor store in nearby Milford? And he'd headed north on foot. Tricia couldn't imagine what business would attract him. The day spa? No. He was going in the wrong direction for that. Besides, his hair had looked perfectly coiffed and his beard neatly trimmed. Did he need a chocolate fix from the Sweet as Can Be candy store?

Tricia shook her head. She'd just have to wait until Ian visited her store or they could speak more candidly at the dinner he'd proposed. She frowned. It had been a lonely six months since she'd had a date or even an intimate conversation with a man. She wasn't sure she was ready for another relationship—and wasn't she jumping the gun to even be thinking about Ian McDonald in that way? He'd most likely be here and gone within days.

The spring in her step had vanished and Tricia slogged along the sidewalk until she reached Haven't Got a Clue. With a heavy heart, she yanked open the plate glass door. It looked like it could be a long day.

About the Author

LORNA BARRETT is the *New York Times* bestselling author of the Booktown Mysteries, including *A Deadly Deletion*, *Handbook for Homicide*, and *A Killer Edition*. She lives in Rochester, New York.

CONNECT ONLINE

LornaBarrett.com
🅕 LornaBarrett.Author
🐦 LornaBarrett

Ready to find
your next great read?

Let us help.

Visit prh.com/nextread

Penguin
Random
House